WHEN DARKNESS FALLS

SIDNEY WILLIAMS

The hounds pushed through the trees, running in a pack. There were six of them. They were big. Very big dogs. Their heads were massive, wide and flat across the top with slobbering jaws and ears that flopped back as they ran.

Their black fur made them almost invisible in the darkness, but their weight made the pounding of their feet audible, and their breath snarled through their throats.

They relied on their sense of smell to locate Budd, almost aiming for him as he slowed to a walk upon nearing the end of the wood line. He wasn't far from home.

He didn't see them coming, not at first.

Acknowledgments

There are always so many people to thank when a project is completed.

People helped in many ways to make the completion of this book possible as I huddled alone in my dark little office. Some names are always left out, but here goes.

Thanks to Adele Leone for pushing this project, and to Ann LeFarge for sticking by it.

Thanks to Wayne Allen Sallee for the steady stream of goofy mail to bolster my spirits.

Thanks to Douglas Johnson for encouragement and enthusiasm about my work.

Thanks to Clifford V. Brooks for the *Azarius* T-shirt.

Chapter 1

The hounds came on an autumn night, a late October night when the chill was just starting to creep into the air and the leaves were just beginning to rust and rustle.

Darkness tugged the afternoon down slowly, dusting its charcoal shroud across the sky. Usually the Louisiana weather remained hot into November, but sometimes there were cool snaps that made the season feel the way it was supposed to feel.

Tonight was one of those; Budd Hagan noticed that as he walked toward home, the collar of his army fatigue jacket turned up to protect his neck against the tickle of the breeze. The jacket had been his older brother's, but Budd was big for his age and able to wear it. He looked older than thirteen, his hair cut short on the sides with a shaggy tousle in back like a tail and spikes on top that needled porcupine-like from his scalp, bristling around the Walkman headphones which piped Madonna into his brain.

The teachers didn't like his hair, but that was sort of the idea, and it managed to meet dress code regulations. Budd didn't intentionally set out to agitate people in authority, but he didn't mind that they didn't like it either. He didn't care much for teachers.

Even though the school year was young, Budd had come close to suspension twice at Petittville High—once for smoking, once for skipping afternoon classes. Neither offense struck him as particularly subversive. He'd picked up smoking two years earlier, snagging the butts his father discarded when the old man happened to be around.

His dad had trouble holding a job, and the family moved around a lot. They had family here, though, so they usually drifted back to live with his grandmother, his mom's mom, when things got tough.

The old man's last stint had been as a Bible salesman in Houston, a job much in demand when you considered the Gideons gave them away whether you wanted them or not. It had been some deluxe study Bible which could be personalized with gold letters on the cover, but the bucks hadn't come rolling in from that one. Budd had realized that when his mom and dad had their argument. That was around the time they moved back to Petittville.

While he didn't have many friends, it was nice to be back in familiar territory. He could keep the local kids scared enough of him to leave him alone most of the time. His size and his occasional flares of temper made him seem mean to most of them. That suited him because he didn't have to put up with much bullshit.

A plus in coming home this time proved to be that Delia Rhodes considered him the new guy, and Delia always got crushes on the new guy. An added bonus was that Delia seemed to have received a genetic blessing in her breast development. That and her long blonde hair consoled Budd significantly. While she was pretty selective about what she'd allow to go on below the waist, she didn't seem to mind having her breasts kneaded and kissed on a regular basis.

Delia was the first girl who'd allowed Budd that honor, the first girl who'd allowed him *any* honors, so he was pretty happy about the recent turn of events.

She'd met him after school this evening, and they'd slipped into the storage room behind the stage in the girls' gym. One of Budd's talents was picking locks.

As was their regular Wednesday afternoon ritual, they slipped in there, sat side by side on the tumbling mats, and necked. After a little tongue dueling, he'd usually let his hands creep up to her breasts. She'd resist at first, but then his activities through her clothes would be allowed, and gradually she would consent to further exploration.

Today she'd been wearing a short denim skirt and pink pullover that hugged her shapely form perfectly. As she'd gradually let him peel it up over her head, he'd watched the white cups of her bra come into view.

2

Her breasts swelled out of them, and he buried his face in her cleavage while she reached behind herself for the hook.

As her breasts tumbled out, he moved his mouth quickly down to their swelling pink crests, and her arms curled behind his head, pressing him against them. It was the closest thing Budd had ever known to true ecstasy, and he almost died when she instructed: "Do it harder. Suck hard."

He'd been only too happy to oblige.

They'd been together three weeks now. The memory of each of their liaisons produced a throbbing in his jeans, and as he cut across the vacant lot near Archer's Acres, the subdivision where the family lived, he wondered how long it was going to take to convince her there was more excitement to be had.

He'd heard she'd allowed a couple of guys some other privileges, though reportedly no one had experienced the true consummation of a relationship with Delia. Derek Quinn had been expected to be the man to claim her virginity, but she'd tired of him when Budd arrived.

Derek had cornered Budd in the locker room one day and threatened bodily harm. Budd had slammed his elbow into Derek's nose and ended the discussion. Once the bleeding had stopped, everyone agreed Derek had bumped into a locker door.

Delia developed a new respect for Budd after that.

The other good thing about being back in Petittville wasn't quite as exciting as having Delia to play with, but Budd was happy that he had met Charlie Black.

Charlie wasn't exactly a nerd, but his mother was overprotective and that tended to make Charlie a little shy. Coupled with the fact that he read too much and was too studious, he was a bit of an outcast. That made him a good candidate for friendship.

Normally, since they didn't have much in common, Budd and Charlie weren't the types to pal around together, but having Charlie was better than nobody. Charlie rattled on about the science fiction books he read and the shit in *Fangoria* magazine, but Budd could tolerate that. It meant he didn't have to sit alone in the cafeteria—Delia was on the other lunch shift—and it meant he had a lab partner for general science and a buddy to hold up the wall with before classes started.

Budd gave Charlie a hard time sometimes, kidded him really, but he liked the guy. Charlie was a little naïve for fourteen, so he couldn't offer much advice about Delia, but he was the only one Budd had to talk to about her, and Budd liked the way Charlie's eyes got wide when exploits were described.

While Budd considered it pretty lame that he hadn't scored with Delia, he enjoyed the chance to impress Charlie. That kind of made the waiting more bearable.

He knew Charlie's parents didn't like him, particularly his mom, but they didn't forbid them to hang out together. They just made it unpleasant for Charlie, heaping on more questions and warnings and the other weight parents could dump on a kid.

He had to appreciate Charlie sticking with him despite all that.

As Madonna broke into "Like a Prayer," Budd began to jog, his Nikes kicking up leaves on the vacant lot. He and Charlie were going to build a fort here when they got the chance. Then he'd have a place to bring Delia, away from school. One of these days a janitor was going to catch up with them if they maintained residence in the stage room.

As he pumped his legs, his lungs began to rasp in the damp night air, and he felt a knot of phlegm forming in his throat. His cheeks were already cold. Normally it didn't get this cold in this part of the country.

Well, he'd be home soon. The old man might bitch a little, but at least the house would be warm. He'd hide out in the room he always had while at Grandma's and play tapes. Maybe Charlie would call. Sometimes he did that, and they talked.

His jogging carried him past the edge of the woods that bordered the subdivision. Sooner or later they were going to clear them for more houses, but Budd had heard that would be a while. The economy was bad, his dad said. It was usually an excuse, but the fact had been confirmed in a civics class discussion about current events.

It suited Budd to have the woods here. If they put up more houses, they'd be filled with rich kids. That was almost all there was in Petittville now. People who worked in Aimsley and Alexandria settled here, people with good jobs and sons who knew it. The other kids were shit-kicker townies who figured knowing how to hunt and fish was all that was important. Total assholes, hick assholes.

4

Following the line of the forest, Budd tried not to think about things that would make him angry. He had enough to worry about.

He might have heard the footfalls if he had not been listening to the music, but the volume was almost to the max. He liked Madonna. She kind of reminded him of Delia. Or maybe Delia reminded him of Madonna. Whatever. He was on the verge of accomplishing something which he'd been thinking about for a good while. He'd be fourteen in December, just in time to keep him in ninth grade. As long as you were the right age for your grade by December 31, you were okay.

One of these days he'd be eighteen. Then he'd be out of the old man's way, and then he'd do what he wanted. Would Delia still be around by then?

Probably not. The family would move ten times before then. They'd be on the move as soon as the old man thought up some new scheme designed to make him a somebody.

Pop figured all the other people in Petittville were somebodies, and that's what he wanted. That's what he always said, every time he started selling a new study Bible or got into some real estate deal.

Budd was wondering what it would be like to have his dad in some regular job, a job in one place anyway, even if it didn't make them somebodies.

The hounds pushed through the trees, running in a pack. There were six of them. They were big. Very big dogs. Their heads were massive, wide and flat across the top with slobbering jaws and ears that flopped back as they ran.

Their black fur made them almost invisible in the darkness, but their weight made the pounding of their feet audible, and their breath snarled through their throats.

They relied on their sense of smell to locate Budd, almost aiming for him as he slowed to a walk upon nearing the end of the wood line. He wasn't far from home.

He didn't see them coming, not at first. He was unaware of their presence until the paws thudded into his back, pitching him forward. He had been struck near his shoulder blades by the lead hound, which had sprung, forcing all its weight into him.

Budd was toppled face first into the moist grass and weeds. Leaves crunched under him, and the wind was forced from his lungs. He felt it go and struggled for several seconds to breathe again.

Then he rolled over with his arms swinging, uncertain at first of what had hit him but determined to fight back.

Why were they after him? Did they kill for food? They didn't look like pets or strays. They were too vicious for either. He could see their eyes glowing red, and wisps of breath shot from their nostrils, taking on a smoky look in the chill. They looked a little like the Rottweilers he'd seen on television, but they were bigger. They were bigger than any dogs he'd ever seen.

Before his mind could question further, they were on him, their thick bodies weighing him down, their jaws seeking exposed flesh. He felt his body pressed down into the grass, and the pressure on his rib cage made him gag.

He threw an arm up, blocking the first dog that went for his throat. Its daggerlike teeth dug into the thick fabric of the army jacket, but he didn't feel pain. The teeth didn't make it to his arm. Frantically, Budd began to hammer the side of its head with his free hand.

Once.

Twice.

Three times he struck the dog before another's teeth sank into his wrist, holding fast. He tried to shake it loose, but the jaws were too powerful, and this pain he did feel as blood began to ooze out around the mutt's teeth.

He screamed, drawing new breath in an effort to make his voice carry. The music still pounded in his ears, so he could not fully hear the dogs' growls.

6

Somebody in nearby houses must be able to hear him, though. It wasn't that far away, and nothing ever happened in this piss-ant town. If anyone heard screams, it would be so out of the ordinary they'd be sure to come and investigate.

The smell of his blood, which now smeared their snouts, filled his nostrils. It sickened him, and he almost vomited. As he choked on the bile in his throat, a massive paw ripped across his face. He felt his cheek tearing. It would leave a scar.

If he survived.

Tears filled his eyes now, nightmare tears, tears of the fear of death. He tried to twist his weight around, hoping he could work his body out from under the dogs, but the effort didn't work. He felt teeth sinking into the meaty portion of his hip.

He screamed again, still hoping someone would come to his rescue, but everybody was inside watching television by now. It was too late for anybody to hear.

He wondered how hard people would try to help him if they knew it was Budd the troublemaker anyway. Most of them would say good riddance. He was a punk. He wouldn't be around to defy teachers now or corrupt the good kids.

They might even have a party tomorrow in the teachers' lounge. The parents might even be invited. They'd have coffee and cookies and rejoice, oh yeah. Budd Hagan wouldn't be here to bother folks anymore.

He stopped screaming when a bite severed his jugular.

As he felt the hot blood pouring onto his chest, he wondered if Delia and Charlie would miss him.

Chapter 2

Charlie Black awoke before his alarm clock sounded, the pressure of his bladder intense, as if it were about to burst. He thought about getting up, but when he rolled over and looked at the face of the clock, he saw that he would have to rise in fifteen minutes anyway.

No need to stir with 6 A.M. so close. He could suffer for a few minutes, just to let the pleasant grogginess of almost-sleep continue. Sometimes his brain conjured vivid dreams in the last moments before truly waking, and he was thrilled when that happened. Charlie loved ideas. He wanted to be a filmmaker, and the vivid, early-morning images were inspiration. They made him think of ways to set up shots and ways to light a scene, all of which were important, he had learned from the magazines he got at Kroger. It was the only place in town that had a really good magazine selection, and while people sometimes complained, he was able to find things like *Cinefantastique* there along with *Fangoria*. They didn't carry *GoreZone*, so he'd had to save his money and get a subscription. Fortunately it arrived in a white envelope. If his mom ever saw the covers, that would be the end of his reading of that publication. She'd already vetoed *Prevue* because of the advertising pages featuring pinup calendars, and risqué comic books.

Charlie's mother treated him like a kid. He'd learned to accept that and work around it. Crossing her was only good for creating more problems, so he just accepted her protective tendencies and appeased her as much as possible.

He didn't want to anger her now because, while it was not quite November, Christmas was drawing close. His dad was supposed to buy a video camera this year.

While the present was one of those dubbed "for the family," Charlie had big plans for it. He and Budd were going to use it to make a horror movie.

It wouldn't be Hollywood quality, and editing it was going to be a problem, but they would at least have the fun of putting something together. To cut it, they would use the VCR at Budd's grandmother's, hooked to Charlie's VCR. That meant the quality would suffer some—each new generation of video lost quality—but it was the best they could do.

Charlie was working on the script, and Budd and Delia would be starring in it. They wouldn't be able to do much with special effects—SPFX as they said in the business—but it would be Charlie's first chance to try anything like this, and he'd get to experiment with some makeup he'd been reading about.

That was why having *GoreZone* was so important. It had articles on how to do makeup and that sort of thing.

With those thoughts in mind, he drifted off, and an image of Budd running filtered into his brain. *What was he running from?* He looked scared; he kept looking behind him at something. He looked like the Devil was after him.

The alarm clock buzzed through the dream, jerking Charlie awake again. He sat up feeling a little uneasy. He'd probably dreamed it because he'd been thinking about Budd and the movie, but seeing friends in danger was frightening.

He'd tell Budd about it at school and Budd would laugh it off, but Charlie hated it when he had dreams about his friends. His mom said psychic stuff was phony, but he found once in a while he dreamed things that came true. Usually it was only pieces of the dreams, and things didn't happen with enough frequency or accuracy to make him feel he was truly predicting the future, but they did happen often enough to make him worry when he dreamed bad things.

Once he'd dreamed the family was driving along the roadway, and his father had taken a wrong turn and crashed the car. The next night when they were coming home, his father had accidentally turned into the driveway of the house next door. He hadn't wrecked the car but Charlie's dream was close, if not exact.

He'd have to tell Budd to be careful. That would make him feel better, even if Budd did laugh. Budd could be pretty shitty at times, but that was just his nature.

Charlie's mom always worried Budd was just using him, figuring Charlie helped him with homework and things, but he knew Budd was his only real friend.

Slowly, he threw back the covers and climbed out of bed, feeling his muscles stretch. He yawned, rubbed his eyes, and turned on the light. Pinhead, the scary guy from the Clive Barker movie, stared down at him from the wall, his hands offering up a mysterious-looking cube.

It was his best poster, ordered from the classifieds in the back of *Fangoria*. It shared space with posters from the "Scream Greats" fold-out series in *Fango*; they had been selected carefully since many of those would have upset his mom too.

"Pumpkinhead," No. 46, and the Dracula guy from *The Monster Squad*, No. 61, weren't too bad. He'd passed on such selections as No. 54, which featured one of the victims from *Halloween III: Season of the Witch*, and No. 58 from *Phantasm II*, which pictured one of the guys who fell prey to the dreaded silver ball. After some consideration, he'd also withheld a poster from *Elvira Mistress of the Dark* from public display. It wasn't gory, but sexy stuff had resulted in the dismissal of *Prevue*, after all.

Charlie gave Pinhead his usual morning salute and hurried to the bathroom to take care of the pressing matter which had awakened him before the dream.

Charlie was a quick dresser. He took his shower, fussed with his light brown hair—which was a little long in back—with the blow dryer for a while and then put on jeans, a stylish shirt, and tennis shoes.

He was thin and fairly tall, nice enough looking with blue eyes and smooth features. He kept hoping some of the girls would notice, but so far he'd been basically ignored. He kept expecting that to change. Delia had picked Budd out. Maybe there was somebody waiting for him.

Heading into the kitchen, he sat down at the table, where his mother had a bowl of cereal waiting, an off-brand of corn flakes. Betsy Black always bought the economy brand even though his dad was an executive at the soap plant in Aimsley and made a good salary. She didn't see any reason to throw money away.

She was stirring around in the refrigerator as he began to eat.

"How's it going this morning?" she asked.

"Fine."

She shut the refrigerator door and brushed an imaginary spot from her robe. At thirty-four, she was still pretty, though beginning to put on weight, which she fought with diets and exercise videos.

Her blonde hair was cut in a short, pixielike style. Wearing it long would make her look older, she claimed. His dad hadn't liked it last year when she'd had it clipped, but she'd kept it that way because it was easier to manage than at shoulder length. Charlie was happy that at least his mom was presentable when she had to attend school meetings or whatever. She had a few of the kids his age lusting. That didn't gain him much ground, but it didn't hurt.

"Any tests today?" she asked. It was a frequent random question. If he'd waked up sick, it would have been the first thing off her lips.

"Not today," he answered.

It was true. Today was a typical day. No special projects due, no extra demands. All he had to do was survive the hoods, gym class, and the upperclassmen. Piece o' cake.

Petittville High School was one of two schools in the small town. The other was a combination elementary and junior high. Charlie had not attended there, and that was part of his social problem. Almost everybody else had gone to school there, and the cliques had been formed long before his father's transfer had brought the family to Petittville six months earlier. Even though everybody in the freshman class was technically a new student, Charlie was "the new guy." He'd found that out quickly and formed an alliance with Budd.

The school was a new building by school standards, constructed in 1977. It was only a couple of blocks from his house, so he chose to walk most days rather than ride the school bus.

The bus was just an extended version of school and the feeling of alienation, while walking was at least a chance to let his thoughts wander without having to put up with any bullshit from the seniors who were pissed that they didn't have cars and took it out on the underclassmen.

Besides, after school, free from the meandering route the bus followed, he could stop by Video Exchange and see Nell Devery, the part-time clerk.

After a final check of his hair, he put on his black windbreaker, tucked his books under his arm, and picked up the used Graham Masterton paperback from his dresser. He secreted it in his inside jacket pocket. Mom didn't like him taking his paperback books to school, but he needed them to pass the time between classes or at the end of classes when the lectures finished early. He usually managed to keep them hidden inside his textbooks if he read while the lessons were still going on, though Mrs. Morris, the history teacher, still had one she'd found him reading while problems were being explained on the board.

He hadn't figured out how to get that one back yet, because he was afraid if he asked for it, she'd be reminded to call his mother.

As he headed for the front door, he passed his dad, Daniel, coming out of the master bedroom. His tie was already knotted perfectly into place, and he was fastening the cuffs on his starched white shirt as he headed toward the kitchen for his coffee and eggs.

"Morning, Charlie."

"Hi, Dad."

His father was two years older than his mother. Gray was starting to show at the temples of his black hair with sprinkles in his neatly trimmed beard, but he was still a nice-looking man with boyish features.

His mind was usually on his work. He even had a home office upstairs where he worked on projects after hours. Charlie sometimes used the photocopier, but most of the time he played it safe and stayed out of there.

He was out the door by the time his father made it to the kitchen. Along the walk to school, he watched for Budd. Sometimes Budd accompanied him on the journey, but sometimes he was running late or skipping altogether.

Some days it was almost as if Budd weren't there because he kept his Walkman on and moved his head in rhythm with the music, leaving Charlie to walk silently at his side. That usually happened on days that Budd had had fights with his old man.

Charlie wandered around looking for Budd when he arrived at school, fifteen minutes before bell time, but there was no sign of him in the hallways.

The place was already crowded with kids at the mercy of the bus routes. Jocks in button-down Oxford shirts walked with their girlfriends, the beautiful chicks. They draped their arms possessively around the girls' shoulders.

Hoods lingered here and there, shoulders slouching as if they expected to be rousted by teachers. He didn't spot the Asshole Squad.

Clusters of giggling girls were strategically located.

Charlie eyed them secretly as he walked past, tracing the form of their slender legs and firm behinds, displayed in the tight, stylish skirts they wore.

None of them seemed to give him a passing glance. He bowed his head slightly, easing on along the hallway to the row of lockers outside his first class. That was where he always hung out in the mornings, whether Budd was around or not; sometimes Budd was off with Delia, but Charlie preferred to have the door of his first class in sight. He avoided late charges that way. You had to stay a half hour after school if they nailed you for tardiness.

Taking out his paperback, he began to read, losing himself in the scary passages that always enthralled him.

He was still reading when he heard the stir at the end of the hallway and looked up. A couple of the guys standing there were snickering. Charlie's eyes quickly looked in on the reason.

She was walking down the center of the hallway, ignoring the hormonal reactions she was creating. A slip of paper in her hand seemed to indicate she was looking for a particular classroom, but there was no mistaking her for a student.

She had to be around thirty, though she looked younger, a slender woman with brown hair and piercing dark eyes.

Charlie saw her moving in slow motion, taking in the bounce of her hair, the spring in her step, and the soft beauty of her features. There seemed to be a sharpness about her face, a pert, exciting look — even her eyebrows had a hint of it, arched slightly.

Her lips were full, her cheekbones pronounced. He didn't feel inclined to turn back to his reading.

He just continued to look, watching the slight bounce of her breasts beneath the dark blouse she wore.

Her waist was slim, and she wore a short brown skirt with dark stockings, so dark that skin was not really visible through them, but that didn't really matter. They were a second skin. He could see the ripples of muscle in her calves, could make out the perfect form of her thighs.

In an instant an image of the two of them entwined filled his thoughts. He was no stronger to fantasies, but this one seemed to form full-blown, as vivid as one of those early-morning dreams.

He pictured his mouth against hers, his hands on her breasts, those muscular legs wrapped around him. He blinked, taking charge of his brain again. This was not the place.

He tried to remain casual, leaning there against the lockers, pretending he was looking somewhere else without actually letting her out of his sight. When she drew even with him, he found it impossible to look away; he had to look at her. Because she was looking at him.

It only lasted for an instant, but her face turned toward him, and a smile crossed her lips for an instant. Was it real or had he imagined it?

As she walked on past, he followed her with his gaze, watching her legs and the gentle sway of her hemline, hinting at the form of her ass beneath.

A new image of her, beckoning to him, pushed into his thoughts. He shook it away and tried to watch where she was going, but she disappeared down the hallway before she had selected a room.

Then the bell rang, and the hallway was a sea of bodies. It was too late to try and find her if he wanted to be in class on time, but she would probably be around all day. He'd run across her again. She was certainly a nice surprise.

Attractive young teachers were a deviation from the norm. There were some cute ones mingled in with the ones pushing retirement, but none to compare with the woman who had just walked down the hall, none in the realm of beautiful.

He couldn't get her out of his mind as he strolled into his first class and took his seat. From what he heard from the other guys, she was on their minds too, and they were voicing activities in which they would like to engage her. They weren't intellectual pursuits.

He made it through his first two classes without dying of boredom or getting lost in a fantasy. When third hour—general science—arrived, he sat in his seat waiting for Budd to walk in.

By the time the bell had rung, Budd hadn't appeared. As roll was called, Charlie looked over at his friend's empty seat. It seemed to serve as some dark omen as he recalled his morning dream.

The teacher, Mr. Briggs, called Budd's name, which was really Horace, three times, finally looking up to see the empty desk. He marked the absence in his grade book and moved on.

Charlie wondered where Budd could be. Could he be somewhere with Delia? He hoped Budd hadn't had some skirmish with his father. If he was skipping and they caught him, this time he would get the old three-day vacation.

Word would get back to Charlie's mom, too, and she'd be even more concerned if she heard he was palling around with Budd. Everything was a problem.

After science, he joined the flow of bodies, elbowing his way to English class. He didn't mind English class too much, especially the literature portion. They'd read one Sherlock Holmes story, "The Adventure of the Speckled Band," and a couple of the other selections hadn't been bad either. There was one called "The Monkey's Paw" that was kind of like Stephen King.

While everybody bitched about the poetry, he kind of liked that too. When he wasn't trying to think up movie scripts, Charlie worked on poems in a spiral notebook. He wrote some about girls he thought were pretty, trying to come up with rhymes that described his feelings of longing. So far he hadn't come up with anything to rival the classics, but he was trying.

Today they were supposed to discuss a kind of dull story by Sherwood Anderson called "Sophistication." Charlie had identified with it a bit, but not enough to keep it from seeming slow. He knew it was from a collection. Maybe all of the stories together made more sense.

He liked discussions about stories. The other kids tended to think he was snobby and intellectual, but he didn't let that bother him. Mrs. Dennison wanted students to bring up ideas. She was one of the good teachers, in Charlie's opinion. She was in her forties and not pretty, but she was pleasant, and that made up for it.

He'd get through this Sherwood Anderson stuff, and then they would be into some good stuff again. He'd flipped ahead in the text, and an Edgar Allan Poe story was coming up, "The Cask of Amontillado." He was looking forward to that. He hadn't read much of Poe, not as much as some of the newer horror writers, but he knew it was Poe who had started the party.

He was peeking over at the Poe story when the door closed with a slight rumble, the glass pane rattling.

He looked up, expecting to see Mrs. Dennison, but instead he found his eyes locked on the new teacher, the one from the hallway. She stood at the front of the classroom, her hands clasped behind her and a smile on her face.

He felt a sudden shudder run down his backbone, and he let his book fall closed. His mouth was open slightly. He shut it as she began to speak, trying not to let his expression reveal his awe.

"I'm Miss Nielson," she was saying. "Mrs. Dennison is ill and may be out for a while, so you have me to keep you from getting behind in your perusal of the literary classics our textbook has to offer." Her voice was light. She was only partially serious.

Charlie gripped the edge of his desk, doing his best not to act out of the ordinary. She was just a new teacher.

Only when she turned to the board to write down an assignment did he look up again. He watched her calves as the hem on her skirt moved

16

with each stroke of the chalk in her hand. She was certainly an improvement over the usual run of teacher.

When she had finished writing, she turned and looked back at the class. "I'm going to give you the period to read this story." She had written "The Cask of Amontillado" on the board. "That way you won't have an excuse tomorrow when we talk about it and 'Sophistication.'"

With that, she turned and walked to her desk, hiding her legs as she sat down behind it.

As she looked down at her gradebook, Charlie studied her face. Petittville High had its share of pretty girls, but there was something unique about Miss Nielson. Maybe it wasn't just her features, which to Charlie's way of thinking were as close to perfect as they could get. Maybe there was something more about it. What was it he'd read about, an aura? That seemed kind of cosmic, but maybe that was the definition for the quality he saw in her. He allowed himself to stare over his book for a while, wondering what she would look like in a bikini … or less.

Then, reluctantly now instead of with anticipation, he turned to the Poe story. There was magic in the report of the thousand injuries of Fortunato, though not magic to compare with the magic Miss Nielson was generating.

He read the first few paragraphs and realized he had no idea what had been said in the story. His thoughts had drifted. Once more he returned to the top of the page for another attempt. He concentrated a little better on the narrator's desire for revenge this time, but by the time he had read to the bottom of the page, he was ready for another glimpse of the new teacher.

Cautiously, he rolled his eyes upward, peering over the edge of the book. He almost started when he focused on the desk.

She was looking at him.

He locked his eyes back on Poe, feeling like Charlie Brown out of *Peanuts* when that red-haired girl was around. He let his hand rest on the surface of his desk, running his nail into the carved letters which must have been cut a couple of years back? "Quiet Riot Rules." The letters had been filled in with a red felt-tipped marker. Beside it was another deeply etched message. "Sawyer Sucks." He suspected that was Mr. Sawyer the math teacher, not Tom.

After a while, he looked up again. She was looking at the lesson schedule before her on the desk. Her long hair fell loosely around her face. One finger was pressed against her temple, and her eyebrows were slightly arched.

She probably hadn't been looking at him at all, just looking up to make sure everybody was reading. *Wishful thinking again, Black. That's all.*

He read a little more of the Poe story, but he didn't manage to get through it. He was almost relieved when the bell rang.

Chapter 3

Charlie was in Mr. Sawyer's algebra class, dying of boredom, when word came of Budd's death.

Sawyer had a way of making everyone comatose when he explained equations at the board, and Charlie was staring out the window when Bethany Quinn, a junior who worked in the front office, came in.

Sawyer, a thin, lanky man with glasses that probably would have seared his eyes if he looked into the sun, looked up from the board, reluctant to pause from X and Y.

He closed his book with chalk inside it to mark his place and listened as Bethany talked to him. She kept lacing and unlacing her fingers in front of her as she spoke. Her weight was balanced on one foot, but she shifted it to the other, then back again, nervously.

Bethany had long blonde hair, was a little pudgy but had managed to get her acne under control.

As she whispered to Sawyer, her expression produced a furrow across her forehead that informed the entire class something was wrong.

The news didn't do much for Sawyer's expression, either. He seemed to lose some of his color, and he shook his head sadly.

Bethany said something else, turning then to leave the room. Sawyer walked back to his desk and sat down. He had the attention of every student now in a way he would never achieve with his lectures. He kept a solemn expression on his face.

"Some of you may know Budd Hagan," he said, searching for words.

Charlie sat up and stared at the man intently. His palms suddenly felt clammy, and his eyes began to throb in their sockets. He could sense bad news was coming.

"I'm afraid I've just been given a report about him," Sawyer said slowly. He pursed his lips as if he was uncertain about how to go on.

It seems that, um, they found his … him a little while ago on the vacant lot on Allen Street. It was apparently some dogs. I know some of you were probably his friends, and this is difficult news. Mrs. Ross will see any of you in the guidance office if you need to talk about it."

Charlie looked down at the graffiti again. It couldn't be true. He had things to tell Budd, things to talk about. He wanted to hear Budd's comments about the new teacher. They'd be rude and crude—Budd would brag about how crude and rude, in fact—but they would be funny too, Budd's brand of funny. He'd have remarks about her appearance and probably suppositions about her social life.

But he never even got the chance to see her. That wasn't fair. And he'd just started dating Delia. That had made him happy, maybe the only thing that had ever really made Budd happy. He'd had a miserable life, and now it was over.

Charlie fought back his tears. He'd never hear the end of it if he cried over Budd. You couldn't cry over another guy no matter how good a buddy he was, not unless you wanted everybody to figure you were queer.

"I'm sorry to break the news to you this way," Sawyer was mumbling. "We, that is, the front office figured rumors would get around. This way you have the true story. I'm sorry."

After a few moments of silence, he tried to turn back to the lesson, but he wasn't very successful in capturing attention again with equations. Even the people who didn't like Budd—most of them—had stark, shocked expressions. Their faces were colorless.

Budd may have been mean to them, may have cut in front of them in line or made snide remarks about their clothes. That was Budd's way, his shield, but the fact remained that he was one of them, their age, their size, and the last time they'd seen him he'd been breathing.

Now, though he still breathed in memory, their thoughts were conjuring images of the reality that had been reported to them, images horrifying and ugly.

Charlie's mental picture was vivid. He had walked the lot off Allen Street with Budd many times, their feet kicking up crumpled brown leaves, the weeds scratching at their pant legs.

Now, in his thoughts, Budd lay there, half hidden in the clumps of brown grass, a ruined form. Charlie thought of his friend's dead eyes staring up toward the sky, and he imagined the blood on the ground and the rips in his flesh.

Though he had not seen much of death in his fourteen years, he knew that when it came, especially in this form, it was not pretty.

He wondered where the dogs had come from. Many people had pets in the Petittville subdivisions, but they were well fed and pampered. There weren't many strays, and he had never seen any roaming in packs. Did tame dogs form packs?

There were woods on the fringe of the lot, but Charlie had never seen any animals there. He'd never heard of any problems with dogs in the neighborhood, not even with them tearing up newspapers. He shook his head, frightened at the thought that wild dogs might be waiting out there somewhere, waiting for anybody who got in their way.

Chief Lucius Rice eased his police cruiser over against the curb in front of the vacant lot on Allen Street. Things were quiet now. Yellow strands of police tape, which bordered the area of the death, flagged in the breeze, and leaves rustled, but there was no sign of other movement. The dogs had not returned to the scene. Apparently that rule applied only to human criminals.

Reaching over to the seat beside him, he picked up his hat, feeling for some reason that he needed to be as official as possible.

He had worn it for the unpleasant task of informing Budd Hagan's parents. Now he would wear it to look over the scene of the carnage once again.

He fit the band into place over his thinning hair as he climbed from the front seat. He was a tall black man with a heavy, muscular build. His hair was going gray at the temples, making it look as if tufts of cotton had been pasted there, and he wore wire-rimmed glasses over his stern features. He looked capable of dealing with criminals far tougher than Petittville had to offer.

He would have preferred criminals like those he had faced in New Orleans for eight years. They were more predictable.

Walking to the edge of the lot, he stepped over the yellow tape and rested his hand on the butt of the pistol in his holster as he walked toward the spot where the body had rested. The blood was sticky and brown on the grass where the body had lain.

The parents had not taken it well. Rice had driven over as soon as the sheriff's department crime scene unit and the coroner's men had left, feeling it was his duty to go in person.

The mother, in her forties with graying dark hair, had wept. The father, a thin man with a seedy look about him, had reacted with less outward emotion. Only in his eyes had Rice detected the pain, and then only for a moment.

He'd wanted to know who the dogs belonged to, and Rice had suspected that was because visions of a lawsuit were dancing in the man's head.

The grandmother had taken the news worst of all. For a while the police chief had feared he was going to have to put her in the cruiser and try to get her over to the hospital in Penn's Ferry, not the best facility but the closest at hand.

Her face had reddened as the tears ran down her face, and she had laced her fingers into the blue curls of her permanent. Finally her daughter had settled her down, giving her water and whispering comforts.

He'd left after that. Grief was a private thing, and he had intruded longer than he had wanted. He wasn't sure exactly what he was supposed to do about the death, but he knew people were going to look to him.

Petittville was a quiet place. That was why people lived there. They wanted an easy place to raise children, a place where drugs were not a worry and the only negative influences were on television.

After leaving the house, Rice had cruised the neighborhood streets, looking for signs of stray dogs, but he'd seen no sign of any animals that were not on leashes or in pens in compliance with the village statutes. Technically, by Louisiana incorporation laws, Petittville was a village, not a town. It was a distinction on paper more than in reality.

Standing over the spot of the death, Rice felt a queasy spin in his stomach. He'd watched kids die from knife wounds and gun blasts, and every time the life oozed out of somebody, it was awful. He wasn't sure why he felt worse about this one.

Maybe because it was the first death he'd seen in three years in Petittville, other than those from natural causes.

The dogs had done terrible work on Budd Hagan, ripping and gnawing, leaving flesh and blood scattered and splashed. Rice had to force himself to kneel and search through the grass once more for some sign of fur or other indication of where the dogs might have come from. The coroner's men had confirmed there had been more than one.

It was too much to hope that some loose veterinarian's tag might have slipped from a collar or some other easy sign would appear to lead him directly to an owner.

He rose and walked to the edge of the woods, looking for signs on the ground of a trail or tracks, but he spotted nothing. He wasn't sure if they had come through the trees or from somewhere else, though the trees seemed the logical place. He'd ruled out the neighborhood. There would have been other evidence of them, even sightings. Perhaps they had sought refuge in the trees. He didn't know much about dogs' behavior. Animals perplexed everybody, especially in Riverland Parish. In the northern region the animals had gone wild during a drought a couple of years back, and only the mixed blessings of a forest fire had seemed to quell their assaults. Nobody had ever satisfactorily explained that as far as he knew.

Maybe the phenomenon was being repeated. He took his glasses off and rubbed his eyes. He hoped that wasn't the case.

With his hand still on the butt of his gun, he walked a short distance into the forest. His ears strained to pick up sounds of animals.

He heard wind, nothing more, and after a few more steps he decided it would be useless to wander through the trees hoping to stumble on the dogs. They were probably long gone by now.

At the back of his mind, he was wondering if the dogs might be pit bulls. Dog fighting was not unheard of though it had been a couple of years since the sheriff's deputies had smashed a ring.

He'd heard about it, and it sickened him. There was something less than human about the bastards that could perpetrate such an atrocity, and if he found out this boy had died because some idiot had trained a bunch of dogs to crave blood, he'd nail the son of a bitch to the wall.

He might not be able to put glue on a first-degree murder charge, but he'd damn sure find a way to stick on something as severe as possible.

Charlie caught up with Delia between classes. Her eyes were red, and she clutched a crumpled tissue in one hand. She was still beautiful, and as Charlie looked at her in her white blouse and short denim skirt, he couldn't quite avoid thinking of the stories Budd had told about her.

It had never seemed like Budd was betraying her when he told his stories, but now, seeing her hurt, knowing how she must have felt about Budd, he felt a little ashamed about his secret knowledge. It was as if he possessed something that belonged to her.

He said, "I feel real bad."

She brushed the white-gold bangs off her forehead and nodded. "Me too, Charlie. Me too."

Petittville High allowed only five minutes between classes. Violators spent thirty minutes in detention, so they walked hurriedly along the window-lined front hallway past the courtyard toward their classes in the new wing. Their sneakers squeaked on the tile as they moved, sounding to Charlie like screams of pain.

"We saw each other yesterday afternoon," she said. "He must have been on his way home from seeing me when it happened."

"Yeah. He didn't call me last night," Charlie said. "I should have known something was wrong."

Delia looked at her shoes. "Everybody thinks I have a thing for the new guys," Delia said. "I guess there have been a couple, but I liked Budd. You know that, don't you, Charlie?"

"Sure. Sure."

"Nobody I've known has ever been killed like this. I feel like I'm real cold, Charlie."

"I feel funny," he agreed. "Sad but worse. Empty kind of."

They reached the door of her classroom. She hesitated a moment, her books clutched against her. "It's terrible."

Charlie nodded in agreement. He had to get on to class. She seemed to want him to say something else, but he couldn't think of anything that didn't sound silly.

He patted her shoulder, and she touched his face softly before he turned away, heading on to his classroom. In the hall, he could hear voices buzzing about the death. Kids didn't know what to think about it. Some of them sounded scared.

Charlie wasn't frightened. He didn't really think about the same thing happening to him. He just thought about how bad it must have been for his friend. Poor old Budd.

More than anything he wanted to talk to Nell. The guidance counselor might smile and be polite, but she wouldn't really help even though she meant to.

Nell might not help either, but she was the one he wanted to talk to. He always felt better talking to Nell about things that he didn't understand, things that bothered him. Only a few hours to go.

One of those hours was unfortunately P.E., the torture tomb of every kid's existence except the Neanderthals who counted on it as the only "A" on their report cards.

It was tough being a freshman anytime, but P.E. was the worst. The coaches, not noted for being sensitive types, tended to turn everyone loose in the gym, leaving the younger kids at the mercy of the seniors.

Charlie headed for the gym with the same apprehension that seized him every day before class. He thankfully had it sixth hour, so he was at least able to get the hell out of there after everything was over.

Pushing the door of the locker room open, he walked inside. People were already getting changed. With his books under his arm, he walked on down to the locker he usually used.

Mark Morris was at his usual place beside the next locker. He was a small kid with brown-rimmed glasses that were too big for his face. He was a sophomore but that didn't seem to matter to anyone. He tended to get the brunt of the jokes in many rituals because he did well in most classes and the Neanderthals took P.E. as an opportunity to get even for that.

He wasn't exactly a friend, but Charlie got along with him. "That was too bad about your friend," Mark said. It wasn't an easy remark for him to make because Budd had picked on him, too.

"It's rough," Charlie said before turning and walking over to the wire baskets where the uniforms were stored.

He always had trouble with his combination lock. He spun the dial as he was supposed to, stopping at each number, but it never opened on the first try. It was new and the numbers had to be exact. Older locks might fall open if the numbers were close, but not this one.

Today was no exception. He had to repeat the process three or four times while listening to chuckles behind him. Finally the lock popped, and he was able to get changed.

Then he and Mark walked out into the gym. A cluster of other freshmen were standing near the doorway. Charlie and Mark were about to join them when a volleyball whizzed past Charlie's head, slamming into the wall with the force of a cannonball. The impact made a ringing sound as the ball bounced off the wall.

"It's Tessman," Mark warned before Charlie had a chance to turn and look in the direction from which the salvo had come.

The other freshmen were scattering. Mark and Charlie also began to look for cover as Tessman, one of the top senior terrorists, wound up for another blow. He already had another volleyball in his hand.

Tessman was an average-sized kid with sandy hair cut in a flat top. He was wearing only his blue shorts today, no shirt or shoes. That was his usual attire, in fact, giving him more of a wild-man look.

If Charlie made contact with a volleyball, it probably wouldn't do much damage, but he knew that with the force Tessman was using, it would sting like hell.

He and Mark jogged along in front of the bleachers, trying to weave as other kids clambered for cover of some kind.

A few inches behind them, a volleyball thudded into the wooden seats, rattling the flaps on the collapsible accordion structure.

Charlie headed for the end of the bleachers. There was a nook between the seats and the wall which would offer cover.

He could hear Mark behind him, following his lead. Meanwhile, Tessman was laughing, and behind him his friends were too. That encouraged him.

He retrieved the first volleyball and mounted another attack. Charlie looked back over his shoulder just as the ball flew, hitting Ronald Hodges on the left side of his face.

The blow let out a loud slap, and the force of it twisted the kid's head around. His hand flew up to his cheek, and tears came out of his eyes as the skin began to discolor.

He wasn't damaged, but it definitely hadn't done him any good, and the seniors were getting a big laugh out of it. Humiliation was a form of pain too, Charlie was reminded.

Nearing the end of the bleachers, he stepped up on the lowest bench, then the next, and ran along it until he was at the edge. Then he stepped down into the corner, ducking his head just as a volleyball whizzed over.

Not a good sign, he thought as it slapped the wall. That meant Tessman was following him.

Mark was behind him too. He joined Charlie, huddling against the wall. Another volleyball slammed into the bleachers. It seemed to have more force than the last.

Tessman was pitching harder.

"You think he's after us?" Mark asked.

"Must be. Everybody else scattered."

"Did you see what it did to Ronald?"

"The one he hit?"

"Yeah, his nose was bleeding."

"I didn't see that part."

"Wasn't pretty."

Another volleyball thudded against the wall, and peeping out through the bleachers, Charlie could see Tessman calculating the angle. Apparently slamming it directly into the corner at them wasn't enough of a challenge. He was trying to figure a way to bounce it off the wall.

"The stupid fuck'll be fat and unemployed in three years," Mark predicted. If we live through this, we'll have to visit his hovel and taunt him."

Charlie nodded, feeling stupid. This couldn't last much longer. Sooner or later one of the coaches was going to get tired of reading skin magazines in his office and check on things.

In Charlie's experience, coaches—usually former bullies—tended to side with bullies. Bullying was about sixty percent of coaching anyway and almost all of physical education supervision. Still, they couldn't stand by and let this kind of shit go on for long. If somebody got badly hurt, it would complicate the comfort of their positions.

Eventually, without an appearance of a coach, Tessman got tired and wandered away. Deeming it safe to emerge, Charlie and Mark stepped out of hiding into the worst of it—humiliation and a round of applause from the seniors and others on hand who'd watched them cowering.

"Did you girls have a good time back there?" Carl Gremillion asked. He was a blond-haired guy with smooth features and an attitude.

"They were probably back there swapping blow jobs," said Mickey Wilson, a skinny junior with lean muscles.

Charlie felt his face redden, but he ignored their taunts. He felt a little stupid, but when he had walked back up the court and saw the blood smeared across the shiny varnish, he felt a little better. At least he and Mark had escaped that.

One major ordeal per period wasn't too bad. At least they hadn't tried to stick his head in the toilet like they had Donald Walker.

"We made it," Mark said, unperturbed by the jeers.

"Yeah," Charlie agreed, climbing onto the bleachers near the locker room door. He wasn't in the mood to try and get into any of the basketball games going on, and as long as the coaches weren't around, it was safe to sit.

Sitting and brooding about Budd seemed to be as good a way as any to pass the hour.

"Did you ever read anything by Arthur C. Clarke?" Mark asked, sitting beside him. He didn't want to play basketball either.

"I read a short story, I think," Charlie said absently. Normally he liked comparing notes with Mark, but today his mind wasn't geared to small talk.

Chapter 4

Nell Devery slipped a new stack of *Ghost Rider* into the designated slot on the rack that lined one wall of the video store; the fiery lettering and a portion of the cover art remained visible.

The rack was carefully arranged, with Marvel titles divided from DC, and independents catalogued separately. Matt didn't purchase many independents because the distributors didn't have a return policy, but he did make an effort to carry some offbeat titles. Petittville didn't have a big demand for comics, but Matt Bordelon, the store owner and manager, had grown up on superheroes and wanted to make sure kids had them if they wanted them.

Nell was thankful for that passion because there was no way she'd get to read all the titles if he didn't stock them. She was squeaking through college with a student loan and the money she earned here at the store, so she couldn't buy many.

She was able to collect issues only since Matt usually let her keep a few here and there rather than ripping the covers to be returned for credit. That was also due to his respect for the medium. He hated to destroy books, so it allowed her to pursue her interests.

That was half of why she kept the job here even though she was going to school at Pine College over in Penn's Ferry. She probably could have landed another job closer to classes, but she would have had to give up her comics habit and that didn't strike her as viable.

She wanted to become a comic book artist when she finished her degree, so it was better to drive a few miles. She had a garage apartment here in Petittville that was reasonably cheap too, cheaper than campus housing.

That suited her since it kept her away from her old man. That was the major reason she'd selected Pine College for her education. It was a three-hour drive from her pop's trailer in Monroe, where she'd already spent more of her life than she'd wanted to. If she'd gone to Northeast where he wanted, it might have been cheaper, but she would have had to stay home.

That didn't do it for her because her dad was a slob, and he drank. He didn't hurt her or anything physically, but she didn't care for being around him either.

Besides, Pine had a decent art program. She had to suffer through basics and worry about forms she never planned to work in, but they also let her get a good foundation for commercial artwork. That was something to fall back on while she worked on developing a style for comics work.

The job helped in building contacts too. She'd gone to a couple of comics and sci-fi conventions with Matt, who also did a little trading in back issues, and she'd met a few guys in the business who had given her some pointers.

They liked giving nineteen-year-old redheads help, she'd learned fairly quickly. Most of their groupies were teenage boys, and she was a far sight prettier even if she didn't agree to go up to their rooms with them to see their original pencil work.

That usually made it clear she was serious and wasn't just another fan saying she wanted to be an artist in order to make it with a pro.

She was cute enough to make them wish that wasn't the case. She wore her hair brushed long and straight, and she had a cute, youthful beauty that made her look younger than her age. Her blue eyes were clear, her lips full, her build lean with just the right flare at the hips and roundness at the buttocks.

Her taste in clothes tended toward casual dresses, a tad old-fashioned in their look, and she always wore her lucky hat, a round-brimmed black job with an upturned brim.

That signaled that she was a little different, avant-garde. That didn't do much for a lot of guys around Penn's Ferry and Petittville. When they got to know her and judged her weird, they were kept at bay. Strange wasn't what they were looking for.

It might have been nice to date some of the comics guys, but most of them lived far away. She wasn't interested in an occasional one-night stand in Dallas or New Orleans when they came down to push their works and shake hands with the fans, so she was lonely, waiting for somebody with common interests to turn up close at hand.

If that didn't happen, there'd be time for men later, once she had the ball rolling on things she wanted to do.

With *Ghost Rider* on display, she opened another box and discovered the new DC releases. She put *Batman* and *Detective* in place, then mined for other titles and pulled up *Sandman*. She enjoyed that one quite a bit, both the art and the story.

Slipping one off the top to read, she put the others in their slot and was working on the paperwork related to ordering when the front door sighed open. She looked up to see Charlie Black headed in, his face sullen.

She'd wondered when he would be by. Matt had called from home to tell her about the death, but she'd already heard. It was all any of the video rental customers had been talking about.

She had wondered how Charlie would take it. She knew it had made her feel bad, and she didn't know Budd well at all, had just seen him a few times when Charlie brought him around. She'd always sensed the kid had problems, but he had usually spent the time he was in the shop gaping at her so she hadn't tried to get close to him.

Charlie wasn't that kind of problem. She caught him looking at her sometimes, but he was quiet and never suggested anything even if he was thinking it. That made it easy to be his friend.

He was way too young for anything else, and their tastes differed, but their mutual interest in comics gave them something to talk about.

"Too bad about Budd," she said when Charlie gloomily approached the counter.

"Yeah, they told us about it in the middle of algebra class."

"Dogs, huh?"

"Yeah, that's strange, isn't it?"

32

"There's still a lot of woods around here. Probably people toss out puppies they don't want. They grow up, and dogs are pack animals. They band together."

Charlie placed his books on the counter and ran a hand through his hair. He was cute when he was sullen. He was cute anyway and would probably get cuter, she decided, as he put on weight to cover his almost lanky frame.

"I never thought Budd would die," Charlie said.

"I had a friend when I was in high school. She didn't die, but she had to have her leg amputated because of cancer. She was this sweet, pretty girl, and after that she had to get around on crutches. They gave her an artificial leg, but you can imagine what it's like for a girl. Legs are one of women's big three features."

"Three?"

"Tits, ass, and legs."

"Oh yeah."

"She didn't take it very well. I remember feeling really bad for her."

"Guess that's how I feel for Budd. And I feel really lonely."

Nell leaned on the counter. "You still got me, kid."

"You're not in school with me."

"And I'm thankful for that. I know it's tough for you. I didn't exactly fit in in school. You felt like Budd was kind of in the same boat, right?"

"Something like that. We were different, and I don't know if he really understood all of it, but we were friends, and we were kinda alike."

"Eloquently put."

"Well, you know what I mean. Kinda like you and me are alike. Inside sorta."

She nodded, sincere without being solemn. "I know, Charlie." She nodded toward the magazines. "The new titles are out. Why don't you look them over."

He fished in his pocket, checking his money before nodding. Charlie didn't like to look if he couldn't buy, but he usually had enough lunch money saved from the days he skipped meals to pick up a couple of titles. What he couldn't afford she usually let him read from her own collection. What Matt didn't know he couldn't behead her for. He made enough money from Charlie, anyway.

33

He selected the *Ghost Rider* as she expected and a *Sandman*, then flipped through some others without picking any of them up.

She accepted his money for them and rang up the purchase on Matt's computerized cash register. It was the latest thing available. Matt liked gadgets.

Once his comics were bagged, Charlie continued to lean against the glass counter, looking down at baseball cards, Justice League button sets, and Scream Queen Trading Cards. Matt ordered a lot of things that didn't sell in this area.

Charlie wasn't looking at any of the items. He was just staring through the glass. Nell drummed her fingers on the glass near him since she didn't have anything to say.

His eyes flicked up at her, and he smiled when he realized she was watching him.

"What are you looking at? Linnea Quigley?"

"Bobbie Bresse is on top," he said.

Nell looked down at the Scream Queen cards featuring pinups of actresses from horror films. Most of their movies were in stock on the video side of the store. She and Charlie had watched many of them on the television set in the stock room. He was always studying camera angles and makeup effects, commenting about the believability or lack of it.

"You want to watch *Blood Salvage* again?" she asked. It was one of their favorite low-budget movies, one of the better killer redneck pictures with John Saxon and Ray Walston of *My Favorite Martian* in supporting roles.

"I don't feel like a film right now," Charlie said. "I can't quit thinking of what a film of what happened to Budd might look like.

"I hate that he had to go like that. You know he suffered."

Nell nodded. She'd never known anyone who was murdered, but a loss like that must be similar to this death. It was abrupt, unexplained, and brutal.

If they found the dogs and put them to sleep or whatever, that wouldn't make anybody feel better, not the kid's parents, and not Charlie. That didn't put breath back into Budd's lungs, and it didn't give Charlie a friend to endure school alongside.

He was going to be contemplating it all for a long time. She knew him and knew he would never arrive at any reason for the random, senselessness of it all. The world was a chaotic place, she decided. That was the only answer there could be.

"What else is going on?" she asked, trying to get Charlie's mind off the loss.

"I got a new teacher for a while. My English teacher is sick. This one is cute."

Ah, bit of a schoolboy crush there, Charles? Oooo and ahh on an older woman."

He grinned, turning his face slightly in an effort to hide his blush.

"Ooo, Charlie does have a thing for her."

"She was looking at me. I mean it was weird. I'm not sure what to make of it. No teacher has ever done that."

"Were you doing anything wrong?"

"No."

"Maybe it was just wishful thinking. Have you been watching the teen comedies? We've got several about teachers and students. It's usually the French teachers, though. Did she look like Sylvia Kristel?"

"No." The blush deepened, his grin widened, and he turned his face away from her. She wasn't hitting far from the truth.

"Sounds like you're not going to have any trouble with grades in English," she judged.

"Stop it. It's probably nothing."

She made a few more playful remarks. At least it seemed to keep his mind off Budd.

"What are you working on?" he asked finally, trying to sidetrack her. She teased him a minute more but then pulled out her sketchbook to show him the work she'd been doing.

She didn't have much of a storyline, really. It was mostly a tale told in pictures, a mystical black and white of a lonely girl and a ghost she fell in love with at the point of her own death. It simplistically represented some of her own loneliness.

Charlie didn't key in on that. He just studied the pictures with an eye trained by his own comic reading.

He made some suggestions that were valid. As he looked over the drawings again, his brow furrowed with the intensity of his perusal, she was reminded that she was glad he was her friend.

She would hate to lose him, and now, more than she had earlier, she understood how it must feel to lose Budd.

Charlie saw the curtain in the front window flutter as he headed across the front lawn. His mom had been watching for him, worried because of Budd no doubt.

She was standing in the living room when he walked in even though she had probably been working in the kitchen on supper earlier, checking through the window between cooking steps to watch for him. She was wearing jeans and a blue cotton blouse with a pale blue scarf in her hair, her usual afternoon attire. Even in her casual clothes she looked immaculate. She was always careful about her appearance.

"Hi, Mom," he said in his best Jerry Mathers voice. He couldn't get the pitch that the Beaver had always used anymore, though; his voice had deepened too much for that.

"How are you doing?" she asked. Her dark eyes showed her concern. She didn't want to set him off if he was on the verge of tears, but she did want to find out how he was handling the news.

"Fine," he said. He really didn't feel like crying anymore. He felt sad, but not consumed by the feeling.

"I'm sorry. Maddy Rand called me about it. I know he was your friend."

Charlie swallowed. He was still standing near the door, his books and comics tucked under his arm.

His mom had never liked Budd, had tolerated him while he was at their house but not much more. He thought better of bringing that up. She was trying to be understanding and wanted to help.

"Do you need to talk about it?" she asked.

He shrugged. "I don't know if there's much to say." She walked over to him and hugged him. "You didn't see any sign of any dogs out there, did you?"

"No, Mom," he sighed. "The coast was clear."

"Well, it's dangerous until they figure out where they came from. I want you to be extra careful. It might be a good idea for you to ride the bus."

He pulled away from her, a twisted expression of exasperation on his face. "Come on, Mom. It's only a couple of blocks. The dogs are probably long gone by now. Besides what happened to Budd was at night. I'm out in broad daylight."

"We'll discuss it with your father, but I think it's a good idea."

"Yeah," he nodded and headed for his room. He didn't like the idea at all. It would be like prison riding the bus, hell to get out of the house once it deposited him at home, and tough to get to go see Nell.

His mom might be protecting him physically but the protection was mental cruelty. He put his schoolbooks on his desk and carried his comic books with him to the bed.

After finishing the bus duty assigned her as the new teacher, Barbara Nielson headed home to the small apartment she had rented. The first day had not been as trying as she had anticipated.

Most of the time had been spent quelling advances from would-be senior studs with hormones on overdrive, convinced she must want the attentions of musclebound youngsters as much as they desired a liaison with an older woman.

She fit well into the lead role of their fantasies. She wondered how many sexual acts she had committed in their imaginations today. They had probably projected her into every position imaginable, forced on her every act they had witnessed in skin magazines and X-rated flicks.

She felt only a flicker of emotion about it. It was not flattery because she knew she was only an object in their dreams, not real, not loved.

They found her beautiful. That wasn't enough. They didn't know her, did not know anything about her soul. And what did she need to know about their souls? Did they have them?

She had known plenty of men who thought only with their cocks. Boys of the same type would be no different. That was not what she needed now.

Once, perhaps, they had seemed exciting, the savage edge of their masculinity drawing her, seducing her, compelling her to trade to them the allure her beauty and sensuality exuded.

Those couplings had felt rewarding once, the sweaty groping, the passionate connection of mouths and bodies. Now in memory it produced more a sense of emptiness, swelling the feeling of loneliness.

The feeling was enhanced as she unpacked the boxes she had neglected upon her arrival. Each item she removed seemed generic, impersonal with no memories attached, not real memories, not recollections of people she cared about or wanted to see again.

She did not see her arrival in Louisiana as a flight away from anything because she did not feel there was anything from which to run. The past seemed meaningless, scenes strung together like a film the viewer regretted watching. All of that was over now. It was gone. She didn't want to watch it again, unless she had to when her thoughts forced her.

When she had finished with the remainder of the boxes, she concentrated on straightening the apartment, making it look like home. She put the quilted, floral bedspread into place on the bed, hung some pictures, and arranged vases with silk flowers. The generic feeling did not ebb, but the touches did brighten the place a bit.

Now this was home.

The conclusion did not immediately elicit an emotion, but she accepted the reality. Though she had not been born here, and though she had lived in other places, this was the place.

There was no need to look back on the unpleasant things, the forgotten lovers, the regrets, no reason to attach significance to items carried with her from other places and times.

Perhaps a generic feeling was the first part of starting over and creating a world that was as it should be.

Matt let Nell off work at 6 P.M., taking over the store for the evening shift himself. Business would probably not pay for the electricity burned during the evening hours, so he never expected her to stay very late. He only kept her on the payroll to have someone on hand so he didn't have to hang around the store all day.

She walked the four blocks to her garage with her portfolio tucked under one arm, scanning her surroundings for ideas. Finding things she wanted to draw sometimes proved to be the most difficult part.

The trip was usually bland, but tonight she watched the shadows which were well formed in the autumn evening. The village council had approved sidewalks the previous summer, so her walk carried her in front of houses without demanding that she move near wooded areas or vacant lots, but knowledge of the dog attack was acute.

Though she'd spent time trying to console Charlie and had not concerned herself much with danger during the day, now she kept imagining the footfalls of hounds and felt a mysterious eeriness.

As she neared her house, she realized the eeriness had conjured inspiration. She would sketch the scary image of the hound which formulated in her thoughts while dead leaves scraped across the concrete and the wind rattled through the bare oak branches.

They were the claws of a massive black beast, leader of the pack which had attacked Budd. He was a foul monster, jaws shiny with saliva.

She looked back over her shoulder, just to make sure it really *was* just leaves then stepped up her pace the remaining distance to home.

Seeing a light on in Mrs. Carpenter's window, she felt a little relief. The elderly landlady was in there, probably watching television already. After the news she would watch whatever game show came on to bridge the gap into prime time. Then she would switch to her evening program based on the night of the week. It never varied.

Nell didn't try to look through the window as she moved up the driveway. The old woman deserved her privacy. She allowed Nell a fair amount most of the time. Moving around the old Chrysler, Nell scaled the wooden steps to her door.

Fishing into her skirt pocket, she found her key and opened the fragile door. In any other town in the world, she would have worried with a door like this, but here it was all she needed.

She pushed it shut behind her and switched on the living room light. A She-Hulk poster, another of Matt's whims, greeted her from across the room. The green-skinned beauty was hoisting a heavy weight over her head.

Nell had appreciated it as a gift when Matt had given up on interesting any of the local kids in it. It was hard to find good posters, harder still to find heroines in a world still dominated by superheroes. She'd never cared for Wonder Woman, and many of the other female comic characters didn't appeal to her.

That was one of her goals, to come up with an interesting female character. She hadn't decided on the superpowers she wanted her to possess, however. Or their origins. Everything had been done before.

The wind rapped an oak branch against the window across the room, and she almost exhibited some superpowers of her own, climbing the wall perhaps.

One thing her heroine would be able to do was take care of killer dog packs, probably beheading the lead monster. That piqued a new notion in her head. Maybe her heroine could carry some sort of battle-ax.

Maybe she should buy an ax. She'd been meaning to get something to protect herself here. She was frightened by guns and not really sure of how to use one. With an ax you wouldn't need instructions.

She went into the kitchen and plopped a Lean Pockets Chicken Supreme into the microwave. The timer was sounding when the phone rang.

She expected it to be Charlie, but instead Michael Langley's voice came through the receiver.

"Hi, Nell."

He was the artist and writer on a book called *Devil Ride*, a colorful stream of consciousness piece about a man named Devlin lost somewhere in a realm between Earth and Hell. People were buying it like crazy even though there was debate about its explicit nature.

Michael was one of the people she'd met in Dallas. He was fairly cool with sandy hair and a beard, given to wearing jeans and sports shirts rather than black T-shirts and skull jewelry as some artists did. He was practically a yuppie.

"What's going on?" she asked, grabbing a potholder to take the chicken roll out of its cooking wrapper and plop it onto a plate. She opened a Diet Pepsi and sat down at the kitchen table.

"What exactly does a Louisiana swamp look like?" he asked.

Michael was from Minnesota, now living in Chicago. "Slimy, I guess."

"I want Devlin to get lost in the swamps, but I started sketching some things and realized even though I have this notion of a swamp in my head, I don't know what really belongs in a swamp."

Nell grinned, recognizing an excuse to call. Matt had warned her a while back she could expect guys in the business to pursue her. Many of them were insecure socially even though their command of their work was flawless. Since she was attractive and involved in the same interests, she was a desirable target. She didn't think their work was goofy the way they were used to women reacting.

She had liked Michael when she met him. He wasn't a lech like some of the people lurking in the corners of the world. He was kind of shy and something about her made him feel partially at ease. If he had lived nearby, she might consider possibilities, but she just didn't see a way to pursue anything with him so far away.

She did consider him a friend, though, and tried to be polite when his courage did allow him to call. They talked about the business, artists they liked, and new books they found interesting.

She knew she could count on Michael's help if she ever finished anything really good, too. He was one of the people willing to help others crack the almost impenetrable wall of publication.

"A swamp looks like a swamp," she said playfully, then waited for him to stammer.

He did. She could almost have counted the number of times he repeated the first syllable of his word. "Bu-bu-but, you know, what kind of features does it have?"

"Cypress knees. You can look those up in an encyclopedia." She knew Michael had shelves and shelves of research materials. They'd talked about it over lunch one day in Dallas. He tended to purchase things from closeout catalogs if he thought they'd be useful. He had traditional references, dictionaries, witches' spell books, and historical works as well as volumes on mythology and crime.

"Spanish moss would be good too," she added. "It's like long gray hair with lots of permanent wave in it."

"I see, yeah. That should help."

There was a silence, brief, awkward. He was searching for something to say.

"So, how are you doing?"

"Fine."

"What's going on in Louisiana?"

"Usual stuff."

"I see. Urn, you reading any good comics lately?"

She told him about some titles she'd enjoyed then described some of the things she was working on. That melted the ice, and the conversation flowed for a while. If he hadn't been earning $40 a page, she would have worried about his phone bill, but he could cover it.

After the conversation ended, she ate the chicken roll, which had grown cold. Then she sat in the living room and sketched the hound.

Her imagination guided her pencil, allowing her almost effortlessly to create the hideous jaws and the deep, evil eyes shrouded by a frown across the brow. The nostrils were dark and flaring, the teeth twin rows of bodkins with four daggers jutting out at the corners.

When she had finished the pencil sketch, she placed the picture facedown. It was horrible and made her think of Budd. She pitied him more with the thought of this beast in pursuit.

He must have suffered, and she wondered why she had felt so compelled to draw the face. It was so morbid.

Forcing herself to pick up her drawing tablet, she ripped the pages out and crumpled it into a ball, which she tossed into the trashcan near the window. The feeling of fear it had conjured up was not as quick or easy to erase, however.

Chapter 5

Charlie's appeals to his father failed to have his mother's decision overturned. He was going to be riding the bus for a while, straight home, with the danger of afterschool confinement, unless he came up with a good excuse that would lead to escape.

Something about schoolwork might do. If he could convince them he needed Nell's help with math or something that might allow him to make the now-perceived-as-dangerous trip over to the comics shop.

He sat in his room after dinner, turning over ideas as he worked on his algebra homework. He didn't give a damn about algebra, but for some reason they considered it essential if you were going to college, no matter what you planned to major in. Charlie had no intention of taking anything other than required math after high school.

Arithmetic was the class which gave him the most trouble, but they would never believe he needed help from Nell in math. They knew Nell better than that. She was not good at algebra either. That's why she was an artist.

He listened to his father rambling about the home office, which was down the hall from Charlie's room on the second floor. There weren't many two-story houses in Petittville, but they had managed to find one of them. His dad was setting up a new fax machine, which had just come in. The company had paid for it because he did so much work at home.

Charlie was interested in the possibilities that would afford, but he wasn't inclined to bother his father at the moment. It wasn't a good idea to talk to him while he was trying to concentrate on something. Daniel

Black could be intense, and somewhat cold at times. Charlie preferred not to deal with him during those periods.

He tried not to think about things, about Budd's death or anything else as he worked on his equations. He didn't really understand them, though, so they couldn't do much to take his mind off the pain.

He hadn't cried yet, but he wanted to every time the loss of Budd rippled through his chest. The TV station out of Aimsley had carried a brief report about the death on the six o'clock news, and both stations in Alexandria had also done brief announcements. Charlie had flipped from channel to channel to catch all of them.

One station had a faded black-and-white photo of Budd superimposed over the anchorman's shoulder as the report was read. All of them had video of the accident scene, but it was shot from a distance. The cops hadn't let them get very close. The only thing really visible was the yellow police tape and uniformed people milling around.

The thought of going out to look at the death scene did not occur to Charlie all at once. It sort of seeped into his brain while he struggled with his homework.

His fear mingled with his memories of Budd as well as curiosity about the site he had seen on television.

As he closed his spiral notebook, the idea was in its final form, and it seemed feasible.

He could hear his mother downstairs watching television, and his dad was still rattling around in his office. Charlie—in traditional schoolboy fashion though he might be a tad old for such a maneuver— could ease out his window and scale down the oak tree which grew near the house.

He'd seen it done in a dozen movies, and he was in fairly good shape even though he did avoid skirmishes in P.E. He could scurry over to the scene of Budd's death, look things over for himself, and see if he could figure out what had happened.

Then he could make it back, probably without his absence being noticed. If he did get nailed, it wouldn't matter that much. He was already under house arrest for his own protection. Punishment wouldn't make that much difference.

"What are they going to do?" Charlie asked himself. "I'm already grounded."

He moved over to the window and pushed the curtain back. The oak was a little farther from his window than he'd expected. He looked through the glass at an angle toward the ground.

It was quite a drop, but then his eyes turned back to the tree. Some of the heavy branches weren't that far from the house.

If he stood on the windowsill and jumped, he could reach one, then move along it hand over hand to the tree trunk, which he could shimmy or slide down.

He'd have to move the screen, but that wouldn't be too hard, and it should pop back into place fairly easily. He went to the closet and got his denim jacket, put his tennis shoes back on, then shoved the window open.

The night breeze came in quickly, damp and chilled with the autumn's breath. He was glad he had his coat on, and even with that the night made him shiver.

He turned up his collar, then reached down to the frame and pried the screen free, gripping the edges tightly so that he could ease it inside. He almost dropped it a couple of times before he had it safely leaning beside his bed.

He pushed the curtain aside and climbed through the open window, crouching on the sill once he was through the opening. He held on to the window as more of the chill wind bit at him. It wasn't what he'd expected.

He had to lean out and look at the ground as he prepared to reach for the branch, but that wasn't too bad. For a moment, he thought about climbing back inside, but finally pushed off.

He almost missed the branch. His fingers didn't grip it as he had anticipated, and he felt his stomach defy gravity as visions of plummeting to the ground filled his thoughts.

He found a grip at last, which scraped his palms but soothed his nerves. He wouldn't plummet. He held his breath as he began to inch along the limb toward the trunk. His muscles began to ache more quickly than he had expected. He weighed a little more now than he had in the days when he had performed similar feats on monkey bars.

He tried not to look down, but he couldn't help it. The ground looked far away and hard. He had dropped from trees as a child, and memories of the pain that shot up through his ankles returned to him. The pain would be even worse from this height, acute, agonizing. It would sprain his ankles, maybe even break something.

He gritted his teeth, shutting out the pain in his palms as he concentrated on making it to the trunk. It seemed to take forever.

Sweat formed on his brow in spite of the wind that whipped around him and fluttered at the dry leaves which still clung to the branches.

They seemed to rasp at him or caw like crows. He'd read some story by Jack Finney in a book at school about a man trapped on the ledge of his apartment building in New York. The man kept thinking of plunging to his death and regretting the fact that he had stepped out onto the ledge to retrieve a piece of paper.

Charlie was beginning to reconsider his decision as well, even though he was only two floors up. Then his tennis shoes struck the bark of the tree, and he was against the trunk.

The slide down was far swifter than he had anticipated, and he felt bark rubbing against his chest and legs. More skin was scraped from his hands, but he survived without much serious damage.

When his feet touched the ground, he felt relieved.

Dusting himself off, he paused only a moment to look back over his shoulder at the house. He could see the television screen through the window. Confident Mom was engrossed in the show, he turned and jogged across the lawn.

His house wasn't as close to the vacant lot as Budd's, but it wasn't far. He moved along through back yards, ignoring the barking of dogs he knew to be pets.

Phlegm had formed cold in his throat by the time he reached the edge of the subdivision. He slowed to a walk, letting his breathing return to normal. His cheeks were numb, and his nose was probably red.

A short distance away he could see the trees and brush of the woods. His quest was near. He put his hands into his pockets and began to check in all directions for signs of the dogs.

They might still be around, after all. If they had been able to catch Budd, they might be able to catch him as well if they were still in the area.

Surely they would be gone now, though. There had been people all over the lot today. That should have scared them away.

He pictured himself as a character in a horror movie as he moved closer to the lot. His shoes squished on the dew-dampened grass, and even in the darkness he could see his breath clouds as his eyes adjusted to the dim illumination provided by the moon.

How many scenes had he seen just like this on videos? They were always about teenagers, and unsuspecting kids like him were always easy prey. Just like Budd had been, he thought with remorse—the unsuspecting first victim.

He hunched his shoulders more against the chill and wondered if he would be a victim too. He imagined the dogs, running in a pack, attacking, vicious and brutal as they ripped flesh until the fadeout or dissolve, whichever effect death chose for an ending, but he couldn't turn back. He was drawn here.

He looked toward the forest as he neared the edge of the lot. He imagined the faces of the hounds peering out at him, their eyes watching, tracking. They weren't really there, he told himself, wishing he believed.

Weeds swatted his pant legs, making sounds which first made him think something else was moving besides him, but when he reached the spot where the tape was set up, he was confident he was alone.

Another look toward the trees confirmed there was nothing visible. He ducked under the tape, and with his hands in his pockets, he bowed his head toward the ground.

In the night, he could make out only hints of discoloration which he suspected were bloodstains on the ground. Otherwise there was no sign that this patch of grass was any different than any other.

There was nothing remarkable or mysterious and nothing to offer clues about the reality of his friend's suffering. He wasn't sure which answers he had expected to find here, but if he had been in a film, he would have been able to spot something, some minute detail the cops had missed that would let him understand.

Standing here in the night breeze, he was reminded only of the randomness of the assault. There seemed to be no reason for Budd to be gone. It wasn't fair, and it wasn't right.

He looked toward the sky now, as if the face of God would be there to explain it all. He saw only the vastness of the universe and a pale moon that was masked by a thin veil of clouds. It was intimidating, so he looked down again.

He almost missed the movement in the distance. He was frightened for an instant, worried now that he had spotted the dogs. It wasn't a pack, though, it was a person, heading along the opposite end of the lot.

He strained his eyes, willing them to pierce the darkness and the gathering mist for him. They failed, but he ducked quickly under the tape and jogged through the weeds until he could get a better view.

The walker was stooping slightly against the chill. Though the figure wore pants, he could tell it was a woman. He walked fast, trying to keep a safe distance but trying to get within range to identify the person. Whoever it was must have come to view the death scene also.

He had reached the sidewalk on South Street when he made out the form as she moved beneath a streetlamp. The white light bathed her long dark hair, making it apparent he was watching Miss Nielson.

She was wearing tight jeans and a sweater, and she didn't seem to be in a hurry. She must have been curious about the death, having just arrived in town. He started to turn back toward home, but instead he decided to follow her. He had no idea where she was living, and it might be interesting to know.

Ducking in and out of the shadows, he watched the sway of her hips as she moved. The jeans revealed contours her outfit from school had not.

She had a slender waist, and the shape of her firm legs was not concealed by the denim. Charlie felt stirrings anew, and even as he wondered again why she had been looking at him, he visualized her in the short dress, then wondered how she must look without clothes. Puberty had him firmly in its grip.

His fingers were growing numb from the night air by the time she reached her building. It was the old Foster Arms place, a small set of apartments near the residential section, the area that had always been Petittville even before the subdivisions had been cut out of the forest. Around the time that Charlie's family had arrived in town, somebody had been redoing the place. The family had considered renting a room there until they found a house, but then the realtor had located their home, making it unnecessary.

The two-story building had brown trim. There were only about six apartments there, and it sat just off the street's edge.

She walked along a breezeway between the rows of doors and climbed the creaky wooden steps to her second-floor unit. Standing near some trees which bordered the street, Charlie waited until he saw a light click on upstairs.

Living room.

Another light came on a moment later.

Bedroom.

Finally another light became visible through a small, curtained window at the end of the building. Bathroom.

She would be getting undressed now, sliding the sweater off, easing her slender legs out of her jeans, peeling off her undergarments.

He felt a hint of dizziness creeping through his brain. The thought of her naked, slipping into a shower or perhaps a bath, was overwhelming.

He looked at the thin trees which sprouted near the wall of the building. He'd never entertained such a notion before, but he wondered if it would be possible to shimmy up one of them, just for a glimpse through the part in the curtains.

His scraped palms reminded him that the idea was probably not advisable. The danger of getting caught was too great. People on the ground floor might see, and if he was caught, word would be all over school in no time. He wouldn't be able to walk down the hall without hearing quips.

Half the guys in town probably would have died to get the same glimpse, but they would still deride him. He turned for the walk toward home. He would have to be content with a fantasy about Miss Nielson.

For now.

On the walk home, he began to worry more about his parents' wrath than the dogs. Getting back into the house undetected was probably going to be impossible, and he wasn't sure how he'd manage to get the screen back into place from inside.

This had been a bad idea. Once at the edge of the lot, he began to worry about the dogs again. The short hairs on the back of his neck began to tickle his skin. He stood for a while with his hands in his pockets, watching the tape flutter in the wind.

Staring over at the trees, he spotted no sign of glowing eyes, but the thought of walking the same path Budd had followed to his death was more frightening than it had been before. He'd had more time to think about it.

He knew it was mostly his imagination—or hoped it was—but that didn't really make the fear go away. He'd read a story by somebody named August something about some boys who had to run past a dark alley every night to get bread from a corner store. They ran past that alley with terror in their hearts.

Now he identified with that story more than ever. He felt that terror building in his chest as the frequency between his heartbeats narrowed.

He would have to run across the lot, get to the other side as soon as possible, and skirt through the back yards to home. Running was the only answer, as fast as possible, putting woods and dogs behind him.

After checking the trees once again, he cautiously lifted one foot. The muscles in his calf tensed almost unmercifully, as if setting foot on the lot would immediately draw the dogs. Once he had been mowing the yard, and while pushing the mower along he had spotted a snake slithering through the grass.

His impulse had been to run over it, but instead he just stopped pushing, left the mower, and retreated. He had hovered on the clipped portion of the lawn for a while until determining he was going to have to go on with his job. The mower was just sitting there in the middle of the lawn burning gas, but returning had been agony. With each step he imagined the slimy body of the snake, waiting ready to strike or, perhaps worse, coil around him.

He recalled that fear now. It was almost the same. He felt it hard to breathe, and as the wind bit into his face, his eyes began to water.

First step, he told himself, just take the first step, get it over with. And he did it, placed his foot on the damp grass. The movement served in the same fashion as a starter pistol's audible signal. He was off in a sprint, and as he moved, even with the wind whistling about him, filling his ears, he could hear the dogs' breathing.

It rasped through the corners of their mouths even with their teeth tightly clenched. He knew they had that kind of jaws, like bulldogs or boxers, geared to let them bite down and breathe at the same time.

Your imagination could use any bit of information you'd acquired against you. He tried to step up his pace, but while his legs were willing to work harder, his lungs were beginning to send signals of complaint.

He slowed his pace, breathing heavily but forcing himself to keep going as fast as possible. Now he was sure he heard the footfalls, thudding in unison under the weight of the heavy dogs. How many were there? It was impossible to tell, but he was certain they were there.

Where had they come from? The woods? He had seen no indication of them there, but it was possible.

As his heartbeat thundered, he considered looking back over his shoulder. Just a glimpse would let him know what he was up against. He would be able to tell how close they were and how many of them.

Did that matter, though? If there were two or ten, he was in the same trouble. Oh, yes. They would do a number on him just like they'd done on Budd, and he would deserve it for being so stupid.

Budd had died out here, and he'd come to sightsee.

He stumbled slightly, keeping his footing but just barely. He felt tears running down his cheeks now, not because he was crying, but because the wind was still slashing at his pupils.

He wanted to look back but didn't. He didn't really want to see them. Knowing they were there, seemed to be there, was enough. His mind could do the rest.

He reached the tape. Would they catch him at the same spot where Budd had died? That would be ironic, probably too big a coincidence in a story, but the possibility seemed too real.

If the dogs were really there. Just a look back, and he would know everything was all right, that they weren't present. He couldn't keep up his speed much longer, and even if he cleared the lot, he wasn't going to be safe. There was no magic barrier or refuge. This wasn't a race which ended when you crossed the finish line. They'd follow him across the lawns to maul him. If he made it that far without dropping.

Just look back, he told himself.

What could it hurt to see them? He couldn't be any more frightened than he already was. Shit. He twisted his head back, almost stumbling again in the process.

Behind him he saw only the empty expanse of land. There were a few swirls of eerie mist—could that be the remnants of the hounds' breath?—a few stirring leaves and nothing more.

He hesitated, his breathing improving as he scanned the space before him. Had the dogs been there? He could not be sure. It could have been imagination, but for a few moments he had been convinced they were there.

He set off at a fast walk on the trip through back yards.

In no time he was back at his house. He didn't see police cars, and his parents weren't standing in the front yard or anything. So far his absence had not been discovered.

Going up the oak tree was not as viable as the trip down had been, though, and if he did manage to scale the trunk, he had no way to make it from the limb to the windowsill. Jumping would not work in the same way it had leaving the house.

That left the back door. Looking through the window, he determined his mother was still watching television. A glance to his father's office revealed the light was still on.

He stood a chance. Quickly he moved around to the back of the house. The door opened into the kitchen. Kneeling, he lifted up the welcome mat and found the spare key. At least if the dogs had been behind him, they were gone—he checked over his shoulder to make sure—and he wasn't in the same situation as the little girl in *The Leopard Man* who banged on a locked door as a killer leopard approached her.

He was in no danger of having his blood seep under the crack in the door; at least he hoped not, checking over his shoulder one more time. No dogs.

Fitting the key into the lock, he gently eased the back door open. Before entering, he tucked the key back in place, then he stepped into the darkened kitchen and closed the door.

52

The sound of the television drifted in from the living room. He would never make it through there without being noticed, but an inspiration struck him.

He slipped his coat off and hung it on the rack by the door then opened the refrigerator, pulled out a piece of cake and walked from the room, praying the rosy color his cheeks wouldn't be noticed.

His entrance into the living room coincided with a commercial break. His mother heard him but did not look back.

"Charlie, you're not getting a Coke, are you?" she called. "You're drinking too many of those."

"Just a piece of cake," he said, moving up the stairs. He held his sigh until he was safely in his room. Maybe there had been no dogs, and he had pulled this off.

The indiscretion had worked so perfectly he should have taken a stab at spying on Miss Nielson. It might have worked.

He got a second chance.

In his nightmares.

It happened not in those moments of sleep before rising. Instead it came somewhere deep in the dark hours of the night, and it did not seem like a dream. It was more of an intrusion.

He was suddenly back outside her apartment, standing at the base of the tree, looking up at the lighted window decorated with the frilly curtains. His ears were alert, listening for dogs or other visitors, but it seemed safe.

Now he did not hesitate. He felt no fear of discovery, and silently he moved up the tree, climbing with ease until he was beside the glass.

Gripping the branches with hands that were no longer scraped, he stared through the glass. She was in there, sitting on the edge of the tub in a white bathrobe.

The light made the white fixtures of the room bright, almost aglow. Her hair also shined and looked so soft it might have been satin.

He adjusted his grip on the limb and held his breath as she stood and her hands moved to the tie of her robe. He half expected to fall to his death then, moments before her beauty was revealed to him in its totality.

But he stayed, and the robe parted slowly, sliding smoothly off her shoulders. In an instant she was naked, beautifully naked, naked without any of the shadows or concealing camera angles of movies on HBO.

His eyes caressed her, the narrow waist and flaring hips, the flat, perfect stomach and the thick brown triangle of curls beneath. Her breasts were not large but were firm and rounded, and they moved, bouncing slightly as she lifted her arms, running her hands through her hair to pin it over her head.

He stared at her nipples, hard and brown, and for a moment, her hand reached up, touching one breast absently before she turned to the tub.

The throbbing in his pants was growing now, becoming uncontrollable. He held on to the tree, trying to hold back the building eruption.

He wanted to keep watching her as she slipped into the tub, slowly caressing her body with a bar of soap. The suds coated her skin, creating soft delicate patterns like lace.

He strained to keep watching, strained also to hold back the pulsing explosion that kept threatening to burst out of him.

Then, Miss Nielson looked up, her face turning toward the window. It was impossible to look out a window from a lighted room into the darkness, he knew. She should have seen only her own reflection, but she saw him. Her expression showed it, not one of surprise or anger but one of smug satisfaction. Her lips curled up in a wry, partial smile as she lowered her head back against the tub.

He had to tear his eyes away from her even upon realizing her discovery, and when he looked down he almost lost his grip.

Budd was standing there, Budd covered in blood. His scalp was ripped open, and his clothes were in tatters, revealing ripped-open portions of his abdomen.

From the ruins of his spiked hair, blood spilled down across his forehead and down his face, staining it bright red. It shined in the rays of light that spilled from the window, and his eyes stared upward as if he were looking from behind a mask.

"Be careful, Charlie," he warned. "You might fall."

The words, though simple, terrified Charlie. That and the fact that his friend was there, his dead friend.

He tried to climb down, tried to control himself at the same time, but before he could get a footing, he felt the ejaculation and looked down at the stain on his jeans.

He rattled into waking then, the thoughts of Miss Nielson still, lingering, but the pleasure was marred and incomplete, diluted by the images of Budd.

Budd covered in blood.

He stared at the ceiling, trying to let her beauty chase the fear from his mind. He could feel the fabric of his pajamas plastered to his leg, the moisture now growing cold and clammy.

Chapter 6

Nell sat by her window as the morning light slowly faded through the trees. Mist and dampness hung in the air, smothering any notion she might have had of using the light of the early hours to work on a painting. This light would betray the colors and distort the vision. She had to settle for watching the gray light and the rustle of the orange and brown leaves as the wind seeped through their branches.

As the breeze played with the leaves, she sensed its chill, and a strange feeling of melancholy settled over her, perhaps a deeper sense of loneliness. Autumn for her always had a way of heightening loneliness.

The sense of death must also be carried on the wind, she decided. Autumn was a time of dying—leaves died, flowers died, people died. Sometimes people who should not die passed away.

From where she sat, she could see a short stretch of the street, the sidewalk with the leaves sticking to it and the cracked pavement of the roadway.

The woman was the first sign of human movement she detected. She moved into Nell's range of vision, her coat flapping around her slender form as she moved. She was carrying schoolbooks clutched against her. Long brown hair brushed her shoulders.

She was too far away for Nell to get a good look, but she had to be the new teacher, beautiful Miss Nielson. A young teacher probably wasn't required to be terribly pretty to set teenage boys into a spermy frenzy, but this woman seemed truly attractive.

Nell kept watching her until she was out of frame, swallowed by the swirls of fog. When she had gone, a feeling of uneasiness began to mingle with the sense of loneliness.

The woman was just a pedestrian moving along the sidewalk, yet Nell felt strange. Was it a sense of danger? Maybe it was just the overall strangeness, the fact that a young boy had died and that it was autumn.

As she kicked thoughts around, she saw the police cruiser also drift through the mist. It was easing slowly along the street. It seemed early for Lucius Rice to be about, but it was time for her to get ready for classes. It took twenty minutes to drive up to Penn's Ferry.

She turned from the window, tugging her nightgown over her head as she moved toward the bathroom. Maybe the uneasy feeling was just a symptom of her low mood.

Or maybe, something eerie … was taking place.

———

Rice had not been able to sleep. Too many thoughts of the body and the bloodstains on the brown grass. He'd seen plenty of bodies on plenty of sites, but this was the worst in Petittville.

It was the serpent in the garden, the reminder that there was no paradise to be had. There might not be crazed killers or crack dealers with Uzis here, but death always seemed to find a way to disturb the peace.

He'd risen early, leaving his wife asleep as he dressed quietly in the bathroom. If some lunatic dog handlers had let things get out of hand, he was going to get them. It might not be easy, but he'd handled tough cases before.

Once dressed in his blue uniform, he had slipped into his den, unlocking the bottom drawer of his desk to slide out the Taurus .38 Special, a stainless-steel revolver. It had been a gift from some of his buddies when he'd left New Orleans. It was a nice gift with its shiny look and walnut grip, but it also made him feel more comfortable. He had replaced the service revolver in his holster with the Taurus before heading for his car.

He wasn't expecting a dog attack, but he wanted a weapon with some stopping power if he had a confrontation. He hadn't had to handle anything much more serious than drunks, but he hadn't had to badger people for information either.

He had kept his eyes open since he had come here, though. He knew the people of this area as well as he had known the streets of New Orleans, knew who did what. He had watched with his experienced eye, picking up on indiscretions and weaknesses.

He knew who knew things. He had always figured there would be a time when he would need information. Even in paradise.

He didn't speed to the edge of town. He drove slowly, in fact, though not dreading the questioning. He used the drive to let his psyche assume the mold he had divested himself of when coming here.

He hadn't had to be a tough cop in a while.

He was still steeling himself for the role when he turned onto the rugged roadway which stretched up in front of a row of houses just inside the Petittville limits. All that really meant was that they got city water piped in. Nobody on Rhodes Street considered themselves part of any city.

They were the people who had lived here when there had been only wilderness around. Now they were pleased that a stretch of woods still divided them from the subdivisions where the ones they considered city people lived.

The houses were not shacks. They were average middle-class brick homes. It wasn't appearance. It was something else that set them apart, something that stretched back in their lineage.

He drove on past several of the places, parking finally on the edge of the roadway. He got out slowly, looking down the slight slope toward the house. It was a brown building with green shutters.

The lawn in front was neat, and a thin walkway with an arched lattice covering led to the front door. The rosebushes that lined the lattice were dormant at the moment, some leaves gone to brown. They had not been trimmed in some time.

Just behind the house, he could see some chicken coops, and off to one side, some pens for goats. With the chill morning air, the goats were bunched together, but as he walked down the slope, their wild eyes turned toward him.

One of them shambled around on the joints of its front legs, its neglected hooves sore, in need of trimming.

That meant Pick Gardner probably wasn't doing well.

Stepping around a hole in the front walk, Rice moved up to the front door. He knocked twice before he heard movement inside.

When the door swung inward, he was greeted by a weathered face, leathery-looking really. The skin seemed to sag around the shape of Gardner's features, and his eyes were deep-set as if kept in individual caverns.

He wore a dingy baseball cap cocked to one side, and his shirt and jeans looked like hand-me-downs from a relative about two sizes larger.

His arm rested against the door frame to support him as he peered through the doorway.

"What do you want?"

"I need to talk to you, Pick. Can I come in? It's airish out here."

Nodding, Gardner stepped back, letting the door swing inward. The front room was small and crowded with too much furniture. A wood stove blazing in one corner had chased away the chill and made the room too warm and stuffy.

Carefully, Gardner lowered himself into a brown plaid chair near the kitchen doorway. The radio on an old box monaural was playing a static-riddled morning show out of Aimsley. Rice wondered why Gardner had it dialed there. It was a drive time show and Gardner wasn't going anywhere.

"What do you need?" the old man asked. His voice was hard and gruff and a little too loud.

"I'm just kind of asking around," Rice said. "You heard about the boy who died."

"The kid from the subdivisions?"

"Yeah."

"Dogs."

"Who do you suppose they belonged to, Pick?"

"Wouldn't know."

"There's not any dog fighting going on in these parts?"

"That's illegal. They do some cock fighting."

The thought of all of it disgusted Rice, and he had seen some brutal things in his time. The mistreatment of animals just seemed unusually cruel.

"I'm wondering if somebody might not have had some dogs, you know, for fighting. Maybe they let 'em go for a run and they got out of hand."

"If they did, they probably wouldn't a done it in the city limits." He settled back in his chair, and the spring creaked under his frail weight.

"The limits stretch a ways, Pick."

"Some of us didn't ask for that. Fuckers come around and want to zone and all that shit. No need for zoning."

"We're talking about dogs, Pick. You know somebody out here owns something besides hunting dogs. If they got out and killed a boy, I need to know about it. I don't want them getting anybody else, not even the sick son of a bitch that let them get mean." He'd seen the way they trained the dogs, using chickens or smaller animals, giving them a taste for blood.

Gardner picked up a small paper cup which sat on the floor beside his chair. Raising it to his lips, he spat brown tobacco juice into it before lowering it again to his side.

"You're not from around here, Lucius. You're gonna stir up trouble if you go nosing around. I don't know of anybody that would let his dogs run out through the subdivisions."

"Dogs get loose."

He grumbled for a moment then shrugged his shoulders and looked back in Rice's direction.

"Best I can tell you, you might check at Matt Wilson's place. He has some bird dogs he raises."

"No Rottweilers?"

"None of those."

"Where would I find that place?" Rice asked.

"Next road over, left at the end of it. There's a duck pond out front."

"And a pit bull farm in back?"

The old man didn't answer.

———————

Back in the car, Rice checked the load on his gun before pulling away from Gardner's house. He followed the old road as instructed and located the house in question with ease.

It was built of cypress with a rustic-looking porch. The ducks, oblivious to the cold, skirted in formation across the brown water of the pond.

He parked the cruiser in the muddy, circular driveway and got out. He let his hand fall on the .38's grip as he climbed from the car and walked toward the house. Wind seemed to be trying to keep him away.

A blonde girl wearing jeans and a sweatshirt answered the door, eyeing him suspiciously. She was pregnant, but she was only showing a little beneath the baggy folds of the shirt.

"I'm looking for Matt Wilson," Rice said softly.

Her expression didn't change. "What da ya think he did?"

"Maybe nothing. I just want of talk to him. I'm Chief Lucius Rice."

Behind her, he heard a chair scrape across tile. In a moment a man came into view.

He was thin with a rugged face and a mustache which drooped over the corners of his mouth. His cheeks were covered in stubble matching his brown hair, which was long, almost shoulder-length.

"I ain't done nothin'," he said.

"Do you own dogs?" Rice asked.

Wilson's eyes were hard, his face sullen. He was wearing a blue muscle shirt with an arrowhead necklace dangling from his throat.

He put his hands into the pockets of his faded jeans as Rice continued to stare at him.

"Do you own dogs?" Rice repeated.

"A few."

"Bird dogs, right?"

"They for huntin'. Yeah," he said indignantly. "Mind if I have a look at them?"

He raised a hand to rub his chin. Finally he nodded, and the girl pulled the door inward then.

Rice stepped into the warm kitchen area. The remains of breakfast still covered the table.

"Coffee?" the girl asked.

"No thank you."

Rice followed Wilson through the living room, where the man picked up a denim jacket that was faded almost white with only hints of its original blue indigo around the seams.

They walked back out into the chill. Wilson put his hands in his pockets, shivering against the chill. His back lawn was bordered by untended grass that grew high and brown.

A trail was beaten through it, and they followed it back to a set of makeshift pens. Most of them were occupied by hunting dogs, pointers and several Catahoula Curs, their glassy eyes stark and accusing as they saw Rice approaching.

The barking was almost immediate. Some of them reared up on the fence, their paws clutching at the wire as they let their teeth show.

"They're not too used to seeing a black fella," Wilson explained.

"It's a genetic thing," Rice said. "I got it from my momma and my daddy." He let no sign of humor creep into his voice.

Gradually the dogs settled down, and Wilson squatted and stuck his fingers through the fence, petting their snouts or toying with their ears. They yelped back and wagged their tails.

"Where do you keep the others?" Rice asked.

Wilson looked up at him, his expression an effort of innocence that failed. He bowed his head nervously. "Little further out."

"Let's go look at them."

They followed another trail deeper into the grass. The pens there were similar. The dogs were not. They barked and tried to climb the fences, but they did not have the animated spirit of the others.

As their barking died down, they stood against the wire watching the men in front of them. Some of them were scarred. One was missing a portion of its ear. Another had stitches on his shoulder where the fur had been shaved back.

The look of them angered the policeman. "They look like they've been through hell," he said.

"It's what they're trained for."

Rice jerked his head toward Wilson. "Is it? You get a charge out of watching them tear each other up?"

He shrugged awkwardly and put his hands in his pockets. He wasn't sure what to say.

"Do these ever get out?" Rice asked, moving around the pen. He checked for escape routes, but the wire seemed to be relatively secure.

He looked around in the grass, but there were no signs of other trails. He flexed his fingers on the pistol grip and shook his head at the same time.

"A boy died," he said. "You sure you know nothing about it, Mr. Wilson?"

"Nothing."

Wilson hesitated, looking down at his boots. There seemed to be something he wanted to talk about. "What is it?" Rice asked.

"In here," he said.

He led Rice back up the trail to a small metal shed. The sliding door rattled on its hinges as he shoved it open and walked inside.

Rice kept his hand on his gun, watching Wilson carefully as he moved inside. The chill seemed worse in there, as if the metal walls had gripped it and held it in place.

Reaching upward, Wilson found the pull cord on a bare white light bulb. It fired to life, making looming shadows on the bare walls.

Near the center of the room was a table covered with a camouflage tarpaulin. The light beamed straight down on it, and Wilson seemed to approach it hesitantly.

Rice stayed near the door, trying to be ready if the kid happened to produce a shotgun or some other weapon from beneath the covering. It had been known to happen in these parts.

The policeman hadn't been long away from the shooting range, but he didn't want his reflexes to fail him.

There was no weapon, however. Wilson pulled the tarp back to reveal the black carcass of a dog. It seemed to be a mixed-breed, huge and black with brown coloring on its paws and face.

Even in the cold, the smell of decomposure was beginning to set in. Rice walked forward a couple of steps at a time, looking down at the dead dog.

"Somebody ripped her open," Wilson said.

"What?"

He motioned Rice around to the other side of the table. The dog had been split open, the flesh over its stomach torn back. The cavity beneath its rib cage appeared empty.

"When did it happen?"

"Couple of days ago. I saved the body since it was cold 'cause I was wondering if I should show it to somebody."

"You were afraid to because of your other activities?"

"Yeah, right. I was scared, though, because you hear all this shit about Satanists and animals dying."

"It is weird," Rice agreed. He looked at the opening, and the reports of surgical precision did strike him. He'd attended seminars on this kind of thing while still on the force.

Many of the reports of animal deaths proved to be the work of predators. "Surgical precision" often turned out not to be as precise as morbid fascination would have people believe.

In this case the body did seem to be opened surgically. He put his hand over his mouth to shut out the smell as he leaned closer to the wound.

"I wonder what use whoever did this had for the organs?" he asked when he had straightened up again.

"I looked in there as best I could," Wilson said. "I'm not much up on that, but I don't think they were after her organs.

"What were they after then?"

"Her puppies."

Rice frowned at the words. The notion was somehow strange and frightening, a sick notion at best.

"What do you mean? They took her puppies."

"Well they weren't born yet. She wasn't far along but she was goin' to litter."

Rice shuddered. "You mean somebody cut this dog open and took out the fetuses of her litter?"

"Like I say, I'm not up on this, but I know she was gonna have a litter, and when I looked around her insides trying to figure out what they'd done, I didn't see any sign of the puppies. They wouldn't have been very

64

big, I mean I had a mutt that had some stillborn once and they were small, but they woulda been where you could see them."

For the first time, Rice took his hand from his gun. He used both hands to run over his face now. "Wrap it up in that covering," he instructed. "We're going to put her in my trunk so I can get her checked out by a veterinarian."

Chapter 7

Charlie was a little nervous about going to English class. He knew Miss Nielson would have no way of knowing he had dreamed about her last night and that her catching sight of him in the fantasy had been no more than a dream, but he still didn't want to look her in the eye.

Yesterday had been strange. Today, following the weirdness of the wet dream/nightmare, he knew she was going to make him even more uncomfortable in her presence.

Of course there were other things to worry about than Miss Nielson. Like the Asshole Squad.

The Asshole Squad was composed of five members who didn't like the name applied to them even though it applied quite well. Ronny Minster, Lewis LaBorde, Raymond Garrett, Faulk Carter, and Tom Henry Hoover were from the bottoms, at least most people called the area the bottoms. It really referred to the dense and sparsely populated land outside Petittville. Their homes were on offshoot roads, stashed back in the bends where the trees grew thick.

They missed school when hunting season opened, stalking through the woods with guns they'd owned since they were old enough to walk.

When they were in school, they attempted to assert themselves with their brutish stamina and the fear it generated. They saw most of the students as encroachers. This was the land of their families, and they were threatened by having kids who wore Girbaud jeans or Duck Head styles.

The city was something evil to them, something to be held in contempt, and the city kids were inferior.

Charlie, though not their only victim, was a frequent target. There was something about good-naturedness that they really hated.

He usually managed to avoid them, but once in a while they ran across him and dished up taunts that usually left him upset the rest of the day. He felt weak after being intimidated even though he knew there wasn't much he could do when he was confronted by a crowd of guys, especially those like the Asshole Squad, who would have loved an excuse to beat the crap out of him.

Fighting back just didn't seem a proper avenue. There would be a suspension for all parties, and the Assholes didn't really care if they missed school or not.

He usually just swallowed it and hoped for the best, following the course of least resistance.

He was in the bathroom of fourth hall when they showed up. Fortunately he was in the back stall rather than at the communal urine trough when the door banged back against the wall and they ambled in. He stayed put.

Lewis was in the lead, his long, oily hair hanging shapelessly around his face. He was wearing a plaid flannel shirt with the sleeves ripped out, faded jeans, and tennis shoes. His bare arms revealed the taunt muscles he had developed through various activities over the years.

Ronny was right behind him wearing jeans and a denim jacket. A gold chain, probably stolen, clung to his neck, and his stringy hair fell to brush his shoulders. He had sleepy-looking eyes and high cheekbones which made him seem to sneer, while his pointed nose gave him a weasel-like look.

They were the unofficial leaders for no particular reason. They walked up to the mirrors over the sinks and checked their appearances before moving toward the urinal.

Raymond, who had shorter hair and wore glasses, was carrying a magazine, some kind of fanzine he'd probably swiped out of some girl's locker.

He was thumbing through when Faulk snatched it out of his hand playfully. Faulk had the neatest appearance of any of them. He wore sports shirts and slacks and his sandy hair was clean and well combed.

He was also probably the meanest. He made decent grades and pleased the teachers, but he liked to hurt people too.

He swatted Raymond's cheek and teased him by pretending to hand the magazine back. "What are you reading this crap for?" Faulk asked.

"I just found it," Raymond muttered. He was a little slower and a little less articulate than any of them, though he didn't tend to elicit sympathy.

Faulk began to thumb the pages until he found a foldout poster at the center. "What have we here?" he asked, pulling at the staples.

The poster unfolded to reveal the face of a rock star who had struck a stern expression for the camera, his blond pompadour sprayed and combed crisply into place. His attitude showed in his expression.

"Oh, he's tough," Lewis said, staring at the photo. "You got a thing for him, Raymond?"

"No way, man."

Lewis snatched the magazine from Faulk's and pulled the poster free of the binding. As he let the magazine slide from his hand to the floor, he held the poster up in front of him.

"He's pretty, idden he?"

"He's a faggot," Tom Henry said. "I don't understand what all the cunts see in him."

Lewis fumbled at the crotch of his jeans with one hand while still holding the poster in the other. Yanking his zipper down clumsily, he tugged himself free and began to urinate on the rock star's face.

Hooting with laughter as his fluids streamed down the slick surface of the poster, the others began to follow suit.

Lewis slapped it against the tiled wall over the urinal, and it stuck there so that the others could direct their streams at it. Colors began to melt, and the paper swelled with the moisture as their guffaws and snorts continued.

Charlie held his breath. There was something savage about their assault, and he trembled as he sensed their anger. He was praying they would leave. He waited, trying not to move.

As he listened to their voices, they sounded as if they were about to make their departure, but instead as they turned and began to zip up, Lewis started kicking the stall doors.

There didn't seem to be a method to it; he just had hostility left to get rid of. Charlie gripped his books tightly, closing his eyes as he prayed they wouldn't find him.

It was one of those prayers to which the answer is "No, apologies from the Creator, but it would interfere with the natural order."

When he opened his eyes, he found himself staring into the leering grin on Lewis's face.

"What cha doin', Chaaaaaarlie?"

Charlie swallowed, trying unsuccessfully to control the expression on his face. He knew they could see the fear.

"You hiding, Charlie?" Faulk asked, sticking his head around the wall of the stall so Charlie could see his grin.

Charlie didn't speak. He looked for an opening to dive through them and run, but that didn't seem possible.

Flexing his fingers on the spines of his books, he decided to try anyway and aimed for a space between Lewis and Tom Henry.

They were surprised by his sudden motion, but they closed ranks quickly and blocked him, their hands falling on his arms and shoulders.

He dropped his books as they jerked him around and encircled him. They continued to grin and laugh, and he felt the blood rising to his face and arms. The embarrassment mingled with anger and fear, and he gritted his teeth as they stared at him.

"It's not nice to try to run away while we're talking to you," Faulk said.

"Maybe we ought to teach him a lesson," Tom Henry suggested.

Lewis slapped Charlie's cheek softly a few times. "Bad boy, Charlie."

"What he needs is a good whippin'," Tom Henry suggested.

He reached to the shiny buckle of his Western-style belt and unhooked it, sliding the brown leather strip from around his waist.

"Turn him around, Raymond."

Obediently, the big guy twisted Charlie until his back was to them, and before Charlie could protest, he felt someone's hands closing on his ankles.

He started to kick, but it did little good as they lifted him and held him spread-eagle, facing the floor.

"What do you think?" Faulk said. "Ten licks do it?"

They chuckled and nodded, and he heard other belts being tugged off.

"Apiece," somebody said.

Charlie closed his eyes tightly, bracing for the pain. A single blow struck him. Then another came, then another and another.

"One," Faulk said.

A succession of slaps came again. "Two."

Charlie felt the pain even through the thick fabric of his jeans, a stinging ache that shot through his buttocks and needled down his legs. They were swatting wildly.

He felt more blows, overlapping each other, twisting along his sides and licking under his thighs.

The hurt brought tears to his eyes, but he contained his sobs, struggling not to give them that satisfaction.

His silence seemed to anger them, and they struck harder, putting more muscle into their swings. He jerked his head back with the pain, his body writhing in their grasps. It was stinging worse now, and he had bitten the inside of his lips so that a thin trickle of blood was seeping out the corner of his mouth.

"I've lost count," Faulk said.

The belts slammed into him again.

"Three," Faulk said through his laughter.

They hit again. "Four."

Charlie grunted with the pain, fighting to hold the sound in his throat. He was breathing hard now, and they could tell how much he was feeling it.

"All right, let it flow," Lewis said.

They were trying to make him scream now, putting all they had into it. He could tell the way they grunted when they hit. They weren't laughing now. They were serious, trying to inflict agony.

They were so caught up in it, they didn't hear what he heard over the sounds of leather slapping denim. The door was opening.

At the level they were holding him, he could see feet walking into the room, leather-clad feet attached to legs covered by dress pants.

"What the hell's going on here?"

Mr. Sawyer, God love him. Nature had called him away from his algebra equations.

Charlie had only a second to brace himself as they let go of him. He slammed down onto the floor with a thud, and the tile jarred him. It was cool, though, and its touch was almost a relief.

"What are you trying to do? Kill somebody?" Sawyer asked.

He pushed through the group and knelt on one knee at Charlie's side. "Are you okay?"

Charlie got to his knees and then his feet, wiping his face on his short sleeve. "Fine," he mumbled.

"I want all of you in the office, now," Sawyer commanded.

"Come on, Mr. Sawyer," Faulk protested.

"To the office," Sawyer shouted. His face was reddened with anger. "You five don't run this school, and it's time you learned it."

Without speaking or letting the scowls slide off their faces, they filed out of the bathroom, slamming the door back against the wall as they all pushed through the opening.

Sawyer watched them leave and then turned to Charlie, who was now at the mirror straightening his hair and shirt.

"You sure you're okay, Charlie?"

"Fine," Charlie said. He was trembling and angry and embarrassed, but he didn't want to let it show.

"They pick on everybody," Sawyer said. "They should be suspended."

"Stuff happens," Charlie said.

"This would be a reasonably pleasant school if it weren't for them," Sawyer said.

"I've got to get to class," Charlie mumbled. He headed for the door, hoping his nerves would settle by the time he reached English class.

After a check to make sure the kids had made it to the office, Sawyer headed down to the teachers' lounge. The gang—that was how he thought of them though he knew they weren't that organized—were all sitting on the couch in front of the principal's door waiting for their sentence. They wouldn't be in school tomorrow, Sawyer was assured.

That was music, and it would please the other teachers as well. He stepped through the swinging door into the lounge, catching a whiff of the smoke that hung in the air.

"The Assholes are being suspended," he announced.

That brought a round of applause from the instructors on their free shift who dappled the tables in the narrow, carpeted room.

He gave a brief statement then entertained a few questions about the incident.

As he was finishing, he happened to notice Barbara Nielson sitting at a table by herself. A paperback book was open in front of her beside a candy bar she hadn't finished eating.

She was looking at him, so he stepped up to her. "You haven't had many dealings with these guys," he said, "but they're hell on wheels."

"I can imagine. I have Charlie Black in one of my classes. I can't imagine him doing much to deserve what you described."

"He is pretty good. Doesn't burn up algebra, but he's likable. Those are the ones they go after."

"Guess that's one of the things I have to learn around here." She motioned to a chair, inviting him to sit down.

He fumbled with it a little before he managed to pull it out and lower himself into it.

Like every other male in the vicinity, he'd spotted Barbara when she'd first arrived, but he hadn't expected her to know he was drawing breath.

"Are you getting settled in well?" Sawyer asked.

"Kind of. It's a quiet little town, isn't it?"

He couldn't argue with that. Even for a movie you had to drive over to Aimsley. He'd almost lost his mind when he'd first moved here from Penn's Ferry.

"You adjust," he said, "but it never stops being boring."

He looked into her eyes. She was truly beautiful. He felt his tongue trying to tie itself into a knot. He was glad it was her turn to speak.

"I've been doing lesson plans and reading paperbacks to break my monotony. I've almost got my apartment in order."

She'd slapped the ball into his court. Was she hinting that she wanted to do something? They didn't really know each other, but she obviously didn't think he was a hideous leper.

Still, he'd never had anyone this attractive show interest. Could be she was just being nice. He hadn't had a date in ages, not since he and Laine Murphy, the home ec teacher, had broken up. That had been last summer after she'd met Cliff, a guy from California.

He drummed his fingers on the table. Anne Manley was getting something from the vending machine, and he waited for her to move out of earshot before he spoke again.

"If you'd like to get together one evening," he said, "we could go over to Aimsley to see a show." It was almost a relief just to get the sentence out of his mouth. He could deal with the embarrassment if she offered a polite excuse. He could handle anything now that the words weren't lodged in his throat any longer.

He was braced for rejection, but she said, "I'd like that."

He felt the anguish which had been rising in him begin to subside. A yes. He wanted to sigh with relief. She'd said yes.

Was tonight too quick? Better let it hang. "I'll call then."

She smiled, nothing too bubbly, quite a calm smile actually, but that was enough. It was reassurance that he hadn't misunderstood her. He'd heard the words properly.

"I guess I'd better get back to my classroom," she said.

He watched her leave, watched the sway of her hips and the gentle ripple of muscle in her legs, and his pulse reminded him his heart was there.

The business of calling would mean going through the agony all over again, but at least that initial step out on the ice hadn't resulted in too many cracks.

———

Charlie recovered from the spanking with relative ease. The pain subsided quickly, though he expected soreness tomorrow. The anguish lingered most of all. Word traveled fast in school, and he suspected those who saw him in the hallway had heard about what had happened.

He felt like a rape victim, stigmatized by an assault that wasn't his fault. He'd just been in the wrong place at the wrong time.

His anger was a fiery edge to all of it. They'd had no reason to put him through that. He had been harming no one, and he ought to be able to go to the bathroom in a public school without humiliation and fear.

He made it through his classes, letting the lessons take his mind off some of it, and as time for English class approached, his apprehension about Miss Nielson replaced all other feelings.

He knew she wouldn't walk into the room and confront him about a dream she couldn't possibly know about, but he still felt funny about facing her today.

It would be hard not to think of her in the dream, and in a way he was also afraid of her. He wasn't sure why, but there was something about her, as if she wanted something from him.

He wasn't sure if he could deliver whatever it was. As he walked toward class, he realized his palms were sweating. If he found her staring at him again, he wasn't sure how he'd deal with it.

Would he run screaming? That was a bit extreme, but his eerie feeling almost made that seem a likely response.

As he moved toward her class, he began to find it hard to urge his feet onward. He was like a condemned man heading for his execution, ridiculous. He picked up his pace, working his way through the crowd, avoiding eye contact.

If they were staring at him after hearing about the restroom incident, he didn't want to know about it. He had enough to think about.

He was thankful she wasn't standing in the doorway when he reached the classroom. He wouldn't have to walk directly past her.

He slipped through the door, finding his way quickly to his desk. He didn't look around as he waited for class to begin. He shoved some of his books under his desk and kept his literature text and notebook on top.

He thumbed through the pages while some around him talked and others waited outside until the last minute.

He couldn't keep from looking up when Miss Nielson walked in. Her shoes tapped softly on the tile, drawing his gaze toward her.

He swallowed, watching her graceful movements now while remembering her look last night. Had it really been her body in his dream, had his thoughts really been able to pierce into the reality her clothes concealed.

As she sat down, he cast his eyes back to his books before she could notice him and establish some connection. He didn't want her to look at him because he feared he would interpret it as a look of accusation no matter what.

He didn't want to live with the worry of that. She must know that all the boys were fantasizing about her. She was beautiful, she must be aware of the reactions she caused.

He listened to the conversations around him, but they were meaningless, ramblings about television shows and singers. He bit his lips, willing the moments to tick by.

Finally people filed or scrambled into the classroom, and the roll was called. He intended to be silent for the class, hunching down in his desk, but Miss Nielson announced that they would discuss the Poe story first.

That piqued his interest, but he didn't look in her direction. He kept his attention on the graffiti as she began a brief introduction to the story, discussing the principal characters.

"Why do you think Montresor is angry at Fortunato?" she asked.

"It doesn't say," Jeanette Massey answered. "Just something about insults."

"Do you suppose Fortunato has really done anything to the narrator?"

A few kids shook their heads. A few others shrugged. No one had a specific answer. They were being asked to think rather than recite something written for them in black and white.

"It doesn't say that," Jeanette reiterated.

"You kind of have to wonder," Charlie said without thinking. He caught himself as the words rolled from his lips and he found Miss Nielson looking at him.

He fell silent, but she continued to look at him. The accusation wasn't present, though. "Go on, Charlie."

Now other eyes turned toward him. "Well," he said, feeling a little relieved. This wasn't so bad. "I mean he finds him out at a carnival dressed up in what's really a jester's outfit if I understand it. How bad could this guy have bothered anybody?"

"Maybe he's jealous of Fortunato, who is having a good time," somebody suggested. Miss Nielson didn't turn. She kept looking at Charlie.

"It could be he feels Fortunato is better than he is," Charlie continued, stumbling only slightly. He hadn't given this concept deep thought, but it seemed to make sense.

"He hates Fortunato because he knows about Amontillado," he continued. "Because he knows about other things probably."

"Because Fortunato is a superior man," Miss Nielson suggested. "Could it be the narrator is envious of that?"

Charlie realized the conversation had turned into a one-on-one conversation. Her eyes were locked on him, and they were connected. He felt it. He couldn't understand it, but she seemed drawn to him.

They went on, talking, discussing the spirit of irony in the story, and he sensed she was trying to tell him something, hinting without actually revealing just as stories did.

When class ended, he was relieved that the intensity was broken. He got up from his desk as the rest of the kids bolted. It had been fun talking to her, but he was ready to be out of there. He was scared of talking to her, of even speaking to her on his way out of here.

His shyness had clicked in again. Dealing with her on classroom level was one thing. Interpersonal communication scared the hell out of him.

He tucked his books under his arm and headed for the door. "Good discussion, Charlie," she said before he escaped.

He had to turn. He forced himself and managed to smile. "Thanks."

She smiled back, playfully, and it made him relax a little. It also reminded him how beautiful she was. He calmed slightly, enough to feel good about the conversation and the bonding.

He grinned slightly as he stepped into the hall. "Got a crush on her, Charlie?" somebody asked.

He ignored the suggestion. Let them be jealous. They didn't understand him anyway. They were like the guy who walled up Fortunato. They were lesser people, inferior, just like Miss Nielson had suggested.

Chapter 8

The smell of antiseptic filled the air in the little veterinary shop, but it didn't completely mask the mingling odors of fur that lingered. Rice could hear pets yapping in the waiting room as he stood beside the metal examining table watching Dr. Morris Wade peer into the black dog's empty belly.

"Sure was a clean job," Wade said, leaning back from the examination and peeling off the rubber gloves he'd slipped on to probe inside the animal. He dropped them into the pocket of his white coat.

"Surgical precision?" Rice asked skeptically.

"You might say that," said Wade, a heavyset blond-haired man in his late thirties. His cheeks bulged, making the top of his head seem narrow, and his haircut only complemented the suggestion. His cheeks were ruddy, giving him a look of being perpetually overheated.

"Was she sliced up or what?"

"Looks like it could have been a scalpel."

Wade leaned against the wall, placing his hand flat against a heartworm poster. "That old boy you got her from was right," Wade added. "They took her puppies. How far along did he say she was?"

"I don't know."

"Well, a dog carries for about sixty days. She must not have been too far along. They opened up her womb and slipped 'em all out."

"You're telling me she was mutilated by a person?" Rice said.

"'Pears that way."

Rice tucked his thumbs under his belt with a heavy sigh. That wasn't the news he'd wanted to hear.

"You're sure she wasn't mutilated by other dogs?"

"Oh yeah. I can guarantee you that. It wouldn't be near this neat if that had happened."

"Is there a history of dogs doing that sort of thing?"

"No. Cats are meaner than dogs and that wouldn't be likely to happen with them, not that I know of. A Tom will mess up a male kitten if it gets a chance, but not a pregnant female. Same with dogs. Now males don't do much as fathers, and I've seen father and son dogs light into each other if they're jealous or whatever, but this is an oddball thing you got here."

Rice lifted his hands. "Is there any reason somebody would fool with a bunch of canine fetuses? Research or anything like that?"

"Nah. No reason for anything like that in these parts. There's not exactly a shortage of dogs in the world, Chief. Not so's you'd have to cut open somebody else's dog and swipe them."

The coroner talked to you about the Hagan boy. "Is she the kind of dog that might have attacked him?"

Now the heavy man threw up his hands. "Could go either way. It was pretty big dogs based on the size of the bite marks. I had to go look at the body, and the bites were big. This kind has the right jaw for it, but so do several breeds."

Rice thought about slamming his fist into the wall. This seemed to be a dead end, but it was odd. Wade was right about that. Why mutilate a dog like this? Could it be to cover something up?

Wade was shaking his head. "We don't need a whole bunch more baby dogs in the world, but I hate to see an animal treated this way. God didn't intend that."

"Do you think the man could have done this to her himself?"

"Hard to say. What reason would he have to do this to his own dog? Maybe one of his competitors if he was a dog fighter. Might not have wanted him breeding more opponents or whatever."

"It wouldn't surprise me if these guys played vicious games," Rice agreed. "I guess it could be some kind of warning." And that could be tied to the boy's death. Somebody could also have let a group of the dogs run loose as some kind of game or practice run.

He rubbed his face. It felt sticky, and the smells of the place were getting to him.

"It was the mutilation that killed the dog, wasn't it?"

"Oh yeah."

"No other damage but the removal of the fetuses?"

Wade stuck out his lower lip and shook his head. "Everything else is in place. They had to cut down to her uterus, and they didn't worry about doing damage to other organs, but it was done to get to the puppies. There's no other sign of intentionally ripping her apart."

"It was practical cutting, you're telling me."

"Mm-hm."

"If they were trying to collect fetuses, how many would they get from a dog of this size?" He wondered if that made a difference.

"It's hard to tell with a dog. They can have anywhere from two to three to twelve, thirteen. They've had cases of some up to twenty-two, twenty-three born alive. A lot of times they'll have some mashed or stillborn when they're a lot of them. Then again you get some smothered by their mother's body while they're nursing. It's hell to be born a dog."

Rice looked over at the still form on the table. "Have you got something you can do with her?"

"I can have her buried with the ones put to sleep at the pound tomorrow. I'm supposed to go give the shots."

Rice nodded grimly. He didn't care for this business at all.

Obediently, Charlie rode the bus home from school. The trip was mercifully uneventful, a relief considering the rest of the day. The incident with the Assholes and then English class gave him enough to think about.

He sat with his head against the glass watching the roadside speed by. The attack had left him unharmed though he still felt angry about it. It was supplanted in his mind by the look in Miss Nielson's eyes, and he allowed himself to think about the dream again. He was careful to block out the images of Budd.

At home his mom greeted him. She'd been doing some kind of oil painting in her workroom, and she wore the stains of it on her sweatshirt.

"Let me show it to you," she suggested, trying to interest him.

He followed her into the room, where she had a variety of other hobby items on display. She tended to move from one thing to another without spending much time on any of them.

She showed him the canvas on her easel. She had actually been working with watercolors, he realized.

"Not bad," he said, looking it over. It showed children with brightly colored umbrellas playing in the rain.

"I saw it in the newspaper," she said, displaying a photo. He looked at the clipping. She had reinterpreted the work while retaining the composition it offered.

He wasn't sure if that was really good artistically or not, but he nodded. She was apparently making an effort to be nice since he had been upset about having to ride the bus.

"I'd like to call Nell at the store if it's all right," he said.

"Sure."

"Can I sit in Dad's office?"

"As long as you don't disturb any of his papers. You know how he is."

"Right," Charlie said. He climbed the stairs and walked down the hallway to the office, dumping his books on a table beside the door.

Moving over to the desk, he sat down in the swivel chair and propped his feet on the blotter. After tapping out the store number on the punch pad, he pressed the handset to his ear.

He imagined himself in a film studio office placing a call to an important backer.

Then Nell came on the line.

"Hi, it's Charlie."

"Hey. You're not coming by?"

"My mom made me ride the bus."

"Because of Budd?"

"Yeah."

"I'm sorry, Charlie."

"You sound like the commercial."

"So sue me for plagiarism. What are you up to?"

"Surviving. I had a rough day. Some guys at school gave me a hard time. It got better by English class."

"The new teacher."

"Yeah. We started talking about Edgar Allan Poe, and it was like we were the only ones in the room."

He expected her to make cracks, but she was silent. The lack of sound on the line made it seem awkward for a moment.

"What did she say to you?"

"We just discussed the story. 'The Cask of Amontillado.'"

"I think I saw her this morning," Nell said. "She must have been on her way to school. She was walking."

"She had dark hair?"

"Yeah."

"That must be her. What'd you think? She's pretty, eh?"

There was another pause. "Yeah, she is, Charlie. You can't really expect anything, though. She's in her thirties or so."

"Oh, I know. She's just nice. Some people teased me when they heard about class."

"Is she kind of strange, Charlie?"

He thought about that a moment. "Yeah, sort of."

"Where'd she come here from?"

"I'm not sure." He told her where she was living, leaving out the fact that he'd followed her there and the fact that he'd seen her out walking where Budd had been killed.

"I don't know what it is," Nell said, "but I've had this funny feeling about her since I saw her walk by this morning."

"It's nothing," Charlie said. "She's just the new teacher."

"You weren't so sure about that yesterday."

"I guess I was just upset about Budd."

"When is the funeral, by the way?"

"Tomorrow. It's in the afternoon. Are you going to be able to make it?"

"I'll probably have to run the shop."

"They're letting school out early," Charlie said. "Nobody ever liked Budd, but now he's everybody's hero. Most of them won't go to the service."

"It'll be all right, Charlie."

"Yeah, I miss him, but you have to go on."

He hung up, wondering why Nell was acting funny about Miss Nielson. She must be a little jealous because someone else had some of his attention. She'd been like his big sister for a long time. Maybe she felt threatened in the role.

Nell checked out some guy in an army flak jacket who was renting from Matt's hard R collection. Hardcore was against the law in Riverland Parish, but Matt had a selection of titles which had been edited and were labeled "cable version." They helped to pay the bills.

The guy tried not to make eye contact as she took his money and gave him his change. She remained polite as she thanked him for his business. He mumbled a response and made for the door, embarrassed.

That left the store empty and her free to brood. She sat on the stool behind the counter and picked up an issue of *The Huntress*.

Why did she feel so strange about this woman? She'd noticed nothing out of the ordinary in just the sight of her, but somehow Charlie's confirmation that Miss Nielson was the one she'd seen this morning seemed to validate the nagging feeling she'd had all day.

Matt would attribute it to too many comic books. People in comic books had nagging sensations that proved true. In real life they were usually unfounded.

She wondered if she was really just creating the feeling for herself to break the Petittville monotony. Imagining some sensation worthy of Time-Life Books certainly took the edge off boredom, and since she did have an interest in fantasy, how far did her imagination have to leap to construct a mystical sensation?

When Matt showed up, she didn't talk about her feeling at first, but after he'd been puttering around for a while, adjusting things on the shelves and rearranging titles, she walked over to him.

"What's up?" he asked, looking up at her from a crouched position on the mystery row.

"I was wondering what you'd heard about the new teacher."

"Pretty good-looking woman," he said. "Lives over in the Foster Arms."

"Where'd she come from?"

"Somewhere in the East. I'm not sure where."

"Did she teach there?"

"I guess so."

"What brought her here?"

"Just takin' the job," I guess. "Bill Grant said she saw the ad they put out in the teachers' journals."

Grant was the school board representative for the area. He'd managed to stay in office in spite of challenges to the board's sex education policies and other controversies which kept the meetings rocking when they convened in Aimsley.

"Isn't it a little odd to hire somebody from way off like that?" Nell asked. "I mean there must be people from the parish who are qualified."

Matt straightened up and dusted off the knees of his jeans. His eyes had a kind of knowing gleam in them. It was a look he always got, as if something was brewing in his brain. The corners of his lips curled up around his Fu Manchu mustache in a grin. "Folks in the parish have had more opportunity to make enemies," he reminded her. "Those board members don't forget if people sign petitions or raise hell. Then their kids finish college and want jobs, and the powers make sure they don't get 'em. Lots of other stuff goes on too. You can't tell what makes things happen."

"You think they did much of a background check on her?"

"What do you think she did, murdered her students back East and came here to hide?"

He walked past her to begin straightening boxes on the horror shelf, pushing the brim of his Bogart fedora back from his brow. "Well, you have to admit this is not exactly a garden spot," Nell said.

He chuckled. "What brought all this on?"

"Charlie Black said she seems a little weird."

"You and your buddy Charlie both have too much imagination," Matt said. He plucked a *Salem's Lot* box off the shelf and fluttered it at her. "Maybe she's a vampire." He put the box back in place. "Couldn't be that. If she was a vampire, she'd have to teach at night school."

"I just think there are some things about it that don't seem right."

"Could it be that you're bugged a little that Charlie's smitten by somebody besides you?"

"He's just a friend. He's a kid."

"Yeah, but it never hurts your feelings when somebody thinks you're hot stuff."

"Okay, I'll admit it's a boost to my ego."

"Uh-huh. And this new babe is a challenge to it."

She leaned against the counter, folding her arms in front of her. "I know it looks that way, and maybe I am a little jealous, but I think I saw her walking by my house this morning on her way to school. There's something weird about her, Matt. She exudes something."

"What does 'exude' mean?"

"Send out strange vibes."

"Beats me. I'll listen around, but maybe she just looked a little too good when you saw her. "

"Get off that track."

"Sorry." He arched his eyebrows. "Guess it's really a sore spot."

She walked back behind the counter as a customer entered the store. Matt's comments were stinging a little, not because they were true but because she didn't want him to believe they were true.

She liked Charlie, that was all. She didn't want him getting hurt by some strange woman. She'd have to see if she could do some checking on Barbara Nielson.

Maybe Matt was right, reading her better than she understood herself. She'd had a communications class once which mentioned a Johari Window, a diagram which identified self-awareness and noted that there are things others can see about an individual that the individual cannot see herself.

If Matt was wrong, and it wasn't jealousy but intuition, however, something might be dangerous about the woman.

———

Barbara Nielson wasn't feeling dangerous as she finished outlining her lesson plans and closed the workbook on her desk. The plan was a school requirement, a tedious one. She rubbed her eyes as she leaned back in her chair.

She had been on her feet much of the time the last couple of days, and with the tension of settling into a new place and job, she felt weary.

She didn't really like it here. The students were not particularly stimulating. They went through the motions, struggling to earn a grade rather than actually gain knowledge. She found them trying to tell her what they thought she wanted to hear in class discussions rather than digging inside themselves for anything profound. That was not really a surprise.

As she got up from her desk and slipped on her coat before gathering her books, she thought about Eugene Sawyer. He was, on the other hand, a pleasant surprise. She had misgivings about entering into anything; she had not taken her new job with romance in mind, but he was different. His manner and his glasses made him a bit nerdish, but he was a nice man, nice enough to make her wonder about possibilities.

True, she had been thinking about giving up men, forgetting about finding that kind of happiness, but that was in part because of past experience. Most guys weren't nice when you scratched the surface.

Meeting him didn't really change her mind, but it did make her think, at least mentally exploring fantasies of a world where romance could be real. Her life experience usually tended to contradict that notion.

As she walked from the building, she looked around but saw no sign of movement in the vicinity. With her books tucked against her chest, she began her walk home at a brisk pace.

The streets were peaceful. She liked that about the area. She was used to crowded streets and noise. Here there were only leaves and occasional children playing, although the children were being kept indoors of late.

She couldn't blame the parents with the reports of the hounds, though she'd never had to care for a child herself.

When she reached home, she ditched her books and changed into jeans and a T-shirt. She wanted to be comfortable and not sexy for a while.

Sawyer had broken the ice, and she found herself wondering if he would call tonight. If he reached her and asked for tonight, she would have to say yes because she didn't want him to be discouraged. It was probably difficult for him to work up his courage.

She didn't really feel like a date tonight, however. Acting before he could have a chance to call, she unpacked her answering machine and hooked it up to the newly installed telephone.

She recorded a new message and flipped it on. Let him think she was out shopping or whatever. That wouldn't be a rejection, just bad timing.

Night came down, and the wind quickened, its dampness adding an edge to the chill while the moon glowed through a dusty covering of clouds.

Faulk Carter stood at the edge of his family's garage watching the treetops waver. He held a Miller Lite in one hand. The other was tucked into the pocket of his jeans, and his long shadow cast by the interior light reminded him of a scarecrow as it stretched across the concrete apron that spread to the driveway.

Behind him, Tom Henry was fumbling with tools. They had been working on the old 1980 Camaro, which had been their project for some time. So far they'd had no luck in getting the bitch running properly. It continued to sputter and complain when they drove it.

They had bought it, chipping in money they had earned on summer jobs. It was a flashy-looking car with a bronze paint job that still gleamed, so there had been no debate about the purchase.

They'd picked it up cheap off a used car lot in Aimsley, mainly because the engine had been ragged by its previous owners.

"What you see out there?" Tom Henry asked. "Nothing."

No sign of Miss Nielson? I wouldn't mind seein' her walk by. We could invite her into the back seat for a sip of beer." He grabbed the crotch of his jeans. "And a taste of boudin. Bet she's never had any Cajun sausage."

Faulk smiled coyly. He didn't find the crude joke amusing, though he couldn't object to Tom Henry's sentiment.

She was unlikely to make an appearance, however, so he started toward the front of the car.

"Close that door, will you?" Tom Henry suggested. "The wind's comin' in."

Faulk grabbed the garage door's edge and pulled it down before moving around the car. He leaned into the vehicle to look at his friend's work. A drop light hung from the hood latch, shining down into the engine block.

"It's not ready to win any races," Tom Henry said.

"Not quite," Faulk agreed. "Just get it so we can drive it to school and I'll be happy."

"Then we can give a few chicks rides home."

"Or detours."

They eased back from the engine, and Tom Henry walked over to the workbench, where an Igloo cooler awaited. They'd stocked it with a fresh six-pack earlier. He pulled two cans from the ice and handed one to Faulk as they sat on the bumper of the car, smiling as Tom Henry pulled the tab on his can.

"That kid nearly shit his pants today, didn't he?" Faulk grinned and nodded. "It was almost worth detention."

Tom Henry poured some beer into his throat. "Wouldn't have had to do that if it hadn't been for Sorry Sawyer."

"I know. We'll get him for that."

"Yeah, we ought to nail old Charlie too. It was his fault."

Faulk shrugged. They *had* been picking on the kid after all. Still it wouldn't be that big a deal to make his life miserable.

Tom Henry was still laughing when they heard the howl. It stopped him. Everybody had been thinking twice about dog howls, and this one sounded close.

"Think that's the one that got Budd the Scud?"

"Probably just a neighborhood dog," Faulk said. "They howl all the time. We're just jumpy."

The next howl sounded closer, at least close enough to make them get up from their seats.

"That's not Old Man Sallee's mutt," Tom Henry said. "Just relax," Faulk said. "It's just a dog."

He put his hand on Tom Henry's arm to calm him, and they stood like statues, silent for several seconds. When no more howls sounded, they continued to sip their beer.

"Shit, we are too jumpy," Tom Henry said.

Then something slammed into the side of the building, rattling the paint cans on the shelf there. A putty knife slipped over the edge and clattered to the concrete floor. The impact reverberated through the room. They could feel the force. There was a lot of weight behind it.

Tom Henry moved to the center of the room without any reason except panic. He seemed disoriented, and Faulk rushed to him, fearing he might try to open the door.

They were standing shoulder to shoulder when something struck the rear wall, rattling the tools that hung on pegs over the workbench.

Some empty oil cans on another shelf were jarred about but they remained in place.

When their eyes met after surveying the effects, Faulk saw Tom Henry's were full of terror.

"This ain't right," he said. "Must be them hounds, but what are they after?"

"I don't know," Faulk said, swallowing.

There was no sound of barking. No howls. For a moment they could hear only their own breathing.

The scratching began a split second later, scraping against the outer side of the door, raking along the corrugated metal.

"They're gonna git in," Tom Henry moaned.

"They can't claw through that," Faulk said, though his voice quivered as the racket repeated. The door buckled inward with the pressure, rattling within its frame.

But it held, even as the clawing continued. Whatever it was, was trying to dig its way inside.

Tom Henry's hand shot into his pocket, fumbling for the car keys. When he yanked them free of the denim, he wheeled around to the trunk. His hands were shaking so badly it was difficult for him to get the key into the lock, but when the lid popped open, he leaned inside and yanked the tire iron out of its housing.

Faulk began to look for a weapon as well, finally spotting a lawn mower blade on the worktable, where someone had been sharpening it with a file. He snatched it up and wrapped an oily cloth around one end of it for a handle.

The scratching continued as they moved back toward the door. The weight from outside seemed tremendous. Something was lunging against the metal, frantically trying to gain entrance. Faulk held his breath, not believing the metal could be compromised even as the assault made him doubt.

"We could be trapped in here," Tom Henry said. "Better that than being ripped apart."

The door rattled again, harder, and they spun around, impelled to move past the car and climb up on the worktable. They crouched there, their weapons raised as their eyes locked on the door.

It bounced inward, returned to its place, then bounced again with each new assault.

A moment later the rattling stopped. They waited. Seconds ticked by. Then a minute had passed without any scratching.

"You think it's gone?" Tom Henry asked.

"I don't know," Faulk said. His ankles were starting to hurt from the position he was holding, and the blade was heavy in his hand.

He realized now how fast his heart was beating, and he could feel the blood tingling in his ears. They were hot with fear.

Slowly, he edged off the bench, lowering his feet to the floor. He moved past the car and leaned against the wall beside the door, listening.

He could hear no sound now, not a hint of movement outside. He motioned for Tom Henry to join him.

Still crouching on the worktable, Tom Henry's eyes widened. He wasn't fond of the notion of coming down.

Showing his frustration with his expression, Faulk motioned again, jerking his hand harder this time.

Moving like an old man, Tom Henry climbed down and walked forward, clutching the tire iron in front of him with both hands.

"We'll open it just a crack and look out," Faulk said. "Then we'll know if they're gone or not."

Tom Henry's eyes opened even wider, and he shook his head. "I don't know that that's such a good idea."

"It's okay. We won't give them room to get in."

"You sure."

"You want to set up residence here?"

Reluctantly, Tom Henry crouched beside the door, gripping one of the handles. With his other hand, he kept the tire iron raised, ready to start hammering away if salivating jaws appeared.

"Ready?" Faulk asked, gripping the other handle.

Tom Henry gave him a nod. "Yep."

They lifted, stopping with the base of the door only about six inches above the concrete. Faulk dropped onto his stomach about a foot back from the door and peered through the opening.

No head shot through the space, no claws appeared, and within his range of vision he could spot nothing living outside.

"It's clear," he said.

Tom Henry let go of the door and let it slide shut anyway. "You sure it's safe to go out?"

"Dogs aren't smart enough to hide around the corner," Faulk said.

"I don't know."

"We'll get our asses in the house," Faulk said. "At least from there we can call the police."

"Agreed."

They gripped the handles again, shoving the door upward. It rolled up on its track, and they stepped through it quickly, blade and tire iron ready.

Their lungs relaxed when they were not attacked. Standing back to back, they scanned the lawn and roadway, then the lawn next door.

Nothing.

"Where the fuck did they go?" Tom Henry asked.

"I don't know."

They were about to walk toward the house, when Faulk happened to look down at the concrete. He put a hand on Tom Henry's shoulder.

"Look at this."

The footprint was as big as a man's hand, a perfect outline of the padded foot that had stepped in the dew-soaked grass.

"Jesus Christ," Tom Henry whispered.

It dried before they could show it to anybody.

Sawyer paced his living room nervously. He hadn't been able to sit for most of the evening. Watching television had done nothing to calm him, and he hadn't been able to concentrate on the work problems in the back of the Algebra II textbook. He usually did those when he was bored.

Tonight he wasn't bored. He was apprehensive. No woman as attractive as Barbara Nielson had ever paid attention to him. He wasn't sure what he should do about it.

She'd left the door open for him to call, to ask her out, and he wanted to. Except he was frightened. What if he'd misinterpreted her kindness? That would mean embarrassment. He would have to face her when they passed in the hall or bumped into each other in the lounge. That would be enough to melt his stamina.

It was safer to let it ride, let it be just a casual thing—friends, buddies. He could be polite when he saw her, and it wouldn't matter if he didn't really ask her out.

Something inside him wouldn't let him accept the complacency, though. She was pretty, beautiful, and she had shown interest. He'd long ago figured if he ever got married, he would have to settle for someone who wasn't beautiful and probably someone who didn't have the best personality in the world either.

He was a math teacher after all, nothing exciting. Why could he expect someone who had other options to want him? Women, especially attractive women, but even women who weren't prizes, always seemed to have plenty of men after them, bird dogging.

He had nothing extra to offer to put himself above the crowd.

Yet now, here was Barbara, and she had indicated she liked him, dammit. That couldn't be his imagination. It was nice and safe to think about not calling, but he might never get an opportunity like this again. If he let her get away, he'd kick himself the rest of his life and wonder about what might have happened.

"Unacceptable scenario, Sawyer," he told himself.

He paced around his apartment's narrow living room, bumping into the coffee table occasionally as he rehearsed his end of the conversation in his head.

He would begin simply, talk about school for a while, compare notes until he was ready to suggest that they get together.

Simple really, just a matter of talking to another human being. His palms sweated, a knot formed in his stomach, and his breathing wasn't all it should be. It was akin to agony, not pain but discomfort beyond belief.

He had to force himself to sit down at the end of the couch. The cordless phone rested there in its cradle, menacing.

He picked it up, pressed out the digits he'd received from Information earlier, and waited. The purr began. He was committed.

He counted three rings, not enough to give up on. She might be in another room. The fourth ring sounded. He had to give it at least five. The knot in his stomach tightened.

He was ready if she answered. He could speak; he could be articulate. He closed his eyes, while he balled his free hand into a fist and punched the arm of the couch.

Finally he heard a click, and then her answering machine came on. He listened to her voice explaining that she was away.

They were never home the first time you called, the law of the jungle. You had to go through the agony at least twice.

At the sound of the beep he said: "Hi, this is Gene Sawyer. I just called to say hello."

He hung up wondering where she might have gone. Was she already out on a date with someone else or just out doing something routine?

Chapter 9

Charlie was playing a swords and sorcery game on the home office computer when his dad came into the room to work at the desk. Dismissing himself before his dad could grumble, Charlie headed down the hall to his room.

He was still bummed out by the attack from the A-holes. If it had been the real world and not school, they probably would have been arrested for assault. Now they were just vacationing, and they'd be pissed off at him when they came back to school.

He shoved his bedroom door open and then pushed it shut, dropping down on the bed. He lay back on the pillow and stared out the window, though he had no desire to climb out it tonight. His palms stung at the thought of it.

Through the oak branches, he could see the silver face of the moon, glowing, watching benevolently. Budd had died under that moon. Budd covered in blood. Tomorrow he would be buried, what there was left of him.

Poor Budd. Nobody had liked him, and now nobody gave a damn that he was dead. He was just a half-day off from school.

People like the Assholes survived. He thought of them, snorting and guffawing as they tortured him. He hated them, and his anger boiled again.

He had done nothing to them, yet they had to bother him, had to upset him and leave him with a bad feeling. He had no way of fighting the crowd of them. That didn't make him weak; it was just a fact.

He tried to let that comfort him, but he wished he had some way to strike out at them, to get even. They were always picking on people, and everybody had to take it.

It shouldn't be that way. He propped his tennis shoes on the foot of the bed. Lewis Laborde's leering face filled his thoughts. The big jerk was brainless and subhuman, a total waste of tissue.

Charlie shifted his weight. His ass was sore, thanks to that bastard and his friends. He wouldn't be sitting comfortably for a couple of days. His hands were sore, too. If things kept going this way a couple more days, he was going to be in traction.

While Charlie was aching, Lewis was taking advantage of the fact that he didn't have to go to school the next day. He'd talked his girlfriend, Corzie French, into meeting him in the little park in the center of Petittville. There were only a couple of benches and some hedges, but there was also a pavilion. After dark, Chief Rice was off-duty, and there wasn't much traffic, so it was a good place for making out.

Corzie's father kept a pretty close watch on her, but she could usually manage to escape the house if Lewis was insistent enough. Tonight he had been, and since she didn't like the thought of losing him and not having anybody, she consented.

He lit a cigarette and turned up the collar on his denim jacket while he sat on the edge of the pavilion waiting, impatient. It was almost nine, and she wasn't going to be willing to risk staying out much later than ten, so there wouldn't be much time.

Midweek liaisons were largely unsatisfying for Lewis. Corzie had to be in the right mood to deliver anything substantial, and she never arrived at any decision to grant liberties quickly.

He'd always thought that once ground was covered, it could be revisited without discussion after that point, but Corzie was prone to allow something one time and disallow it the next occasion they were together.

He only tolerated it because he knew he wasn't going to find anybody much better than she was. The cheerleaders weren't accessible. Corzie was a little heavy, but she was cute with round cheeks and dark hair even though her features were a little hard-looking.

His cigarette smoldered down toward the filter, still without any sign of Corzie, and he cursed her under his breath.

She cost money. He'd made pretty good cash the last couple of months, working with his older brother cutting firewood. The new people in the subdivisions loved their fireplaces even if they didn't work as well as their central heat. They shelled out good money to have a bunch of oak logs stacked in their back yards.

Lewis and his brother took their old Chevy pickup back into the woods, sawing away at logs and filling up the truck bed and the little wagon that trailed behind it. It was hard work, but it was worth it.

Except that the money went fairly quickly taking Corzie to movies or to eat over at the Dairy Queen or McDonald's in Aimsley. On nights like this, he wondered if it was worth it.

When he heard footsteps, he got up and turned around, expecting to see her standing there with an excuse. He thumped his cigarette away and was about to bark at her.

The dogs snarled first.

He froze.

They stood there, a pack, shoulder to shoulder. Their jaws were already dripping with saliva that stringed out the corner of their mouths where their fangs were bared.

He'd never seen dogs like this before. They were big, massive in their shoulders like a cross of bulldogs and bigger mutts.

He tried not to look into their eyes, but he was mesmerized. They were eyes full of hatred—glowing with it, in fact. Their brows wrinkled into what looked like frowns, and their heads dipped low as they watched him.

He'd seen a show about dogs. They said you didn't turn and run. They'd chase you. You backed away slowly. That way they were less likely to pounce.

He tried that now, picking up one foot, lifting it as if he were loosing it from a quagmire. With his eyes still locked on the hounds, he slowly

96

began to move his foot backward. The growls that followed came from somewhere deep inside them, warnings. They somehow knew what he was doing. He could see that in their eyes. They knew he was trying to escape, had sensed it.

Lewis felt a cold snakelike fear coiling through him now. These were the things that had ripped Budd Hagan apart, and he didn't have any real way of getting away from them himself.

The pavilion offered no cover, and there was nothing else within a hundred yards. The only thing he could do was try and scramble onto the pavilion's roof.

It was his only shot. Turning, he jumped onto the decorative railing which circled the pavilion and started reaching for the rafters.

He was balancing precariously, reaching with both arms, when the lead dog lunged for him. They both went spilling into the center of the pavilion floor. It was made of planks, and with the dog's weight on top of him, Lewis hit the floor hard, slamming his left shoulder painfully into the wood.

He tried to raise his arm to make his forearm a shield, but the dog's face shot past it and teeth dug into the flesh over Lewis's collarbone.

Tears came to his eyes as the pain pierced his consciousness. He could feel the teeth going all the way to the bone, clamping there so that he could not pull away.

Corzie found him a half hour later. He was all over the floor.

Rice had been asleep when the call had come. Exhausted from the day and the tension, he had packed it in even before the ten o'clock news. His wife had taken the call and awakened him.

As he climbed out of his police cruiser, he aimed the spotlight on the driver's door toward the pavilion, where a cluster of people had already gathered.

He left the blue lights on top of the car spinning to signify they were at the scene of a tragedy.

The mayor met him as he walked across the grassy lawn with his hand resting on his pistol.

"I can't believe this happened in the middle of town," Malcolm Keys said. He was a big man with graying hair and hard features. He wasn't wearing a tie but he'd put on a sports coat over his sweatshirt and blue jeans. It was plaid and made him look like a used car salesman, which was convenient considering that was his job.

"Doesn't make much sense," Rice agreed. "They're pretty bold if they just waltzed up Main Street."

He unhooked his flashlight from his belt and stepped up into the pavilion. He shined the light down onto the floor only a moment before switching off the beam.

"I've got somebody getting a blanket," the mayor said.

"Good."

He walked silently back to his cruiser and radioed for the coroner. Then he hooked the Motorola mike back into place and returned to the cluster of people gathered around one of the benches.

They were sitting and standing around a chubby brunette girl who had someone's jacket draped around her shoulders.

"Are you Corzie?" Rice asked, squatting in front of her.

"Yessir."

"Tell me what happened."

She had been crying, and her eyes were swollen. In one hand she clutched a tissue someone had given her, but her sobs seemed to have subsided.

"I was meeting him here. He wanted me to come see him. I was scared of the dogs, so I stayed at my house a long time. I was late, and when I got here he was … he was torn up." She closed her eyes tightly.

"Did you see the dogs when you arrived?" Rice asked. "No sir. I guess they were already gone."

"All right." He looked at the people. "Can somebody take her home?"

He picked a volunteer and dismissed them. The mayor was waiting for him near the pavilion.

They positioned themselves with their backs to the carnage to talk. Malcolm folded his arms in front of him and looked off toward a tire

98

store across the street. The showcase lights gleamed through the veil of fog.

"Do you think somebody could have brought the dogs in?" he asked.

"Girl said she didn't see them when she got here. There's no way of knowing right now how long the boy was dead before she arrived."

"Could somebody have turned them out, then put them back in a cage and carted them off?"

"I don't know. It seems a little unlikely. A lot of trouble. I'll check with the people and see if they saw any strange vehicles."

"I already asked some of them," Malcolm said. "Nothing."

"The dogs probably made off like they did before," Rice said. "These kids shouldn't have been out here. You probably need to get a special meeting of the council called and set up a curfew."

"That's a good idea. We've got to do something to keep this from happening again. My God, it's awful."

Rice moved over to the crowd and asked a few questions while he waited for the coroner. No one had seen any vehicles.

That soothed him a little. Malcolm's idea that someone might have carted the dogs in did seem farfetched, but it had also occurred to Rice. He'd been worrying since finding the mutilated dog.

Removal of the fetuses did seem ritualistic, and he'd read stories about dogs being used in occult rituals. Could he have some strange band of Satanists in town? Perhaps they were using the dogs to perform what they considered sacrifices.

He raised his hand to the back of his neck, massaging the tightness that was developing there. There had been too much attention to this sort of thing, and his imagination was going into overdrive. He'd had seminars in New Orleans on this sort of thing, but it was overblown.

Wild dogs, he had wild dogs on his hands and that was all.

———

Charlie sat up in his bed. Moonlight streamed in through the window, creating familiar shadows which allowed him to orient himself, but he realized he was shaking.

He couldn't remember the nightmare, but it had been filled with blood. He couldn't remember Budd being in it, and he couldn't remember what had caused the blood, but he knew there was a lot of it.

He had a vague feeling, sort of the ghost of a feeling, that Miss Nielson was in it somewhere too. The thought of her suddenly moved to the forefront, pushing other images away.

He thought of her eyes and her body, and the feeling warmed him even as he shivered in the cold sweat that bathed him.

What was it about her? He had seen other beautiful women, but she had more of an allure.

He searched his mind, wondering what part she had played in the bloody dream, but he could think only of her face, her eyes, and her body, that wondrous vision unveiled to him the night before.

It replayed now, and he stared at the ceiling, thinking of her, the water and soap gleaming on her flesh.

In a way it felt as if his own thoughts were not in control. He sensed something was driving them to her, shaping her in his brain.

He didn't fight it. He let the image linger as he drifted back into a dream, and this time the dream was far more pleasant with Miss Nielson at its center.

———

Nell sat on the edge of her bed long after the sounds of the sirens had faded from the night. She couldn't sleep. She knew someone else had died.

That intertwined with the feeling that something was wrong in this town. It had begun with Budd's death or just before, and she could sense it in the wind.

She didn't believe it was any psychic ability on her part. It was somehow much simpler, just a primal feeling that something in the fabric of reality was rippling.

She worried about Charlie, and she wondered about this woman who was captivating him. Matt was wrong. It wasn't jealousy. It was concern.

Her family was far away by choice, and without family or a boyfriend or anyone else particularly close, Charlie was like a little brother.

She had decided late in the day that she would go to the funeral, mostly to be there for him. Matt had agreed to fill in himself at the store.

Now there would probably have to be another funeral. Sirens and bright lights didn't occur in Petittville if there wasn't something bad happening.

She got up and walked to the window, sitting on the sill as she stared down at the twisted shadows cast by the oak. She could hear the wind playing with the leaves as well.

She had thought about going out, walking toward the sound of the sirens, but she had deemed it unnecessary. Was there any doubt the hounds had struck again? There would be even more attention and hoopla now, and heaven could only guess what would happen next. They'd try to hunt them down, and people would wind up shooting themselves in the foot.

Everyone would be afraid to step out of doors. Matt would curse that because it would be bad for business if kids weren't allowed to roam around.

Someone had been roaming tonight in spite of the warnings. If this kept going, there would be others, because some people never listened to warnings.

As she sat there watching the leaves and the sidewalk, she wondered if Barbara Nielson could account for her whereabouts of the evening.

Probably not.

Chapter 10

The halls were abuzz with the news the next morning, and there weren't too many kids who were unhappy to hear one of the Assholes had died. While there was a grim feeling of fear and an even more awakened sense of youthful mortality, the spirit fell just short of rejoicing.

Charlie couldn't help himself for feeling a certain satisfaction, especially since Lewis had led the attack the day before. It was almost poetic justice that the buzzing about Lewis's death came on the same day they were to say goodbye to Budd.

Charlie drifted through the morning classes without paying much attention to lessons or people. He wasn't looking forward to the funeral, but there was an anticipation. It was an event that loomed at the end of the day.

He listened to kids talking all morning about what they would do with the time off. He had no question about how his afternoon would be spent.

When the final bell rang just before noon, he walked zombielike out to the bus, not even thinking about the fact that he would not see Miss Nielson today. Budd was in his thoughts, the Budd that had been his friend, and the Budd who had looked up at him in the nightmare.

Budd covered in blood.

He rode the bus home silently, leaning his head against the glass and staring out at the passing roadway. He had nothing to say to the kids around him.

When he reached his house, he walked up to the door and grunted a hello to his mother. She was already dressed to accompany him.

He went up to his room, where she had put his suit on the bed. It lay there like a flat silhouette of his body.

He changed into it quickly, noticing that the sleeves were getting a little short on the coat. They'd have to go shopping for a new one soon over at Aimsley Mall. He hated trying on suits. He hardly ever wore one, even to church.

For Budd, he figured he could stand it. He'd learned the previous summer to handle a Windsor knot. He managed to get this one on the first try. The collar of the white shirt rubbed at his throat, but he ignored it.

He felt stupid walking down the stairs. His mother looked up at him and smiled. He tried to smile back.

"You look very handsome," Betsy Black said.

"Thanks," he said grimly. They walked out to the car in an even heavier silence. He thought about saying something to her about how she'd never liked Budd, but he refrained.

He didn't even turn on the radio as they headed over to the funeral home. He just stared out the window. He wasn't surprised when he didn't spot many cars in the parking lot.

They parked next to a gray Chevy Celebrity and walked across the cobblestone walkway to the front door. The smell of flowers hung in the air when they stepped into the reception area. Several people who must have been Budd's relatives were standing around talking. Charlie and his mother moved on into the stateroom, where the casket sat on a draped bier. The lid was closed, and on it a framed yearbook photo of Budd was displayed.

Only a few people sat in the chairs which ringed the room. Near one corner sat Budd's father, a dark-haired man in a brown suit long out of style. He was sobbing. His black hair was worn with too much oil, and locks of it hung down over his forehead.

Budd's mother, with her brown hair neatly set, was beside him. She wore thick makeup, but it was holding firm. Charlie was wondering if he should go over to them when someone touched his shoulder.

He turned and found himself looking into Delia's blue eyes, their beauty unmarred by her tears. Her hair was brushed loosely to her shoulders, and she wore a short black dress and high heels. He couldn't speak for a moment, and then she was hugging him, gripping his shoulders tightly. He could feel her breasts against him for a moment before she pulled away.

"We won't even be able to see him, Charlie. How can we tell him goodbye?"

Charlie stammered. "I guess he knows," he said finally.

Her perfume was fresh, and it tingled in his nostrils, reminding him of her closeness. He didn't really need a reminder. He could sense her warmth, and the stories Budd had told him about her edged their way into his thoughts.

He kept looking at her as she spoke, trying to explain the sadness, and a tingle of guilt crept up into his throat, as if he was betraying Budd by feeling the attraction toward her.

She wouldn't like him anyway. She was too pretty and had too many options. He tried to think about other things, about his own sadness, but he was reminded that she was his age. It was more appropriate to feel something for her than for Miss Nielson. The way things were supposed to be was important. His mother would be far less upset about Delia than if she knew about Miss Nielson.

"Maybe we should go ahead and sit down," his mother suggested. He hadn't introduced her to Delia, and he felt rude.

"Are you with your folks?" he asked Delia.

"No. I'm by myself. My mom dropped me off."

"You want to sit with us?"

"Sure."

They walked from the stateroom and along the narrow hallway to the chapel. Some people were already lining the pews, and men from the funeral home were transferring the flower sprays to the front of the room.

Sunlight played through the stained-glass windows, casting dazzling reds and violets. They were not colors of death, and yet they seemed grim.

Mrs. Black led the way into the room and they sat on a pew, sliding along it so that they were not directly on the end. Beside Charlie, Delia crossed her legs, and he watched the hem of her skirt slide upward, revealing her thighs, clad in dark, sheer stockings which made them seem even more forbidden.

Budd would hate him for thinking about Delia, but he couldn't help it. She was too close to ignore, too perfect in her black dress. Just being present, she numbed the feeling of loss, and he regretted that. He had come here to mourn.

———

Nell was wearing her own black dress when she went by the video store on her way to the funeral home. The garment was ankle-length, and she wore black stockings with it. She had taken the time to curl her hair into a tangled, flowing mass, and donned black wraparound shades.

You look like you take to death well," Matt said.

She didn't respond to that as she leaned against the counter, shades still in place to shield her expression. "You think you can manage here without me?"

"Guess I'll have to. I guess it's good to have you representing the shop there. It is a shame about the kid. He was sort of a customer."

"What's the word on the new killing?" she asked.

"They're talking curfew. They're gonna have to do somethin' since this one was right in the middle of town. I can't believe it."

"Not as many people crying about Lewis?"

"It's the thought rather than the loss, I guess. He was a troublemaker. Still, nobody wanted him chewed up and spit out."

Nell rested her chin in her hands. "It was that bad?"

"Real mess. Lot of talk's going around now too."

"You got your feelers out, do you, Matt?"

"Always. Some folks think the dogs belong to a cult or somethin'."

"Don't we have a tape like that?"

"Not really, they think some Satanists or something are turnin' them loose on kids for sacrifices."

Nell shook her head. "That sounds kind of farfetched," she said.

Matt eased the brim of his hat back over his forehead. "Well, all I know is Lucius Rice tracked down a guy who had a dog mutilated."

Again Nell shook her head. "That could have happened for any reason. That doesn't mean there's a cult. The dogs that killed Budd and Lewis could have done the mutilating."

Matt shook his head, pursing his lips at the same time. "More to it than that. It was a pregnant female. Somebody surgically removed her fetuses. You're usually the one that's wantin' to believe in black magic. That doesn't sound to you like something ritualistic?"

"Sounds pretty sick," Nell said.

"Hard to think of why somebody would want to do that sort of thing, you know? If they weren't in a cult."

Nell didn't like the feeling the information elicited. It made the uneasiness grow so that it was greater than she'd experienced in the last couple of days.

With a parting wave to Matt, she headed out the door. She didn't want to be late for the funeral, but she would have to check on what he had said.

Was there some black magic that called for the fetuses of a puppy litter? She'd never heard of such a ritual, but then anything was possible.

As Delia's perfume played in his nostrils, Charlie listened to the minister's generic sermon, and the words brought memories of Budd. He felt his throat tighten as he recalled going to movies in Aimsley or playing Nintendo or just hanging out.

He felt tears coming, but he fought them. There were a few other people from school here, guys he didn't want seeing him cry. He'd never make it down the hallway alive again if word got out he was crying for Budd. He could hear the innuendos stinging in his ears.

He was curling his lip inward, biting gently on the inside of it to control the sobs, when he felt Delia's hand fall onto his own, which was resting on his leg. He didn't resist, couldn't resist the electricity that traveled through his hand. He closed his eyes, letting the warmth course through him.

As the minister spoke of life eternal, he felt some of the pain ebb even as he missed Budd. Maybe Delia would date him now. Again he felt guilty thinking that, but it was inevitable. They both felt the loss; they were both left with an emptiness.

Nell arrived late as she had feared and had to take a place on a back pew during a song. She tried to concentrate on the condolences offered from the pulpit. Instead she wound up examining the sparse crowd. She spotted Charlie with his mother quickly and recognized Delia next to him. She was a little curious about that, but not jealous. It wouldn't hurt Charlie to have a girlfriend, even if it did mean he would become less dependent on her. That had to happen at some point, and at least Delia was his own age.

She looked toward the front of the room then. The flowers on top of the casket were fresh, a cluster of blue and pink. They seemed too bright and fresh to decorate the departure of one so young.

Nell didn't want flowers at her own funeral. Let the ceremony be shrouded with grim colors. Death should not be treated as smooth and beautiful. She thought of how much hurt it brought.

And shock. Petittville usually lost only the old. Now in two days' time, two young men were gone, savagely taken. Though there were few mourners here, there were many who felt the hurt and the accompanying fear. There should be no fresh pink flowers.

She looked back at Charlie. He wasn't crying, but she knew how he must feel, far worse than he'd been able to tell her over the phone. It must be settling in today, becoming real.

She wondered how he felt about the news of Lewis's death. Charlie wouldn't be happy about it. She knew him better than that, but it wouldn't be something he would feel a loss over.

It was a small town. Everybody knew everybody, yet it was strange to her that both of the people had connections with Charlie—Budd a strong link of friendship and Lewis enemy status.

Matt would say it was her imagination overreacting again. Probably true, just coincidence stimulating her thoughts, but the strangeness of it all remained.

As the minister finished and the final hymn was sung, the people began to get up from the pews as the trek to the cemetery began. That would be left for family, she suspected. She began to make her way through the crowd toward Charlie and his mother.

She got the usual disapproving glance from his mom, and Delia eyed her as well, showing suspicion more than contempt.

Charlie, to her relief, brightened at the sight of her. She took his hands in hers, conveying support with touch she could not offer in words.

"I didn't think you were coming," he said.

"Matt let me out of my cage."

He looked at his mom, and ignoring her stern expression, he said: "We're going over to the Blue Bell. You want to come?"

"Sure," Nell said. She hadn't eaten, and the café had fairly good sandwiches. She checked Delia's expression, and she didn't seem to mind. That made it easier. She didn't want to breed friction, but she wanted to be there for Charlie. He'd eased many an hour of monotony for her, and he was her friend, one of her few true friends.

She turned and walked with them down the aisle, making the way through the sprinkling of family members. In the lobby they paused for a few moments while Mrs. Black spoke to Budd's father.

"We're parked out front," Charlie said.

"Okay," Nell said. "I'm on the other side. I'll meet you there."

She watched them head for the door before turning, planning to head down the hall to the left.

She froze when she saw Barbara Nielson. She was detached from the crowd, standing with her back resting against the wall near the business office.

Her gaze was locked on Nell. It was not vitriolic or angry. It was just consistent, not a stare exactly, but unwavering. Her arms were folded beneath her breasts, and her flowing brown hair was pinned back on the sides, the length of it spilling down her back. She wore a short black dress with long sleeves, its shape hugging her flawless form. A single string of pearls were draped around her neck.

She was unquestionably beautiful, yet it was not her beauty that struck Nell. She sensed something deeper, something that chilled her inside.

She looked back at Miss Nielson for a moment without trying to be defiant, just looking. While the teacher's gaze seemed nonchalant and would not have been noticed at all by those passing by, Nell could feel it. There was a warning being issued here, a strange territorial announcement.

As the chill sank deeper, she broke the connection and headed for the door. It was strange that Miss Nielson would be at the funeral. She hadn't been in the school long enough to know Budd.

She must have come because she knew somehow that Charlie would attend. She'd wanted to see him, perhaps observe him with others around. Why? What did she want from him? It couldn't be sexual, could it? He was just a kid.

You heard more about older men molesting youngsters, male or female, but accounts of women doing the same were rare. Part of it, she realized, was society. A glamorous picture was painted of an older woman fulfilling the lusts of a pubescent male, teaching him, making him a man, but the fact remained it wasn't natural.

Barbara Nielson could have anybody she wanted. She didn't need to seduce teenage boys, if indeed that was what she wanted.

Was that what Nell had sensed in the gaze? That she wanted Charlie and didn't want any rivals for his affections? Perhaps everyone's mind was just trained to look for sexual explanations in human behavior—Freud again.

What other explanation could there be? At the end of the hall, Nell pushed open the door and stepped into the sunshine that had burned back clouds and chill, making the afternoon warm and golden.

That took away some of the queerness. The looming oppression of a funeral home could fuel the imagination, but the sunlight didn't end the contemplation as she moved toward her car.

If Barbara Nielson wasn't some female pedophile lusting after Charlie's affections, what did she want? She was going to have to find out. Something, the same intuition that had been thriving the last few days, was telling her Charlie was in some kind of danger.

The café was a large room on Front Street with a rounded counter which jutted out from the kitchen like a peninsula decorated with glasses and pies on display in glass domes.

Tables were scattered on both sides of it along with displays of Louisiana cookbooks, crawfish posters, and other souvenirs. Occasionally people passing through on the way to Aimsley or on to Alexandria stopped and made the displays worthwhile.

The tables were covered with red-checkered tablecloths and decorated with napkin dispensers and saltshakers. A painting near one of the large plate glass windows depicted a 1950s Chicago diner with a lone man in business suit and hat at the counter.

It reminded Nell of a picture from one of her literature textbooks, something that conveyed notions of Fitzgerald or perhaps Sherwood Anderson.

Near another window was a painting of the Blue Bell itself, the lines of the work clean and antiseptic like renderings from the fifties. They set the tone for what the place was supposed to be, and it came close. It was a perfect creation of a Southern diner.

The tables were occupied by a variety of people, all being tended by waitresses in shapeless beige uniforms.

Nell found her party in a booth. Delia had positioned herself on one side beside Charlie. That left a seat open beside Mrs. Black for Nell.

Delia wasn't touching Charlie as she sipped a Coke through a straw, but she was sitting close. Charlie seemed aware of it, but he wasn't giving away much in body language, probably because Mrs. Black was watching.

Nell didn't know Delia very well, but the girl was pretty with the potential for beautiful. If she distracted Charlie from Barbara Nielson, that would be fine. She felt odd about the thought, but it was valid.

"I can't believe he's gone," Charlie said. It was nothing profound, but at least it broke the silence.

"It doesn't make sense," Mrs. Black agreed. "I hope they find those things."

"It'll be hard," Nell said. "Some strays have probably been shot already by well-meaning citizens, but how do they know if they've got the right ones?"

Mrs. Black shook her head. "It's terrible. That boy that was killed last night was a troublemaker, but it's still horrible."

A glance at Charlie told Nell he hadn't let her know about the school attack. His mother was so overprotective he probably hadn't wanted her worried about that too. She probably would have marched to the principal's office with demands and the results would have made more hell for Charlie when other kids heard about it.

Nell couldn't figure out why someone Mrs. Black's age was so obsessive, but everybody's parents were strange. That was one of the facts of life.

When the waitress came over, Nell ordered a Coke and watched Lucius Rice come in and sit at the counter. They brought him coffee, and while he was sweetening it, several people gathered around him.

He nodded, apparently offering reassurances as he tried to drink.

"I don't envy him," Mrs. Black said. "I don't see what he can do."

"It's not a typical case to investigate," Nell said. "Keeping people off the streets at night is the best they can do."

"I hope all the parents do their part," Mrs. Black said. "If they appreciate their children, they will."

Charlie remained silent. Nell realized he didn't want his mother going on in front of Delia.

"So what did you think of the new issue of *Ghost Rider*?" she asked to steer the conversation in a new direction and silence Charlie's mother.

He perked up a little. "It's pretty cool," he said.

"Do you read a lot of comics?" Delia asked.

She didn't give a damn about them, but she wanted Charlie to think she was interested. Good enough, Nell thought. The conversation droned from there for a while until everyone was ready to go.

Charlie, his mother, and Delia set off in one direction after paying their check. Nell lingered for a while, waiting for Rice to finish his coffee. When he did, she followed him from the diner.

"Chief?" she asked.

He turned, ready to offer another reassurance or deal with another irate complaint. He seemed relieved when he saw it was Nell.

"You got my videos in yet?" he asked.

"We're still looking for them." He was interested in black movies from the fifties, and they were hard to find, but she had been scouring catalogs. Not many people realized there had been black Westerns, romances, and adventures, but she was learning about it as she helped him with his hobby.

He walked toward his cruiser, which was parked against the curb at the end of the street.

"I guess you're worried about the dogs too," he said.

"It's scary," she admitted.

"I'm doing all I can."

"Uh, Matt said there's talk about a dog that was mutilated. Somebody took her puppies."

"I'm trying not to talk about that too much," Rice said. "That blasted Morris Wade can't keep his mouth shut."

"Do you think it's occult?"

He smiled. "That would be nice and eerie, wouldn't it? I'm not inclined to believe that sort of thing. They always talk about it at police seminars, but it's a bit too strange for me. It's hard to explain some things. That's all I can say."

Chapter 11

She had missed Sawyer at school, but when she returned from the funeral home, Barbara found a new message from him on her machine. This time it was just a perky attempt at humor. She rewound to the message of the previous night and found his phone number then called him.

He answered on the second ring, and when she identified herself, his voice brightened.

"I just got in from the funeral," she said.

"I thought about going," he said. "I just decided it would be too depressing. I didn't know the kid that well. Did many people from school show up?"

"It was mostly family. I stayed in the background."

"I should have gone," he said. "He wasn't a bad kid, not as bad as Lewis. I feel kind of funny now that he's dead, after disciplining him the same day."

"Oh, it's not your fault. He was attacking that other poor kid."

"I know. He was a real bastard. I guess really we're all better off without him. I know that sounds terrible."

"It's easy to feel that way about some of them," she agreed.

"Well, we've certainly gotten morbid," he said. "I was wondering if you wanted to go to the movies tonight. It would get us out of all this insanity."

She smiled to herself. The quaver in his voice was barely audible, but she knew the nervousness was there, the fear of rejection.

"I'd love to go," she said softly.

There was no sigh of relief, but when he spoke again, he did seem calmer. He suggested a film which she'd seen advertised in the newspaper. It wasn't something she'd have gone to on her own, but she wasn't going to reject his suggestion. She had no desire to make this process hard on him.

"We could pick up dinner," he suggested.

"Anything's fine with me," she said. "Sandwiches would be okay." She didn't want to force him into a large expenditure. She knew what teachers were paid.

"Well, there's a Subway near the theater."

"That would be good."

"I guess we could catch the seven P.M. show. That way we won't be out too late on a school night."

"True. So you'll be by around sixish?"

"Yeah, we'll drive over, see the movie, eat afterwards."

"Sounds good," she said. "I'll see you later."

She thought she could hear his whistle as he hung up. She placed her own handset into its cradle, a slight smile flickering across her lips. He was quite boyish. She found that refreshing. She'd never really known a man quite as polite as Sawyer.

Her father had certainly not been that way. She tried not to think about him, but sometimes she remembered the fights he and her mother had had before the divorce.

For a long time she had believed that was what marriage must be about. The thought of it had not appealed to her. Though in school she'd had friends whose parents functioned together, she had never believed it possible for her.

A part of her suspected deep down that all men were like her father. He had been a big man, brutish in a way. Around the house he tended to drink and slouch, vegetating in front of the television or sleeping on the living room couch, his snores rasping through his puckered lips.

On weekends he never shaved, and the stubble spread across his jaw like a blue mask, his stomach bulging against the ribbed fabric of his undershirts.

He had started his advances toward her when she was thirteen, as if she had crossed some line of demarcation. She had resisted, and that had worked for a while.

She suspected her mother knew about him, but his growing interest in Barbara was beginning to relieve her mother of some unpleasant duties. While his attempts on Barbara were not being rewarded, they were taking some of his energy.

When she was fourteen and her beauty was beginning to blossom along with her feminine qualities, his attempts to coerce her became more and more frequent and more and more intense. She had no choice but to leave.

She moved into the home of a friend for a while, hiding there until she found a job using a forged work permit. It wasn't a bad job, better than the work in fast food restaurants. She ended up in an avant-garde bookstore, clerking. It was in the Little Five Points area of Atlanta—that's where she had lived—and it was also there that she discovered that men took an interest in her.

She began to let them buy her meals. At first that earned them no rewards other than her pleasant company, but then the man named Crowel came along. He was big and handsome, and he took her to his home, a small little apartment in an otherwise deserted building. The walls were peeling, and the carpet was beaten down. The bed was a large single, sagging in the middle, the sheets threadbare.

Their contact was not rape, not quite, or perhaps she only told herself that later. Although she resisted for a long time before he half convinced her, half forced her, she nodded in agreement finally as he tugged off her clothes.

He was not gentle. He handled her roughly with his hands and his kisses, and when he entered her, it was painful.

The hurt eventually melted into pleasure and she accepted his plunges, burrowing her head back against the pillow.

Afterward, he turned his back to her, and she silently slipped from his bed. Briefly, she used his bathroom, cleaning the blood that had seeped from her ruptured hymen before leaving.

She found it easier after that to be with men, found she enjoyed their bodies and the electricity they bored into her. Some of them reminded her of her father and others of Crowel, even the ones who first seemed gentle.

She hated herself in a way after each liaison, feeling as if all she could offer as a person was sex. Things came later, harsh things that made her want to give up men.

Now, she looked at Sawyer, and he seemed different. He was attracted by her beauty—he was male after all—but he was not like many of those she had known before, not so quick with advances or pleas.

She'd become convinced she would never meet a man who wasn't like the ones before. Just as some children had normal family lives, some girls found pleasant, gentle men, but that wasn't in the cards for her.

Cautiously, she let herself wonder about Sawyer. Could he be different? Could he really come to know her?

She sat down on her sofa with a sigh. She was expecting a great deal. They hadn't even been on a date yet.

She had been considering herself jaded, unaffected by such thoughts, but let the possibility of romance flower and she was as dreamy-eyed as a college freshman reading Bronte.

Her lips curled into a smile, a reflex. She was smiling at herself, at her own silliness. It was better not to let hopes develop. Hopes were dashed too easily, but perhaps for a little while she could enjoy a little taste of happiness.

―――――

Nell kicked off her shoes as she entered her apartment, glad she could let her feet relax at last. At least she could find some vestige of comfort in that, though she still had a weird chill from the look Barbara Nielson had given her.

What was it about the woman? She knew now it wasn't just a jealous feeling about Charlie. There was something more, something subtle yet very real.

On her way to the couch, she scooped up the phone which rested on the floor. Its long cord allowed her to move freely.

Tucking her legs under her, she dialed Michael's number. Even though it was late afternoon, she figured he would probably be working in his home office.

He answered on the second ring.

"It's Nell," she said.

His voice brightened. "Hi there."

"Are you working hard?"

"I'm kind of stalled," he said. "I was trying to do a funny storyline to break up some of the monotony, but I'm finding comedy isn't as easy as I thought it was."

"Well, down here dying seems to be pretty easy," Nell said.

He chuckled. "What do you mean?"

"A lot of people are doing it."

"You're serious?" His voice grew solemn.

"Two are dead now. The dogs again. I don't know how to describe the feeling I have to you, but it's odd. I sort of had a vision about them. I sat down and drew one."

"So wild Louisiana swamp dogs are attacking people?"

"Something like that. Maybe worse. You do a lot of work about mystical things, Michael. How much of it do you think is real?"

He laughed a bit nervously. "I make up stories. I read a lot of things for ideas, you know."

"But I'm serious. What do you think is real?" There was silence. It lasted for a moment, then longer.

She could sense his discomfort on the line, and there was a rustling, as if he was shifting about.

"It's hard to say on that kind of thing, Nell."

"I'm not asking for all the answers."

"I've talked to people," he admitted finally. "They've told me about things that are way out. None of it really confirms, you know."

"Could you do some checking for me, see what you might come up with as far as dogs?"

"You really think there's something supernatural? Could you really have had a vision?"

"A boy died, and I was kind of seized to draw a hound. Besides, there's this new woman in town."

117

"Oh, I forgot. You're down where a stranger in town must be Beelzebub."

"Right, we're just dumb Southerners. She's strange, okay? She shows up, the dogs show up. All hell breaks loose. And they found a dog mutilated, cut open and her puppies taken out of her. See if there's anything in ritual books about that kind of thing. Who knows what could be going on?"

He shifted again, then nervousness evident once more. "Do you have a fax at that place where you work?"

"Oh yeah. This is 007 central. Matt would never be without a new gadget."

"Let me have that picture you did, then."

She curled her fingers into the telephone cord and swirled it around. "You think it will do you any good?"

"It'll give me another sample of your artwork."

"I crumpled it up."

"No problem. Just let me see what it is that's got you acting so strange. You are, you know?"

"I guess so, calling, you up talking about swamp dogs and witches, but you're the logical choice to turn to on this. You're the one who has zombies and werewolves tap dancing through his brain."

"I don't do anything that trite."

"Well, shape shifters and wraiths or whatever, then."

"I'll be watching for your fax. You have the number for mine, don't you?"

"You'll get it tomorrow when I go to work. For once I'll look forward to hearing from you."

He only laughed at the insult. Sometimes she was amazed at what she could get away with.

⸻

After dropping Delia off, Charlie and his mother drove home. She went to fix some dinner, and he went to the office computer, loading in a fantasy game. It was not an arcade disk but more of a strategy game. If a monster or other enemies were encountered by his band of adventurers, he had to contemplate a battle plan, mixing magic spells and brute force to score a kill.

It was a good deal like fantasy role-playing games which Charlie would have loved to try, but there were never enough people around interested in that sort of thing to get it going, not in places like Petittville.

That was probably for the best. The people he had known who did play were a bit too strange for his tastes anyway, and his mother would have been worried about the reports of damaging effects caused by gaming.

As the game booted, and he began his travels through the adventure, he found himself missing easy clues and warning signs, causing him to lose a couple of his favorite characters in battle.

He couldn't force himself to devote the proper concentration. Too many outside options were available to snag his thoughts.

The anguish over Budd's death was just beginning to take root, while at the same time, images of Miss Nielson stirred him. Delia was there too. Sitting across the table from her at the café, he had really been reminded of how pretty she was.

She had a creamy complexion and eyes blue enough to seem clear at some times. He liked her eyes.

"She's a pretty little girl," his mother had said after Delia had climbed out of their car.

As she'd driven home, Mom had suggested that Delia might like him. He felt that might be true, even though he couldn't quite understand it.

She could've had any of the jocks she wanted or whatever. He wasn't any prize, at least not in terms of the high school social scene.

He found it hard to believe she wouldn't forget him if someone better came along. Maybe she wasn't really interested either; maybe it was just politeness because he'd been a friend of Budd's.

Budd.

Poor Budd.

Budd covered in blood.

He felt the pressure of tears and fought them back. He wouldn't cry. It wasn't that he felt he was too big, just that he didn't want to right now. What was really accomplished by crying?

Spinning in his chair, he picked up the telephone on the desk and slid the telephone book from beneath it. The glue used for the book had softened in the Southern climate, so the page ruffled loosely as he thumbed through it.

When he'd located Delia's number, he dialed before he had the time to lose his courage. After a couple of rings, her father answered, his voice a bit gruff. He informed Charlie that Delia was taking a shower, but dutifully wrote down Charlie's number.

Feeling a bit dejected, Charlie turned back to the computer after hanging up. He was just about to get involved in the game again when the phone rang.

"I'm sorry I missed you," Delia said. "I'm so embarrassed my dad told you I was in the shower. He could have just told you I couldn't come to the phone. I mean really."

"It's all right," Charlie said, instinctively wanting to quell her embarrassment. "I just wanted to see how you were feeling."

"Okay. I miss him, but I'm okay."

Charlie nodded silently, then managed: "Good."

"I enjoyed going to the café with you," she said. It made it feel less terrible."

He took that as encouragement. "I liked it too," he said. The handset was slippery in his palm, but he felt some of the tension in his abdomen ease.

The conversation lasted only a little while longer, but it made him feel cautiously excited. Perhaps he could stay in touch with Delia, and perhaps something might open up. Maybe they could date. Charlie had never really had a date, and except for Nell, he'd never had a good friend who was a girl.

When he hung up and tried to turn back to the game, he found Miss Nielson still snared his thoughts. He was still wondering what she wanted from him.

Did she think he was special, as special as they had talked about when discussing the story? He didn't quite understand it.

He killed the power on the computer game, effectively undoing everything that had transpired in it thus far. Then he turned it on and started it again, restoring to life those characters eaten by dragons and destroyed by trolls.

Too bad he couldn't bring Budd back as easily.

Delia lay on her bed for a while after Charlie's call. He seemed to like her, and that made her feel better. She hated that Budd was gone, missed him, but she didn't want to be alone.

There was a feeling of security if you had a boyfriend. It might not mean you were popular, but it did mean you didn't have to be alone. You had at least some social life guaranteed that way.

Charlie was nice, and cute in his way even though he was only a few pounds heavier than skinny. She would like going to movies and things with him, or just to basketball games at school.

A twinge of guilt touched her since she was thinking about Charlie so short a time after Budd was gone, but that would pass. She couldn't spend a lifetime mourning him even though she felt a heavy sadness now.

She felt cold too in a way, chilled when she remembered kissing him and then considered that he was dead now. What a morbid thought! She tried to let her thoughts turn back to Charlie.

When she had come out of the bathroom and her father had told her of the call, she had come straight to her room, still wearing her pink terrycloth bathrobe. Rising now, she walked over to her closet, slipping off the robe and selecting an old, oversized Bon Jovi T-shirt from her closet.

When she had slipped it on, she returned to her bed, switching off the night table lamp before tossing her white teddy bear to one side and pulling back the quilt.

She slid beneath the covers quickly, her head sinking down into the pillows with the same swiftness that she sank into sleep.

She dreamed of Budd, and the funeral, and bad feelings curled through her body.

She was thinking of cold, icy cold kisses from Budd when she was awakened, or at least she thought she was awakened. She could hear something outside her window, heavy footfalls on the ground.

They weren't the footfalls of people. They were padded, the footfalls of a dog or several dogs. Fear contracted her muscles, and pinpricks began to dance across the surface of her flesh, as if someone were grabbing and pulling every hair on her body, stretching tauntly against the follicles.

She pulled the covers up to her chin, as if the thin fabric might truly shield her against some assault. She knew better than that yet still derived some sense of security. It kept her from feeling exposed as she strained her ears to detect sounds from outside.

She thought she heard snarls, and then something thumped against the screen outside her window. She dug her fingers into the hem of her covers, biting her lower lip. Her eyes twisted tightly closed.

Another thump, scratching followed. Something was outside her window, but the scratches were not diligent. Was something trying to get in, or was it only letting her know it was there?

She lay for a long time, listening, waiting for another scratch to come, but there was nothing.

Then she awoke, wondering if she had dreamed the whole thing or if she had heard it and dozed after the sound stopped.

With a quivering hand, she lifted the covers and after some hesitation slid from the bed. The calves of her legs trembled as she walked toward the window, and she felt the pinpricks return.

She didn't want to look out the window, didn't want to draw the curtain back, but something compelled her. She had to step forward, had to raise her trembling hand to the edge of the curtain.

Holding her breath, she pulled it aside, looking forward into the darkness. Enough moonlight filtered down through the pine trees to let her see the emptiness of the lawn. The old swing set, the birdbath, the flower bed, all were still. There were no signs of any life out of the ordinary, but then her eyes moved from the distance to the close-up. She could look through the glass at the screen, and as her eyes trailed downward, she saw the small flaw near the corner. The tiny wire threads had been disturbed, not cut or separated, but something had tangled within them, separating them slightly in places.

Perhaps it had not been a dream.

She jumped back into bed and covered herself once more, wishing Charlie were there to hold her.

Chapter 12

After the movie, Barbara and Sawyer discussed a walk along the quiet streets as the soft night breeze drifted through the damp air, but the thought of the hounds stifled that idea.

Instead she invited him up to her living room. While he sat on the couch, she brewed some tea in the kitchen and cut up a lime. She had learned it offered a different flavor which she liked. It turned out to please too when she served it.

Sitting in an armchair which faced the couch in order to avoid sending him signals for the moment, she smiled and let him talk for a while about school. He liked his work in spite of the tough kids and the grueling pace of the workday coupled with the agony of lesson plans and faculty meetings. Working with the mathematical puzzles, trying to impart some of the understanding of them to his students, was a challenge which made it all worthwhile to him.

That made him seem more charming, even with his nervous edge and uncertainties. He was basically a good man, not glamorous or overly handsome, but she had learned long ago how little those things mattered.

As he talked, and they laughed and sipped the tea, she allowed herself to fantasize. Though she had just met him, she wondered what it would be like to marry him, to live in a house somewhere with him, a quiet house where they worked on the lawn together and shared housekeeping duties.

It was a vision as alien as a science fiction story, the stuff of fantasy and imagination, yet sitting here with him, it did not seem impossible. It was the kind of world Sawyer was born for. It showed.

He would never make a ladies' man. He needed the stability of a wife and family. He might not realize that yet, but that was the way he would be happy.

She watched his eyes as they talked, trying to determine if he was interested in her, not just attracted to her—she could already sense that—but interested in her as a person, interested in more than dating.

There had been a time when she had not worried about that. Signs of attraction had been enough, because when those were present, she knew what direction things would take with a man. It might not mean anything lasting, but it did afford momentary closeness and other rewards.

Now she wanted to be more than someone he wanted to sleep with. She felt the attraction in herself, but that was not enough, not this time. Passion was expendable.

Could you love me? she asked him mentally as he talked about some incident from school. She willed an answer as she studied his eyes and the soft lines of his face, but of course there was no reply.

After a while, he checked his watch. "Well, tomorrow comes early," he said.

She nodded, glad he was polite. She walked him to the door, and they hesitated for a moment, facing each other. She could read in his expression that he wondered whether or not he should kiss her. Finally he opted for safety, told her good night, and stepped outside.

When he was gone, she went to the window and watched him get safely into his car. Then she sat down on the couch, enjoying the warm feeling that settled over her.

Sawyer's feelings were similar as he drove home. A portrait of Barbara Nielson had been painted inside his brain, and he savored the vision. She could not have looked more perfect as he remembered her sitting there in her armchair. Her hair, her eyes were captivating.

He had dated some women who always seemed cautious, afraid that he *was* interested and might, God forbid, ask them out again. She was at ease and seemed interested in the things he talked about.

He fought the urge to whistle, but he did have a grin on his face when he reached his apartment. He allowed himself to hum as he walked on into his kitchen and poured himself some milk. As he sipped, it did nothing to quell his giddy feeling. He hadn't felt this way in a long time.

Sawyer rarely fell in love because he was rarely allowed to. Women didn't usually give him positive vibes, and so there was no reason to feel encouraged.

Tonight was different. He had the indication that if he asked Barbara Nielson out again, she'd be glad of it.

He started to plan things in his head. On the weekend they could drive down to Ville Platte. It wasn't that far really, just a quick trip down through Evangeline Parish, and there was a great restaurant there where they served crawfish and other seafood.

She probably hadn't been around long enough to have much Louisiana cuisine, so he'd be able to introduce her to some Cajun cooking. It was a small thing, but it was a gesture he hoped she would like.

He tried to think of other things they could do. Movies were fun but would get old quick, and he didn't want to get them in a rut. Sometimes it seemed hard to find things to do in Petittville and Aimsley if you didn't want to go to a truck pull.

There were things at the Aimsley Museum, but he rarely attended those. He might with Barbara, however. She might enjoy seeing the touring art displays they brought in. He reminded himself to watch the Clarion for announcements.

At least there were possibilities now. For a long time there hadn't even been prospects. He had forgotten how lonely he felt because the feelings had been submerged for so long. Now he felt alive again, anticipating happiness if not actually happy. It was amazing how much difference a person and a chance meeting could make.

Lucius Rice stood at the window of his den, looking out across his back yard. It was another of the blessings he had counted when he had moved here. It took him a couple of hours on a riding lawn mower to get the grass trimmed, but it was still nice to have the room. In New Orleans this much property would have been far too expensive for his consideration.

Here he had room for a picnic table and some lawn chairs, and room just to spread out. He was gradually doing some landscaping, and he had begun a rose garden in one corner.

He liked the woodland feel his yard possessed, and he had purchased a birdbath sculpted to look like a small tree. It had an electric pump in it that kept a trickle of water flowing all the time, and it created a placid feeling.

At night it looked even more peaceful. The moon had set now, so the shadows were heavy.

He ran a hand over his face. The look of peace offered him no consolation tonight because he knew it was an illusion. That depressed him.

It was a reminder that no place was isolated from violence. It was a fact of life to be accepted and dealt with. Attempts to run away with it—though he didn't really see his retirement and move as running—were futile.

Those ponderings were not what had kept him up into the wee hours, however. He could accept violence. He was not immune to it, but he had toughened himself to it long ago. That had been the only way to survive when he went out on the streets in New Orleans, knowing he might have to kill in order to stay alive.

What troubled him now was the suggestion the kid, Nell, had made, the suggestion that had been made the night before as well. Suppose some crazy cult was turning dogs on people.

It seemed unlikely, like the stuff of horror movies, except that nothing could be ruled out in an investigation.

He'd found no signs of anything but dogs in the park even on a second search after talking to Nell, but it did seem odd that wild dogs would wander into the middle of town to attack someone.

Trained dogs could have been released somewhere at a distance. He wasn't sure if they could be sicked on a specific target, but if the selection was random, he didn't find it inconceivable. The dogs might be starved until the time for the release.

He'd have to check the medical examiner's report to determine if the remains had been devoured or simply mangled in the attack.

Other questions remained. How had the dogs been rounded up and taken away without someone seeing? Were they trained to return to a specific point? Was that possible? He'd seen a movie once where bandits controlled dogs with silent whistles.

He ran his hands under his collar, where a ring of perspiration had formed. This was all speculation, nothing but speculation.

Tomorrow he'd do some checking with official sources. There were people he could call, but he wasn't sure about how he'd phrase questions without sounding like an idiot. He knew intelligence officers in New Orleans with cult experience; they could recognize symbols within routine graffiti and interpret what the markings would mean to Satanists or bruja priests or whatever group made them. Yet how they would react to a query from a retired cop in what they considered the sticks was another matter.

"Come on, Lucius. You had somebody killed by dogs? You live in the woods. It means they're wild. It doesn't mean there are people in black robes performing rituals."

Maybe he could just spell out what he had and let them run the information through their database. That way he'd be able to find out if anything similar had occurred, and if there were suggestions of the occult, let them make them.

He turned from the window. Let that suffice. He probably was letting his imagination play a little freely anyway. He had to check out possibilities, and questioning similarities was more tangible than just hoping the dogs didn't show up again.

It would feel good to take action. He could pursue normal channels tomorrow as well. He would talk with Wade again, possibly even get him to try and figure out what might be causing the dog attacks if they were random. He'd never heard of anything like this. Dog attacks were usually spur-of-the-moment things, prompted by hunger or by some provocation. He could not let go of the feeling that these were somehow calculated.

He realized he'd had that feeling all along. It had just been nestled somewhere in his subconscious, not really acknowledged until Nell made her suggestion. Perhaps that was why her idea had seemed at least slightly plausible to him, not something to be dismissed as the ramblings of some strange kid.

Suddenly he was thirsty. His throat was dry, and his mouth had a tightness, as if he had not had anything to drink for a long time. It was as if the crystallization of the idea had drawn all of the moisture from his throat.

From the moment of his first phone call, that late-night, half-hysterical report that Budd Hagan was dead, he had felt some instinct engaging, something that told him there was more going on than there appeared. It was what TV cops might call a hunch, a gut instinct, but it was something he'd learned from his years on the street. Perhaps it was something like a sixth sense that cops developed, not mystical but pragmatic, not inborn but acquired, honed through experience. It was that intuition that told you when a punk was lying or that tingling feeling that let you know when there was danger and that you needed to watch your back.

The fact that he had not recognized the sensation before now indicated that he was going soft. He'd been away from the city and its challenges long enough to lose touch to some extent.

The fact that the feeling had finally surfaced heightened his concern. Something was really wrong, something more than a pack of wild dogs. But what? His instinct couldn't tell him that.

He walked through the house slowly, contemplating possibilities. When he reached the kitchen, he opened the cabinet which held the old glasses, the ones his wife allowed him to use for every day. The others were for company and thus were cloistered in another cabinet to preserve them from chips or outright breakage. For some reason around the house his hands always seemed to be slippery.

On the shooting range he could score marksmanship medals for his steady hand, and on the street he could function with bullets flying at him, but in his wife's kitchen or in the living room he was dangerous. Vases, glass countertops, and drinking glasses were his frequent victims, and his wife never let him forget his destruction of the orange pottery pansy ring they'd bought one year on vacation in Arkansas. He'd dropped it after filling it with water and flowers, watching it crash down onto the glass-topped coffee table to shatter into a thousand pieces and send a network of cracks spider-webbing across the entire table surface.

He selected one of the safe glasses, an old Burger King promotional giveaway item with a faded image of the Duke of Doubt on its surface. Numerous trips through the dishwasher had baked all of the color out of the Duke's clothes, but it hadn't affected the way he held water.

Rice held the glass under the tap, filled it, and drank it down. When he'd finished drinking, he was still thirsty, and he knew more water would not do any good.

Charlie dreamed.

He had dozed off while still thinking of Delia, and the images had stayed with him as he sank down into sleep. Her eyes, her smile, and her laughter made the first phases of his sleep cozy and pleasant, tinged with just a hint of the warm ache of longing.

He thought about touching her, of letting the golden strands of her hair slide softly through his fingers, and the dream of that sensation, imagined since he had never experienced it, was more thrilling than anything he had ever considered, better than being offered a chance to direct a horror film.

Memories of Budd's descriptions filtered through the surreal veil which surrounded the vision, the words fueling with fantasy. Charlie felt as if he were seeing something he was not allowed to see as the vision of her body took form, but he looked anyway, and the ache intensified.

He couldn't stop looking. She was too beautiful to disregard, even if there was a matter of feeling guilty. He could deal with that as his eyes eased over the pale flesh exposed to him, a smooth flat stomach, perfect flaring hips, and high, full breasts just as Budd had described them.

He was still looking when Miss Nielson invaded his brain. It was as if he were standing somewhere and she had approached from behind. Turning, he looked into her eyes—sultry, seductive eyes.

Her hair was disheveled, making her look wilder than she did at school, and she wore black, not a black skirt, but a long, flowing black gown that gave her an appearance of being at once dangerous and more alluring. The neckline plunged between her breasts, forming a V that almost reached her navel.

She beckoned to him, and he felt as if he should go, as if there was something more than her beauty and his desire for her, as if there was some bond.

His wish was to spin around and to go to her. The gentle ache of longing and desire for Delia turned into a need, a powerful, agonizing want. Miss Nielson was so beautiful, but it was more than beauty.

He did not quite understand the vibrations that emanated from her, but they were powerful, like fibers shooting into him, entwining somewhere inside him, linking with his need.

He looked into her eyes and saw more than their deep blackness. He looked at her lips, at her form beneath the gown. How wonderful it would be to go to her, to let her embrace him and draw him into her.

He imagined his hands sliding over her hips, his face nestled against the soft flesh of her neck. It made his heart quicken and his breathing become sharper.

Did she want him to touch her? Was that why she stared at him, why she beckoned to him? What else could she want from him?

He couldn't just ask her, not in the real world because it would be crazy, and not here. He was too afraid of her answer.

He had some deep-seated fear that it was something horrible, something that would shatter him. He sensed she wanted something from him he did not perceive. That was terrifying, more than anything else had been.

Yet as frightened as he was of her, he could not simply turn away. The ache was too great, and the wondering. He needed to know why and what this was all about.

She understood that too. He could read it as clearly as he could read a short story in the literature text. It was printed in the expression, an expression more readable here in the dream than in the classroom.

He kept looking at her, standing, wanting to move toward her but too frightened to, and an electrical finger of anger needled through him.

He had not asked for this. He had been meandering through his life when she had arrived, and suddenly everything seemed out of kilter.

His best friend was dead, and he was being twisted from side to side by confusion. Miss Nielson could see that too. He realized it from the look in her eyes.

Then a faint, calm smile formed on her features. She understood, that he was confused, that he was not ready for whatever she was offering. She nodded slightly and turned, the dark swirling mists of dream enveloping her, for now.

He awoke, sweating, breathing hard, feeling as if he had just been dropped down onto his pillows from a great height.

For a second he was disoriented. Then he stared up at the corners of his room and realized he was back in his bed.

The confusion seeped back into his consciousness then. He wasn't sure what he wanted to do with himself or which path he wanted to follow.

For a while he was angry at everyone, and after that, for some reason he didn't quite understand, he was frightened.

Chapter 13

Before driving over to Penn's Ferry for classes, Nell stopped by the store with the drawing of the hound. She had smoothed out the crumpled form as well as she could, and she hoped it would feed properly through the fax machine.

Matt was puttering around in his office when she entered, his hat tilted back on his head. He looked up and smiled at the sight of her outfit.

She was wearing tight black pants and a long, loose black shirt over them. The hem of the shirt fell unevenly to just above her knees, and she had pulled her hair back with a black headband.

"The Midnight Woman arrives at dawn," Matt quipped.

"I need to use the fax," she said. "Long distance. You can take it out of my check."

"No biggie," Matt said. "It's not gonna bankrupt me. What you got to go anyway?"

Knowing he would tease her, she passed the page over to him, and Matt's face flared as he looked into the eyes of the snarling monster.

"This what you think the killer dogs look like?" he asked. "Maybe Lucius Rice could circulate this like they do on TV."

"I'm sending it to my friend," she said.

"Oh yeah, the comic book guy." He grinned and asked no more questions. If it was going to a comic book person, that was fine with Matt.

He walked over the fax and put the page into the feeder shoot. "What's the number?"

She gave him the area code and then the number from her note pad, and he dialed and set the fax into motion. Slowly the paper disappeared

133

into the machine, glowing green lights from inside the device visible through the opening where the paper fed.

Gradually the paper emerged again, not jamming at all. She picked it up from the floor when it fluttered free.

Matt had returned to his desk now. A copy of *Paul the Samurai* was open on top of the blotter, and he scanned the pages, chuckling.

Nell checked her watch. She needed to be heading to school, and Matt didn't seem to have any more conversation to offer. Asking questions would probably facilitate more jibes.

Still, she asked: "Have you heard much more about this Barbara Nielson?"

"Your competition for Charlie's affections or at least adoration?"

"She's not alone. Budd Hagan's girlfriend seems to have taken a shine to him too. "

"Damn, the boy's getting popular for a skinny little shit. You just let him slip through your fingers, didn't you?" He snapped his fingers. "That's why you're trying to make up with your comic book buddy. Better a long-distance boyfriend than none at all."

"It's not like that. You know that."

He grinned. "Don't get so defensive." His swivel chair squeaked as he propped his feet up on his desk top.

"I did hear she's originally from Atlanta," he said. "She taught at a high school out there."

"Do you know the name of it?"

"It wasn't really in Atlanta. It was one of the suburbs. Dunwood or something like that."

"Why'd she come here?"

"Beats me. Maybe to snare that buddy boy of yours. Not enough men in Atlanta to satisfy her. Course if she gets tired of Charlie, I think I'd volunteer."

"Petittville is a long way from Atlanta. Do you think they might have run her off?"

"No way of knowin' that. I just know what Ray Manley from the school board said when I talked to him again."

"Maybe she had a thing for her students out there too."

"Maybe so. If so, she likes 'em young. Must be somethin' wrong with a woman that looks like who wants young boys."

Nell couldn't disagree with that. Barbara could have her choice of men. Desperation would not drive her to seek affection from a youngster enamored by the thought of an older woman.

Some flawed sense of desire was the only thing Nell could imagine that could attract a woman like Barbara to someone as young as Charlie. If she had that sort of disorder, this would not be the first time it had occurred. Those things didn't just happen suddenly.

That could be at least part of the explanation for her leaving Atlanta and traveling halfway across the South.

Perhaps that could partly explain her weirdness as well, but Nell was anxious to find what Michael had turned up.

Something, perhaps the same feeling that had compelled her to draw the hounds, indicated the matter was more complex than a May-December attraction.

She looked down at the snarling face of the hound and crumpled it again to hide it from her sight.

The hallways were always filled before school, as crowded as a street in New Delhi and almost as distinguished by caste. The popular kids clustered in one area, the hoods in another, and the nerds in still another section.

Charlie did not suffer from agoraphobia, but he always felt a tense knot in his stomach when he had to make his way through the hallways in the mornings.

The people made him nervous, and things were never safe, not really. There was always a chance of humiliation. You never knew when one of the Assholes or just one of the other hoods was going to pull something.

There was a prick named Rudy who'd tried to steal his watch once and punched him in the mouth when he'd tried to get it back.

It was just the nature of things. High school was hell so that the real world seemed like a relief when you got paroled.

He passed an alcove where a couple of kids were making out and was heading toward the spot he usually hung out before his first class when Miss Nielson eased alongside him.

"Morning, Charlie," she said brightly. Her smile was warm, brightening her face. The expression from the dream was gone, and he had to remind himself of the difference between dream and reality.

He felt a little tense standing beside her, but he managed to smile back.

"Going my way?" she asked. Her long hair was pulled back over one ear, and she was still wearing her coat and carrying her books.

"I guess so," he said, managing to make his words audible with only a little effort to keep from choking.

"Mind helping me with some of these?"

She had more books than she could handle and a briefcase as well. He took some of the texts for her and tucked them under his arm with his own books.

"Thanks," she said. "You're sweet."

The remark was very basic. She was just being polite, not seductive at all.

He walked beside her through the sea of people. She turned the heads of all the guys but ignored them. Charlie didn't find it as easy because he caught the glint of jealousy a time or two.

When they reached her classroom, she fumbled in the pocket of her coat and finally drew out a large golden key ring. Several golden charms dangled amid the keys, but Charlie couldn't see them well enough to determine what they were.

Then the door was open and she was dropping the keys in the pocket again. He followed her inside and placed her books carefully on her desk top as she shrugged off her coat.

She looked better than she had in the dream, dressed now in a short dark skirt, white blouse, and sheer black hose. He tried not to look at her, but he couldn't help it as she hung her coat over a chair and then leaned against the desk, one buttock resting on the edge.

Sunlight filtered in behind her through the windows, a few golden rays catching the auburn strands that mingled with the darker locks of her hair. Her expression was still bright, but she seemed less removed from the woman of the dream.

He felt tingly inside, and his palms broke out in sweat almost immediately. He tried to conceal his nervousness by averting his eyes from her, though he wanted badly to look at her legs, one dangling slightly, the other firm, foot flat on the floor, generous portions of her thighs revealed by the hem of the skirt as it rode up an inch or so with her position.

"You seem to like class, Charlie," she said, folding her arms. "You like reading?"

"Yeah. Er, yes ma'am."

She laughed. You don't have to be so formal. "I'm not that much older than you."

"Sure." Best he could manage, but her remark wasn't lost on him. Was that some kind of hint?

"I thought you were a reader," she said. "It kind of stands out from some of the kids. I've always read a lot myself. There've been some tough times for me when reading was all that pulled me through, just being able to escape from everything."

"I like to read," he agreed.

"Is school tough for you, Charlie?"

"Not the schoolwork."

"It's tough around here, though, isn't it?"

He shrugged nervously. "You know. I'm not a hood or a jock, so I have to watch it sometimes. They like to pick on you if they think you're a good student."

"Some of them would like to drag you down. They figure they're going nowhere in life, and they don't want anybody else to either."

"I guess that's true," Charlie said.

"Good students like you ought to be able to function without putting up with all of that crap," she said.

"Well, I manage," Charlie said. "Sometimes it's scary, but you know, you get by."

"I heard about the incident with those boys who attacked you."

Charlie made a face of dismissal. "They're jerks. They bother everybody. It's tough being a freshman. I never have figured out why seniors think they can pick on you just because they're older than you are. It happens all the time, though. A guy named Tessman started slamming a volleyball at all of us in gym the other day."

Miss Nielson dipped her head slightly, the hair falling across her cheek. "Let me know if you're bothered," she said.

"Thanks," Charlie said, "but I guess it's better if I just deal with things myself."

He felt himself at least becoming more comfortable with her. She wasn't like the dreams. She was nice, well intentioned.

"If I let you turn them in or whatever, I could get into more trouble. Like Mr. Sawyer finding out, that was no big deal. They were caught in the act. If they think I'm being favored, though, I'd be in worse shape than ever."

She nodded. "I suppose you're right. I just hate to see you have to endure aggravation. It's so unnecessary."

Charlie only shrugged again, wondering about her concern. It seemed genuine. He ventured a look into her eyes. They sparkled, warm, deep, and she was stirring as she leaned there, arms folded under her breasts. Maybe the attraction was not what he had thought it to be, but why did she have an interest in him?

The bell rang before he could become mesmerized. He looked back over his shoulder at the door where kids were flowing quickly past. He flashed a quick, half smile at her. "I better go."

"See you in class," she said.

He headed for the door.

"Be careful," she said, just before he stepped into the hall.

He allowed himself one quick final look back, one quick sweep of her legs and figure, before plunging into the crowd to face the day.

———

As his students worked problems, Sawyer sat at his desk and looked out the window. He had hoped to talk to Barbara before school, but she'd had Charlie Black in her classroom when he passed by. Rather than interrupt a consultation with a student, he moved on through the masses of kids to his own room, unable to quit thinking about Barbara.

She was still in his thoughts now. He had really rushed through his explanations of problems this morning just to get the kids quiet so that he could daydream, and he wasn't easily distracted from algebra.

She looked fabulous today, however, hair perfect, the black skirt sexy on her. There were pretty women, but she was more than that.

As the kids whispered and mulled over their assignments, he slid his chair back and walked to the door. Her classroom was only a couple of doors up the hallway.

He glanced back at the kids. They were busy. If he stepped out, they would get rowdy quickly enough, but if he was quick, it would be okay.

Teachers weren't supposed to leave students unattended, but it would only be a moment. The water fountain hung on the wall just past her door. He could make a trip there with a dry throat as an excuse.

Perhaps she would turn and notice him at the window as he passed. He could wave to her, and she might step out for a moment on his way back. Best case scenario.

Worst case, she didn't come out to speak to him, didn't even notice him as he passed, but he still got a glimpse of her. That wasn't perfect, but it was enough.

He made one more check of his students, and assured that they would remain diligent with their variables for a little while, he lowered his hand slowly to the doorknob.

He pulled the door open, glancing in both directions to make sure the principal wasn't making rounds or anything, then set off.

He didn't rush. He walked slowly, moving past Nuke Ruddy's classroom. Nuke, who was part of the coaching staff, taught history and was probably the only one in the universe with the ability to make the Roman Empire boring.

Sawyer was surprised the kids weren't dozing as he moved past the windowed door. He could see Nuke, a nickname from the coach's college football days, standing at his podium with the textbook spread open in front of him.

Nuke referred to his lectures as reinforcing the text. To everyone else, that translated as rereading the material to the kids without any further explanation. It wasn't exactly teaching, but it allowed Nuke the illusion of doing something constructive besides just training defensive ends, another job for which he was exceptional.

Lectures and busywork were visible in each of the other classrooms as well. Sawyer picked up speed, slowing only as he approached Barbara's door. He could hear her voice as she discussed romantic poetry.

He felt the flutter in his chest as he listened to her words describe the depth of emotion felt by Byron and Shelley. She made him want to write romantic poetry of his own, describing her beauty in sappy, inept, metaphors.

She was looking at her students when he walked by, sitting on top of her desk with those wonderful legs crossed, one foot cocked upward as she spoke, the calf of that leg tensed and firm.

He drew in his breath as he moved on past. He needed the water now. He stepped up to the fountain, drank quickly, and spun on his heels, setting the same slow pace as before.

He looked through her door without hesitation this time, expecting her to still be speaking to her students. He almost jumped when he saw she was looking directly toward him.

He felt like a schoolboy caught with a copy of *Playboy* and wondered if she could see the blush he could feel on his cheeks.

A smile formed on her lips, removing the embarrassment, replacing it with fresh excitement. The look in her eyes sent a charge through him, as if he had grabbed an exposed electrical wire.

He smiled back. There was no need for speech, no need for her to come to the door. She said everything in the silence.

He felt a warmth settle over him as he walked back to his own classroom. He tried not to grin as he opened the door again.

More of the students were whispering now, but several still worked on their math problems. He'd returned before things had had time to become rowdy, and it had been worth the trip.

He was on his way to his desk when he noticed Charlie Black was looking up at him. The boy turned his attention back to his book when Sawyer glanced in his direction, but it was as if there had been a look of accusation on his features. Could he have sensed something?

He kept his smile inward. Maybe Charlie had a crush on her. He had been in her classroom, and perhaps he was already aware somehow that Sawyer was smitten as well. He probably watched Barbara and bristled if he noticed anyone paying attention to her. *Too bad, Charlie*, he thought. *You're pissing with the big boys.*

Sawyer pulled his chair out and lowered himself to the cushion. It didn't matter if someone noticed. If a romance developed with Barbara, the kids would talk about it soon enough, embellishing.

Barbara looked out at the faces of her students, a mixture of masks from animated to disinterested. Some of them didn't even bother feigning interest. They leaned their heads against their palms and stared into space.

She found the ones who tried lifted her spirits. At least they realized there were opportunities for them if they seized them. She'd had to create her own opportunities, so she had little respect for those without ambition.

She couldn't really call her desires ambition, however. Her efforts had always been aimed toward survival and picking up pieces.

Especially after Doss.

She closed her eyes as the image of his face touched her thoughts. It was a fright mask in her memory.

Once he had seemed so handsome, his face rugged with firm cheeks that were frequently unshaven, and there was a faraway look in his blue eyes, as blue as the Caribbean. They almost seemed glazed, but she had always felt that was romantic, as if he could see distant horizons.

He was romantic in his way, though it was not his romantic nature which had first attracted her. She'd seen him edging his way through a crowd in a bar—tall, broad shoulders, looking massive compared to the skinny guys who stood around her.

He'd seemed beautiful, as beautiful as any man could seem with his golden hair brushing the shoulders of his brown leather jacket. He wore

141

a white sweatshirt beneath it and jeans that fit tightly, accenting the muscular roundness of his buttocks.

He had also seemed to have money. He was getting rid of plenty of it anyway. She saw a wad of bills when he paid a giggling waitress for a drink.

She'd decided then to get his attention. He seemed more interesting than the other men trying for hers. She'd worked her way through the room, dodging waitresses and elbows before purposely bumping into him.

She knew by the look on his face when he turned to her, by the way the expression crawled across his features, taking away the annoyance at being disturbed, that he was impressed by her appearance. His lips curled up into a smile, and he raised the brown Miller bottle he was holding in a salute. "Excuse me," he said, taking responsibility for the collision.

"It's all right," she said. "I wasn't watching where I was going. I'm kind of trying to get away from a guy."

"Oh?"

"He's trying to pick me up. You know how it goes."

"I could see why somebody would be trying to pick you up," he said, raising his voice to be heard above the crowd.

She picked out a balding man across the room and pointed back over her shoulder with her thumb. "He seemed decent enough, but he's just not what I'm looking for."

Doss turned his back to the table where he'd been standing so that he could face her fully and do a complete examination.

She was wearing a summer dress with little flowers in the print. It fit tightly over her breasts, accenting without revealing.

"Can I get you another beer?" he asked.

She wrinkled her nose, "White wine would be better. I'm kind of tired of beer."

The conversation had remained energetic. With very little effort she was able to keep it flowing. Leaving her imaginary pursuer behind had been no problem. He was exchanged for very real interest by Doss.

The conversation had moved from the bar to his car, where they didn't have to shout. He drove a red Porsche, drove it very fast in fact.

They went on a spin around the perimeter. There was something savage in the way he handled the car, the way he took it through dangerous curves with casual ease. If she hadn't been so infatuated—so young back then—she might have seen it as a warning.

Instead it only made him more beautiful. They'd ended up at his apartment, a nice place with a sunroom and a living room dominated by his stereo system and projection TV.

He fixed a pitcher of margaritas while she looked over his tapes, but they drank only a little bit before they began to neck.

His lips were warm, and his touch urgent. She let him peel the dress down over her breasts quickly so he could explore her with his lips.

She lay naked on the living room's soft carpet, letting her eyes close as he moved his hands over her breasts and down her sides.

He was gentle as he kissed her belly, and she giggled as he made a hungry sound when he buried his face in her pubic hair, letting his teeth toy with the curls. It tickled, but he didn't stop, and soon she didn't want him to as she slid her fingers through his hair and pressed him urgently against her, letting her legs drape over his shoulders.

Her first orgasm came from just his kisses there, but more followed when he carried her to his bed. The men who had used her, and the ugly memories of her father, were kicked away as she entwined with Doss.

He was a bastard and a savior, and he filled her time after time that first night, pounding his manhood into her. She had accepted it willingly, and it had sent throes of pleasure through her, but it was only later, when he held her and they talked and she told him everything, that she felt something happening inside her.

She had never fallen in love. She had never loved her parents, had never had siblings, had never felt that close to friends, but now she felt her spirit reaching out, enveloping the warmth he provided. He laughed with her, told her stories of his own, and they kissed and caressed even after other contact was spent because of exhaustion.

She hadn't let herself believe it would be more than what it was. She had expected him to drop her off at the place she was living in Little Five Points the next day and go on his merry way without ever calling her again.

She was prepared to go back to her waitress job in a natural food place and squeak along, but he took her name and phone number and the next evening she had found him waiting for her after work.

She never called it dating. It all happened too quickly. They spent little time on courting. Before she knew it, he was taking her away from her small, cracked place, moving her into his apartment.

It had seemed as if things were turning into a dream for her.

"Miss Nielson, I don't understand where to put this gerbil."

She looked up from her desk at Roland Joseph. He was trying to complete an assignment along with the rest of the class. She unfolded her arms and walked to his desk to briefly explain it was a gerund he was dealing with. She hated the grammar portion of teaching.

Turning, she walked back and sat down. She felt a tingle of humor as she thought about the boy's mistake. Her life had a touch of normalcy here. She liked that. She was glad the voice had dragged her back from Menesmone's clutches.

When she remembered Doss, all she could think about was blood.

Chapter 14

After school, Nell relieved Matt at the video store and took her usual place behind the counter. A couple of kids were in the store sorting through the science fiction stock, and an old man was looking for a classic, the title of which he could not remember. It was the first film he'd seen with his wife. She had died the previous summer, and he wanted to remember their early years.

Nell finally decided to help them all. Rounding the counter with her hands in the pockets of her billowing black pants, she approached the kids first, talking them into *The Last Starfighter*. It wasn't classic science fiction, but they'd never seen it, and she convinced them it was good.

The old man she talked into *Anatomy of a Murder* with Jimmy Stewart. He liked the actor, and it was a long movie which would fill up a good deal of his evening, chasing away some of the loneliness even if it wasn't the film he wanted. It was probably better for him since it wouldn't bring back as many memories.

When she finally had them checked out, she pulled out the telephone book, riffled through the loose pages, and found the Atlanta area code, 404. She then dialed information, 404-555-1212, and asked for Northwood High School's number.

Matt had left the school name on a note pad for her after talking to someone he knew with the school board.

When the operator gave her the number, she dialed. It was late in the day there, but the staff was still on hand.

A secretary with a Georgia drawl deep enough to fry potatoes came on the line. "Northwood High School. What can I do for you?"

Nell deepened her voice slightly, pronouncing her words precisely in a manner she hoped made her sound older. "My name is Nell Bordelon," she said, throwing in Matt's name to give the lie a good Louisiana ring. "I'm with the Riverland Parish School Board, and I was calling about some records on a teacher you used to have there, Mrs.—"

"Miss Williamson," she said. "What was the name?"

"Barbara Nielson. She's teaching here now at Petittville High, but we either had a mix-up or something but we don't have a file on her."

"We usually forward personnel files when they're requested, but I don't have a record of a request. That would have come through me, but I think there's a mistake."

She put Nell on hold and returned a moment later. "I checked the files," she said. "Are you sure you've got the right school?"

"This is Northwood High?" Nell asked.

"That's us. Home of the Blue Demons."

"I was told you were her last place of employment."

"I'm sorry. We've never had a Barbara Nielson teaching here."

Nell hung up. She wasn't surprised by the news, but the feeling that she had now identified as dread seized her a bit more firmly.

She picked up the phone again and dialed the Atlanta School Board office. They had no record of Barbara Nielson either.

Miss Nielson had never worked in the Atlanta school system. Whatever credentials she had presented to obtain her job here had been forged.

Nell leaned on the counter and twisted one finger into the locks of her hair. That meant a couple of things. First of all, since it was a job in a small school, the woman had been fairly confident they would not do much of a background check on her, especially if she managed to be charming in person.

The second thing, the thing that made the knot of concern inside Nell draw tighter, was that with such a thin line of defense behind her, Barbara Nielson, or whoever she was, probably didn't intend to stay here very long.

Nell wasn't sure what that meant, but she didn't believe there was no need to worry. If Barbara Nielson was only planning to stay for a short time, whatever damage she would do would be accomplished quickly.

146

John Tessman had never had any desire to play football. Running into 200-pound guys wearing shoulder pads and helmets didn't appeal to him. It just didn't seem prudent.

He found track far less insane if not any less grueling. Despite studying hard in order to get into a good school and keeping up with other responsibilities, he maintained his training. Even with the beginning of track season a while away, he didn't decrease his effort. He had held to his program through the hot summer months, and now with the air turning a little cooler, it was actually easier to stick to schedule.

His specialty was cross-country, so he tried to jog a few miles every day. He saw no reason to alter his plans as he suited up after school in the locker room behind the gym. The dogs usually came after dark, and he should be finished long before then, and he could keep training even if the talk of a curfew proved true.

He pulled on gray shorts and a sweatshirt since it was a little airish as evening approached, but he also slipped a terrycloth headband around his forehead to keep the perspiration from stinging his eyes.

He wasn't sure when he had realized he loved to run. It had been sometime in his earliest childhood, playing games with neighborhood kids. They ran, and they laughed, and he found out he was fast and that he loved the feeling of the wind rushing around him.

It was liberation; it was like flying. He could feel himself floating away from everything when he ran.

In junior high he had been able to do some running, but that had only been preparation. In high school he had truly found his calling, winning meet after meet, claiming district trophies for his school as well as respect from friends and chicks alike.

It set him apart from the other mindless jerks who wandered through the Petittville halls, and it would distinguish him when he went to college. They might look at him as a kid from some Podunk town, but they wouldn't be able to deny his record when he was up for scholarships.

They wouldn't have to worry about his academic eligibility either. He'd kept his grades up. He was an A and B student in senior courses, and he could do the same in college. He wasn't worried about the course load at all.

He was looking forward to college, probably LSU. That was seeming like the place best suited for him. He'd talked to the coaches there and the paperwork was underway for his admission even though he hadn't heard anything about how much money would be provided for him.

It didn't really matter. The scholarship was just a matter of personal pride. His father was a lawyer and would cover whatever he needed. He'd be getting a new car in the spring; he felt certain of that.

College was going to be a good experience. He could feel it. He just had a few more months to endure. He had enough points to graduate easily, so he looked forward to finishing things and moving on.

A little pain on his runs didn't matter. He walked from the locker room and did his warm-up behind the gym as he always did, careful to stretch his muscles and ready them for the exertion. He'd heard too many stories of people hurting themselves without warm-up, especially when it got a little chilly.

He waved to a couple of freshmen girls, then began to bend and twist, smiling to himself. They were probably impressed.

When he finally began to trot along the roadside in front of the school, the sky was turning to a dusty gray color. It was later than he had realized. The sun was dipping. He'd have to be careful. Any sign of dogs and he would run like the devil.

He started up the hill that rose just past the school, moderating his breathing so that he could pace himself. He breathed through his mouth to provide moisture for his lungs, trying to ignore the bite of chill that was carried on the building breeze.

A car passed and the driver honked. It was Dan Guillory. Tessman waved back then noticed Guillory was grinning through the glass and extending his middle finger.

Without breaking stride, Tessman cocked his fist into the crook of his right arm in answer to the salute.

Guillory, a dark-haired guy with freckles, only grinned back and gunned his motor. He was driving a reasonably well-put-together MG which he'd bought from his brother with money he earned working at McDonald's.

It was worth about half what he'd paid for it since it was old, and Tessman had challenged him a time or two to running against it.

Now Guillory had Tracy Moore sitting beside him, and he was ready for the challenge. Tracy was a freshman, blond, pretty, and rumor had it, ready to rid herself of her virginity so she could join the crowd.

Word circulating was that she was auditioning candidates for her deflowering. Rumors were usually exaggerated, but something like this could be a test, Tessman considered.

He wasn't particularly interested in Tracy, but if he could make Guillory look bad enough not to get her, it would be an accomplishment, a matter to brag about, a source of pride in his abilities.

As he saw the car's brake lights flare red, he picked up his pace, moving forward until he was alongside the slowing vehicle.

Guillory grinned at him through the glass again, and nodded toward the roadway, raising his eyebrows inquisitively.

Tessman nodded in response. He had no hope of outrunning the car, but if he could keep up his pace for just a short distance, he would feel good about himself. It would be a nice workout, a challenge for his abilities, and it might impress Tracy, which couldn't hurt. Even if he didn't earn her first honors, she might find she enjoyed the activity and decide to take other samples.

Guillory slowed the car to a stop, giving Tessman a moment to get positioned. Tessman looked at his friend's leering face, then glanced past him to the passenger seat. Tracy was watching it all with fascination.

Maybe she respected him just for having the sheer audacity to take on a car. He brushed some hair from his eyes, letting the headband hold it into place as he drew a few quick breaths.

He was warmed up, ready.

Guillory held up his hand, all five fingers splayed apart. Then he let his thumb fold into his palm, followed a second later by his index finger.

As the middle finger curled down, Tessman raised himself onto the balls of his feet.

They were near the rise of the next hill, but the road moved through an S curve before climbing. He might be able to outrun the car since Guillory would have to navigate the curve. That was his major hope.

The ring finger dropped.

Almost time.

The pinkie came down, and Tessman charged just as Guillory floored the gas on the MG, grinding gears as the rear wheels began to spin, spewing loose dust and gravel.

Tessman had a split-second lead, and he used it, pumping his legs hard and raising his knees high. As the car began to move, he was already flying, swinging his arms loosely at his side for minimal labor.

He heard the wheels of the MG grinding and the motor flaring, but he didn't look to his side. He kept his eyes focused straight ahead. The first curve was coming.

He shot into it full blast, adjusting his weight only slightly to keep his balance as he moved. He heard the car's movement, knew Guillory was braking to keep the vehicle between the ditches.

He let his breath build and kept his legs churning. He was moving out of the curve before Guillory was halfway through it, and he poured it on, making the most of the short stretch before the beginning of the next curve.

Once he got things together, Guillory would wax him, but for the time being he was doing okay, making a showing. Sweat beaded on his forehead from the extreme exertion, but the headband quickly absorbed it.

Tessman's legs were lean and muscular, but he was also aware they were strained. This was really a sprinter's job, and he wasn't a sprinter, so he was pressing himself in a way to which he wasn't accustomed. He usually paced himself for a long haul, but he wasn't half bad, he decided. All of the training didn't hurt, and when he went to competitions for scholarships, he was glad to know he would have these reserves on which to draw.

As he heard the roar of the MG a short distance behind him, a very short distance, he churned his legs harder, preparing for the next bend in the road. He stuck close to the shoulder, avoiding the gravel but trying to minimize the distance he traveled.

Pine trees and a ditch lined the roadway to his side, and a fence was stretched along the edge of the trees protecting timber land which had not been cut in a while. Lumber companies had trimmed out the hardwood and replaced it with the faster-growing evergreens, which shot up close together.

He moved parallel to that, watching the hill that he was approaching. That was where Guillory would overtake him. The little car was just behind him now, and he didn't have the steam to make the rise quickly.

He weaved through the next curve as fast as possible and started his ascent, but the car shot past him, the engine coughing but then roaring as Guillory put the transmission through its paces.

His hand shot out the window, waving over the top of the car as he peaked the hill. The contest was over, and he braked, waiting for Tessman.

Slowing to a jog, the runner gasped for breath. He was panting heavily because he had expended a good bit of air.

He was almost upon the car when Guillory gunned the motor and shot away. Tessman imagined his laughter, but he knew he couldn't really hear it over the engine.

He wasn't really worried about the laughter anyway because the sudden movement of the car made him twist, instinctively avoiding the brush of the fender.

As the car disappeared down the slope, Tessman teetered back, putting too much weight on his left foot at the wrong moment. His ankle twisted, and he stepped off the edge of the roadway.

The shoulder was made of soft red gravel which was depressed a couple of inches below the rim of the asphalt, so Tessman's balance was endangered further.

He flailed his arms, but things were too far out of kilter, and he went sliding down the grassy ditch bank beside the shoulder, skinning an elbow as he went down.

He landed against the ground with a thud, feeling the remaining wind in his lungs expelling. He was already tired, but the blow made him feel instantly exhausted.

He lowered his head back to the ground, wondering if everything that had happened in the past instant had been real. Guillory was long gone.

He'd kept pace with the MG, perhaps one of the best runs of his life, only to have things go crazy in a split second. He hadn't even had a chance to see if Tracy had realized how well he had done.

As the pain shot up his calf, he felt stupid. He should have known better, but she was pretty. It should have been just a momentary thing, but now he was hurt.

"Shit," he muttered as he sat up and began to massage his ankle. He didn't think it was broken or even that badly sprained, at least not so bad that it couldn't heal before the season, but he hated the thought of taking time to recuperate.

He forced himself to one knee and then managed to get his right foot under him. It felt okay, so he pressed the ground with his hands, lifting himself upward.

Putting weight on his left foot wasn't pleasant, but it wasn't as bad as he'd expected. He made himself take a step, then another, and soon he was making his way back through the curves.

If he could get back to the gym, he would be able to slip into his car and drive home. No problem. He moved slowly, but he made progress. His first trip through the curves had taken far less time.

He cursed Guillory as he felt the breeze. It chilled the sweat on his body and made a clammy shudder run down his backbone as the sun settled behind the pines.

He realized tears had formed in his eyes from the pain. It hurt worse than he'd first realized as he placed his steps, and he wanted to curse out loud. There would be no one to hear him scream.

People cleared away from the school when they didn't have to be there.

He spat out the phlegm that was forming in his throat and dragged the headband off his hair. He used it to wipe the sweat from his face as he limped along.

If he was hurt badly enough to mess up college, he'd kill Guillory. No questions asked, dead on the spot.

He reached the end of the first curve and started moving toward the edge of the school grounds. He probably could have dragged himself on his stomach faster than he was moving, but he didn't let himself think about that. Just a few more feet and he would be able to slip into the locker room and get some hot towels to wrap around the now throbbing ankle. He probably needed to get his shoe off of it because it was definitely going to swell. That fact was making itself apparent.

He looked toward the rear door of the gym, but even with his goal in sight in the glow of the dusk-to-dawn light which hung like a cyclops' eye over the parking lot, he decided he'd better unlace now.

Kneeling, he began to fumble with the knots. He'd seen a guy last spring with a sprain that had swollen to the size of a softball. They'd had to cut his shoe off at the emergency room in Aimsley. Tessman didn't want that happening to his Nikes. He'd paid for them out of his own pocket.

He grunted with the pain as he bent his legs, and he had to get into a sitting position to function. He couldn't just squat. The pain was too much.

He chewed his lower lip as he bent his leg toward his body so that he could reach his laces. The knot seemed impossible to untangle. It had slipped and was no longer a bow. He cursed again and began to fumble with it, trying to untangle the strands.

The dogs came then.

He heard them—their footfalls and the rasp of their breath—only a second before they were upon him.

The instant he heard, he scrambled forward, but sound wasn't enough warning. One of them clamped onto his shoulder.

He felt the teeth sink through the thick cloth of his sweatshirt, but there were only pinpricks from the teeth before he jerked forward. Landing on his stomach in the gravel, he began to drag himself along, pushing with his knees and ignoring the pain as his skin was raked off it by the rocks and coarse sand.

The dog at his shoulder didn't pull away, but he managed to keep it busy trying to wrap its paws around him, and that prevented it from biting a piece out of him through the sweatshirt.

He wasn't sure how many of them there were, but he told himself it didn't matter if he could somehow reach the gym. Damn, he should have waited until he was there to unlace. It wouldn't have made that much difference. Better a swollen foot than no foot.

That notion hit home when one of the dogs bit into his right calf. Bare, exposed, the leg was vulnerable, and the pain overtook the throbbing in his left leg. He felt blood flow, and knew the jaws were making hamburger of the muscle.

He cried out and swatted back at the dog. God, it was big, a monstrous black thing. He'd heard the reports, had thought it was too bad about the other kids, but he had figured they were pit bulls or something.

He'd never imagined the pain, or the fear—he was crying now full force—and he'd never thought about the fuckers being as big as lions. That's what they seemed like, big heads, big jaws. They clamped on him with more force than he could have imagined.

He dug his hands into the gravel, splitting fingernails and completely ripping the one off his right middle finger as he sought to claw himself toward the gym's door.

A dog tried to bite the crown of his head, but it wasn't able to get a grip. He screamed at the very notion of the monsters biting into his brain.

Was there any hope here? It didn't seem likely that he would be able to escape. They had killed the others. Why not him?

When he had started his run he had not been worried, but now it was clear he had no special dispensation of invulnerability.

He was *dead meat*, as he might once have said facetiously. Now *dead meat* didn't seem such a dark joke. It was a dark reality. He was going to be meat, was already meat. They were biting into him as if he were canned dog food.

He pulled himself another inch and felt another piece of skin tear. The door, maybe he could make the door, just maybe. He had given up hope but not the struggle.

Spittle streamed out of his mouth now, and the tears ran down to meet it. He had pissed in his pants long ago and just now realized it.

He was sopping in his own piss, humiliated as well as devoured. And the door was so close, so frigging close. He was stretching his hand toward it. It wasn't within reach, but he wanted to reach out for it as if reaching would transport him the final feet to his destination.

A dog's paw made a swipe at his arm, and he braced himself for the teeth. He knew they could clamp on to the flesh, would probably bite through; so fine, let it be over, let them bite it off and let him bleed to death and get it the hell over with.

He was thinking that when the headlights swept across the parking lot. He saw them on the gravel, saw their beams bounce off the rear wall of the gym, and his heart picked up a beat it had lost.

He felt the jaws relaxing, felt them letting go. The bastards were scared of the light or something. He felt teeth sliding out of his wounds, and he let his face fall down into the dirt, sobbing.

Someone was coming.

The dogs pulled away from him, spinning on their paws and trotting off from wherever they had appeared.

He felt dirt in his mouth but couldn't manage to spit as he heard someone step out of the car. Two people climbed out. He moved his face slightly so that he could look in the direction of the vehicle.

He saw Guillory's shoes and Tracy's. He wanted to tell her not to come any closer because he didn't want her to know he'd lost control, but he only managed a croak before Guillory knelt beside him.

No warning was necessary to keep Tracy back. She lingered near the car's front fender, in shock at the sight of him.

That was okay. Shock was good. Shock meant she could respect him because of what he endured.

"We'll get you a doctor," Guillory said through quivering lips. "I didn't know. You gave it a hell of a run back there. I didn't know."

"It's okay," Tessman managed to say as he curled into a fetal position and closed his fingers around the rut in his calf. The dog had mangled muscle and tendon. He wasn't going to be putting weight on this foot for a long time. The chunk they took out of him might never grow back.

He didn't have to worry about scholarships. He wasn't going to be running track anymore. He could see that, and his sobs were exchanged for deeper, painful weeping.

Barbara picked up her phone to find Sawyer on the line. She detected a slight quiver in his voice, and that brought a smile to her lips as she pressed the receiver to her ear.

"How are you doing?" he asked.

"Okay."

"Have you been out?"

"I stayed late grading some papers," she said.

"Oh, well, I was wondering if you'd want to do something over the weekend. I know you must be bored here."

She sat on the couch, curling her legs under her. She couldn't quite define the feeling that his suggestion gave her—it was warm, pleasant. It seemed so special that he wanted to do something for her.

Men had always offered to do things for her, but she had never doubted that they expected something in return. With Sawyer that motive was not so apparent, and it wasn't that he was subtly masking it.

She let her head fall back on the arm of the couch as they talked, and she knew from the tone in his voice he was falling for her. It was happening quickly, but that didn't matter. She was glad he cared because she cared too.

He was not like Doss. He was an opposite. He was a lonely little schoolteacher who wanted someone in his life.

Where had he been ten years ago or five? There were never answers to those kinds of questions, only the irony that the good men came after those who made you suffer.

She supposed it was better just to enjoy the fact that he had appeared. Love came when you weren't searching for it. It came when you were looking the other way with your mind on other things.

Love had hurt before, but she didn't let herself feel fear now, not with Sawyer. She couldn't find anything wrong with him, none of the savageness or anger.

Still she wasn't sure what she wanted. "I'm kind of tired," she said. "I'd love to see you if we could plan something quiet."

"Sounds good," he said. "We can decide a little later."

When Sawyer rang off, she placed the phone back in its cradle and folded her arms, hugging herself as a broad grin forced her cheeks to rise.

She'd never believed things in her life would feel this stable.

———

Nell was still behind the counter at the store working on some sample sketches for a comic book story she had outlined when she saw Matt come in with a grim expression on his face. He leaned against the door, shaking his head.

She dropped her pencil. "Did they get another one?"

"Not dead, but hurt. The Tessman boy, one that ran track."

"Oh shit."

Matt took off his hat and rubbed his forehead with a red bandanna he had tugged from his jeans. "Mincemeat of his calf," he said, sticking his chin out slightly as he spoke, as if his tone and expression were adding weight to the news.

"Where was he?"

"Close to the school. He'd been running. That's a good ways from where the last two were hit, but there's some trees over that way. They figure maybe the dogs hid there after killing the boy at the pavilion."

Nell picked up her pencil again, holding it between her thumb and middle finger. The eraser bobbed from side to side because she could not hold it steady.

She knew Tessman. Everybody saw him running along the roadsides at some time in Petittville.

She'd heard Charlie talk about him too. Here was another one that Charlie wouldn't mourn that much.

On a sketch pad, she began to doodle a small sketch of Charlie's face, cocking one eyebrow up and wrinkling the other downward, giving him a suspicious expression for no particular reason. Then she thought about that, and she felt as if she had stepped into a walk-in freezer.

It was a small town. There weren't that many people. Everybody knew everybody more or less, yet each of the people harmed by the dogs had a connection with Charlie. It was coincidence, of course, nothing to think twice about. She had known all of the people too.

But she hadn't had close contact with them. She began doodling another face beside Charlie's and realized it was Barbara Nielson.

Things had seemed to coincide with her arrival here, and she had some mysterious interest in Charlie.

She was at the school, so she would know at least about the incident with the Assholes. Word would travel among the teachers. She might also have heard about Tessman.

Nell put her pencil down again. She had jotted down the eyes on the drawing, and they seemed to stare up at her, cold and angry with a glint of jealousy. She was looking at the smudges from her own pencil, but it was as if she was really looking into the eyes of Barbara Nielson.

She tore the sheet out and threw it away. Matt watched her and shook his head, grin spreading.

"You let go of that like it was something hot," he observed.

"Guess I scared myself," she said.

"Drawing dogs again?"

"No, something more frightening, I think."

She watched the second hand tick by on her watch. If her shift ever ended, she was going to have to go and talk to Charlie.

Chapter 15

The fog had descended again when they closed the video store. As she watched Matt lock the front door, Nell looked around through the darkness, but she could only see a short distance.

The fog had more density than smoke. Even the streetlights were only blotches of white, their shapes distorted in the mist.

Nell tried to look along the sidewalk, half expecting glowing eyes to appear, emerging slowly toward her through the cloud. The fog's damp touch on her skin felt the tingle of a ghost's veil, giving the night a mystical atmosphere conducive to further imaginings of the macabre. As if she needed her imagination stimulated further in that direction.

When Matt had the door locked, he turned and put his arm around her. It was a fatherly move, not an attempt at a pass, but she stiffened.

On most nights he let her close, but he had returned tonight, concerned for her safety. Guiding her gently, he walked her to her car, but she did not relax.

"Thanks, Matt," she whispered as she fumbled with her keys. She didn't want him thinking she had to have him present. She could have made it to her car safely, and even though she was glad he'd been there, she didn't want to show it. She didn't need a surrogate father to replace the one she didn't like, not even a well-intentioned one.

"Be careful," Matt warned as she climbed behind the wheel. "The hellhounds probably thrive on a night like this."

She nodded. As he walked away, a feeling of eeriness settled over her. The feeling worsened when she slid behind the wheel, an unusual uneasiness, almost an overwhelming feeling that things beyond imagination were taking place. Some uncontrollable ball was rolling, and trying to stop it was futile.

She thought about going home and locking her doors and hiding under the covers, but she knew things wouldn't be all right just because they were out of her sight. She slammed her palm against the steering wheel. She hadn't come here to get involved in weirdness. She had come here to get away from her father and the quicksand of her life. She wanted to develop her talent and find a ticket to a better life, to find a way to move ahead.

It wasn't her responsibility to face all this, not her responsibility to try and understand it or unravel whatever was going on.

People like Rice were supposed to do that, put the pieces into place, determine what was happening. But he wasn't in a position to spot things the way she was, at least not in this situation. How could he know about Charlie?

She was Charlie's friend, and she could see things nobody else could notice, not even Charlie himself. He wasn't outside looking in. She was an observer here just as she was when she did artwork, looking into a character's world.

The Contessa, her heroine, might not be able to see somebody sneaking up on her, but Nell could. She knew the evildoer was around the corner, and the same was true here.

She didn't have as good a vantage, but she could sense when things were awry.

She opened her purse, fumbling for her keys. She was about to dump her purse when she realized that she'd already slid them into the ignition. She expelled a breath, curling her lip so that the air shot upward to toy with her bangs. "Your frustration is showing," she told herself.

Cursing, she shoved the key into the ignition and fired the reluctant engine. As the motor idled, she thought again about going home. She could avoid all this. She could settle in at her apartment and work on school matters or play with artwork. Creating new superheroes would keep her mind off the madness.

Charlie wasn't her responsibility. He wasn't her brother. He should be figuring out his own situation. Except he was her friend, her only good friend. He was the only one besides Matt who didn't think she was ditzy, the only one in the real world anyway.

She popped the car into gear, and slid the light switch back. The beams blazed, and she began to ease the car forward. The lights seemed to do little more than make the fog glow, however. They couldn't penetrate the gray wall.

She tried the brights, but that seemed worse than the dims. At least with the beams aimed downward, she didn't have the glare off the pale swirls coming back at her.

Hunched over the wheel, she put her foot on the gas but pressed it only slightly. She knew the street well, so she navigated almost from memory.

Finally the stop sign at the corner appeared. She applied the brake and sat there for a moment. A right would take her out to Charlie's, but a left would take her back to her apartment. She wouldn't have to fight the fog. She could make a few turns and be there, and she would be safe from the dampness. It would be warm and quiet at home. The thought was inviting.

But she turned right.

The radio was blaring Guns 'n' Roses. She'd had it on for the drive from Penn's Ferry earlier. Her hand shot over and switched it off. She had to concentrate as she inched through the darkness.

She wasn't a particularly cautious driver, but she did okay most of the time. She'd never had an accident. With the strange feeling tonight, she kept the car at 15 miles per hour, following the route out toward the subdivisions. It was a winding road, something she never paid much attention to in the daytime. Tonight it was like a carnival ride, snaking from side to side.

She couldn't remember the S curves because she'd never expected to be driving them by Braille. She held her breath.

It wasn't just the fear of crashing. The feeling, that damned eerie feeling, was doing it, making her wary. She began to wonder if it was the same second sight which had allowed her to sketch the dog.

Was she experiencing some premonition that something was going to happen? That worked wonders for her stomach.

She rounded another curve and saw headlights. She slowed almost to a stop as the car passed, then picked up only a little speed to move forward.

The sensation worsened. Normally it would take just a few minutes to reach Charlie's from the store; it was walking distance when you cut across yards. She wanted to curse.

Then realization settled. Even as she told herself she could not be aware of it, she knew the dogs were watching her. She glanced out her window, expecting to see their eyes.

No glowing orbs greeted her, but she was certain the dogs were there, loping along the roadside, keeping pace with her vehicle.

She waited for them to attack in some way. She expected to feel the jolt of the car as they slammed into the door or to see their huge paws suddenly scraping down the windshield as they leaped on the roof and tried to get at her.

That didn't happen as she rounded the curve and drove through the archway into the subdivision, but she checked her rearview. She thought she detected movement in the fog. She couldn't be certain, but she was convinced, even as she told herself over and over it was just imagination, that they were after her.

The street seemed empty. There were no other cars. A few houses had porch lights turned on, but they were no more that white blobs lost otherwise in the gray.

She'd be lucky if she could find Charlie's house. She couldn't see the numbers bracketed over the doors, and the rural route mailboxes didn't have separate addresses printed on them. In most cases the carriers knew the houses by location and didn't have to watch for numbers.

She chewed her lower lip until it hurt. Maybe it would have been better to go home. She could have avoided this confusion, and what if the dogs were out there? What if they came lumbering up on her little car? Their weight would probably allow them to slam into the rear glass and gain access. Locking the door wouldn't keep them out.

Her heart thundered. They were back there, behind her, trotting along the narrow subdivision drive, keeping pace with her slow progress, ready to leap.

She pressed the gas pedal slightly. She didn't think speeding up would do much good, and the subdivision road was a circle, so she couldn't build much speed, but at least she would make it a little more difficult for the bastards.

As she moved into the first curve, she checked the rearview again. Were they back there? She couldn't see movement. She hit her brake as she moved around the roadway, watching the taillights turn some of the mist pink for a second, yet there wasn't enough light to penetrate the dense shroud.

She tried to count driveways. At least if she could reach Charlie's she could honk the horn, and he could call the cops, if he didn't get mauled by coming out first to see why she was honking.

She could pull into any driveway and do the same and hope the residents looked out and wondered before opening the door. Maybe they would spot the dogs in her headlight beams.

She refrained from pulling over because she was still telling herself the dogs couldn't be there, couldn't be following a car. Dogs couldn't read license plates or recognize colors.

No, but they damned well seemed able to single out people that messed with Charlie Black. If they were smart enough for that, they might be smart enough to track a vehicle.

She spotted the driveway that had to be Charlie's and turned without signaling. A car behind her might have hit her, but another vehicle would have been a blessing because the fucking hounds would have had to move out of its way. However, there were no headlights. The animals couldn't be bright enough to understand turn signals, but why give them any help? She felt crazy trying to outwit mutts, but she didn't have many options—maybe a few more than the guys the dogs had killed, but not many.

She could see the glow of a light in the front window, but the porch light was off. She killed her engine but left her headlights on and waited for impact.

They would strike the car any moment, would be pawing at the doors or slamming against the fenders. They might be big enough to force the car over. Ridiculous. Dogs? But who knew? They had to be big to do as much damage as they had. They might be as big as tigers.

She held on to the wheel, afraid it might bend with the tension. The fog was too thick. On any other night there would have been enough light to let her look around and relieve her fear. She would have been able to determine if there were dogs within fifty feet with light from the moon, street lights, houses.

There would not have been total blackness in a subdivision, but with this fog she was effectively blinded. The porch light came on.

She closed her eyes and prayed. If the dogs were here, please God, she hoped no one would open the front door.

She thought about rolling the window down to yell a warning, but that would have made it possible for the dogs to dive in at her without even having to break the glass. Even a crack might give them enough opening to rip at her.

Concern had turned to fear which had become terror inside her without her awareness. The process had churned too quickly for understanding.

She had tears in her eyes, and she could feel shudders running through her flesh. She wondered if the dogs were out there, but she couldn't wait to find out.

She threw open her door and ran for the house. Her feet sank into the soft winter rye grass that covered the lawn, and as the dampness of the fog touched her flesh, she knew the dogs must be coming, must be running after her.

She could hear them. Their breath was there; they were coming. But she also heard the front door opening. The chain was sliding back. Someone was turning the knob.

Nell ran, grabbing a handful of her skirt so that it didn't tangle with her legs. She traversed the lawn like a sprinter and moved up the steps.

Charlie was standing in the doorway, looking at her quizzically. She pushed him inside and shoved the door closed, but even as she did, she knew the dogs were gone.

If they had ever been there. She told herself they hadn't and knew that they had. Sweat covered her face and she wiped it with her palm as she leaned against the wall beside the door.

"What's wrong?" Charlie asked.

His mother was in the living room watching television, thank God. The sound of the program carried through the house. At least she was engrossed in it and not aware that some half-crazed nineteen-year-old girl had just shown up on their doorstep. That would endear Nell to her sure enough.

"Dad's upstairs," Charlie said, still wondering what was wrong.

Two strokes of luck. Mr. Black wouldn't be on hand to decide she was out of her head either.

"Let's go into the kitchen," Charlie suggested.

She didn't object. She followed him. He led the way into the golden room, and Nell settled down at the table, resting her hands on the plastic top as she let her composure return.

Charlie pulled some homemade cookies out of a Tupperware container and got two cans of Cokes out of the refrigerator before joining her.

She took a napkin from a little silver holder beside the salt and pepper shakers and wiped her eyes while he popped the cans open.

He seemed a little depressed, but his anxiousness about her state brought a little more animation into his eyes.

"What happened," he asked.

His voice trembled a little, revealing that he was worried about her. She was reminded he didn't have any more friends than she did.

"I just got scared," she said. "I decided to come see you, and the fog was thick. I was worried the dogs were after me."

He nodded, probably thinking about Budd. "I guess they're still out there somewhere."

"You haven't heard?"

"Heard what?"

"About tonight."

He shrugged, leaning forward. "Mom's been watching TV. Dad's upstairs. Nobody's called. What is it?"

She took a swallow of Coke to wash the dryness from her throat. "Your friend John Tessman was attacked by the dogs."

Charlie's eyes widened, and he almost let his own Coke slide from his hand. "How'd it happen?"

"He was running and they got him and chewed up one leg really bad. They didn't kill him, but he was on the track team. It messed him up so he can't run."

"Wow. God, he was a jerk, I told you what he did in the gym the other day, but that's almost like Budd."

"Almost like Budd. Think about it, Charlie."

He frowned, setting his can down. "What?"

"Budd was your friend, right?"

"Yeah."

"The Asshole guy had bothered you personally that day."

"Right."

"Now Tessman gets it, and he messed with you just the other day."

Charlie looked away from her, contemplating her words. His left index finger moved along his lower lip as his eyes stared into nothingness.

"We all knew all of the people that were killed."

"Think about it, though. It could be coincidence, or it could be some connection. None of this happened before Miss Nielson showed up, either."

An adult might have quickly scoffed at the notions she was throwing out, but Charlie gave a little more thought to them. He was still young enough to have an open mind. He read comic books too, and things happened in comic books that matched this activity. Weird people arrived out of the nowhere and strange things started happening in the four-color pages.

Was it possible that the same could be going on here? It would be nice to think that the issue would end and all the bad things would be over for a while, but an end didn't seem evident.

They still had to identify the evil and figure out what to do about it. Only then could they think about straightening things out.

"Where do I fit into all this?" Charlie asked. "Miss Nielson said something about me seeming special. Do you think that's it, that she's got some special purpose for me and she's trying to protect me?"

"I don't know."

Charlie slapped his palms down on the table top. "I told her about Tessman. I was talking to her, and I mentioned what he did with the volleyball."

For Nell that was another sign that things were falling into place. He told Miss Nielson about someone who'd tried to harm him, and then Tessman had been attacked. He had actually bothered Charlie before the Assholes had attacked, but he had fallen victim to the dogs later because Barbara Nielson learned about it later.

All of it could be coincidence. Tessman was out after dark. If the dogs were attacking at random, he would have made a nice candidate, but he was a long way from the downtown area where the dogs had previously attacked, and a long way from Budd's death site.

"Charlie, we need to check her out. I called the school where she was supposed to have worked before she came here. They never heard of her. She didn't come here just to take a teaching job."

"Maybe she's trying to get away from someone. Maybe she had a husband who treated her bad."

"Or maybe she came here looking for you, Charlie."

"Why me?"

"That's what we've got to figure out. Something's weird here. You know it, and I know it. It might be fun to have your enemies, but the dogs bumped off Budd too. I think they were following my car tonight too."

"You saw them?"

"No, but I've sort of been sensing things the last few days. I drew a picture of the dogs after Budd died. I've had a feeling, about her, impressions about everything."

"Have you ever felt anything like this before?"

"No, but maybe this stuff triggered something. I don't know, Charlie. It's not that I've been reading too many comic books."

"I know," he said, trying to be reassuring.

He looked at her, as if he expected her to be able to provide answers now that she had introduced these ideas. She could only shrug.

"What are we supposed to do?" he asked.

"I wish I knew, Charlie. I asked a friend of mine to do some checking, but otherwise I don't know. Somehow we've got to figure out what's going on."

"With Miss Nielson?"

"And the dogs. What could she want with you, Charlie?"

He held up his hands. "I don't know." Part of him seemed to want to cry. She couldn't blame him.

His best friend was dead, others were dying and somehow it all related to him.

She took his hand. "It'll come together, Charlie. I had to let you know. I don't know if you're in danger or not."

"Maybe I am," he said, bowing his head. "Maybe I am."

"It's okay," she said, squeezing his hand. "We'll figure something out."

"What can we do?"

"We can check on Miss Nielson some more. Tomorrow I can talk to my friend. Maybe there's some more checking I can do on her. People leave paper trails, you know. If I can figure out how to check on that, that might tell us more about her."

"That's if she's behind it. You think she trained the dogs or something?"

"It's weird, Charlie. I don't know. I talked to Chief Rice. They found a pregnant dog with all the fetuses cut out of her. I don't know if that makes sense or not."

He drew his lips up tightly, folding them inward, biting them. "How else can we check on her?"

"I'm not sure."

"Do you think we should spy on her?"

She studied his face for a moment. There was no gleam of anticipation. He was asking earnestly, not looking for an excuse to sneak glances at the subject of an infatuation. Miss Nielson was beautiful, and Charlie was an adolescent male, but concern and confusion weren't being superseded by lust.

"Maybe we could learn something from that," she agreed. "But we can't just go out sniffing around. Especially not tonight."

"The fog is too thick?"

"And it would be dangerous if we're not careful. Suppose she spots us."

"I guess you're right."

"We have to figure out where to park the car so that we can get back to it easy and get away without being seen." She thought a moment. "And we need an excuse for what we're doing out. I think the council wants to set a curfew."

"We could go Monday, though," Charlie suggested. "I'll have to sneak out of my house too, but I've done it before."

"Monday, then. We'll see what we can find out over the weekend."

"Yeah. I'll talk to you later."

She slipped out the kitchen door. The fog was still thick, but she heard no sound of hounds. She edged along the side of the house and charged from the corner to her car.

Once she was inside, she locked the doors and waited. The dogs didn't show, all the way home, she watched for them to come out of the fog.

Weekends in Petittville were quiet times. Nothing much happened. People traveled to Aimsley for shopping and movies or rented videos.

That provided Nell with a busy day on Saturday. She sat behind the counter and checked out people steadily. With the rain that began shortly before eleven, people had little else to do.

She chatted with Matt some, but things remained fairly hectic in the afternoon, putting on hold many of the things she had planned to check on. She didn't get a chance to call Michael.

It was late afternoon when she saw Mr. Sawyer from the school come in. He was followed by a woman with a dark umbrella. When she folded it and placed it by the door, Nell realized she was looking at Barbara Nielson.

The woman looked up at Nell, as if sensing the stare. For a moment, their eyes locked, and Nell felt a quick sense of malevolence emanating from the woman.

Then Barbara Nielson smiled at Sawyer, and they walked down an aisle together. Nell had to turn and check out another patron, but she watched the woman the entire time she remained in the store.

When they finally moved to the counter, she forced herself not to look over at the woman even though she felt Miss Nielson's eyes on her. She checked out their movie, and when they departed, Nell realized she was shivering.

She felt as if Barbara Nielson had looked into her soul.

Chapter 16

Sawyer spotted Barbara in the hallway Monday morning and paused at the end of the corridor to watch her make her way through a pride of kids. She moved gracefully, dodging elbows and delivering warning stares to guys who ogled her. She was wearing a dark blue skirt with a red jacket and white blouse. The skirt stopped well above her knees, and he couldn't imagine her being any more beautiful. Her hair was brushed slightly to one side, and her captivating eyes were more electric than ever.

She finally broke through the crowd and almost bumped into him. He would have welcomed her touch. When she saw him, he smiled.

He was glad to see the smile she offered back. He didn't know much about women, but he'd watched the kids enough to know when smiles were real and when they were bogus. The weekend had been fun and quiet but you never knew what the post-date reaction would be from a woman. There was always a moment or two of awkwardness.

"How're the equations this morning?" she asked, reaching out to pat his forearm gently with her fingertips.

The charge jolted up his arm, and he felt the stirring of hormones he'd forgotten about. A vision of the two of them intertwined touched his thoughts. He could see her flawless body almost perfectly in his mind, and his imagination did a pretty good job with the touch and taste of her also.

He shifted his weight, trying to concentrate on the Barbara in front of him. Her eyes had almost a glow within them. She was, it seemed, as infatuated with him as he felt with her. A good sign. That should serve to move things along. Sawyer had waited a long time to find someone, a woman to have in his life. He didn't have many doubts about details. He was unquestionably crazy about her, and since she seemed to feel the same about him, he saw no need to wait to form a relationship. While rain had spoiled the trip to Ville Platte he had hoped for, they had had a fun time watching a tape together and then talking.

On Sunday he had spoken with her on the phone after church, and the conversation had filled up more than an hour without seeming to take any time at all.

He wasn't in any hurry to drop to one knee and put a ring on her finger, but he didn't mind the thought of having her as a girlfriend. They could spend their evenings grading papers and snuggling on his couch while they watched television together.

"Walk me to my classroom?" she suggested.

He nodded with a smile and moved with her through the tangle of kids. They were all talking about Tessman s injury.

The rumor had had two days to fester. Some were saying his leg had been chewed off. Though the truth was probably bad enough, exaggeration would continue until the boy could return to classes.

Sawyer had taught the kid and thought him a good student if a bit arrogant. He felt sorry for the boy and mentioned that to Barbara.

"I heard he had a mean streak," she said, her voice hard.

"Most kids do," Sawyer said, wondering if she felt any compassion at all for him. She didn't normally seem so cold.

"I suppose that's true," she said. She dodged a kid that was rushing ahead of a couple of pursuers and barked a warning for them all to slow down, and the subject was effectively changed.

They spoke of the aggravation of standing duty until they reached her classroom. Then as she settled behind her desk, Sawyer lingered for more small talk. There was no need to get into intimate conversation here, but at least there was more opportunity for them to get comfortable together.

He was in midsentence when she stiffened. Her eyes grew wide, almost as if she were angry about something. He glanced over his shoulder to see if a murder was being committed outside the door.

He only saw Charlie Black and a blonde girl moving by, talking with each other. She was gorgeous wearing a short pink dress and a pullover that hugged her breasts, a hotter number than he'd ever expected Charlie to be escorting.

He turned back to Barbara, who was watching them as they smiled and spoke to each other. The roar of the crowd kept their words from being audible as they moved out of sight, but Barbara seemed to be straining to hear.

"You have any tests planned today?" Sawyer asked.

"Hmmm? Oh no. No tests for a while." She began to bother with her hair for a moment.

"You want to do lunch?"

"I have duty," she said, still a bit stiff.

"How 'bout coffee in your free hour?"

"That sounds good."

The bell rang. He thought about a peck on the cheek, but the students would notice for sure. He settled for a quick grasp of her hand, then he skirted out the door and joined the flow of the crowd.

He wondered why she seemed so concerned with Charlie. Maybe it was that Charlie had displayed signs of a crush and now the flattery she must have felt was challenged. That was human nature.

Or it could be that she knew Charlie was a good student and she didn't want his mind turning to romance and screwing up his grades. She was a good teacher. She cared so that seemed plausible.

He couldn't think of any other reason she would be so concerned about male and female students taking notice of each other.

That was to be expected. You couldn't leave boys and girls together for long without chemical reactions developing.

"How are you doing, Charlie?" Miss Nielson's voice was unusually sharp as he entered the classroom.

He offered a startled: "Fine."

He also smiled, receiving his usual smile in return, but in her eyes he noticed something different, as if she were angry. The gaze made him shiver, and as he moved to his seat, he wondered what was wrong. Could she somehow know about his discussion with Nell and their plans? They had talked more about them on Sunday and wondered if they should have acted over the weekend.

He decided it wasn't possible for Miss Nielson to suspect, but her reaction did seem to confirm his original suspicions and Nell's concerns that there was something unusual about the teacher's interest in him.

As he waited for class to begin, he watched her, feeling the same strange stirring inside as she walked from her desk to the door, hips swaying gently, muscles in her firm legs rippling, straining against the dark stockings. He had talked to Delia for a while this morning, pleased with what seemed to be her blossoming interest in him, yet he could not help being excited whenever he thought about Miss Nielson.

She was an older woman, forbidden, and she was somehow sinister. Perhaps it was that hint of danger which had Nell so upset, which actually made Miss Nielson more alluring.

He rested his chin in his hand and let his thoughts drift back to those early fantasies about her. They seemed to be more than his imagination. They seemed real, as if he had been sent telepathic images of her body. The dream rushed back stronger now, enhanced by his willingness to accept the visions and supplement them with his imagination.

As he watched her walk back from the door, he envisioned himself in her arms, kissing her and moving his hands across her flesh. As she settled down behind her desk, she looked up at him, one eyebrow cocking upward as she smiled.

He felt as if he'd been caught at something bad, as if she'd just looked up and seen him touching himself. It was like—*oh God*—she knew what he was thinking. She couldn't know, but it was a knowing smile, a smile of satisfaction.

Nell was headed up the stairs of her apartment, her backpack dangling from one shoulder, when Mrs. Carpenter, her landlady, stopped her. The old woman's gaze darted over Nell's outfit—black hat and shapeless black dress—with disapproval before she spoke.

"Your phone was ringing off the hook," Mrs. Carpenter said. "I finally went up there and answered it. I was working in the garden, and it just kept blaring, and I was afraid there might be an emergency."

Nell's phone didn't ring. It made a more shrill, whirring sound, and she had left her bedroom window open. She was glad Mrs. Carpenter hadn't stumbled on the clothing piled on the floor as she'd waded in to answer.

There had been no chance to straighten up with school, work, and Charlie on her mind, but the landlady didn't seem concerned with the apartment's condition.

"It was a young man," Mrs. Carpenter said. "He sounded very ... excited, I guess you'd say. Almost desperate."

That had to be Michael, but Mrs. Carpenter was fumbling into the pocket of her gray gardening slacks for a message.

"He said he'd been trying to get in touch with you with some information. I thought it might be about schoolwork."

Nell nodded. Let her think what she wanted. She began to move. She didn't need Mrs. Carpenter's note, but the older woman seemed intent on finding it.

"He sounded like a nice young man," Mrs. Carpenter said. "I hope you're polite to him."

"I am," Nell said.

"It would do you good to get out more. I know you work so hard. Maybe someone to go to the movies with or whatever would be good for you. "

Nell wanted to bolt up the stairs. If Michael had sounded urgent to Mrs. Carpenter, he must have discovered something important. She wanted to rush up and dial him, but she felt trapped, not wanting to be rude. Mrs. Carpenter had been nice to her since her arrival here, and while she was nosy, she was well meaning.

"I know it's not my business, but you don't have family or anyone to look out for you here," Mrs. Carpenter said.

She looked down at the note in her hand. "Oh, that's my seed list," she said, pocketing it again and delving into her other pocket.

She drew out a piece of notepaper from one of the pads Nell had brought home from the store. It featured superheroes around the border in various action poses. Matt had had them printed over in Alexandria at a place called Printer's Ink.

Mrs. Carpenter offered it over to her. Michael's name was there along with his number, meticulously transcribed.

"That's not a local number," Mrs. Carpenter said. "It's a different area code, 312. Where is that?"

"Chicago," Nell said.

She wondered what Michael had learned. He must have turned up something he felt was significant if he'd called enough times to annoy Mrs. Carpenter. That was calling every few minutes. That was more than just an excuse to talk to her again.

He didn't just want another opportunity to flirt. He had something to tell her.

"Is he a relative?"

"Just a friend," Nell said. "Not a boyfriend or anything. He draws like I do."

"That's nice. So you have common interests?"

Nell nodded politely to Mrs. Carpenter, ending the conversation after evading a few more prying questions. She thanked her and tried not to run up the stairs. She took them two at a time, hoping the landlady wouldn't think she was being too eager to call a suitor.

Michael had learned of the little shop from his buddy Wayne Sales, who worked in a little comic book store. Wayne knew about the place because he'd met a Celtic witch selling jewelry at a science fiction and horror convention he'd attended recently to push comics.

Over coffee at a Rable Ranch outlet on Saturday, Wayne had given him directions.

"You already delve into some strange things in your work," Wayne noted while they watched the short-order cook who looked like a longshoreman fix their meal.

"I need to delve a little deeper," Michael said.

"Just be reminded these folks are strange," Wayne had said, and then he'd taken out one of his own business cards and scribbled an address on the back of it.

"How strange is strange?" Michael asked.

"They make those fringe folks at science fiction conventions look like normal, well-adjusted people," Wayne observed, shoving a bite of waffle between his lips.

Michael looked at the address for a moment before slipping it into his pocket. He looked at it again when he found the street listing. He thought at first he was turning into an alley, but it was a street, narrow and damp. On the corner was a cluster of youths who looked like their hobby would be stealing Social Security checks.

As the breeze drifted between the buildings that lined the stretch, it tickled crumpled paper cups and cans and rattled crushed newspapers which scratched across the pavement like bird claws.

Michael couldn't convince himself that the temperature did not drop when he stepped forward. That was mainly because it did. It was chilly as he moved along between the buildings, past narrow, shadowy doorways and barred windows.

He kept an eye peeled for winos. He didn't want to trip over anybody. He was beginning to wonder at which point he had stepped out of the known universe.

When he found the door to the shop, he didn't feel any different. A black drapery covered the inside glass, and strange golden markings decorated the panes. He saw no Open sign or even credit card stickers, universal confirmation that one was on Earth.

He wasn't sure if he should knock, or if he should just walk inside. He finally tried the knob, and it turned without resistance.

Stepping inside was like stepping farther away from reality. Crimson drapes of crushed velvet lined the walls, and displays cluttered the front room, gathering dust which added to their arcane strangeness.

A table with tarot cards laid out in a Celtic cross was set near the door. The brightly colored faces of the cards seemed to leer up at him, while beyond the table stood a brown, old-world globe on a pedestal.

Old maps had born the legend "Here there be tigers." He wondered if that same warning would apply to this dark little corner of the universe.

Behind the globe were shelves lined with musty, leather-bound books, their gold lettering flaking off. They reminded him of H. P. Lovecraft stories as he caught a whiff of their odor.

Beneath the leather volumes were newer books. Michael recognized some of them, including a book he'd been meaning to read—something called *Azarius* by Gable Tyler.

What appeared to be actual icons of saints hung on a rear wall, their rich colors shadowed in the dim light from the old, overhead fixtures dangling from cords. It had the look a tourist would expect, but it was too out of the way to be anything but sincere.

He was standing on the creaking wooden floor looking around for some sign of life when the old man appeared. He was wearing a white Neru jacket and white slacks, and he moved from behind a curtain in the rear wall. His steps were placed carefully, and he held his hands together in front of him. He looked like he belonged in a *Weird Tales* pulp story.

His skin was like the cracked leather on the books though a richer shade of brown, and hair the color of sterile cotton swirled about his head in wisps that stretched to his shoulders.

Despite his age—he could have been a thousand—his eyes were sharp and clear, and looking into them was like looking into the night itself.

Michael introduced himself. He thought about smiling, but when the old man didn't, he felt no obligation to try one in return.

"I am Vinoba," the old man said. He did not offer his hand nor make any other gesture of Western salutation.

Michael nodded toward him, a sort of bow, he hoped. "I was told you might be able to help me," he said.

The old man nodded, waiting.

Michael looked around the shop again. On another shelf trinkets, or what seemed to be trinkets, were on display. A statue, something like a mummy in a flowing red robe, walked near the edge, while beside it was a black miniature obelisk. A statue of Shiva stood beside it, dancing the creation once again.

The air seemed heavy in the place, and he could not seem to relax. He detailed bizarre worlds all the time in his work, but here, in this place in the real world, he did not feel at home.

"It's about dogs," he said. "They've killed people, and there's something mysterious. We think there may be black magic involved."

"Indeed?" the old man's snowy eyebrows arched upward, as if punctuating the odd stresses his accent placed on the word.

"You... might know something about this kind of thing?"

"Perhaps."

The old man moved forward and took his arm. "Come, we will speak with Father Alison."

He led Michael through the black curtain. Michael held his breath, half wondering if they were about to move through some dimensional doorway.

Instead, as the curtain pushed aside, he found they had stepped into a quite normal sitting room with Victorian furnishings. There was less dust here, and a marble-topped coffee table sat in front of the ornately carved sofa.

As if company had been expected, a silver tea service had been set up on the table, and a silver-haired priest in a dark shirt with Roman collar leaned over it.

When he heard the rustle of the curtain, he looked up and stood when he saw a guest. "How do you do?"

"I'm fine," Michael said.

"This is Father Jules Alison," Vinoba said.

"I believe they've caught him," Alison said.

Michael frowned. "Caught who?"

The priest chuckled. "The man who stole your barber's clippers."

Michael felt his cheeks flush as he brushed a lock of hair from his eyes. The priest seemed quite amused with his joke for he continued to grin.

Then he did offer a hand. After a pause, Michael shook it and found the grip somehow comforting.

"I'm given to the occasional jest. Forgive me."

He showed Michael to a seat and poured him a cup of tea. "What can we do for you?" There was some trace of accent in his voice, though Michael couldn't place it.

"I have a friend," he said. "She lives in Louisiana, where they have had some dog attacks. There seems to be something more to it than just wild animals. She asked me to see what I could find out because I write comic books and I do some occult research. The books I owned didn't offer much."

Father Alison nodded. "So you write about superheroes?"

"No. Scarier stuff, but I've never really thought of it as real."

"Do you know who we are?"

Michael shrugged. "I was just told you might be able to help."

"Perhaps. Vinoba and I may seem like a strange combination to you. A Hindu holy man and a Christian priest?"

"Yes."

"We met long ago," Father Alison said. "I was a young missionary in India. It was under British rule in those days. I'm afraid I'm a bit older than I look to you, older than Vinoba looks to you for that matter."

Michael nodded.

"We began to seek to determine the true nature of evil," the priest said. "First it was just a casual conversation as I sought to understand Vinoba's beliefs with a notion of converting him.

"We soon became intrigued by each other's concept of evil, however. We realized that we wanted to understand true evil in an effort to facilitate its defeat."

Michael nodded again and sipped the tea, more to have something to do with his hands than because he desired its taste.

"We have encountered evil in many forms over the years," Father Alison said. "We have met many people in similar quests. Have you ever heard of a man called Danube?"

"No."

"We met him long ago, and he taught us much. He works with an organization, an order of nuns which seeks to defeat evil also. We spoke to him recently. He had been to Louisiana. That's why I asked."

"I don't think my friend knows him either," Michael said.

"No matter. You have a problem."

"Well, these dogs have apparently killed some people, and my friend believes she may have picked up some kind of hint of psychic energy, I guess you'd say. She felt led to draw a picture of them, and they seem to be awful. The deaths caused by the dogs coincided with a woman's arrival in town. She seems mysterious."

"People have often wondered if animals could be evil," Father Alison said. "Many have thought black cats to be demons or witches' familiars. Goats have long been symbols of Satan or similar figures of evil, and other animals are discussed in various harvest rituals."

"What are the chances that something besides wild dogs could be on the prowl?"

Father Alison smiled. "Nine times out of ten things believed to be supernatural phenomenon, or super-science for that matter, prove to be unfounded. No one has proven ghosts exist or that UFOs are real. The Catholic Church still performs exorcisms and those have received a good deal of publicity in recent years, but what does that prove? Perhaps they're performed on people with psychological disorders."

"You're saying in all of your research you haven't found evidence of the supernatural?"

"He is only saying that we have learned to check things carefully," Vinoba interjected. "Much that seems in the realm of the paranormal is not."

"Well, there have been a couple of dog attacks. That could be natural, but Nell is convinced there's something more to it, partly because of this premonition. Partly because of other signs."

Father Alison was on his feet. He walked across the room as he listened to Michael's words. As he moved, he sipped from his cup and then returned it to the saucer from time to time.

"What other signs?" Vinoba asked.

"Well," Michael hesitated. "There have been some animal mutilations."

"Oh, that's always a sure sign of Satanic activity," Father Alison said, lifting his eyebrows. He was jesting again. "God did create scavengers, you know."

"I know there are plenty of scares about that sort of thing," Michael said. But when Nell explained it to me, I thought it sounded odd."

He paused a minute, watching Father Alison pace about. "They found a dog, a pregnant dog that is, with her puppies surgically removed."

The priest almost dropped his tea. He turned, juggling the saucer and cup, and stared at Michael, his piercing blue eyes threatening to sprout from the sockets.

Vinoba seemed disturbed by the news as well, but he didn't look at Michael. He looked at Father Alison, who looked back at Vinoba when he had finished staring at Michael. Apparently the priest was convinced Michael wasn't making it all up.

"You've heard of this kind of thing before?" Michael asked.

Slowly Father Alison nodded. "It could be a prank," he said. "It's not something that could not be dreamed up by schoolboys."

"But what?" Michael asked. "You're acting like it's, I don't know, something you've seen before."

"It has been known before," Vinoba said. "There are rituals you would not learn about in writing funnies. Not even in studying the occult in traditional volumes. There are things mentioned, dark things. Our friend Father Danube encountered hounds once. Long ago."

"It would be possible for you to make it up, but then again, there is a reality," Vinoba said. "We can do more research on it. If some ritual is being practiced, it would seem someone is pursuing the darkest of magic."

Nell dropped her books on the table beside her bed and snatched up the telephone, collapsing to a seat on her mattress as she dialed Michael's number from memory. She let it ring several times before his answering machine clicked on. At first he spoke in a voice that was supposed to be Devlin's, reporting that he couldn't come to the phone because he was battling the devilish hordes of Eldran.

Then Michael's real voice came on the line, asking that she leave a message at the tone. She started speaking when the answering machine beeped, but before she could finish, another beep sounded.

"Nell, I was wondering where you were," came Michael's real voice.

"I was at school. I take it you picked up on something."

"I went down to this little shop of horrors and talked to these magic men. I think they're authentic."

"I didn't tell you to go find con men, Michael. I asked you to see what you could dig up in your spell books."

"I don't have spell books. I looked through my books, and I didn't see anything that fit what you'd described. Then I went to see these guys, and they recognized the business about the mutilation, or at least they seemed to."

Her eyes widened, and she leaned sideways against her crumpled pillows. "They did?"

She could hear him rustling pages. "I made some notes," he said. "I didn't scribble down all of the names because I was trying to get the basics. There's an ancient ritual, traced back to Sumeria, maybe further. It speaks of doglike spirits."

She pressed the receiver harder against her ear, making sure she didn't miss anything because of the usual buzz on the line.

"Doglike spirits?" she asked, making sure she'd heard him correctly.

"Dogs for lack of a better description. They're supposed to be fierce demons, probably the basis for the phrase 'hellhounds,' probably the basis for legends like Cerberus too."

"Did you show them the picture?"

"Eventually. After I had them convinced I wasn't full of bullshit. Like I said, it was when I told them about the fetus removal that they started believing me. The hellhounds or whatever you want to call them are demon spirits, so like all demonic creatures, they don't have a physical form. Someone summoning them, using this ritual I mentioned, would have to provide them with vessels."

"And what better vessels than canine features?" She felt something worse than a chill wrapping around her.

"The really scary thing is that these demons are among the most difficult for a conjurer to control," Michael said.

"Did your friends offer any suggestions for stopping these monsters?"

"They said they'd look," Michael said. "They wanted to try to talk to another priest too."

"I hope they do it fast," Nell said.

All of this was beginning to feel more real than comic books.

Chapter 17

Charlie began to get nervous as soon as the bus dropped him off from school. When Nell had first mentioned it, spying on Miss Nielson had seemed exciting. Now, as the moment approached, things like the fear of getting caught were setting in.

The notion of spying on the teacher was fine in theory, especially when coupled with fantasies like the one from the dream, but after class today, it didn't seem as neat. Not after that look she had given him. If she could read his thoughts—*of course she couldn't but what if?*—what was to keep her from knowing they were watching her, trying to find out secrets about her?

If she had secrets, dark secrets, she wouldn't want them delving into her life. She wouldn't want them doing so anyway, invading her privacy, but if her privacy involved something bad, retribution became more likely.

The fear of Miss Nielson wasn't the only thing to consider either. The dogs were still out there, still striking, and he hadn't forgotten the last time he'd gone out. Maybe the sounds when he jogged across the vacant lot had been imagination, or maybe they'd been real. And Nell had been scared shitless the other night, even driving in a car. That must mean something was out there. Mass hysteria wasn't chewing up kids—*kids who had something against you, Charlie.*

Something real was doing that, so probably the fears he and Nell, and possibly others too, were experiencing were real.

He went into the kitchen and got a canned drink from the refrigerator. He was headed up to the office to play computer games when his mom met him in the living room.

"Just thought I'd check on how you were doing," she said.

"Fine," he said, not exactly grumbling but not exactly chipper either. He *was* just in from school. He couldn't be expected to be energetic.

"I just know you've been through a lot," his mom said. There was a genuine sound of concern in her voice. "You were quiet all weekend. Your father and I both noticed it."

He had been quiet, worried about everything. He hadn't been able to concentrate on reading or anything else. His mother's concern was unexpected, however. Sometimes she seemed so caught up in her own business that she didn't notice him.

"If you need to talk, I'm here," she said.

He nodded, then headed on upstairs. He thought about calling Delia but decided he could do that later when she'd had time to rest. They hadn't had much chance to talk at school today, and they had only spoken briefly over the weekend. He'd been too nervous to ask her out so soon after the funeral. She'd had some kind of club meeting to go to today.

Barbara felt sticky when she got home, so she peeled off her clothes and stepped into the shower, taking her time to soap herself with a bar of Dove. If she saw Sawyer later, she needed to be freshened up anyway.

For a long time she hadn't wanted to shower. Not after Doss. The shower had been the first sign he wasn't what she'd thought he was.

They'd been playing one afternoon, lounging around the apartment, tickling and necking on the couch. She liked snuggling with him, and he could be so gentle. He liked to run his hand through her hair.

When he'd suggested the shower, the idea hadn't sounded unpleasant. She'd peeled her clothes off, then his, kissing his chest and running her fingers over his cock as they moved into the bathroom.

While he sat on the closed lid of the toilet, she turned on the water, holding her fingers under the tap until it was warm. She smiled at him as they waited. He smiled back, hungrily.

When the water was right, she pulled up the stob, letting the needlelike spray begin.

Then they had stepped beneath it, letting the water wash over them as they embraced and kissed and ran their hands over each other. They had known each other's body well, but there was something different as they became wet and slippery. It was new again, fresh, exciting at once. She ran her hands over his smooth chest, watching the water shine on his tanned skin.

Leaning forward, she kissed his shoulders and nipples, his body blocking the shower spray from her eyes. She felt his hands slide behind her, and he massaged her shoulders. As she pulled back, he let his hands slide to her breasts, fondling them while he looked into her eyes.

He had a predatory look. That was fine. She loved his touch. Sometimes he could almost bring an orgasm with his fingertips against her cheek. There was something about him, a magnetism, an air, that made him as desirable as any man she'd ever seen.

She leaned forward, meeting his lips, biting at his mouth without using her teeth. His kiss back was almost passive. She slipped her arms around his waist, gripping her forearm with her hand behind his back, pulling herself to him. Her breasts flattened against his chest, and she moved her hips, letting her pubic hair brush against him in an effort to bring more arousal.

He grunted slightly.

She kissed his shoulder again and his neck, sticking out her tongue to lick at the water. A tight grin formed on his lips, and she felt him hardening. Results.

"I love you, baby," she whispered.

He slid a hand around her, cupping one cheek of her ass and squeezing it softly. She felt little pleasure needles there, as if his fingertips were electrically charged.

She kissed his ear, closing her eyes against the spray of the water that came over his shoulder, and she ran one leg up and down his side, moving her knee over his hip.

Her own nipples were hard, and she felt a throbbing desire inside her. She wanted to impale herself on him and wrap her legs around him.

She rubbed her face against his shoulder, then inched back from him so that she could kiss his chest again.

He stood almost like a statue, letting her make the efforts, apparently enjoying her advances.

She slid her hands over his pectorals, then downward, caressing his hard stomach. She sensed in his lack of resistance that he wanted her to take him in her hands.

She didn't mind complying. She encircled his hardness with one hand, caressing the foreskin. It was easy to slide her palm up and down its moist length.

She then brought her other hand around, cradling him between her palms, handling it almost gingerly. It had brought her so much pleasure.

He grunted again, and she touched the tip with her thumb. It was warm and hard, giving only slightly.

She started to manipulate him with more aggression, pulling in an effort to intensify his pleasure.

His hand dropped down then and held her wrist, pulling her right hand away. For a moment she thought she had hurt him and looked to his face, pulling her hair back over one ear as she let him see her puzzlement.

The expression he gave in return showed that he had not felt pain. No, it wasn't a matter of his being hurt, just a matter of her doing the wrong thing. It wasn't her hands he wanted to produce his climax.

She felt her throat tighten, and something inside her also clenched. She'd never thought of him wanting … that, but …

She slowly bent her legs until she was kneeling, her knees sensitive to the hard tub bottom. She kissed the flat muscles of his stomach, holding him with only one hand now, trying to get ready.

She wanted to please him, and his hands slid into the wet tangles of her hair, urging her to proceed. She closed her eyes …

… opened her mouth …

… took him in.

His hand cupped the back of her head now, forcing her forward, and an even louder sigh and groan issued through his lips.

She felt some of the water spattering down onto her shoulders, heard its soft rap against the shower curtain, but those sensations seemed far away.

He was filling her, the organ throbbing inside her mouth, jamming into her throat. She felt the muscles contract. She had seen this kind of thing in porno movies, had even thought about it, but with all her experience this was her first time to perform this act.

She thought she would choke. A couple of times she gagged but managed to contain the convulsion. He might get mad if she expelled him before he was ready.

She groaned herself, somewhere down in her stomach. The pressure of his hands hurt her scalp, and the wonderful slippery texture that had felt so exciting in her hands was different on her tongue. It tasted ugly and seemed alien. It didn't belong in her mouth, and she felt degraded for having it there. Why had he wanted this from her? If she had offered willingly, that would have been one matter, but to be coaxed into it—*of course if he wanted it he had to coax because that was the only way it was going to happen*—seemed almost like a violation.

It was a violation, she decided. He was taking advantage of her because he realized how much she cared about him and how much she was attracted to him, as well as how much she needed the security he provided.

She'd never realized that he had that side to his nature. He was doing this not for the pleasure it provided. It was more a matter of domination. It was to subdue her, to conquer her.

She was about to pull back when he burst inside her, hot lava coursing into her throat. The taste of it was awful, sickening. She'd read what men ate could affect what their fluids tasted like. He must have been eating something rank and sickening.

She pulled back now, spitting, trying to get it out of her mouth. She was leaning forward, eyes closed and stinging from the water, head tilted down, reaching with one hand to find some of the shower spray. His hand caught her on the cheek, slapping her face to the side. Her other cheek brushed along the shower curtain, and her brain reeled.

The pain was not severe, but there was a sharp rush of hurt, emotional more than physical. Tears came immediately, mingling with the water on her face. She still wanted to get the taste out of her mouth but she couldn't manage to spit.

She started to move, was trying to pick herself up, when his hand fell on her shoulder, pushing her back down. Her knees slammed painfully against the hard porcelain. She was afraid a kneecap might have cracked.

She didn't try to rise anymore, but he still slapped her again. She slumped down onto her side now, crying. She hoped he wouldn't hit her more or kick her. She waited, eyes clenched, wondering if he would attack again. He didn't. Not immediately.

He just stood there for a moment. She didn't try to peek up at him, not even through the corner of her eye because the water was stinging. She wouldn't make it worse or give him more satisfaction by seeing her cry.

She felt her heart pounding as she waited for him to move, or hit her again. But he was a statue.

Then, he finally turned, and she heard the squeak of the shower faucet as he shut off the water. She felt some relief as the spray stopped. Maybe he was about to leave. She would be glad when he did. Then she could get this taste out of her mouth and begin to stop feeling so degraded.

If she could just get her throat clean, it would make a difference. She wouldn't have something lingering to remind her of this humiliation. She would forget it as she had forgotten all assaults. She'd leave this place and find her a rich man, someone to buy her dinner at The Abbey and a nice penthouse in Buckhead.

The hell with this bastard. The hell with him. He'd hurt her all he could. She ached at the thought of love being lost, but it was false love. How could she love this man? He was attractive, but he was cruel, so cruel and mean.

She willed him to leave her. She wanted to be alone. She would stay curled here in this place for a long time. Alone, safe.

She heard him laugh.

She didn't move, but she felt anger growing. Damn him. Damn him to Hell itself.

She was about to move when she felt it, hot and sudden. She was still, but as she realized what was happening, the hurt burned into her soul, deeper, to the very core.

His urine ran off her shoulder and down across her neck and breasts.

She felt tears in her eyes as she rinsed the Flex conditioner from her hair. The scent of it, fresh and clean, made her feel washed and pure, but the memory was ugly and more vivid than it should have been. She had thought by coming here she would escape some of the past, but it was with her after all.

When she stepped from the tub and wound a towel around her hair, she called Sawyer and told him she wasn't feeling well.

Matt noticed Nell's impatience and decided to let her go early. He didn't know what she had to do though he suspected it was something involving her investigation of the deaths. If it made her happy, that was fine, as long as she didn't get into trouble. He warned her to be careful.

He figured whatever she was up to was harmless. It probably gave her a sense of adventure. He couldn't argue with that as he leaned back with a comic book.

Nell drove home as the darkness began to settle. She felt the nervousness returning, but it wasn't as severe as it had been. Maybe she was getting used to it.

She managed to make it to her room without attracting Mrs. Carpenter's attention. There she changed into black pants and a black turtleneck. If they were going to lurk in the shadows, it was best to be prepared for it.

She tried Charlie's number after she was dressed. Busy signal.

She went to the bathroom, returned, fixed herself a snack, ate. Dialed again.

Busy signal.

She tried some homework, did some sketches, read some comic books. Dialed again.

Busy signal.

She started a letter, crumpled it, and thought about what Michael had said. Dialed again.

Busy signal.

She doodled, paced, considered the dark secrets of Barbara Nielson, and felt her anxiety growing. What could be behind the conjuring of some forgotten demons, providing them with canine vessels for modern life? This had to be dangerous.

Dialed again.

It rang. Charlie answered.

"Who the hell have you been talking to?"

"Delia. I didn't get to see her long at school today."

"Great." Something terrible was going on and he was falling in love. That was good, but distractions were dangerous.

"Sorry," he said. He sounded genuine.

"It's okay. I didn't mean to snap."

"I'm feeling weird about going tonight," Charlie said. "I was daydreaming about Miss Nielson today, and she looked up like she knew I was watching. What if she expects us tonight?"

"We'll be careful. I don't think she's that kind of mind reader, but she is playing with magic."

She told him what Michael had learned.

"Weird," Charlie said. His voice cracked, revealing his fear. "What if she knows we're investigating her?"

"She's bound to suspect. We have to figure out what she's up to before she can do something to us. Charlie, you're one of my best friends. I don't want anything to happen to you."

Was he her only friend? Besides Matt, whom did she really have? She couldn't let Charlie be lured into some bizarre relationship with Miss Nielson.

"We need to check her out," he agreed finally. "My mom will never let me out after dark, though. I'll have to take the tree down like I did the other night. Can you meet me at the road?"

"Sure. That'll be best."

"What time?"

"Eight-thirty?"

"Yeah, that should be good. That should be plenty of time."

While he waited, he worried. The conversation with Delia had been fun, exciting. There'd never been a girl interested in him before.

She had rattled on about her club meeting and they had talked about doing something together, something like the visit to the café except without Mom in tow. The tingling anticipation that created made him feel almost like leaping into the air.

He felt a fresh twinge of guilt when he thought about Budd, and he felt another little pang when he considered the things Budd had told him about Delia. He couldn't really be jealous of his dead friend, but he did feel something, a discomfort when he remembered Budd's descriptions of Delia's anatomy and their liaison.

That could be overcome, though. She was nice and sweet, and she didn't seem to mind that he wasn't a jock.

The next step was for them to have a real date, or at least for them to get together after school.

Hopes for that would be destroyed if he got nailed tonight. He'd be grounded for spying on the teacher and being out with the hounds around. That would mean no chance of getting a reprieve from the precautionary afternoon trips straight home.

He had no way out of going with Nell, however. She was right. There was something odd about the way Miss Nielson acted toward him, and the people attacked by the dogs were all connected to him. They had to come up with some answers.

If they could just get this mess out of the way, find a way to stop anybody else from being hurt, he could get back to normal.

He watched the second hand on the clock in the office roll slowly around the dial while he tried to play games. He wasn't successful. Nothing seemed to occupy his already busy thoughts.

As the time approached, he began to worry that his parents were not going to be in their respective places. If they were still bustling around the house as they seemed to be now, sneaking out would be hard. They were looking for some kind of paper right now. He could hear their voices occasionally in the hall.

Not good. Not good at all. They needed to be settled. If not, they might come into his room and find the screen missing.

He wanted the risks at a minimum. Facing the hungry dogs was bad enough. Having his parents angry was a nightmare.

As the clock ticked closer to the rendezvous time, his parents were still milling about. He swore at them under his breath. Why did they have to pick tonight to vary their routine? Normally his father would have run him out of the computer room by now, and his mother would be settled in front of the television set.

He drummed his fingers and then tapped his feet, trying to handle the anticipation. After a while he climbed from the chair and walked down the hall to his room. He could hear his mom and dad talking at the foot of the stairs, squabbling because something was misplaced.

Each was trying to blame the other. Maybe that would keep them busy. If he closed his door, they probably wouldn't bother him.

Of course it would only take one knock for them to figure out something was wrong. He sat on the foot of the bed, looking at his posters. He hadn't thought about movies or anything related in days. He needed to try to work on a horror script or something if he was ever going to get anything accomplished. He'd been distracted, though. Good excuse.

He looked out the window. It was dark. Almost time for him to head out. He felt a shiver. The dogs were out there somewhere, no doubt about that.

There was plenty to worry about even if he didn't think about Miss Nielson telepathically realizing an intrusion. He listened for sounds of howling.

———

Nell found the same terror from the night before creeping over her as she pulled her car to a stop near the roadway's edge. Mist swirled around her, and she kept imagining the dogs were concealed by it but watching her.

Since there was no sign of Charlie, she had to kill the engine and wait, and she decided not to play the radio. She didn't want the battery dead if the dogs attacked. She wanted to be able to get the hell out of there.

She watched the second hand on her watch, occasionally glancing out through the windshield, straining her eyes as she tried to pick out Charlie's form.

It was impossible with the fog and the darkness. She imagined it must be like being at sea. She needed a yellow slicker and a rain hat, and a lantern. That would make the combination complete.

A lantern might not actually be a bad idea, she decided.

Charlie knew the designated spot, but how easy would it be to find in the darkness? She leaned over and opened the glove compartment, fumbling for the flashlight she'd stashed there.

She had to dig through a dozen scraps of paper, but finally her fingers closed on it, an Eveready plastic job, aquamarine in color. Matt had given it to her because he worried about her driving home after dark.

She was disappointed in the beam when she flipped it on, but it was better than nothing, and better than risking running down the car battery by turning on the headlights. She rolled the window down quickly and placed the flashlight's flat end on the hood so that the beam aimed skyward.

When she decided the light was balanced, she jerked her hand back inside quickly, praying it wouldn't be nabbed by hounds' jaws. She could tell the light above her made a bit of a glow on the fog, the best beacon she could offer. If it attracted any other attention, it wouldn't matter. It would only make people curious. If Rice happened to be on patrol, he'd only find she was out here trying to take some action, going out of her mind in the meantime.

She wished she'd brought a sketch pad or something to kill time, but she hadn't thought about needing something to keep her busy on an operation like this. The Dirty Dozen never needed time killers on their intricately planned missions. Of course they did have some little poem they'd said in the first movie. Her father had let her watch that on the VCR because it was his favorite film.

Where the hell was Charlie? She'd be doing math problems in her head in another five minutes.

She felt a tingling sensation on the back of her neck and jerked around in the seat. She knew the dog was there, knew he'd placed his front paws on the rear bumper so that he could peer through the windshield.

She knew she'd see red eyes glowing as he peered at her, knew she'd see his hot breath fogging the glass.

She knew she would see all of these things.

But she didn't.

She saw …

… nothing.

Nothing at all.

She turned back into her seat and tilted her head back with her eyes closed, telling herself to calm down.

If they tried for her, they'd have to hit the car. They wouldn't make it inside on the first try—the glass wouldn't shatter that easily—so she would have time to start the engine and drive away.

She said that over and over to herself, making it her mantra.

She was clutching the steering wheel and breathing heavily when Charlie tapped on the glass. She almost yanked the wheel off the dash.

"You scared the shit out of me," she said as she reached over and opened his door.

"That was kind of obvious," he said.

"Sometimes I restate the obvious for effect."

He pulled his door shut again and locked it. She was starting the engine when she remembered the light.

She rolled down her window and grabbed it, flipping the switch as she handed it to Charlie. He was wearing a blue windbreaker that was damp from the night.

"Much trouble getting out?" she asked.

"Not really. My parents are looking for something, probably the savings bond for my college education."

"Least they care."

"Sometimes I wonder."

She leaned over the wheel, trying to keep the car on track. The fog was worse than the other night, and her headlights still didn't do much good with it.

"We need a foghorn," she said.

"Yeah," Charlie agreed. "I guess that'd scare the dogs."

Chapter 18

The fog was lifting some when the car eased to a curbside stop a few hundred feet from Miss Nielson's apartment building. The streetlights were beginning to become visible, their rays illuminating the ground beneath them rather than just glowing like dragon's eyes through smoke.

Nell killed the engine, but they didn't climb out immediately. Neither had to contemplate what was in the other's thoughts. They sat, both nervous, both considering turning back.

"What can we really learn from this?" Charlie asked.

"Who knows?" Nell whispered, a loud, tense whisper of frustration.

"Maybe there are other things we can do to check her out," Charlie suggested.

"Like what? I've already tried looking into her past, but it doesn't go that far, at least not in the places I can check."

Charlie swallowed. "That's what's scary," he said. "That and what your friend said about the dogs."

"Yeah. Scary."

She looked at Charlie. "Shall we?"

He shrugged. They were here now. They might as well move ahead. They climbed slowly from the car, meeting in front of the grill. Nell took the flashlight back, and they started along the sidewalk.

They fought impulses to creep forward hunched over. They were just walking along a sidewalk. They weren't supposed to be out, but just walking here didn't mean they were doing something wrong. They weren't, Nell reasoned. Yet.

There was not a lot of need for stealth at the moment, anyway. The town seemed deserted, and the darkness and fog offered more concealment. There were lights on in a few houses, and now and then they passed one with a television screen visible through the front window, but others were dark and empty, looking haunted.

When they reached the front of Miss Nielson's building, they paused. The windows in her apartment were dark.

"A bit early to be in bed," Nell said.

"I guess," Charlie agreed. He was looking at the tree. It was the one from the dream, and if he climbed it, he was worried he would look down and see Budd's walking corpse. *Budd covered in blood!*

They'd buried him. Charlie had seen the funeral, but that didn't mean anything. He'd look down and see that face covered like a mask with dried blood. The stark eyes staring up at him in accusation.

Could Budd blame him? Was Budd's death somehow his fault? That was part of why he had to find out if Nell was right. If she was, then they had to do something.

He couldn't mourn for the others as much though he felt bad about them being hurt, but for Budd he could feel the anguish. Dammit.

"We'll see what we can find out," he said, leading Nell across the damp ground in front of the building. "Keep the light off."

They did crouch now, ducking into shadows while looking over their shoulders. Now they were where they didn't belong. They needed to avoid detection.

When they reached the tree, Charlie looked up the twisted trunk. It had plenty of handholds and knots. He could climb it. Nell could stand watch. She'd notice any walking corpses that looked like they belonged in a George Romero movie. Of course they would approach in color, which would mean they belonged in the Tom Savini version.

No matter. He had a lookout. He hesitated only a moment, then started up the trunk. His skinned hands were sensitive, but the bark was a bit smoother on this tree. He found the bends and twigs to grip, and his sneakers provided traction.

In only a couple of minutes he was able to settle into a nook on a limb which provided a vantage straight into the living room. The curtains were open there but the room was dark except for a small night light, something plugged directly into a wall socket, probably so she didn't stumble over the furniture if she got up in the middle of the night. Or was it there to let him know the room was empty? What if she was setting a trap?

He let his gaze move sideways. The bedroom curtains were drawn. He could detect no sliver of light behind them either. All seemed still in the apartment.

"What do you see?" Nell asked from below in a loud whisper.

"Nothing. She's not in there."

"You sure?"

"Yes."

He scrambled out of his nook, descended a few feet, then dropped to the ground. He landed in a crouch that drew complaints from his ankles, but he straightened quickly and dusted himself off.

"If she's not there, maybe we should go inside," Nell suggested.

"You mean break in?"

"Maybe she didn't lock the door. We're in Petittville after all."

"What if she did, and we get caught?"

"You'll get a slap on the wrist for hanging out with a girl who's legally adult. I'll be the one in trouble."

"I don't want that either."

"Charlie, people are dying. This woman could be responsible."

"I know. I know." He thought of Budd again. The sigh that followed conveyed his agreement.

They followed the shadows into the breezeway between rows of doors where wooden steps led up to the second floor. After checking the mailboxes on the wall, they started their ascent. The steps creaked beneath their weight, but they didn't make enough noise to draw attention. People in the other apartments weren't going to look out just because somebody walked up the stairs. That happened all the time.

When they reached the door with Miss Nielson's number, confirmed by the mailboxes, Nell knocked softly. There were no bells or buzzers to press.

Even in the chill night air, Charlie's skin seemed hot, hot the way it felt when he got into trouble. When he was fussed at or about to be nailed for something, his skin always burned this way. He could feel buckets of sweat pour out his armpits too. In biology they'd learned that sweat, perspiration they called it in the textbook, wasn't always because of temperature. Anxiety could trigger it also. That wasn't something new, everybody was aware of that, but he was confirming it tonight. Hey, he was becoming a B&E artist and completing a science project in one connected effort.

He sighed again while they waited for an answer at the door. If Miss Nielson showed up, dressed in a nightgown with a robe clutched closed around her, he'd need an excuse.

He tried to come up with something while the seconds fell like hammer blows. It would be hard to convince her they were here selling cookies. Nell looked a little old to be a Girl Scout.

And *shit*, even if she wasn't here, but that mind-reading business was accurate. She'd know what they were up to. And if that business Nell had found out about the dogs was true, if they were some kind of mystical hellhounds, then maybe Miss Nielson could make them materialize inside the apartment.

He felt his bladder straining, and he held his breath until they decided the door would not be answered. Then, Nell tried the knob. It turned only a fraction.

Locked.

That made Nell hesitate all of two seconds. Then she reached into her hip pocket and slipped out her driver's license. It was a couple of years old, laminated in sturdy plastic. After tapping Charlie on the shoulder to urge his service as a lookout, she began to work on the door.

He was peering back down the stairs, watching the fog swirl outside the breezeway, when he heard the door ease away from its facing. She'd managed.

Gripping his arm, she pulled him inside, closing the door again before switching on the flashlight.

As the dim beam swept across the room, there seemed to be nothing out of the ordinary. In one corner were some boxes, indicators that she hadn't been living here long. She hadn't finished unpacking.

That made him feel guilty, reminded him they were invaders here, stepping into someone's private world. Nell apparently didn't feel the same thing.

She moved toward the room's center, aiming the flashlight here and there, studying the walls and looking over the furniture. On a table near the door were the schoolbooks and a planning calendar. Miss Nielson's coat was draped over a chair at the table almost tucked into a corner of the room. It was the dining table, looking a bit rickety.

The couch and matching chairs had also seen better days. Charlie for an instant felt bad that she did not have nicer things.

Over the couch on the wall was a painting of a conquistador, acrylic caked thick on the canvas to give the hard features a dark reality. Nell shook her head as she focused the flashlight on it. Then she moved on.

"What are you hoping to find?" Charlie asked.

"Something we can take to Chief Rice, I guess, something that will confirm the occult angle on this. If we can convince him, maybe he can do something about all this."

Charlie still felt humbled. They were invading someone's privacy, intruding on a private world.

They moved on into the bedroom, where the sheets and blanket were still in a tangle atop the mattress. A nightgown hung across the bottom of the bed, and some socks were strewn on the floor near the brown dresser.

A few bits of jewelry were spread on the countertop along with some pennies. An assortment of perfume bottles was also there. Most of them had barely been used while a couple were almost empty. No mystery about her favorites.

Nell made a quick check of the drawers and found only clothing. Closing them back carefully, she turned to the closet, a walk-in with louvered doors.

She folded one of them back. Inside there were dresses and skirts hanging neatly on the hangers. Rows of shoes lined the closet floor.

Nell shined the light on the shelf above the hangers, but it was almost barren. She would have missed the box if she had not knelt on the carpet and aimed the light past the shoes.

It was almost hidden beneath the hemlines, sequestered in a corner, a small brown corrugated box with the flaps folded over each other. She reached inside and began to pull it open.

"That's her private stuff," Charlie warned.

Nell looked back over her shoulder at him with an exasperated expression. Realizing he might not be able to read it in the darkness, she put the light under her chin. "That's kind of the idea," she said. "We're looking for secrets. Now give me a hand."

Reluctantly, Charlie helped her tug the box out, and when they had set it on the bed, she peeled the flaps open. It was stuffed with a variety of junk. Playing cards and dry cell batteries, a couple of old issues of *Vanity Fair*, a can of stain protector like they always pushed to you at shoe stores and a McDonald's Christmas tree ornament. It played "Jingle Bells" when Nell pushed it.

Beneath the junk she found some things that were more interesting. Photographs and some letters.

The pictures were snapshots, stacked together and bound with a rubber band. She untwisted it and held them in front of the light. The colors were beginning to fade.

They showed Barbara Nielson posing or caught in candid moments in an apartment somewhere. In one she had her hands in dishwater and she was laughingly trying to prevent the picture.

In another, she wore denim shorts and a T-shirt and was pretending to look sexy. In another she was standing with a blond-haired man. It was a sunny morning, and they had apparently been washing a red sports car that was in the background.

Nell studied the man's face. He wasn't from Petittville, at least he'd never come in the store. Yet something was familiar about him. She looked at his eyes, but they were hard to make out in the photograph. It was too small.

"Recognize him?" she asked, showing the picture to Charlie.

"No." He pursed his lips, not pouting, not quite.

She shuffled on through the snapshots. There were none conveniently snapped at coven meetings. Nothing came that easily.

Putting them back in their original order, she wrapped them in the rubber band again. Then she began to shuffle through the letters. One was the letter of acceptance from the Riverland Parish School Board office. It was addressed to a P.O. Box in Dunwoody. All she'd had to do was rent a P.O. Box in the right place. What an easy façade.

Another was a piece of junk mail. The third was signed by somebody named Tigges. The first name was a scrawl or perhaps just an initial. She couldn't make it out.

It proved to be just a note of thanks. Apparently she'd lived next door to him at some point and watered his plants while he was on vacation.

Naturally the return address was a scrawl as well, and the post mark was faint, the ink smeared. Was it an Atlanta address? It was hard to tell.

"What do you think?" she asked Charlie.

"Looks like Athens, Georgia."

"What about the street?"

"Shriner?"

"Could be. A Mr. Tigges on Shriner Street in Athens, Georgia. Hope we can locate him."

"You're going to call him?"

"I'm going to try."

She put the box back, trying to make it look like it had when she'd found it. Then she eased the door back into place. Her nerves were tingling a bit too much for her to do any more searching rationally. This was probably the one chance to locate information, though. If Mr. Tigges didn't pan out, she had nothing.

Nothing to help Charlie.

Nothing to restore the town to normal.

She swept the flashlight across the room again. Anything? Anything at all? Papers that indicated Barbara Nielson's real identity? Maybe she was too smart for that.

She was obviously too smart to have anything resembling an occult icon on hand. The closest thing Nell could locate was a cotton ball holder in the bathroom with a golden unicorn stenciled on its lid, hardly something that could serve as evidence. Otherwise the bathroom was filled with the usual toiletries. Some soap in the shape of seashells, Edge shaving cream, a lady Gillette, a Tampax box, towels, wash cloths. Aim toothpaste.

Leading Charlie literally by the hand, grasping his palm for security as much as to reassure him, Nell moved back into the living room.

Newspapers were piled on an end table, recent issues of the *Aimsley Daily Clarion*, nothing special about them. The reports of the dog attacks were not circled or highlighted. In fact the papers did not seem to have been read.

The anxiety was becoming too great. They had to get out of here. Wherever Barbara Nielson might be, she could return at any time.

They moved back to the front door. Nell eased it open and peered out before deeming it safe. They scrambled outside, pressing the lock mechanism before leaving.

Nell felt a rush of relief course through her. They'd made it. Trying to maintain the silence, they scrambled down the stairs and back outside.

With the shadows, she felt better. All was going well. As they headed back for her car, she felt like skipping. Charlie heard them first.

One moment he and Nell were walking along. The next he was standing still. His hand shot over and clutched Nell's forearm. She almost dropped the flashlight.

Then she realized why he had grabbed her. She could hear the thundering approach also, and she was not deluded this time. It wasn't imagination. There were dogs coming.

"Run," she said. She started forward, switching hands with the flashlight so that she could take Charlie's hand again.

They charged forward, skirting off the sidewalk and ducking through a narrow driveway. That took them across a couple of front lawns until they found a hedge and followed it a short distance back to a narrow street.

Cracked and less traveled, it snaked over a couple of hills. It was the one that connected with the Aimsley First Bank branch drive-through, Nell realized.

They sprinted along it, figuring there'd be no cars on it. The houses along this stretch were dark. Even in daylight this part of town seemed dark and deserted. Tonight it was like a cemetery.

She began to get reminders that she hadn't had strenuous P.E. classes in a while as they hurled themselves forward. Their pace slowed as they moved up the hills, but they made better time on the way down, and the bank's parking lot was flat ground.

They charged across it, rushing through the narrow drive-through channel. Nell considered the possibility of scrambling up onto the drive-through's overhang, but discounted it. The dogs might be able to jump that high. They weren't normal dogs after all.

She looked back over her shoulder as they moved onto the next street. The hounds were still in pursuit, traveling almost as a single black entity, a pursuing cloud visible in the parking lot's white lights.

With Charlie still at her side, she moved across the narrow street outside the drive-through. Another parking lot stretched out on the other side, neglected and cracked since it was behind a closed Riverland Parish Library, branch.

"We're never going to get away," Charlie said, panting. This run wasn't doing him any good either.

"We've got … to … try," she managed.

Their shoes echoed on the concrete …

… echoed because …

… the damned place dead-ended. It was like a canyon.

A brick wall stretched along the edge of the lot, separating it from the tire business on the other side. The top edge of it was well over their heads. Even jumping, Nell couldn't reach the edge. The chances of scrambling up the sheer surface were unlikely. It was brick, smooth red brick with the indentations slight.

"Leg up?" Charlie asked.

The dogs had to be getting close.

She nodded. "I'll go up and then help you."

"Fine. Hurry!"

He dropped to one knee and laced his fingers together to create a stirrup. He was shaking badly and he kept looking over his shoulder.

The dogs were coming!

She missed his hand the first time she tried to place her foot, and they almost tangled in each other's limbs. "We've got to move," Charlie warned.

She dropped the flashlight. It rolled about, beam bouncing and finally stopping, aimed at the dogs' end of the lot. Without looking back, she slid her foot into Charlie's hands and stuck her hands heavenward as he lifted.

Holding her breath, she tried to help him by clawing at the wall. It was too smooth for her to do much good, but she soon felt her fingers edging over the top.

She draped her arm over the brick and pulled, kicking with her feet, grinding them against the wall with as much traction as she could manage.

Finally she was able to swing her knee up over the wall's edge. Using that grip, she hoisted herself upward. Her first inclination was to jump immediately to safety on the other side.

She knew the dogs were coming. In a moment they would be at the base of the wall, and they might be big enough to jump up at her.

She lay on the narrow brick surface and forced herself to turn her head, knowing she couldn't leave Charlie. Leaning down might give the hounds access to her arm so that they could sink their teeth into her and drag her back into their jaws, but she couldn't desert her friend.

"Give me your hand," she screamed as she reached down for Charlie, but he wasn't looking up at her.

He was standing with his back to the wall now, frozen by the sight of the approaching pack. They were thundering across the lot, their red tongues lagging out the corners of their mouths as their pounding feet drew them closer and closer.

"Charlie," she screeched.

He jerked his head upward and reached for her hand. She realized as his fingers closed around hers that they weren't going to make it. The dogs were too close.

She pulled, but even though Charlie was skinny, he was heavy. Lifting him wasn't easy. She reached down with her other hand, gripping his wrist.

He tried to push off, tried to help her, but they couldn't manage. Not in the time available. The dogs were coming.

The dogs were here.

Charlie looked back over his shoulder as they formed a semicircle around him.

Nell felt a scream forming. Her lungs tightened, and the sound started trying to struggle out of her throat. She sensed her grip on Charlie's hand relaxing, and he let go of her as well.

His hands dropped to his sides, and he breathed heavily.

The dogs were only looking at him.

One lay down, almost humbled. Others turned their heads, and a couple of them whined.

"What is it?" Nell asked. When she spoke, one of the dogs looked up and snapped. Its paws scraped the bricks as it tried to climb up at her.

She jerked her arms in and prepared to dive off the wall on the other side if necessary.

As Charlie looked at it, however, the dog did not seem interested in pursuing her. It rolled onto its side at Charlie's feet. In his presence, all of them seemed as gentle as puppies.

"What is it?" he asked.

"I don't know." She gripped the edge of the wall and looked down at them. She couldn't believe it either.

"Get out of here," Charlie commanded.

The dogs hesitated, looking at him, cocking their heads inquisitively.

"Go on. Get out of here."

They did as they were told, turning and running back across the parking lot, disappearing into the night.

Chapter 19

His parents were waiting in the front yard as he approached the house. He felt a spasm in his chest when he saw them. There would be no slipping in the back door or shinnying up the tree trunk. The fog had lifted enough for him to make them out clearly in the light cast by the porch bulb. They had the look of two worried people.

His father was still wearing his sports shirt from work, but the sleeves were rolled up and it was open at the collar. His mother must have already changed for bed before they discovered him missing because she was wearing her long quilted robe. She had probably gone in to kiss him good night and discovered his absence.

He knew when they saw him there would be trouble. He watched his father check his watch, watched his mother pacing along the front walk at Dad's side. The terror he'd felt while he and Nell were trying to escape the dogs didn't compare with the anguish that wound its way through his intestines.

Its intensity grew as he moved forward, emerging from the darkness into their line of vision. The porch light's glow reached a long way, so they could watch him approach. Their relief had turned to anger by the time he was upon them.

"Where the hell have you been?" his father demanded.

"I was riding around with Nell," he said, bowing his head slightly.

"Do you have any idea how dangerous it is out there? Those dogs could be anywhere."

Charlie knew. He wanted to tell them that, that he had seen them and they hadn't bothered him so there was no reason to keep him in protective custody. He almost blurted that out, but he knew it wouldn't be believed. Also he and Nell had decided they wouldn't discuss the dogs' reaction with anyone. At least not until they understood it better.

It didn't make sense. Why would they attack others and leave Charlie alone? Unless they were tied to Miss Nielson somehow and the way she reacted to him.

"I'm okay," he said.

"Let's go inside," his mother suggested. She was looking around as if she expected the dogs to show up on the front lawn. She was probably worried about the neighbors too.

Gruffly, his father ushered him into the house. As they moved into the living room, Betsy Black closed the front door, dead-bolted it, and slipped the chain into place. Even if the dogs had lock picks, they wouldn't be getting in here. Unless they wanted to use the windows.

In the living room Charlie sat in an armchair beside the TV set. The witness stand, he thought.

"Why did you have to run off with a twenty-year-old girl anyway?' his mother asked.

"She's nineteen."

"Small difference."

"She's my friend."

"She's strange," Mom protested. "Why doesn't she have friends her own age? Why doesn't she have a boyfriend? You're too young for her."

"She's not like a girlfriend," Charlie said.

"Delia is a nice girl. How would she feel if she knew you were out riding around with Nell?"

"Nell is a friend. We were just talking. Comic books and things like that. It's lonely, you know." That wasn't a lie. He didn't want to lie. He just wanted to hold back a few truths, selective revelation rather than full disclosure.

"We can't take this lightly," his father said. "You can't go wandering around in the middle of the night."

"It's not the middle of the night."

"It's late enough. You're too old for me to spank, so I'm going to cancel your privileges on the computer, and you are definitely to come straight home after school." Black jabbed an index finger toward him. "You won't be reading comic books either."

The computer was the only thing that prevented the boredom from becoming unbearable. As for the comic books, he would miss important issues if there was a buying ban. He'd have holes in his collection which would cost even more money if he had to fill them in later by ordering from back issue houses.

If he was grounded, that was going to make it hard to get together with Delia, harder than his mother's worry that she would be jealous of Nell. He slammed his fist down on the arm of the chair.

"Look at him," his mother said. "What's wrong with you?"

He bit his lip to keep from saying something nasty. This was unnecessary. He wasn't a child. He had known it was dangerous to go out, but he'd been trying to figure out what was going on. He'd calculated the risks along with Nell. It hadn't been an irrational outing.

What kind of lesson were they going to teach him? All they were doing was meddling.

"Didn't that girl have any idea what kind of danger she was putting you in?" Mom asked.

She was in danger too. "Her name is Nell," he said tersely. He didn't like them referring to her as "that girl." She wasn't Mario Thomas, and Mom had a way of making it a derogatory term.

"Whatever her name is I don't know if she's such a good influence on you," Mom said. "You need to concentrate on school more than you do those funny books."

He clamped his mouth shut. No need to correct her on another point that seemed trivial to her, comic books not funny books. He stood up.

"Can I go to my room now?"

"Go ahead. Get used to it. You're going to be spending a lot of time there," Black suggested.

"Fine," Charlie said and stomped up the stairs. They were sure making things hell if they loved him and were trying to protect him. He closed his door hard so they could hear it. Then he dove onto the bed, raising his head only long enough to look up at the dripping jaws of a monster poster. Next to the hounds, this guy didn't look so bad.

As he tried to let his anger ebb so that he could fall asleep, he heard his parents voices raised. They were arguing about something, probably him.

He tried to make out what they were saying, but they were too far away. He fell asleep wondering.

———

Nell scurried from her car up the driveway and the steps. She fumbled only a moment with her keys then rushed inside and slammed her door, locking it. The fear had boiled since she'd dropped off Charlie.

After seeing the dogs, she had felt at least secure while he was with her. On the drive home she had expected a full-scale assault.

Now as she sat in her living room, what there was of it, she wondered if she was about to go into a fear seizure. The monsters were out there somewhere. They were real, and they definitely weren't just wild dogs. They were too big for that, and they didn't behave like wild dogs. They wouldn't have turned docile toward Charlie if they were just mutts.

She tugged off her jacket and went into her bedroom. Looking out the window, she expected to see them clustered on the ground outside, looking up at her, waiting for an opportunity to clamp their jaws on her. The ground was empty. Just the usual leaves and grass.

No dogs, no monsters. She took off her hat too and pitched it on the bed, fuzzing her hair because perspiration had dampened her scalp.

She realized as she let the curls drop through her fingers that she was pacing. Understandably, she felt. This was nightmare territory.

She sat down on the bed and picked up the telephone. It was getting late, and the rates were lower. She dialed Michael's number.

She figured he would fail to pick up since she really needed him to. She let it ring several times before he came on the line.

"Hi," she said, letting the sound of her voice tell him who was calling.

"Hi," he responded, voice brightening from a quizzical hello.

"Are you busy?" she asked, trying to keep her voice steady.

"Just trying to meet my deadline. I always manage. What's up?"

"Michael, they're real." He would hear the quaver now, but that was all right. He could think she was crazy; he was hundreds of miles away.

"You saw the dogs?" he asked.

"Yes." She had trouble controlling her breathing as she explained what had happened.

"They actually cowed to the boy?" Michael asked when she had finished.

"Yes. It's crazy, I know. But that's what happened. They've been attacking people who were mean to him, and now they bow to him."

"Kind of confirms what you were wondering about," he observed.

"That it does. It discounts the idea somebody trained regular dogs, too. Have you heard from the men yet?"

"When you go back there, see what they think of this."

He hesitated a moment. Apparently he wasn't looking forward to the idea of visiting the strange shop again. "I guess I could," he said, relenting. "Sounds like the mystical is more real than we've expected."

"I'm scared, Michael. Scared for Charlie and for me."

"What are you going to do?"

"I may try to talk to Chief Rice. I guess I'm going to have to try to find out more about Miss Nielson too. I found a name, name of a friend of hers from Atlanta. Maybe I can turn something up from there."

"Well, I'll go talk to the guys when I've given them time for their research. For God's sake, be careful."

"I will. Really."

Faulk and Tom Henry were being careful.

They'd fixed up the old Camaro, had it running again, and they weren't going to let the dogs keep them hiding in the garage. They'd taken the precaution of making sure the garage door was locked while they had completed repairs on the vehicle, but now that it was working, they felt pretty safe. Dogs wouldn't get into cars. Besides, they had the .32 caliber revolver which belonged to Faulk's old man in the glove compartment.

They frequently used it to pump lead into the green and white Louisiana road signs which displayed maps of the state along with the highway numbers. Their goal was to put holes through the maps of Louisiana at the point where Petittville existed. Sometimes they missed and pinpointed Aimsley or Alexandria, but once in a while they got lucky and planted one just about right for Petittville, garden spot of Riverland Parish.

The gun was handy tonight, because they had a date with Denny Morris, and they weren't going to pass that up. It wasn't a date actually, but Denny had the most famous snatch in all of Riverland Parish.

Or at least her freedom with it was legendary. For enough beer or Jack Daniel's she would spread her legs for anybody. Faulk and Tom Henry had both heard about this and were ready to take their turn. They had a twelve-pack icing in the trunk, and a fifth to entice her.

As Tom Henry gave the Camaro gas, his black outlaw cowboy hat tilted back on his forehead, Faulk anticipated the pleasures which awaited them.

He recalled his old pal Ruddy Maxwell had dated Denny for a while and was fond of saying: "It's a bitch dating Denny. I have to fuck her so much to keep her happy it makes my dick sore."

Ruddy was not known for his spontaneity with words. His other favorite phrase he'd heard on *Hee Haw*. It applied to his luck, and he spouted it when they played putt-putt golf and he screwed up his shots.

If there was any accuracy in his reference to Denny, however, Faulk was willing to investigate. "She sounded like a damned good way to relieve tension. With Lewis dead and all the other shit going on, he needed some relaxation. Tom Henry did too, although he wasn't as eloquent in his consideration of it. He just wanted to get into some," he told Faulk.

When Denny had told them at lunch that she'd love to go for a ride in their newly repaired car, they'd felt like doing a do-si-do in the bathroom to celebrate.

She wasn't dating anybody at the moment, which meant she would probably be cooperative.

Things looked good when they found her waiting at the appointed spot, inside the old Petitt's Garage. They'd agreed it wouldn't be safe for her to wait out in the open anywhere.

Tom Henry pulled in where the gas pumps had been once upon a time, and Denny stepped out from the dark old building. She was wearing a pair of jeans faded almost white, but they fit her hips and thighs nicely. The sweater she wore had also seen better days and fit loosely. Her hair was blonde but hadn't had much attention, and her face was devoid of makeup. She was a pretty girl, but she didn't take care of herself. There were a couple of blemishes on her cheek, and she looked kind of pale.

Faulk couldn't help being a little disappointed that she hadn't bothered to fix up just a little bit, but Tom Henry didn't seem to mind. It wasn't her face they were concerned with anyway.

"Step right up," Tom Henry said, gesturing toward the Camaro as if it were a royal coach. Faulk noted Tom Henry wasn't given to creative use of the language either.

That didn't really matter. It got Denny into the front seat. That was the desired result. After they opened the trunk and pulled out a few cans of beer, they climbed back into the car. Faulk took the back seat and handed Denny her first can.

She thanked him and wasted no time popping the top. That was good. Faulk sipped his own beer while Tom Henry gunned the motor and shot the Camaro back onto the roadway.

As he turned up the radio, he seemed to be trying to match the throb of the music with the car's speed. They wound through curves and twisted around corners for a while, giving Denny time to down several beers.

She was humming pleasantly in an almost euphoric state when the boys agreed with a quick glance at each other that she was conditioned properly for submission.

Selecting a side road, Tom Henry slowed the car and guided it back along a twisting stretch of gravel. At the end of the roadway, they found a cluster of trees at the edge of an open field.

He parked the Camaro near an oak, and as the engine died, he turned to Denny. She smiled at him, her eyes drooping slightly.

"Wanna get in the back seat?"

"I wan 'nother beer," she said, slurring her words badly.

"Well, get the lady another beer," Tom Henry said. He nodded toward the trunk while indicating to Faulk that he should move her into the back seat.

Faulk climbed out of the car and walked around in front of it to Denny's side. Opening the door, he took her arm and coaxed her out.

"Let's get in the back," he suggested. She brushed against him, and the warmth of her body aroused him.

Seconds away from fulfillment.

As he was helping her slide into the back, Tom Henry returned with the beer. He handed it to her and then slid in beside her.

The Camaro's drive shaft cut through the back seat, a large lump dividing the two cushions. Denny was not going to have a comfortable ride, Faulk decided as he watched her sip her beer.

A trickle of it seeped out the corner of her mouth, and he decided she would probably awaken tomorrow morning and wonder where her bruises came from. No big deal.

As Tom Henry slid in on the other side, he gently took the beer out of her hand and sat it on the ledge beneath the back windshield beside one of the stereo speakers.

She giggled as Tom Henry slipped his hands around her waist and began to nuzzle her neck.

Faulk, however, began to scan the darkness. They were quite a distance from the other dog attack sites, but he had no idea how fast or how far packs roamed.

"Maybe I ought to get the gun out," he said.

"I need to get my gun out," Tom Henry said as he slid his hands over Denny's body.

Without replying, Faulk eased the front seat forward and reached up to the glove compartment. The gun rested there on top of some road maps. Taking it out, he placed it on the console between the front bucket seats. It could be grabbed easily if the need arose. Since the car was so cramped, the doors needed to be open for space as much as air.

The night breeze drifting through was chilly and damp, but he suspected things would get warm soon enough.

Once he had the gun within reach, he turned to the important business of getting Denny's clothes off. She wasn't uncooperative, but she wasn't particularly helpful either.

She was sort of rubbery, resting limply against the back seat as Tom Henry fumbled with her shirt. Faulk helped him tug it up over her head, and they pitched it into the front once it was free of her head. Beneath she was wearing a functional white bra with wide straps and smooth cups, no lace or frills.

"Look at the tits on her," Tom Henry said, sounding astonished.

"She's blessed," Faulk agreed. He put his hand against her forehead to keep it from banging into the console as Tom Henry hurriedly leaned her forward to work on the hooks.

He was in such a hurry his fingers didn't function properly. He was yanking at the fastener when Faulk reached over with his spare hand to help.

They let her lean back as they peeled the bra off, letting her large, soft breasts spill out. Faulk had to admit they were impressive, pendulous with large pink areolae and budlike tips.

They hung down to the waistband of her jeans, and Tom Henry couldn't stop himself from bending over to nestle his face between them.

"Man," he said, words muffled as he kissed the valley between them before working his way over to her left nipple where he began to nurse. "Make a sandwich of these and my face," he suggested.

Faulk couldn't blame him. There'd be time in a few minutes to get her pants off, and they were so excited they would probably end so quickly it would be a nonevent.

Might as well make the most of the foreplay, he thought. He bent forward cupping the soft flesh between his hands, kneading as he brought his lips downward.

She giggled as he began to kiss her and lap his tongue across the bud. He felt her squirm slightly. He wondered how she felt, being mouthed by two guys at once. Maybe she didn't feel anything.

"I want another beer," she said.

"Get her another beer," Tom Henry said as his hands moved to the button at the front of her jeans. He was ready to move on to other pleasures.

"Fine," Faulk said. Reluctantly he let the soft globe slide from his grasp, a bit mystified by the way it lolled softly against her body. There would be time for more. They could keep her as long as they wanted.

Prying himself from the back seat, he moved around to the trunk and opened the Igloo. He peeled a can loose from the plastic ringlets which held them together and was popping it open when he heard a sound.

It was just the wind through the drying autumn oak leaves, but he turned anyway. A prickly feeling played across the back of his neck.

He ran his hand across the short hairs there, smoothing them as if he had just had a haircut that left an itch. He didn't take the sensation as a premonition, just nerves.

He was headed back for his side of the car when he heard Denny's moans. He thought at first Tom Henry must already be slipping it to her, but then he realized they were sounds of resistance.

"Don't wanna," she said, and she came falling out the car door, thudding softly onto the soft grass.

Her jeans were tangled around her ankles, but she kicked them free and was on her sock-clad feet before Faulk knew what was happening.

She went scurrying off across the field, her skin and the pale outline of her white cotton panties visible in the darkness. Torn Henry came scrambling out of the car, holding his jeans closed in front with one hand.

"Why'd you let her get away?" he demanded.

Faulk shrugged, fighting not to laugh at him. He looked like an old farmer trying to catch a chicken thief.

"Dammit, now we've got to go find her. She'll probably think it's funny to hide."

Faulk popped the beer for himself and leaned against the car. "She'll get cold and come back in a minute. She's buck naked."

"I don't want to wait that long." He grasped his crotch. "The boss is ready now."

He started off in the direction Denny had headed. She was wading through the tall grass which was probably damp with dew. She was going to get her socks soaked and wind up with a cold.

Faulk hoisted himself onto the fender of the car to watch the show. It was a little cold for a beer, but it shouldn't be too bad.

218

Across the field, he could see Tom Henry high-stepping through clumps of grass. Denny was still bobbing up and down. He kind of wished Tom Henry would chase her back this way so he could watch those jugs of hers flop around. Damn, why hadn't anybody told him about those when they'd discussed Denny's willingness?

He leaned onto his side and sipped a little more beer. A nice, comfortable feeling was settling over him.

His eyes closed lazily, and the mellow feeling continued, lulled him. Denny's squeals carried on the wind across the field, followed by Tom Henry's curses. At least she was making things interesting.

The scream made him open his eyes again. It was Denny's. She was screaming in fear. If Tom Henry had been able to scream, his would have been from pain.

The dogs were on him.

Had they come out of nowhere? Faulk dropped his beer as he jumped off the car. He landed and stumbled and watched the dogs ripping at Tom Henry.

They had him down on his back a hundred yards away, and they were not being gentle. They were all over him.

Denny was running forward now. Faulk got his chance to watch her breasts bounce for a moment as he had desired, but there was no thrill in it now. In a moment, she folded her arm across them, pressing them against her body so that she could run without having them flail wildly about.

He turned for the car. He should have acted quicker, he decided, even though only a split second had passed. He should have pulled the gun from the console as soon as he decided to sit on the hood. He'd grown too confident, recklessly confident that nothing would happen.

He scrambled across the passenger seat, closing his hand on the weapon. Then he spun around, climbed out of the car, and ran a few feet across the field.

He met Denny as she approached, and she fell into his arms, clutching at him. She was crying, and she was scared. He could feel her trembling even though the way her breasts felt against him was distracting.

219

Tom Henry was issuing screams now, though they were gurgling screams. Faulk started to move toward him with the gun, but Denny was clinging to him too tightly. She didn't want him to go.

She murmured and sobbed and wrapped her arms around him.

He watched the dogs. They were vicious, determined in their assault.

Maybe going over there wasn't such a good idea.

He raised the gun, pointing it straight up in the air as he pulled the trigger. He hoped the sound would drive them away.

The only effect was that it made Denny cringe. It didn't deter the dogs for a second. They were too busy. He wondered what he should do. He couldn't shoot at them. He didn't want to hit Tom Henry even though the bullet probably wouldn't do much more damage now. If his friend wasn't dead, he soon would be.

"You can't help him," Denny sobbed. She had apparently been sobered by the nightmare.

Faulk wasn't inclined to disagree. He hated to leave Tom Henry but there wasn't anything he could do. At least he could save Denny. All the guys would thank him for that.

He pushed her into the front seat and slammed the door. He gave a fleeting glance toward the attack scene, shook his head, and ran around the car.

He was behind the wheel with the door closed, fumbling with the keys Tom Henry had thankfully left in the ignition, when the hound leapt onto the hood.

Its glowing red eyes bored into him as he looked at it through the windshield.

Blood and slobber dripped from its jaws down onto the glass in sticky strings which smeared into little pools.

He lifted the gun from where it rested on his knee and shot without thinking twice. The bullet plowed through the glass, sending crinkling cracks through the smooth surface.

The echo inside the car was deafening, as loud as cannon fire, a howitzer explosion.

When the lead crashed through the skull between the dog's eyes, there was another explosion. Blood sprayed on the windshield as the bullet bored into its head. As the bullet exited, making a picture window out the back of the skull, the body stood statue-like for a few seconds. Then it slumped over sideways, landing on the hood with a thump.

Faulk fired the engine to life and began to back up as the body lay on the hood twitching.

He kept hoping it would slide off as he spun the car backward, twisting the wheel so that he could aim it back in the direction of the highway.

Denny sat beside him weeping. The blood smeared on the windshield cast strange shadows on her skin.

"It's okay," Faulk muttered as he wheeled the car around. The carcass was still in place. It wouldn't have stayed that well if he'd strapped it there. He'd killed deer and had a bitch of a time getting them to stay in place for the trip home.

As he righted the car, the dog's legs began to twitch, death spasms Faulk thought at first, but then the paws began to claw at the slick surface of the hood. The fucker was trying to get up.

He gunned the motor, but the body continued to twitch and paw until it was no longer on its side. It was standing again, a hideous black beast with half a head. The lower jaw sagged down, the tongue dangling off the side of it as the claws made digs at the hood.

He began to swerve from side to side, hoping he could knock this thing off. T. J. Hooker couldn't have stayed on a hood this long.

"What is it with that thing?" Denny screamed. "It should be dead."

Denny made good grades. Sometimes people forgot she had a brain, but there was no question that she was alert now, and she was seeing the same thing he was. This was unquestionably real.

The fucking thing had killed Tom Henry, and Lewis too, and hurt other people and he'd blown its head off, and it wouldn't die. He jerked the wheel hard, almost spinning the car into a donut in an effort to dislodge the beast. It had the balance of a Wallenda.

As she was pitched about the car, Denny began to curse at the thing. She wanted to be rid of it also, especially as it began to claw at the shattered glass.

Faulk finally slammed on the brakes and picked up the gun after pushing the gear shift to park.

"You're not getting out," Denny said.

221

"I've got to get rid of the thing. There's just the one. The others can't have followed us."

She grabbed his arm, but when the mutilated hound slammed its feet against the glass, she let go. Perhaps it was better to let him do his damnedest with the thing.

Slowly, he grasped the handle and swung the Camaro's heavy door outward. The dog turned on the hood, but he was already standing beside the car now. Before it could leap at him, he fired the weapon, bracing it against the window.

The bullets chewed into the dog's side near the rib cage, causing it to jerk and teeter. Finally it fell backward off the hood.

He was feeling complacent as he lowered the gun. "Got the bastard," he muttered, not sure if he was speaking to Denny or to himself. If she didn't hear him it didn't matter. She could see.

He went down when something struck him behind the knees. He let out a quick complaint, but then the dogs were on him, ripping his throat out immediately so that he tasted blood.

He was drowning in it when he died from the lack of it.

Denny cowered back against the door on her side of the car, too frightened even to move over and yank the driver's door closed. She would have been putting her arm into the midst of the monsters if she reached for the handle.

As they chewed Faulk apart, she waited, knowing they would come for her next. She thought about opening her door and running, but she knew they would take her down. She was too frightened, and the beers were still doing some work in her system.

When they had finished with Faulk, however, they stood for a moment near the car, their breath curling out in wisps in the night chill. One of them looked in at her, cocking his head slightly, his face shining with blood, hideous.

She shivered from the cold against her bare skin as well as the fear. Another of them turned toward her, looking at her for a moment. The ears perked.

It was preparing attack. She tightened her muscles, trying to be ready.

Nothing happened.

They turned and began to run, disappearing back along the roadway in the direction from which they had pursued the car.

When she felt like moving again, when the fear drained gradually from her muscles, she grabbed her clothes from the back seat and hurriedly jerked them on.

Then she slid behind the steering wheel, yanked the door closed over what remained of Faulk's corpse, and drove to Lucius Rice's house.

Chapter 20

Rice collected a high-powered rifle and a state trooper before driving out to the site Denny had described. The girl was too upset to make the trip with him and reluctant to return to the scene regardless. He left her with his wife, who was on the telephone trying to locate the girl's mother.

The trooper, Bobby Landreneau, was young and solemn, meaning he didn't talk. He followed Rice in the dark blue and gold cruiser which matched the state police uniforms. That suited Rice, better to ride alone than in oppressive silence with Landreneau grunting responses to any attempts at conversation.

He'd known cops like him before, almost robotic in their functions. They had no ability to judge situations. All they could do was go through prescribed, by-the-book motions. That wasn't good in unpredictable situations.

He would have preferred some other man working his end of the parish tonight, but you took help where you could find it. At least the guy was packing a .357 and a shotgun. Firepower might come in handy.

The girl's sobbing ramble about dogs that wouldn't die had obviously been tinged by liquor and shock, but something was killing people. He had a new theory. He'd been reading a fax from the state Commissioner of Agriculture about coy-dogs, hybrids of dogs and coyotes. They'd been hell on livestock, and some crazed inbred pack might be the answer to his mystery here too.

He was trying to picture something half-dog/half-coyote when his headlights caught the green glow of something's eyes in the center of the roadway. It froze for a moment, not large enough for a dog, then turned and scurried into the ditch, leaving what it had been examining.

His headlights had no problem defining that for him. He was looking at Faulk's remains. He stopped his car, letting the cherries blaze on top. He figured it was the best way to keep Landreneau from plowing into him.

Reaching over and grasping the rifle at his side and sliding a flashlight from the glove compartment, he opened the driver's door and climbed out. He glanced around quite a bit before moving forward.

He was standing beside the corpse when Landreneau joined him, shotgun at the ready.

"Careful where you point that thing," Rice said as he knelt. There was no question that the kid had been eaten up. He wouldn't have to wait for a postmortem to tell him the cause of death.

Turning from the body, he began to look around for the carcass of the dog the boy was supposed to have killed. He could see the pistol still clutched in the remains of Faulk's hand, so Denny must have been a reliable narrator in at least that aspect of her account.

A quick sweep of the area while Landreneau called in to the sheriff's office produced no signs of any remains besides the boy's. With the rifle raised and the flashlight braced against the side of it, Rice edged along the roadway a short distance. He saw no signs of dogs living or dead.

When Landreneau returned from his car, Rice turned to him. "Their men are tied up. We'd better check for the other body."

Landreneau nodded. After they put a blanket from the trooper's trunk over the body, they both climbed into Rice's cruiser and moved on along the roadway to the field. Tom Henry's mangled body was where they had expected, but there was nothing else.

Rice looked up at the moon and its glow. It was almost opaque through the foggy mists.

He prayed they were seeing the work of wild dogs that had bred with coyotes. That he could handle. If it was something weird like Nell had mentioned, he wasn't sure what he was going to do. Morris Wade couldn't help and neither could a state trooper with a cannon.

Somehow, he suspected there were no hybrid hounds around here.

Nell stood at her window. Unable to sleep, she peered down at the ground below. Leaves rustled. She saw no sign of dogs, but she knew they were out there, waiting for her.

The world felt very empty, as if she were an isolated planet in a solar system with a dying sun. She wondered if she should go to Rice with all that she had learned. Would he believe her?

Perhaps she could go to Matt and convince him. He was a man, and he was older. Even the incredible would sound more reasonable coming from him. At least to another man.

Anything she said would be dismissed for her age or discounted as hormonal, the product of PMS. No one would believe a girl. It was a sexist society.

After a while, she climbed back into bed. She had no plans of going back to sleep. She folded her legs into a lotus and placed the telephone in her lap.

Then she flipped through the tattered directory past instructions for local calling and directory assistance to the area code map. She had checked it before when she'd called Dunwoody, but the number had slipped from her brain.

Georgia had two area codes. In the north, including Atlanta, the number was 404. She punched that in along with the 555 directory assistance number.

She would not call Tigges this late. It would be an hour later in Atlanta, too late to telephone with what would probably seem to him inane questions.

By checking tonight, she would have the number when she was ready to call tomorrow after school.

"What city, please?" the generic voice asked when the connection was made.

"Atlanta."

"Name?"

"Tigges." She hesitated a moment. How common a name could it be? "Dave Tigges."

The search produced a J. Tigges and a Rupert Tigges. She took both numbers, scribbling them down on her sketch pad. When the operator hung up, she tore the page off and folded it, tucking it under her bedside lamp.

She wasn't sure if either of them was the correct number for Barbara Nielson's old neighbor, but at least she had done something, made an effort.

It didn't make her feel any less alone.

Barbara Nielson came into her apartment dripping.

The dip in the apartment swimming pool had been icy, and she shivered as she moved into the living room, peeling off her one-piece as she moved across the floor.

It was like shedding a cold, slimy skin, and she darted immediately into the bathroom to get a towel. Despite the chill, she felt invigorated, cleansed.

She made a quick splash in the shower and was out again. With one towel around her, she began to dry her hair carefully. She didn't want it damaged by the chlorine.

She had been damaged enough. Many times. Too many times ...

After the incident in the shower, Doss had grown tired of her. He had explored all of her mysteries and had no further desire for her. She had thought about leaving after the assault, had intended to escape the cold demeanor he adopted, but she felt like a prisoner. Something had kept her after her initial anger faded. On occasions, when his anger flared, she feared he would beat her again or commit other atrocities. She remained silent most of the time, staying out of his way. That wasn't hard because he ignored her. When he was in the apartment, it was like being there alone.

Besides the fear, she stayed because she feared going back to the street, and she might have given her body to him if he had asked, simply because that seemed preferable to giving herself to strangers to survive.

He was an evil man, but not the worst evil she could imagine. At least she knew what he was. At least there was no more delusion about his greatness and thus no more danger of a long drop from adoration to hatred.

She had adapted to the emptiness, had learned to accept her life and find small joys. Then he came at her with a new horror.

She thought the man was just a guest, one of the many people who dropped in with Doss. "Clients," he was fond of calling them. The new man was a client, but he wasn't there to buy drugs.

Doss introduced him as Manfred Kule. He was only a couple of years older than Doss, but he was heavyset. His curly blond hair looked like a Harpo Marx wig. His face was shapeless, his jaws and chin hidden somewhere beneath folds of fat.

He was dressed in dark jeans and a black V-neck shirt with a sports coat worn over it, and he wore a gold chain on his wrist and another at his throat.

Doss reached into his pocket and brought out a piece of paper. It was typewritten and signed at the bottom.

"Mr. Kule just bought you from me," Doss said.

She didn't argue. If she argued, Doss would attack. He had not been angry or cruel in some time, and she chose not to unleash his anger.

She had decided almost immediately to go with Kule. Anything would be better than Doss, and she had been young. She had believed the sale.

It was, though terrible, the exit she had been looking for, the exit she had been seeking since the incident in the shower.

Kule was obviously sick and twisted, but he looked big and slow. If he was cruel, she could outrun him, she reasoned.

She had quietly collected her things and followed him out to his car. She climbed into the passenger seat and rode quietly out to the house he had inherited from his family.

It nestled amid some pines on a hill, not big enough to be a mansion, not far enough from the roadway to be an estate, but elegant.

Both his parents were dead, and they had left him money. There had been insurance, and there was property and stock, enough to let him do whatever he pleased.

Whatever he pleased was buying women. She was the first, but it seemed to be an idea he liked. He gave her a room with a canopied bed and delicate decorations, and gave her gifts.

It didn't change the fact that she was a prisoner—at least in spirit if not in chains—but he treated her well. He was not as exciting as Doss at his best, but he was not as cruel as Doss at his worst.

She learned to endure sex with him fairly easily, shutting out the sensation of his heaving form on top of her. She resisted his kisses until he stopped trying for that intimacy.

She learned his weight was due to a glandular malfunction. His parents had been thin. He had been thin until his teens.

He was thirty when she met him, depressed because his life was nothing. He could go where he wanted, could do whatever he chose, but he was bored and alone.

Sometimes he wanted her to love him. She sensed that, but without telling him, she let him know that would never happen. She could not force herself to love.

She was thankful that he was not violent like Doss. He was most quiet, and his family had left behind a full library. She sat in there for hours and hours, reading, learning. That was her escape. It was her first real chance for education, other than that of the streets.

Only when the drugs began to get bad did she think about leaving, about finding a way out.

At first his use was recreational, but it became an addiction. What was it Robin Williams said: *"Cocaine is God's way of telling you you're making too damned much money."*

That was what Kule must have known. He sat in the small living room he called his study and sank deeper and deeper into an abyss of despair.

As she watched him dying, she realized Doss was supplying the method of his suicide. The bastard probably knew what he was doing, too.

She had thought he was gone from her life forever, but then he began to visit the house regularly, dropping off packages for Kule, helping him to end his life.

She tried to avoid him when he came by, but sometimes he found her wherever she was in the house. She didn't talk to him, and he didn't do much, but her fear of him did not ebb.

He was dangerous. Remembering his face made her shudder, and she tried to forget his eyes, those horrible eyes.

———

She pulled a nightgown from the closet and noticed the box turned. Kneeling, she looked at it for a moment. There didn't seem to be anything missing. Perhaps she had moved it when she was digging out her swimsuit.

When she had changed into her gown, she slid beneath the covers. Even if someone had gone through the box, there was nothing there that mattered, nothing to steal, nothing that was telling.

She couldn't help but feel a little uncomfortable, however. Her facade was not that secure. What if someone was trying to check up on her? She had obtained her job with minimal interrogation, but could she expect to come to a small town like this without being questioned or without raising suspicions?

She rested her head on her pillow and one thought hovering at the forefront of her brain as she drifted into sleep, trying to forget the past. She had to be careful.

Chapter 21

Charlie's feelings were evident in his stride. He moved along the hallway slowly, his head bowed, one shoulder brushing against the wall. It was hard to get excited about a school day when there wasn't anything else to look forward to.

When he ran into Delia, his mood brightened a tad. She was wearing a short pink skirt and matching jacket, white socks, and tennis shoes with pink markings. The rush on his brain made him glad he already had the support of the wall.

He leaned away from it as he felt his smile broadening. He loved the look in her eyes. It was almost as if she seemed hungry for him, which was fine, a good sign really.

"Walk me in the general direction of my class?" she asked.

"Sure," Charlie said.

He stood close to her as they moved, occasionally feeling the brush of her shoulder and catching a hint of her hair's smell. The wonderful tingly feeling nestled in his brain like a fever, and suddenly the grounding and the strange events with the dogs and Miss Nielson didn't matter as much.

He wished that Delia was the only thing in the world of concern to him. He didn't pay attention to the path they threaded through the crowd.

"We haven't had much time to spend together," Delia observed.

"I know," Charlie said. Was that a hint for a date? He felt the tingly feeling transforming into something with a soft edge of anxiety. Her remark was the kind that called for a response. He didn't want to give the wrong one.

If he asked for the weekend, she might reject him. Yet if he didn't act, she might lose interest or think that he was not interested.

He was searching for the right words when he noticed they had moved out of the crowd. They were skirting along the rear hallway, and in a moment, they had ducked into the alcove where the Coca-Cola machines were sequestered.

Some other couples were there, but they weren't noticing Delia and Charlie. They were locked in embraces.

Charlie stood awkwardly in front of Delia. She stood with her back against the wall, waiting. Almost instinctively, he leaned forward and kissed her.

Her soft lips did not resist. She nibbled gently at his mouth. It was a gentle kiss, an innocent kiss, but the charges it sent through Charlie carried high voltage.

He leaned back, still confused, but pleased that things had happened without the need of speech or explanation.

He wanted to kiss her again, but they were in the wrong place. This was too public for this kind of intimacy, even if the other couples were ignoring them, busy with far more aggressive groping.

He did kiss her again quickly before drawing back, and some of his anxiety melted. This was exhilarating, like finding out you'd made an A but better. He stifled, barely, the desire to jump up and down.

He was contemplating another approach when she asked: "What are you doing after school?"

He felt something in his heart flip-flop. Another dangerous question. He couldn't say he was grounded. That would make him sound like a kid. Junior high kids got grounded.

He managed to shrug.

"I know a place we could sit for a while," she said.

And she wasn't just talking about sitting. Oh no, Charlie boy. She was talking about more of this.

If he just never went home, he couldn't be shackled. Fine, let Mom get pissed. She'd already grounded him. He didn't cherish the idea of her anger, but he could deal with it later. This was worth the risk. She wanted him to get together with Delia anyway.

"When do you want to meet?" he asked.

"After school. The old gym."

"Sounds good," he said. Then he kissed her again and felt the moisture as her lips parted just enough. As he hurried toward class, he decided it would be better not to kick up his heels.

———

Sawyer dropped by Barbara's classroom just before the bell. She was sitting at her desk, so he walked over to stand beside her as he said hello. He had worried since last night, unsure if her announcement of sickness had reflected a desire not to see him. He was never certain what to expect, and since her peculiar reaction the last time he had visited her classroom, he couldn't help but worry.

She looked up at him today with a bright smile, however. "I'm sorry about last night," she said. "I just couldn't get my headache cured."

"I'm sorry."

"It's better now, not a migraine I guess."

He felt a little better. She seemed to be interested. He felt a real desire to touch her in some way. He couldn't kiss her here; that would create talk and God knew what else. Discipline from the principal, meted out as if they were school kids.

He settled for patting her hand softly where it rested on her desk. She smiled in response. "I did miss you," she said.

"I missed you too." It was a giveaway line, but he could be witty later, when he'd had more time to feel relaxed again.

"Can we make it up tonight?" he asked.

"That would be fine."

He smiled. "I'll call."

"Sounds good."

He hurried out of the classroom, hoping that he could escape before enough kids noticed and started rumors.

He was so sincere and insecure. As Barbara watched him leave, she wanted to call him back and hug him. The timing was wrong and the setting, so she let him go, hoping her encouragement had bolstered him enough.

She found herself wishing that he was all that mattered. In a simpler world, she would have met Sawyer long ago. He would have been her first love, her only love, and they would have set up housekeeping to live happily ever after.

That would have been preferable to other adventures, or at least it seemed that way in looking back. She had never been given the opportunity for that kind of bliss.

What if Doss had been like Sawyer? Or Kule? Or Galan? Galan DeSarno? He had shaped everything.

She wasn't sure if Kule had met him somewhere or if Doss had brought him around. He just started turning up one day, a slender, older man.

He was unquestionably handsome with firm features and iron gray hair combed straight back from his forehead. He did not have a widow's peak, but the style made him seem sinister, dangerous.

He dressed casually, though by the way he wore his expensive gray or beige cotton slacks and open-collared sports shirts from Banana Republic, he looked as if he might be accustomed to more elegant clothes.

She became impressed with him quickly. He was intelligent. His eyes had a bright glow that made their gray color seem almost to have a flash of silver. When she spoke to him, he was always polite. When he discovered she read, he engaged her in more discussions. She learned from him as he became a frequent visitor. She wondered about him since he was a friend of Doss, but he lacked the hardness Doss possessed. Kule seemed to welcome him also because he had so few friends.

Soon DeSarno appeared even when Doss was not on hand to transact business. If Kule was busy with whatever hobby was holding his interest, she sat alone with DeSarno, talking about the places he had visited or the meanings hidden in books.

They became lovers about a month after their first meeting. Kule was in another part of the house, and while she and DeSarno sat in the patio chairs, the simmering connection that had been between them since the first meeting drew them together.

She joined him on his lounge, kissing him hungrily, more hungrily than she had ever kissed Doss. He was a gentle man, his hands moving over her in a careful fashion. There was excitement that was different from the savage touch Doss had provided.

She felt her clothes sliding away, and then she fumbled with the buckle of his slacks, reaching beneath the fabric to coax him free. She straddled him as his hands continued to caress her. She was amazed at the gentleness and the power they exuded.

Since Kule had held no attraction for her, she had forgotten that lovemaking could be something more than an experience to be endured, but with DeSarno inside her, she felt shimmers of pleasure she had forgotten.

She found a thrill in the sheer illicitness of it as well. She literally belonged to Kule, yet she was enjoying his friend. It was a revenge for her imprisonment in spite of the indifference she felt toward him, but it was also the most glorious fucking she'd ever known.

She had been attracted to Doss, but their liaison had come about because she needed a place to stay. Kule had been mandatory. DeSarno she loved because she wanted to, because she wanted to feel him throbbing into her. That made the ecstasy he produced even greater, more fulfilling. After their first encounter, she found herself sitting by the front window when she wasn't attending to Kule, waiting to see the sleek black sports car pull into the driveway.

Their lovemaking became a regular occurrence. If Kule suspected, he never let on. He was becoming more and more involved with the drugs, paying little attention to anything else, so perhaps he no longer cared. He was making far fewer demands on her.

She began to wonder if DeSarno could be persuaded to buy her from Kule. He seemed to be wealthy, and with his recent disinterest, Kule might be easily convinced to part with her.

She contemplated how she might ask DeSarno to make the purchase. What if he had a wife somewhere? He wore no wedding ring, but that didn't mean much. He was old not to be married, but perhaps he was divorced. She began to harbor that hope, because "belonging" to DeSarno would not be like being with Kule.

Maybe they could be married. That would be wonderful. She could see herself living happily with DeSarno. He probably owned a place even nicer than Kule's.

The wait seemed endless until he appeared again. She watched him park in the driveway and move up the front walk, his hands casually in his pockets, the sleeves rolled up on his white shirt. A gold bracelet on his wrist gleamed in the sunlight. He was quite easygoing.

She heard him talk to Kule for a while, and she did not interrupt. She waited, biting her lip, biding her time, hoping he would come and find her before leaving.

Eventually he made his way back to the library, where she was sitting. She rose and walked to him, embracing him. She kissed his cheek softly.

"Want to go for a walk?" she asked. The property was not expansive, but Kule's land did extend back a good distance from the house, encompassing some wooded hills. Trails meandered back through the trees.

She had taken DeSarno there a number of times for their liaisons. Even though Kule never paid any attention, she felt better not worrying that he would walk into a room and interrupt.

DeSarno put his arm around her, and they went out the back way, strolling silently across the back lawn.

She put her head against his chest as they walked, listening to his heartbeat. She loved him as much as she'd ever loved anyone, not just because he was handsome and not just because he was gentle.

Part of it was because he was kind to her, but he just seemed perfect, a gallant man. Jesus, he was her knight.

When they reached the soft bank of ground where they often coupled, she embraced him and kissed him hard on the lips, letting her hands slide down his chest to his buttons.

She undressed him frantically before shrugging off the denim shirt and jeans she wore. She sat across his chest then, touching his face and shoulders before bending down to kiss him.

236

He kissed and fondled her for a long time before easing her onto her back, touching her knees with his palms to coax her legs apart.

She curled her legs around him as he plunged into her, and as she dropped her head back against the clover which blanketed the ground, she gasped in quick breaths, all that her body would allow her with excitement.

When he had spent himself inside her and had rolled off to lay beside her with his head on her breast, she asked him.

"Can you take me away from Kule?"

He laughed. Not at her. She thought that only for a moment before she understood his laughter better.

"You don't feel fulfilled belonging to my friend?"

"I don't feel anything. I have a roof. That's all. I have no life."

"So you want to live with me?"

"Yes."

"Do you have any idea where I live?"

"It doesn't matter. You aren't married?"

He laughed again. "No. I'm not married."

"Do you want me? Or am I just that cute little girl that you lay behind your buddy's back?"

"You're much more than that," he said. "You strike me as something of a Lolita, I suppose, but you're more."

"I'm not that young."

"You may be of age, but you're a child, a babe."

"Is this how you treat babies?"

He propped his head on an elbow. "No," he admitted. "No it's not."

"Then take me the hell out of here."

"How do I know you're devoted to me?"

It was a coy question, a strange one. She curled her lower lip. "What do I have to do?"

For a heartbeat, an awful feeling that his idea of devotion might be akin to that demanded by Doss burned inside her. It was hard not to believe that he must want to degrade her.

He shook his head. "Don't worry," he said as if he had looked inside her mind. "It's nothing like that."

"What do you want me to do?"

"Prove you love me."

"I do."

"You love me beyond everything?"

"Yes."

"Then I guess we can think of something to show your devotion."

The kids rambled in when the bell rang, dragging her back from that long-ago conversation. She looked up at the dull expressions on the first-hour crowd. Surely none of them had known what she had known in her lifetime. Surely not.

Betsy Black could not get comfortable. She did some housework, but it did not subdue the growing concern she was feeling.

Charlie was becoming openly rebellious. That was to be expected. He was of an age to confront parental authority, and she did not worry that he was not a good kid. He was good-natured and pleasant, not prone to generate trouble.

She could not help but worry about what he might be lured into, however. Nell was a pretty girl, but she was unusual. It could not be healthy for Charlie to hang around with her.

He couldn't see that. Because she liked comic books and horror movies as he did, she was exciting, but she was also nineteen years old. She should be interested in boys her own age, not comic books and kids.

She couldn't blame Charlie if he was attracted to her, but an attachment to an older, possibly disturbed girl was potentially damaging to him.

She didn't want to think of him groping with any girl, but if he had to come of age, she would rather it be in a normal teenage relationship, not in a seduction orchestrated by a lonely older girl.

She ran her hands over her face. There were other worries too. They had lost the folder with all of Charlie's important papers—Social Security card, birth certificate, the works. They had been tossing the house for it last night when they d discovered that he had gone out.

They didn't need any of the papers now. He was already registered in school and everything, but they were important to have on hand. Some were irreplaceable.

She would prefer to locate the folder, but she couldn't remember when she had seen it last. They had handled Charlie's admission to the new school through his old school, so his record had followed him.

Had she seen the damned folder she kept things in since they'd moved to Petittville? She couldn't be sure. She wanted to kick herself for letting something so important out of her sight.

She couldn't remember Whitney's phone number. It had been too long ago, but she found it easily enough through information. He was out of his office the first time she tried, but she reached him on the third try. What the hell else did she have to do but keep trying?

Finally she heard Whitney Grier's voice on the line. She had not talked to him in a long time, but he was as soothing as ever.

She had nothing to be concerned about, he told her. He had told her that before, but he didn't know everything. She accepted his reassurances, however. She wanted to believe that all was well, that Charlie was not growing up too fast, that he would not fall in love and be hurt by Nell, that he would go on to college and become a success at his chosen endeavor.

Was that too much to hope for?

When she hung up, the phone rang almost immediately. It was Belinda Sebury to tell her there had been more deaths.

Rice kept his hand on the pistol at his hip as he walked the field where the killings had occurred the night before. It was outside his jurisdiction, although the death on the road was in his sphere of influence.

He could still find no sign of an injured dog. He had talked to Denny again this morning. Sober, she still insisted Faulk had shot the dog and that it had stayed alive.

She didn't seem hysterical. Just hung over. Stopping in the middle of the field, he pulled a handkerchief from his pocket and mopped his brow. The midmorning sun was fiery, and the Louisiana , air was as humid as a steam bath. Seasons didn't matter around here. The weather changed on whim.

He ran the cloth across the back of his neck as well. This was the damndest shit he'd ever been through.

The disappearing fetuses and a dog carcass that disappeared after having its head blown off had him worried.

Deputies were trekking through the forest with high-powered rifles and scopes, but he couldn't expect them to find anything. He'd spoken to the Department of Wildlife and Fisheries about coy-dogs, but they didn't have much to offer. Attacking humans didn't seem to be a coy-dog trait. They preferred to feed on livestock.

All this had dashed his hopes that he was on the trail of something that would lend logic to the scenario. He didn't want to accept that something beyond his understanding was going on.

He couldn't stop wondering if Nell was right. He'd never believed the voodoo claims in New Orleans, had scoffed at some of the occult experts they'd brought in on cases.

Now he might need one. He heaved a heavy sigh as he started back toward his cruiser. He had some friends in New Orleans he could call. He wondered what kind of results he could expect.

He climbed behind the wheel of his car and flipped the air conditioner to high before putting the vehicle into gear. As the vent spat cool air into the interior, he wasn't surprised that he didn't stop sweating.

Tom Henry and Faulk were not immediately missed from school since they were still under suspension. They would not have been in the hallowed halls on this day anyway, but shortly before lunch the news began to swing on the grapevine.

Faces drained of color, and once again the mingled feelings swept over the young people. True, the Assholes had been further diminished and would not generate as much terror, but these were young guys who weren't supposed to die. The fear worsened as they contemplated the horror.

Charlie was sitting down when he heard the news, and he was glad. A fierce shudder rippled through his back. They had died last night after the dogs had refused to touch him, and they had been among the ones who had tried to harm him.

"What's the matter, Charlie?" asked Ricky Pierson. They were in the lunchroom, and he was sitting next to Charlie. He wasn't really a friend, but Charlie had a class with him right before lunch. They had walked down to the lunchroom together and Charlie had followed him to a table of his cohorts. One of them had mentioned the deaths.

Charlie shook his head. "Just scary thinking about all the killing," he said.

"I thought you watched all the horror movies," Ricky said.

"That's all special effects," Charlie countered. "This is real."

"Yeah," Ricky agreed. "I bet the morticians have to work a long time to make those guys look presentable."

"Considering what he has to work with in the first place," quipped Joe Bell, slapping the table.

They all laughed. Charlie faked a grin, but he couldn't stop thinking about the things Nell had pointed out. Why was he surviving? Why were his enemies being killed?

Only when he began to look forward again to his afternoon liaison with Delia did he push the awful feelings away, replacing them with warm expectation.

Of course the day seemed endless. Miss Nielson had been silent in class, speaking only a hello. She gave no lectures and no unfounded glances in class.

After class, while he was strolling along the hallway where his locker was located, he encountered her again, however. She had duty on that hall and was sitting in a small chair at the end of it near the wall heater.

Her legs were crossed, the hem of her skirt revealing their firm shape through the dark hose. She was looking over a stack of essays, but her eyes flicked upward when she noticed him approaching.

"Hi," he managed, even though he felt strange as one of her eyebrows cocked upward.

"Hello, Charlie."

He felt uncomfortable, but he didn't move away. She seemed to want to tell him something, or be waiting for him to ask something.

"How are things going for you?" she asked.

"Okay," he said.

"You seem nervous around me, Charlie."

"No," he said. "I don't know what it is."

"I like you," she said. "I think you're a good student. You have more potential than a lot of kids, more than you realize."

He frowned slightly, not sure of what she was getting

"I just want to see what's best for you," she said. "I want you to realize your potential."

"Sure. I do too," he said. "I mean I want to amount to something."

What was it about her eyes? She wasn't looking at him seductively. It wasn't hunger, but he felt like she wanted something from him. He wanted desperately to end this conversation and get the hell out of here. She was beautiful, and he should be honored that she cared about him, especially when you considered she snubbed other guys.

This wasn't normal attention. He'd had teachers encourage him before. They hadn't scared him in the process.

He shifted his weight from one foot to the other, swaying slightly without realizing it.

"I guess I better be going."

She smiled. Pleasant smile, nothing wrong with her smile.

Except it chilled the hell out of him.

Chapter 22

Nell tried Tigges from a pay phone in Penn's Ferry, charging the call to her home number. When she got no answer, she decided she would wait until after 4 P.M., which would be after 5 P.M. Atlanta time.

She went on to work, settled behind the counter, and doodled pictures of the hounds until Lucius Rice showed up. She heard the door open, and didn't look up from her pad until she realized he was standing at the counter.

He wanted to ask something but wasn't sure how to put his question into words. She could read that in his expression.

"You heard about the new deaths?" he asked.

"Yes."

"Has the rumor started circulating yet, about what the girl said she saw?"

Nell shook her head. "What time did the deaths occur?"

"We don't have a ruling on that yet. Why?"

"Curiosity. What did the girl say?"

"She'd been drinking."

Nell nodded. "Denny fucks." Everybody knew that.

He turned his head away, a bit embarrassed by the profanity, at least coming from her lips. "She'd had several beers, but she said Faulk shot a dog and it kept coming, got on the hood of the car and stood even with half its head gone."

"You believe her?" She held her pencil tightly in her hand, gripping it for security as she wondered if she would tell him what had happened with Charlie.

243

She decided to let him play his cards first.

"Nothing adds up to four around here anymore," he said. "I've been a policeman a long time, and I've never believed anything that wasn't hard evidence or eyewitness testimony, and most of the time you can't believe eyewitnesses. I have this feeling, this gut instinct which you aren't supposed to have, but you get."

"That's kind of what I've been experiencing," Nell confessed.

"I thought about calling occult crimes experts, but most of them are trained at the same seminars. They rattle off identical rhetoric and identify unicorn stickers as signs of Satanism. Sometimes satanic groups are associated with dogs, but I have a feeling something else is going on here."

She looked down. "I spoke to my friend, Michael, again," she said. "He's found some people in Chicago. He's supposed to go back and see them again, see what else he can learn."

"What are they?"

"Occult researchers or something, but not like you're thinking about."

Rice placed one hand on the counter. He had a look on his face that pleaded for answers. "You know something?" he asked.

"He mentioned to them what you said about the dog that had been eviscerated. It seemed to jibe with some kind of ancient ritual. They were going to try to do more checking."

Rice seemed to shiver. "Then we could have some kind of Satanists here?"

"I'm not sure if they're Satanists in the traditional sense, but the ritual would have been to bring the fetuses to life."

"That's impossible."

"I know," Nell said. "But something's killing people."

"And I want to know what it is," Rice said. "I just have to be careful. The people are going crazy, and they'll think I have too if they believe I'm looking into crystal balls for answers."

"But you want to know what I find out?"

"It'd be nice," he said. "Maybe we can arrive at something, find a way to stop this. The thing up in Bristol Springs stopped when they had a forest fire. I hope we can do something short of that."

244

"I think we've got a different situation here."

"I hope so."

He turned and walked toward the door. "I'll be talking to you," he said.

Nell nodded, thankful at least Rice was a reasonable man. He didn't want to believe things were out of the ordinary, but he was realistic, and the bizarre seemed to be the only explanation.

When the final bell rang, Charlie headed down the hallway where Delia had her last class. People were on their way out of the building, so he had to buck traffic. It took him a while to weave his way through the flowing bodies, and he was almost trembling as he neared the door.

Normally he would be fighting to get to his bus on time, but he didn't have to worry about that. He had to worry about his mom, but she was already mad at him. What could she do?

He moved to the door and saw Delia there, talking with her teacher. She was nodding, listening, nodding again. It didn't appear to be a lecture, just a discussion.

He wasn't sure what he should do. He felt awkward lingering in the hallway, but he didn't want to barge into the classroom even though it was empty. He wasn't sure how Delia would feel about that, and teachers all had their idiosyncrasies to contend with. You never could tell if one of them might be on a power trip.

He'd had teachers who refused to let students leave when the bell rang noting: "The bell does not dismiss you. I dismiss you."

Others you had to say good morning to before you could make business requests. It probably grew out of a desire for order in a chaotic system, but it could sure be a pain for kids trying to second-guess neurotic adults.

No wonder the public school system was such a mess. Finally, he moved past the door and let Delia notice him. He saw her eyes dart toward him, and he detected a slight nod, an indication she was on her way.

He sighed. That made him feel better. He scanned the hall just to make sure there were no other teachers about to sweep by and lecture him about loitering.

Finally Delia emerged, smiling. The sunlight that made it to the hallway from the classroom windows shined on her hair. She was as beautiful as he had ever seen her, and she was interested in him. Unbelievable but true, something for Ripley, no doubt.

There were still some kids milling about as they moved along the rear hall. Various activities were carried on immediately after school hours, practices or meetings or other extracurricular projects. Charlie worried that the room where they were headed was in use.

Delia assured him it was not. He had to remind himself she'd been there before. She knew what she was talking about. Words from Budd echoed from memory to confirm that and brought along a touch of sadness.

Budd was dead. He had held her in this room where they were going. Charlie thought about turning back. He had been anticipating this all day, or longer really in the form of hoping for it, but now, could he go through with it?

The look of her face and her hair, her perfume's aroma, all told him he could. Budd was gone. This was not a betrayal of his memory.

He followed Delia around to the rear of the old gym. As they moved, he looked back over his shoulder, making sure no coaches or other authority figures were watching.

A narrow flight of steps made of the same wood as the gym floor led up behind the old stage, but the varnish was long gone. The steps were dull and creaked slightly under their weight.

The moisture on his palms felt as if it were going to start dripping as they ascended. He continued to look back, sure they were going to be caught and reprimanded.

Delia seemed quite calm. With her books under one arm, she tried the knob on the old dressing room. The heavy wooden door opened easily, and she pushed it open.

The musty smell of old mattresses filled Charlie's nostrils as she led him into the room. They had been stacked here a long time, tumbling mats. None of the acrobatics for which they had been designed had been performed on them in ages, but a couple of them had been pulled to the center of the floor. Some feats had been undertaken there, no doubt.

A couple of beer cans lay crumpled in the corner, and cigarette butts had been ground out on the floor leaving a stale smell of nicotine to blend with the mattress smell.

"It's not a suite, but it's private," Delia said. She sat down on some of the mats piled against the wall, placing her books at her side. She patted a spot beside her for Charlie.

Putting down his books, he settled into his place, almost but not quite close enough to Delia to be touching. His heart was trying to outrun his nerves.

Contact was not necessary. Her presence sent off charges. He could sense her warmth, and the memory of her taste from this morning and the feelings that touch had triggered resurfaced.

She shifted slightly, adjusting her weight so that she was leaning toward him. "It's quiet here. Don't you think?"

"Sure."

Charlie was eyeing the door. Their access here was possible because the lock was broken, but that was now cause for concern. They were not protected. Anyone could enter.

No one except others looking for the same sanctuary would have reason to come to this forgotten room, but the possibility of intrusion made him nervous. The world would love to hear Charlie Black had been caught with his hand up a girl's blouse, good old quiet, slightly weird Charlie copping a feel. It was natural, part of being a teenager, but they would rib and pester him if they knew.

As Delia moved again, he felt the touch of her hair against his cheek, and concerns were forgotten. He turned to her, and the awkwardness of beginning left them.

He leaned forward so that his mouth touched hers, and she let her lips part, enough for him to feel the moistness without actually penetrating with his tongue. That would come in a moment.

First, other things had to be accomplished, like the embrace.

247

When the bus passed, Mrs. Black pulled back the curtain, but instead of stopping at the walkway's end, it motored on past, no more than a yellow blur in the afternoon sunlight.

As the curtain slid from her fingers, she told herself she should not worry. He could have missed the bus. He could have defied her and gone by the comic book shop to see Nell. Any of those things might have accounted for it rather than his being in danger.

She had never been able to feel comfortable about Charlie, however. She had never felt right when he was out of her sight. She worried all the time about his safety and the solidarity of their family.

Suddenly she felt like her own mother worrying and fretting. When had she grown old? When had Charlie grown away from her?

She was not good at showing affection, but she loved Charlie. He was the only child she would ever know. Her womb was damaged and would not allow her to conceive.

The small hands of her watch moved slowly, but they moved. She watched them creep around the face, ticking off ten minutes and then fifteen past the time Charlie should have been home. She sat in the kitchen for a while, waiting for him to walk through the door, trying not to let her mind come up with terrors. The dogs came at night. They shouldn't bother him at this hour wherever he might be.

She couldn't stop herself from going to the telephone and picking up the handset. She dialed the office after consulting the telephone book in the drawer under the phone. She got a janitor who informed her the offices had emptied out.

There were no kids there either, he said.

She tried the athletic office and got a coach who didn't sound very sympathetic. He didn't know who Charlie was and didn't have anyone fitting his description in the vicinity.

The receiver sounded heavy as it clicked back into its cradle, like the lid of a coffin. She told herself it didn't matter. Charlie wasn't in danger. Her fear was irrational.

She was walking back into the kitchen when she saw the car keys hanging on the ring beside the door.

There was one way to make sure he was okay.

248

Slowly, Delia eased to her side on the mattress until she and Charlie were positioned horizontally, their arms wrapped around each other. He kissed her lips and her face and her neck, careful not to leave hickies but quick and passionate at the same time.

He had never had the opportunity to kiss like this, to enjoy contact with the opposite sex, and it was overwhelming. Her skin was soft and exquisite, her lips warm. He tried to take in as much as possible since he had no idea when they would be able to repeat this.

She thrust her tongue up hurriedly through his lips now as they pressed their mouths together, her breathing quickening.

He could feel the shape of her legs through her skirt, and her breasts were flattened against his chest. Their softness and their fullness were evident.

Charlie had positioned himself so that his leg was against her, keeping his hardness away. He was embarrassed by it, unwilling to let her feel the effect she was having.

Delia could tell his breathing was matching hers, and there could be little doubt he was enjoying her. He ran his hand along her side, feeling the shape of her hip. He was resting his palm on her hip bone, squeezing gently, wanting to do more.

He was hungry for this affection, discovering things he had probably been dreaming about, but he was gentle. Budd had been quick to take what he wanted. Charlie was more cautious, shy and careful not to be rough.

She had been attracted to him first because he was close when she was feeling the loss of Budd, and the loss of security of a steady boyfriend. Now she was impressed with how cute Charlie was, and how nice.

She would have to be careful not to let him slip away. He wasn't a jock, but there were plenty of girls that would spot him eventually.

He was a good guy, a gentleman. She could love somebody like Charlie. She had been judicious with Budd. She'd had to make sure he didn't obtain too many liberties because he would have sought more. Charlie, on the other hand, needed perhaps just a little coaxing.

When she reached down and grabbed his wrist, Charlie thought Delia was angry. He thought she was going to tug his hand away from her, but instead, she guided it gently toward her right breast. He had not expected that privilege.

No reason to look a gift horse though. He let his fingers cup the soft mound. It was encased in her bra, but he could feel the roundness.

"Like a little boy with a new toy," Delia giggled. Charlie didn't speak. He looked at the way the fabric of her blouse conformed to it as he squeezed. Then he discovered she had another and cupped it in his other hand.

She leaned back against the wall, thrusting her breasts forward, sighing as his thumbs found the hardness of her nipples through the cloth.

He buried his face against her collarbone, kissing as he gripped her breasts. Soft sighs issued from her lips, and he barely stifled his own gasps. He had dreamed about moments like this, had watched television programs and fantasized, but he had expected a long wait.

Jocks got the girls, and he had wondered if he might not have to wait until college to hold a girl close. He had never let himself expect to be in the arms of a girl as beautiful and soft as Delia.

She was more than a dream. He felt almost a dizziness. He nibbled at her flesh, moving along her neck to her earlobe. He loved the touch of her skin against him as much as being able to touch her, but he held on, unwilling to relinquish the long-desired access to a girl's body.

He wanted desperately to touch the breasts not through the cloth of her blouse and bra but untethered. He wanted to see them as well, take in their shape and their color.

Slowly, he let his hands slide downward, reaching the waistband of her skirt. Gently, he began to ease out the hem of her blouse.

She did not resist, though he had expected her to stop him. She kept her eyes closed and her hands on his upper arms. She caressed his muscles slightly as he touched the warm flesh of her abdomen.

———

Mrs. Black had to force herself not to speed as she headed toward the school. She had thought about going to the comic book store first, but she decided it might be better to check the school and then follow the route over to the store. She might spot Charlie along the way.

She hoped she would spot him walking and not tangled in the middle of a pack of dogs. They didn't come out in the daylight, she kept telling herself. They hadn't struck anyone in the daylight. They were wild. They hunted at night.

Charlie was at the age to be defiant. That was natural. She didn't have to worry about him being attacked or being taken away from her. That was absurd.

It was always so hard not to believe your paranoia. Your mind conjured up little scenarios, and then you became certain they must be true. If you could deduce something from a set of facts, then that must be the reality.

She assured herself over and over again that she would find Charlie safe and sound somewhere. He would be sitting on a stool at the comic shop reading something that had just arrived on the UPS truck, probably sipping a Coke and swapping tales with Nell.

It did seem unnatural for him to spend time with a girl so much older. Years made more of a difference in adolescence, but they did have common interests. Perhaps she had been too harsh in her judgment. Nell wasn't what she had to be afraid of. She was just a tomboy with a better wardrobe and hairdo. She wasn't out to seduce young boys. She just happened to be excited by some of the things that excited them.

She flipped her turn signal on and turned onto the roadway which wound back to the school. It had been along this stretch that the track star had been hurt, she recalled. A good distance from the other attacks, and this was not the route Charlie would have taken on foot. Still, she began to look out her window, peering into the hedges and ditches. She watched for the eyes of hounds sequestered there and signs of Charlie's form, perhaps mangled and twisted. She prayed she would see neither.

———

Delia held her hands over her head, fingers extended like Superman. It took a moment for him to understand what she was doing. She was going to let him slip her blouse off. He'd never expected things to go so far this afternoon.

Budd had talked about it, but Charlie had never dreamed she'd let him do the same. He hesitated for a second, nervous. The door was still unlocked, but she was here, so soft, so beautiful, and this was the stuff he'd seen and heard talked about.

He reached down to the already untucked hem and pulled upward, peeling the thin pink blouse over her head. Her breasts bounced slightly as they pulled free of the fabric even though they were still encumbered by her bra.

They were larger than he had expected, well rounded, their curve visible above the bra cups. He touched the valley between them, a bead of sweat forming on his brow as he slipped his fingers beneath the fabric.

He was long overdue at home now. His mother would kill him, but at least he would not be dying without experiencing these joys of existence.

He was almost trembling as she reached behind her back to unhook the clasp. He was waiting for the fabric to fall away when the door opened.

He jerked around as the sound of the knob turning echoed through the silence like the crack of a rifle. Delia began to claw for her blouse, grabbing it and pressing it in front of her.

As the door swung inward, Charlie felt as if his chest was about to explode. He had nowhere to run or hide. He had to sit and wait, watching for whoever would step through the door with the humiliation and teasing.

He found himself looking into Miss Nielson's eyes.

She showed no sign of surprise. She had not just happened here, stumbling on them while performing some other mission. He could read that in the way she glared at him.

Charlie stammered, unsure of what he should say. He felt his face flushing, even his ears hot with the rush of blood.

Miss Nielson didn't speak, and she hardly seemed to notice Delia as the girl tugged her blouse on. The woman's dark eyes were locked on Charlie.

With her head bowed, Delia gathered her books, while Charlie could only sit. He had not moved since he had spun around. He was not breathing.

Miss Nielson wasn't moving either. She just continued to glare until Delia realized she wasn't being noticed. Pushing past Charlie, she darted around the teacher and made an exit without Miss Nielson uttering a word.

As the eye contact between them continued, he did not feel fear, not exactly. He realized or sensed that he had no worry of reprimand. She would not turn him in to the principal or speak of this to other teachers or his parents.

The feeling of being in her sight right now was bad enough to make up for that, though. It was more than embarrassment. He felt in a way as if he had betrayed her, or he at least sensed she felt betrayed. The hint of romance that she had seemed to exude at first had faded over the last few days, yet he felt there was still some kind of connection she desired, and she didn't approve of this little endeavor.

"You shouldn't be here, Charlie," she said softly. There was no anger, not even inflection. It was a simple statement.

He could only shrug. What had he done that was so different from what everyone else did? He sat there on the mattress, bowing his head as he rested his hands on his knees.

"I'm sorry," he said.

"You are so bright and gifted, and I find you tussling with that guttersnipe. Do you think you're the first boy she brought in here to be felt up?"

"I guess not," Charlie said.

"Somebody like that can mess up your life, Charlie."

"We were just …"

"Kissing and petting?"

"Yes."

"And how long would it have been until something else happened?"

"I wasn't going to …"

She moved forward, placing her hands on his shoulders and looking into his face. "I know she's pretty and it's exciting to experiment, but it's dangerous too. I've been there, Charlie. I've made mistakes, and I don't want you to see you get into trouble. You're a nice person, and I don't want to see you turn into what some men become."

"She's a nice girl."

"Charlie, nice girls get pregnant too. Nice girls can be just as much trouble as bad ones."

He felt a burst of anger. Maybe they shouldn't have been in here making out, but Miss Nielson was stepping over the bounds of disciplinarian. He almost barked an accusation, but he realized that would be creating a whole new tension.

It was better just to nod and get this over with and get out of here. Perhaps she was just well meaning in her admonition, not really intending to pry.

Yet he could not help but wonder if she was not displaying signs of jealousy. Perhaps she had purposes of her own for not wanting him involved with Delia.

The questions that had been with him since the first time she fixed him with a stare came back again.

"What do you want from me?" he asked. Let the worms come out of the can. It was time to figure out what was going on here.

"I'm only concerned about you, Charlie."

"Why?"

"You're a good student. Good students are rare."

There was something more. He couldn't figure it out, but it was clear. For the first time since the discovery, she was being evasive.

"What is it?" he asked. "What do you want from me?"

She touched his hair softly. It was not a sensual touch, but there seemed to be genuine affection in it, mingled with sadness.

"We'll talk more later," she said. "You're upset now." She pulled back from him and walked across the room.

"What do you have planned for me?" Charlie asked.

She paused with her hand on the door, looking back at him. One eyebrow cocked up mysteriously.

"Y7ou're not ready to know," she said and stepped outside.

Chapter 23

Mrs. Black turned slowly into the parking lot behind the school. This was the place where the boy had been injured. She looked at the gravel but saw no remaining signs of blood. That was a relief, but the fact it had happened here meant the dogs might be close by. Even though she kept telling herself she was being irrational, a new flood of fear that Charlie was in danger washed over her.

She pulled the car quickly into a parking place behind the gym and climbed from the driver's seat. She stood for a moment beside the car, resting her arm against the door as she looked around, scanning the parking lot and the grassy area beyond it for signs of her son. She saw no signs of a mangled body, and when she looked to the stand of pine trees, she detected no dark eyes peering out at her.

She gave the door a shove, letting it clunk closed before heading toward the gym's rear door. She expected it to be locked, but the latch flicked open easily when she touched the handle.

She found herself standing in a long tiled corridor. The lights were turned off, but late-afternoon sunlight filtered in through windows near the ceiling.

One wall was lined with a glass trophy case. Faded photographs of teams long gone and tarnishing trophies filled it. She walked past it feeling nostalgia even though this case did not hold her memories.

It made her think of school and other things from the past. She tried not to look back. The old Satchel Page adage was not lost on her. She did not want memories catching up.

She moved on along the hallway, not sure of where she was going. Would she find Charlie hanging around here? He wasn't that fond of basketball. She found a doorway that opened into the gym, but it was empty.

She turned and walked back along another hallway, past an old concession stand with plywood over the sales windows. She was about to round a corner when she saw the dark-haired woman.

At the sight of her, the woman stopped abruptly. Her head twisted slightly with the start, and her hair fell across her face for a moment.

She reached up and brushed the locks out of her eyes, eyes that were dark and penetrating.

"Can I help you?" she asked. This wasn't where adults were supposed to be.

Mrs. Black forced a weak smile. "I was looking for my son," she said. "I came up the back way. I wasn't sure if he'd be around or not."

"School's been over for a while," the woman said. "This wing isn't used for extracurricular activities."

"I was worried. My son was late. With all this dog business, you know."

The woman nodded, but it was not a particularly knowing or understanding nod.

"I'm Charlie Black's mother," Betsy Black said.

"Oh." There was almost something curt in the woman's voice. Her heels clicked on the tile, echoing through the vacant hallway as she moved a few steps forward. She folded her arms in front of her and tilted her head slightly.

"You're Charlie's mother," she said. "So nice to meet you."

It seemed there might be sarcasm. Mrs. Black was not sure how to take it. She refrained from lifting her hand.

"I'm Barbara Nielson," the woman said. She seemed to be waiting for recognition.

"You're one of Charlie's teachers?"

Her eyes seemed to flare. "Mm-hm."

Mrs. Black folded her arms in front of her. As she did, she realized a subconscious defensive mechanism had been triggered. The woman was intimidating.

257

"Have you seen Charlie?" she asked nervously.

"No. Not since class."

Mrs. Black gave what she hoped was a knowing expression. "He must have gone by the comic book store. I've instructed him to come straight home since all this craziness has been going on." She felt suddenly silly and unsophisticated uttering the last sentence. Barbara Nielson seemed so smooth and elegant, unusually so, maybe too elegant.

"He's getting older," the teacher said, "maybe old enough to make his own decisions."

Mrs. Black started to offer a rebuttal to that remark, which seemed a bit defiant for an educator, but she held it back. She suddenly didn't want to discuss Charlie with this woman.

He was still unaccounted for. She had to check the comic shop. He could still be hurt somewhere or wandering around somewhere that might place him in danger.

"I guess I'd better go," she said. "I still have to find Charlie."

She turned and started back down the hallway.

"Be careful," Barbara Nielson called after her. "The hounds may be about."

While Barbara and Mrs. Black were talking, Charlie made his way out the other exit, never knowing his mother had been there.

He looked around outside for Delia, but he could not see her anywhere. She had departed quickly, and that left him feeling as if he were inside a dark cloud of smoke.

He put one hand in his pocket and felt his shoulders droop. He'd finally found a girl who wanted to be close to him, and everything had fallen apart faster than a decomposing zombie.

All of the excitement produced by being near her rushed out of him now. He would have to call her, apologize even though it wasn't his fault, and try and make sure she didn't associate him with the disaster.

He cursed as he moved outside and along the sidewalk beside school. He would have to walk home now, and his mother would be angry at him. That didn't seem worth it any longer.

He thought about dropping by to talk to Nell, the shop only a few paces out of the way, but he reconsidered. Her understanding would have been welcome, but that would put him even later arriving home. His mother would already be worried, and she would fuss at him when he arrived. If he gave her enough time to think it over, she would have dreamed up some new punishment for him.

Mrs. Black walked out the back door with her car keys in hand, ready to hop behind the wheel and head over to the comic shop, but the dogs were waiting.

One of them was resting on top of the car, its front paws folded across each other while its tongue lagged out over its teeth.

Two others were lying on the hood, and a few more were on the ground at various points around the vehicle.

All of them seemed calm. They panted as they rested, looking around, cocking their heads. One of them scratched his ear. Another sniffed at the ground in front of him.

She might have been looking in a pet shop window, but she knew as she looked at the huge black beasts, that she was looking at killers.

How could they be so docile? She had imagined monsters with matted coats. These were not rabid. They were not foaming at the mouth. They didn't look like the St. Bernard that had menaced Dee Wallace in *Cujo*.

Keeping her feet planted, she reached slowly behind her, hoping to find the door handle easily. If she could slip it open and then dart back inside, she might be safe before they made a move for her.

As soon as her fingers touched the wind-chilled metal, the hounds jumped to attention, however. The one on the car top jumped to his feet, growling as his teeth were bared.

That seemed to be a command, and the others leapt to attention as well, their growls forming a chorus. They had been waiting for her.

She remained as still as possible, trying not to let the fear drive her into a frenzy that would get her killed.

The boy who had been jogging had been rescued, and his attack had occurred at dusk. This was only afternoon. With any luck somebody would happen by, spot the situation and help her, or at least get help.

Maybe someone would call Lucius Rice, and he could bring someone with a gun.

She wondered where the woman she had met inside had disappeared to. Was she still in the hallway somewhere? Surely she hadn't disappeared in the time it had taken to walk outside.

Seconds ticked past. She wasn't looking at her watch, but she knew time was passing even though it was moving slowly. She felt as if she'd been standing still for hours, even though only a couple of minutes could be gone, perhaps only one minute.

She felt the muscles in her calves at the same time she realized there was perspiration on her legs.

The dogs had not changed from their guard positions, and they seemed to be as intense as ever, still snarling, ready to pounce.

They were probably getting restless. Eventually they were going to do something. She didn't know if they were attacking for food. She felt strangely that they had been sent for her.

The way they lingered on her car, they almost seemed to have been waiting for her to emerge from the building.

She was going to have to chance ducking back inside. She could yank the door open and slide behind it, tugging it closed.

They weren't far from her, but they couldn't all reach her at once. One of them might get a piece of her, but she could slam the door on its neck or something. Not a pretty thought but preferable to having the mass of them on her.

She'd heard the talk about the kids that they had killed. She didn't want to be found in pieces.

She remained completely still for a few more moments. She looked into the dogs' eyes. They seemed filled with hatred. Their brows wrinkled into frowns, and their mouths revealed their sharp white teeth.

She could imagine those fangs violating her skin, sinking through tissue, drawing blood.

She would have to move quickly. She didn't want them even getting a chance for an ankle. She paused, glanced from dog to dog, then moved, making the effort as sudden as possible, trying to give them less time to realize what was happening.

With her hand on the latch, she yanked the door back and hurled herself around it, ducking through the opening and grabbing the bar on the inside. She was inside, had made it without being snagged. She tried to pull the door shut, but the closing mechanism at the top of the frame slowed it.

She tried to pull, but the stubborn hydraulic device sighed, taking its damned sweet time.

Before the wood was safely in the frame, a dog's head shot through. It was a huge head, larger at this angle than it had seemed a few feet away.

As she yanked on the door, pressing it against the monster's throat as she had intended to, the beast growled at her and tried to lurch toward her.

She yanked on the pull bar hard, hoping to cut off his breathing and possibly even break his neck, but while he gagged slightly from the pressure, he did not seem otherwise affected.

He kept pushing forward, trying to get at her, trying to force himself through the door. His thick shoulders tensed.

The door's edge began to cut through his fur, but even as blood began to ooze out through the blackness, he did not give up.

Then others of them began to claw at the wood, trying to get it open. Their paws began to dart through the crack over the head of the injured dog. It was as if they were trying to yank it out of her grasp with an effort more determined than she would have thought dogs capable.

She clenched her teeth and looked down into the snarling monster's face. She couldn't hold out against this forever. She had to get his head out of the opening. If she could get the door shut, she could rest and find a telephone or some other way to signal people for help. Even though school hours were over, there should be somebody around to help her.

The question was, how did she get rid of this thing? He was still snarling, still trying to get at her. She didn't like the idea, but the only alternative was to push him out.

She had visions of his mouth swallowing her foot if she stuck it toward him.

But she had no alternative. She lifted her leg slowly, calling on courage she'd forgotten. Placing her heel between the thing's eyes, she pushed.

He resisted, growling deeply, but he had no room to maneuver, no way to get his jaws at her. She heard his feet digging in outside, trying to resist, but she pulled her foot back and stomped.

Something cracked in his head, and his resistance sagged. It didn't subside completely, but she was able to drive him backward.

When he was gone as an obstruction, the door fell easily into its frame, closed at last. She rested against it, sighing as she heard the claws digging against the wood outside.

She let her breath settle for a moment before she moved into the hallway, rushing along in the direction she had traveled before. She was moving past the trophy case again when she heard the sound of the footfalls.

It was impossible, but the dogs were coming, thundering across the floor. She spun just in time to see them slide into the hallway. Their claws did not provide traction on the smooth floor, so they slammed into each other and skidded about as they tried to make progress.

How could they have managed to get inside? It made no sense. Dogs couldn't open doors, but that was academic now. They were here, and she had no cover. She'd never outrun them and find a way into a room.

She turned to the glass case. Trophies with gleaming angels and tarnished basketball players were spread out. Without hesitating, she kicked.

The glass shattered easily. She felt a shard go through her pant leg, but it didn't cut deeply enough to concern her at the moment. There were other things to worry about.

She snatched up a huge metal basketball replica and hurled it down the hall at the dogs, anything to slow them down.

The injured dog was leading the pack, and the metal crashed into his skull, disorienting him. The others tangled into him again, giving her time to snatch up a couple of other trophies. One she threw, hoping the marble base would do some damage.

The three-foot basketball sweepstakes trophy from 1957 she lugged with her. It was the best weapon she was going to find. She was surprised at her own ingenuity, but then she'd watched enough television shows in which heroes improvised.

As blood soaked through her pant leg from the cut, she rushed around the corner where she had seen the old concession stand. The entrance was a thick wooden door with a padlock, a padlock that gave easily when hammered by the base of the trophy.

She flung the door open and ducked inside, slamming it into place behind her. An old metal chair leaned against the wall beside a forgotten popcorn machine that stank of rancid butter.

She opened the chair quickly and placed it under the door knob. She realized she was flowing on adrenalin now, and as she sat down on the floor, snatching up the trophy and clutching it in front of her like a sword that she was near hysteria. And why shouldn't she be?

Slowly she tried to control her breathing as she listened for sounds of the dogs. Her lungs had pumped only a couple of times when the pounding footfalls arrived. For a moment, the dogs scratched at the doors.

When that stopped, she hoped they might be giving up, but then she heard them thudding against the plywood coverings over the serving counter.

Simple metal clasps kept the coverings shut, but they weren't going to hold, not with the size of the dogs. They probably weighed from eighty to one hundred pounds each, and they were taking turns diving at the wood.

Inching back against the cinderblock wall at the rear of the narrow work area, she positioned the statuette, ready to stab or hammer at the dogs with it.

She felt uncontrollable shudders rattling out from the center of her chest, and she thought for a moment she was hyperventilating.

She demanded her brain to take control. Somewhere it found the will to listen, and she braced herself as the loud thuds continued, rattling the clasps, the same kind of clasps used for screen doors.

Finally one of them worked its way out of the wood, and the door swung inward, letting the dog dive through. Its momentum carried it over the counter.

She slid the trophy in front of him as he came down. With the base braced against the floor, it held as the beast's abdomen was impaled.

His weight carried him downward over the sharp, molded angel wings. Blood flowed down over the championship inscription.

She stepped back, letting go of the sides, wiping her hands quickly on her sweater.

She grabbed the counter cover and slammed it down, sliding up on the counter and pressing her shoulder against the wood to keep it in place.

She expected the other dogs to begin another assault, but nothing rattled the other covers, and nothing plowed into the wood she was bracing.

She waited a long time, listening, but she heard no pants or growls. Finally, she decided they must have gone. The smell of the dead mutt and the defecation that had spilled from his collapsed bowels was making it impossible to stay in the narrow, confined space. She climbed over the carcass and carefully moved the chair from the door.

Peering around the door frame, she scanned the hallway. There were no hounds, no sign of them.

She rushed into the corridor and scurried along until she found a pay phone in a small lobby where some unused bookshelves lined the wall.

She called her husband first with her only quarter. He told her he was on his way. She hung up and dialed 911 then. When connected with the emergency operator, she asked to be patched through to Lucius Rice. She still had no idea where Charlie was.

Tigges answered the next time Nell called his number. He had a slow Georgia drawl that made anything she'd heard in Louisiana sound like Bostonian.

Nell told him where she was calling from.

"I didn't know I knew anybody in Louisiana," he said softly. He sounded older than she had expected.

"You know somebody that just moved here," she said.

"Oh? Who's that?"

"Barbara Nielson."

There was a pause, a heavy silence, as if the name surprised him, or shocked him.

"Barbara moved out there?" he said after a moment. The effort to sound casual couldn't have been more obvious.

"She's teaching at the local school," Nell said, waiting to see what response that evoked. Maybe he would tell her the woman had no business being around children.

"Hmm," he said.

She held her breath. He knew something. She just wasn't sure how hard it was going to be to get him to talk. "Who'd you say you were?"

She repeated her name.

"So why are you calling five hundred miles long distance?"

"To see what you know about her. She's teaching a friend of mine."

"She's kind of strange all right. Nice neighbor and all, though."

He wasn't telling all he knew. By his silence it was evident he was wondering if he should.

"If you think she's dangerous, it might help for me to know that. My friend may be in trouble."

"I don't have anything to prove she's dangerous. She's just different. She used to have some strange types visiting her around here."

"What kind of strange types?"

"She wasn't here long. Just a while last year. She was always a nice neighbor. She looked after my place for me. I'm a factory rep for a tobacco company. I have to travel a lot."

"But there's something that has you nervous."

"Well, they were weird people sometimes. An old guy that was kind of odd, some women, good-looking but kind of lost like."

"Did you hear strange noises in the middle of the night?"

"Not like you're talking about. The older man was there a lot. I kind of wondered about him."

He seemed to be growing nervous. "I don't really know who you are," he said.

Nell tapped a finger against the back of the handset. "I'm telling you the truth, Mr. Tigges."

There was more silence. For him to be suspicious was not unusual. This was an odd phone call, but for him to be frightened was revealing. He was afraid someone was checking to see what he knew or suspected.

"Mr. Tigges, I'm trying to get to the bottom of some things. If you know something that might be helpful, I need to know it. Anything, even something you're not sure about. If it will make you more comfortable, I can have our local police chief contact you."

"Barbara is under police investigation?"

"Not exactly, but I've talked to the police chief here. Something out of the ordinary is taking place. We don't know what, but it started when Barbara Nielson arrived."

"I don't know anything specific," he said.

"What do you suspect? Was she performing human sacrifices?"

"I don't know that. That fellow that used to come over there looked like he'd be the type to do that sort of thing, though. He had an evil look about him, a really evil look."

"Do you know his name?"

"No. I never spoke with him, but I know he was like a, well, just like I said, an evil sort of guy."

Nell felt her chest tightening. She had suspected, but now fears were being confirmed. "You think he was a Satanist, Mr. Tigges?"

"Maybe. I mean I never saw him do anything wrong, but I've been hearing all this on TV just like everybody else. I figured if anybody I ever saw looked like they might be a Satanist, it was this guy."

"Did you ever notice his license plate number or anything?"

"No."

She was getting the idea how cops must feel trying to pry information out of people. What was she really learning from this man?

She'd risked a great deal for the shred of information that led her to him, and he had nothing concrete to offer. "How long did she live next to you?" Nell asked.

"Not long. She just showed up one day, and hid in her apartment for a while. Cops came by and talked to her some. That made me wonder about this business, cult stuff, you know. They had a seminar about it at my church. Then eventually she started coming out some, and I spoke to her. Like I said, she watched my place."

"Why did the cops talk to her?"

"I never knew. I figured she might have left an abusive husband or something at first. Then I wondered about drugs. She never said. I never asked."

Nell scribbled down some notes to herself. If the police had checked on something, Rice could make a connection there.

"Is there anything else you can think of, Mr. Tigges? It could be very important."

"That's about all I can come up with. If I'd seen her with Elvis's cadaver or something, I'd sure tell you."

"What about dogs? Did she have any?"

"No ..."

There was a pause.

"You're going to say: but ... ?"

"But several pets in the complex out here disappeared. We thought it was a ring or something, but I think it happened right around the time she moved in."

Nell thanked him and hung up the phone.

Chapter 24

Once he had a paramedic taking care of Mrs. Black in the parking lot, Rice walked back into the school. He rested his hand on his gun as he moved into the concession stand, but the dog wasn't moving.

He knelt beside it, holding his breath as he examined the carcass. He could find no sign that it was anything other than a very large dog. With a chunk of metal driven through its ribs, it had died, just like organisms were supposed to when trauma occurred.

That gave him a feeling of security, or at least reassurance that the world was as he had always believed it to be. He was not required to believe mystical things were real, at least not for the moment.

He would have to let the vet look at these remains, but for the moment all appeared under control. And at least there was one less dog to worry about.

He closed the door to contain the stench and walked back outside. Mrs. Black was sitting in the back of the ambulance summoned by the 911 operator.

A thin, blonde woman in a blue uniform had clipped Mrs. Black's pant leg and was applying some cleansing agent to the small wound on her calf. A piece of glass had lodged in her leg and had continued to do damage as she had run. There was a lot of blood on her clothing, but she didn't seem to be in pain.

She was quite pale, however, and she was badly shaken. Rice was afraid she might collapse before he had a chance to question her.

He'd already heard the basics of her story, but he hoped he might get some more information, something that could lead him to the rest of the pack.

Leaning one hand against the ambulance door, he nodded toward Mrs. Black. "You have no idea where they came from?"

She shook her head. "I was in the building. I came out and they were here, just like they were waiting for me. But the weird thing is that I ran back inside and got the door closed. I thought I was safe, and then the next thing I knew they were coming down the hall."

"Dogs don't open doors," Rice said. "Maybe the door didn't close all the way."

"I made sure it did," Mrs. Black protested.

That's what Rice had been afraid of. Did it mean the dogs had some mystical power, or had someone let the door open to let them pursue Mrs. Black?

Leaving her to her first aid, he walked back and checked the door. There were scratches. He saw no way of determining if it had been latched.

He was looking around on the ground for other signs when the paramedic approached him.

"The woman's worried about her son," she said.

"Tell her not to worry," Rice said. "If anything had happened besides this, I'd have heard about it by now."

He was still looking for signs when Daniel Black arrived.

"What the hell happened?" he demanded. "How did the dogs get into the school?"

"They followed your wife in there," Rice told him. "Some deputies are checking through the woods right now.

He showed Black where his wife was being treated, then leaned against the side of the ambulance. Other people were going to be asking questions.

If the dogs could get into the school building in broad daylight, how could anybody be considered safe? People would be demanding action quickly, or there would be a panic.

They were going to try to cancel school tomorrow without question. He'd have to let the mayor contact the superintendent to deal with that decision. Then some dead dogs better be produced or people would be leaving town and police chiefs and politicians were going to be out of work.

He wanted to spit when he turned around and spotted the television vans.

Barbara was watching the Aimsley station when they broke into their newscast with a live feed from the Petittville High parking lot. She listened to Chief Rice give his account of what had happened while she waited for Sawyer to arrive.

The policeman didn't name names, but he stressed that an adult and not a student had been attacked.

"Was it a teacher?" the exotic-looking woman holding the microphone asked.

"No. A parent." He was beginning to look uncomfortable.

"She wasn't hurt by the dogs. She did kill one of them."

"She had a trophy that had been on display. It had a sharp point, an angel's wings."

"How many other dogs do you believe there are?" she asked, a little of her Southern accent slipping through her polished speech.

"That's undetermined."

"What steps are you taking to protect the citizens?"

"We have help from the state police and the sheriff's office. I'm going to make every effort to be sure that the school is safe tomorrow, and I'm also hoping people will stay in their homes tonight. We're trying to do our best to deal with this and get to the bottom of things."

"Get to the bottom, chief? Do you suspect there's something more here than dog attacks?"

"That's all I can say at this time." He turned away from the camera, leaving the newscaster to finish her standup with a few comments to the anchorman.

With the remote control, Barbara turned off the set, resting her head against one hand as she listened to the cooling pops.

She wasn't sure she felt like seeing Sawyer tonight, but she couldn't keep putting him off. She wanted him close, didn't want him to get away. He was too nice, too good to be allowed to escape.

She needed to draw closer to him before he started to grow tired of her ups and downs.

DeSarno had warned her about her mood swings. He had warned her about many things. In many ways, in the later years, he had been a teacher rather than a lover.

Yet she had loved him passionately. She had wanted him to know that, wanted him to understand she would do anything for him.

Anything.

He had suggested the liaison with Doss, something she had at first been horrified by. She hated to see Doss visit Kule, but DeSarno encouraged her to come on to her former paramour to win his trust.

Only after she had begun to take Doss to the place where she coupled with DeSarno did she understand the older man's purpose. He had given her the knife late one night, explaining to her softly what he wanted, what he expected.

He wanted Doss's drug connections, wanted Doss's business for reasons of his own.

For DeSarno, she agreed. He was all that she could ever think of wanting. He was so elegant, so pleasant. She agreed, listening carefully as he explained that she should hide the knife first, so that she would have access to it when she took Doss out for a rendezvous.

Each time Doss came near her, she thought of the time he had sought to dominate her. She feared that at any time the enjoyment of her body would cease to be enough. She knew he would eventually want to do something horrible as he had before.

That made it easy to hate him, easier to think about killing him.

DeSarno talked to her about it frequently, until he felt she was ready. It would make her stronger, he promised, and then he instructed her that the next time Doss came, it would be the time.

The knife was already in place, hidden in the leaves at the spot she felt her right hand would fall upon as she lay on her back.

Doss was wearing jeans and a denim jacket when he showed up at the house. He was handsome, his roguish style intact. Kule was in his room playing computer games, so she felt no hesitation to fall into her old lover's arms.

She let him feel her body pressing against him for a moment and then took his hand, leading him outside.

He did not resist. He wanted her. He was excited that a woman could desire him again after what he had done to her. To him, it confirmed his masculinity. She read that in his eyes.

Good enough. Let him believe that. With her hand in his, she walked him out to the spot, stopping when she was where she wanted to be.

Quickly she let her hands move over him, peeling off the denim before she shed the shift she was wearing.

His lips were warm on her flesh, and for an instant she recalled the passion she had once felt for him. Her body tingled, became warm with anticipation and she let her head roll back as he kissed her neck and her breasts. As she recalled his evil, nausea replaced stimulation. She hated him, and she wanted to spit the bitter bile from her throat.

They tumbled onto the ground, wrapping around each other. He ran his hands through her hair and then gripped her shoulders as he filled her.

She felt charges of pleasure coursing through her, and she recalled what it could be like, what ecstasy could be. It was the wrong ecstasy, however. As she had learned to do with Kule, she shut off the sensation. Then she reached down and pulled the blade from the leaves and jammed it into his back, forcing it through cartilage, angling it so that it plunged downward into muscle and then a lung. Summoning strength, she forced the blade in to the hilt.

The hoarse rasps that rattled from his throat were like growls, and the twitches of his convulsing muscles made it seem for a moment that he was still thrusting.

Blood and spittle seeped through his lips, stringing down onto her.

The bursting flood of her own orgasm had come then, and she had cried out, letting the scream rise up loud and long through her lips. It was almost savage, primal, a cry of victory as much as pleasure.

That had been a long time ago, years, but she could remember it as if it had occurred just before her last heartbeat.

Only Sawyer's knock at her door brought her back to the present.

He stood on her welcome mat with a bouquet of fresh yellow flowers, their stems wrapped in green florist's paper. The look in his eyes conveyed boyish nervousness. He wasn't sure if this was the right thing, and he was waiting for her response.

She didn't want to disappoint him. She reached out for them, letting her face show surprise and amazement. "Oh, they're wonderful," she said.

After she had taken them, she put one arm around his neck and hugged him, pressing her body against him as she gave him a kiss on the cheek. He had been worried by her behavior, afraid he was losing ground. She needed to reassure him.

"You didn't have to do this." She took his hand and led him toward the couch.

After she had drawn some water in a vase, she placed the flowers on an end table and then sat beside him.

He didn't have the angry strength of Doss or DeSarno's power and sophistication. He was uncertain, a man out of his element when he was not in front of a classroom.

Yet his eyes were so blue, his dark hair tousled just enough to make him look like a boy who'd just come from the playground.

He was dressed tonight in jeans and a gray work shirt with a black vest over it. The outfit made him look stylish, though it was probably based on something he'd seen on television.

She slipped her hand behind his head, letting her fingers run through his hair. What would her life have been like if she had met him long ago, loved him long ago, married?

She brought her lips to his. It was different from old passions, not driven by fire but that did not mean it did not burn deeply into her.

She felt Sawyer's arms move around her, and they continued to kiss as she eased back on the couch.

With his warm kisses on her throat, she forgot all other lovers. She was close to something real here, close to love. If he wanted to marry her, she would give up almost everything else. She had come a long way to this moment, past Doss and Kule and DeSarno.

DeSarno had taught her so much, given her much, but he had not been without demands. He had his reasons for wanting her, but Sawyer only wanted her because he needed love.

She folded her arms behind his neck, gripping him tightly. She could tell he had been a long time without experiencing affection. He kissed her neck and let his mouth move across the hollow of her throat. She tilted her head back, closing her eyes, relaxing. She could hear his breathing accelerating, yet he seemed to be holding back, making an effort to be gentle.

She bit softly at his ear and kissed his neck, trying to signal him that she enjoyed his affection.

He kissed her harder, but he still seemed restrained.

He was not aggressive, not sure of himself.

She let her hands slide across his shoulders, down his back. He felt wonderful, not an athlete but trim, muscular.

She began to kiss the side of his neck as he buried his face in the hollow of her throat, and her fingers glided along his belt, sliding between her body and his.

The edge of the buckle was smooth to her touch, and she began to tug at it. He jerked away from her as if her fingers had become red-hot.

Shifting off of her, he sat on the side of the couch and touched the back of his neck.

"What's the matter?" she asked. She pulled one leg under her and rested her face against his back.

"Nothing."

He continued to rub his eyes.

"Was I being too forward?"

"Ah, it's all right."

He turned back at her, and he looked disappointed. His eyes were clouded.

"I didn't mean to be too aggressive," she said.

"It's not that. I don't know. I guess I just … I don't know."

"It's okay." Here was a new experience, a man who didn't want her to be so ready. It was refreshing, yet it also made her quiver inside. Had she done something that would ruin it all? In only the tick of the second hand, things seemed to have changed.

She bit her lip and tried to prevent tears from escaping. "You want to go get a hamburger?" he asked.

"Sure."

She got a sweater from the closet, and they drove over to the café. It would have been a short walk, but there were the dogs to think about.

He was silent as they ate, and she could think of nothing to say to break through to him.

She had been afraid he was too shy and needed the assurance that she wanted what he wanted. Now she realized she didn't know what he wanted at all.

Rice was back at his house fielding angry phone calls when Nell found him. Mrs. Rice showed her into the living room, where he was sitting in his easy chair. He held the phone to his ear.

"Yes sir, I know you're worried. We have deputies hunting for the dogs right now. School won't be canceled tomorrow. I'm sorry, but we are going to have deputies around campus. Just stay inside tonight. Everybody will be safe."

He hung up and looked across the room at Nell. His eyes looked weary, and a wrinkle of worry rippled across his brow.

"You coming to complain or did you find more voodoo for me to check on?"

"I talked to one of Barbara Nielson's neighbors in Atlanta."

"How'd you find one?"

"I telephoned."

He looked at her skeptically but nodded for her to continue.

"She lived next door to Tigges for just a little while, probably right before she moved here."

"And she played her music really loud and disturbed him, right?"

"The guy used to see mysterious guests showing up at her place, and not long before she left, the police visited her."

"Did they arrest her?"

"No. Nothing like that. They only talked to her apparently, but you're a policeman. You could talk to them, find something out."

Rice breathed deeply. "I suppose I could. What do you think I might learn?"

"Who knows? But it couldn't hurt to check it out."

"I guess not."

He picked up the phone and dialed Information. When he had written down the police number in Atlanta, he dialed. After a couple of conversations, he determined he would not be able to gather any information until morning. Even in big cities bureaucracy slowed down at night, not caring if cops had to work twenty-four hours.

"I'll see what I can do tomorrow."

"I hope that's soon enough," Nell said.

"So do I," Rice said. "I hope those bastards take the night off."

The dog came through Delia's window without warning, its weight carrying it through the screen, the fine mesh surrendering to its claws with very little resistance.

Before she could throw back the covers and scream, it had jumped onto the foot of her mattress. She kicked at her sheet and blanket, trying to free herself of them as she pressed back against the headboard.

The dog moved toward her too quickly for an escape. Its eyes blazed red in the darkness and spittle dripped out the corners of its mouth as it bared its fangs.

The sick, foul smell of its breath swept up her nose, gagging her. She thought she was going to vomit, and she placed her fist over her mouth, trying to hold back the bile as she waited for the monster to rip into her.

She woke with a jolt. She was staring up at her ceiling. Her legs were tangled in her covers, but there was no dog. She had gone to sleep thinking of Charlie, not long after hearing about his mother.

Her mom had told her after talking to someone on the phone. The news had rattled her, so she'd turned in early.

She had not told her mom that she had been with Charlie at school or that his mom was probably looking for him because he was late coming home. Delia told herself it was not really her fault, not her fault that Miss Nielson had found them and not her responsibility that Mrs. Black had been attacked.

It had always been safe in the dressing room. Duty teachers who stayed after school never checked there. No one ever came there. How had she known?

Mrs. Black should not have come looking for Charlie, either. It wasn't that late after school. She was apparently overprotective, definitely not like Delia's mom, who had things of her own to think about.

As she looked around the room, making sure there were no dogs crouching in the shadows, she realized she was sweating. She was also trembling, yet she didn't want to throw back the covers.

The fabric would not stop any attacker, human or animal, but she still felt better, safer beneath the blankets.

She let her head sink back into the softness of her pillow. What bad luck she'd had with Charlie. He was so cute and so sweet. They had just been having fun, not doing anything really wrong. She wouldn't have let him take too many liberties, but then Miss Nielson had barged in.

Hopefully she hadn't said too much to Charlie. What reason would she have to ruin things?

As her fear subsided, Delia felt her trembling ease. She thought about Charlie. She would see him tomorrow and tell him how sorry she was about his mother. Maybe they would at least have some time to talk, and maybe he would ask her out if he wasn't in too much trouble. He could no longer doubt now that she liked him.

Maybe they would start going together, maybe even get married someday. If Miss Nielson didn't mess things up. What was her interest in Charlie anyway?

Finally sleep crept back over her brain, and she dreamed for a while about Charlie. It was not a steamy dream, just a simple image of his features and his smile. He had a wonderful smile that brightened his entire face.

He held her hand and smiled right at her and she felt herself melting. But once again Miss Nielson interrupted.

She stood behind the dream Charlie and the Dream Delia. Delia turned and looked at her, and she smiled at her. It was such a mean, evil smile that Delia began to cry.

Suddenly she was trapped alone in the dream with the teacher's dark image. She looked like a demoness with her eyebrows arched and her dark hair spilling wildly down around her face.

"What do you want?" Delia asked.

"Stay away from Charlie."

"He's my friend. I like him."

The smile left Miss Nielson's features. She looked down at Delia with a glare that seemed to glow just as the dog's eyes had earlier.

"He doesn't need you."

"He doesn't have anybody." She was almost crying. "No friends really."

"He doesn't need you, you little tramp. Leave him alone."

"I like him."

"I'm warning you. If you don't stay away from Charlie, the dogs will come for you."

Her dream self closed her eyes. "I don't believe you. You're just a nightmare."

"Is that what you want to believe? Don't count on it. I want you to stay away from Charlie. If you want to stay alive, you'll do as I say."

She sat upright in bed. Once again she was safe in her room, but she was trembling worse than before. She wanted to cry out.

She felt not just as if she had had a nightmare, but as if someone had been inside her head. It had been too real.

She hadn't just dreamed Miss Nielson. The woman had been there, in her head. That wasn't possible, but that's the way it seemed.

Had she put the dog there too? Had she made her dream of the dog to frighten her?

That didn't make sense. She lay back on her pillows. It was the middle of the night. She was upset about being discovered with Charlie.

Everything would be all right. She'd talk to Charlie about it in the morning.

Chapter 25

The next morning, Delia searched the hallways for Charlie, praying she would find him before classes started. She finally located him at his locker, just a few minutes before the bell.

"How's your mother?" she asked.

"Fine," Charlie said. He looked tired. Dark half-moons were curled under his eyes. "She was out looking for me."

"Are you in trouble?"

He shrugged. "I was already grounded. My dad was pretty pissed, but he was more worried about my mom than anything. They gave her some sedatives, but he sat with her most of the evening. I stayed in my room. I was working on a Tor Johnson model kit I've had for a while."

Delia didn't know who Tor Johnson was, and she didn't have time to bother with asking. "Are you mad at me?"

He shook his head. "We had bad luck," he said, closing his locker door.

"How did she know where we were?"

He tucked his books under his arm. "I don't know."

"Nobody ever goes back there, Charlie. She wouldn't have just happened on that room."

"I don't know what to make of it," Charlie said.

"I had a dream about her," Delia confessed. "I had a nightmare about the dogs first, and then she was in my dream, telling me to stay away from you."

Charlie's eyes widened. "What did she say?"

"She said the dogs would get me. Charlie, the other night I heard something at my window. Maybe they were there then."

Charlie's face lost color, and he placed one hand against the lockers to steady himself. "The dogs have only attacked people I know," Charlie said almost under his breath.

"What?"

"Nell noticed it. Everyone who's been attacked has had some connection to me. The Assholes were mean to me right before they started getting killed, and John Tessman was messing around with me in the gym. Budd was my best friend. My mom, now you."

"Miss Nielson said to stay away from you."

"What does she want?" Charlie asked. "I don't understand. She showed up here and everything started getting weird. First I thought she liked me or something, now I can't tell."

"You never saw her before she came here?"

"No."

"Do you think I was just dreaming, Charlie? It felt so real, like it was more than a dream."

"I don't know. It's crazy, but it ..." He stopped in midsentence.

Delia didn't have to turn around to know what had silenced him, but she looked over her shoulder anyway. Miss Nielson was standing there, watching. She didn't speak, didn't move, but there was a look in her eyes. It wasn't anger. It was more like complacency, a smugness.

"Maybe we can talk later," Delia whispered to Charlie. She pushed past him, hurrying down the hallway. She could feel Miss Nielson's gaze burning into her even as she hurried away.

Rice tried the Atlanta police around 8 A.M., figuring it would be 9 A.M. out there. He was transferred around the building a few times, it seemed, but finally mentioning his New Orleans connections and boiling ire in his voice broke down some barriers.

They put him on with a detective, and he discussed the information Nell had provided. That got him referred to the sheriff's office since the location was their jurisdiction.

Twenty-five minutes after he had begun his calling efforts, he was connected with Red Hanson.

She sounded harried, even at the early hour. He could envision her sitting on her desk, coffee cup in one hand, other hand straightening her inevitably red hair while she pressed the receiver to her ear with her shoulder.

"Where are you from?" she asked.

He explained where Petittville was, certain he wasn't impressing her.

"And what are you trying to run down?" she asked. "I was out late trying to talk to some people, so you're lucky you caught me in here this morning. I have about a dozen reports to file."

"What I'm calling about may be related to Satanism, or at least some kind of occult activity," he said.

He heard her breathe. The sigh was so heavy he was lucky it didn't come through the receiver. "Have you had a seminar or something? Everything may be related to Satanism these days. If you've got some dry bones and funny markings, you've probably got a dead goat and some kids that have been listening to heavy metal records."

"It's a little more than that. I've got some dead kids and dog attacks. I've also got a woman who may have been checked out in Atlanta at one time. I'm operating with limited resources here, but I'm doing the best I can. I know this all sounds like backwater bullshit to you, but I'm from New Orleans. I worked the streets there a long time, so I have an idea of what your job is like."

"I see." Her voice had lost some of the edge. "What's the name?"

"Barbara Nielson. Maybe. I don't know if it's an alias, but apparently she didn't hold the jobs out there she said she did."

"Well, you're on a roll. I know her."

He almost dropped the phone. "You don't even have to run a computer check?"

"Nope. We're familiar with Miss Nielson out here. We haven't been able to charge her with anything, but she's got her background. Nielson's not her real name, but that's the name she's been going by for the last ten years or so."

"You've had an eye on her for ten years?"

"Not me personally, and not for that long. We watch a lot of people. She stands out because she's been involved in the past with some activities you wouldn't hear about in an occult seminar."

"Why's that?" Rice asked.

"The seminars are usually tied in around a couple of scenarios involving fears about devil worship. Your Miss Nielson there, if she's the same one, has associated with The Microcosm for some time."

"That's a cult?"

"Of sorts. They've been involved in criminal activity here for some time. We've uncovered minor members, but we have evidence that the group is involved in drugs and other criminal activity.

"They're sort of like what you're told about Satanists. The pentagram symbol is considered a microcosm, and somehow the name evolved from that but they're different from devil worshipers. Their belief system is descended from a black magic society called The Mopses of Germany. We're not sure how the order reappeared in modern times, but from what literature we have, that seems to be the origin.

"The original symbol of the cult was a dog."

"I don't like what I'm hearing," Rice said. "Have you found them possibly training attack dogs?"

"I wouldn't put it past them. I've known them to own dogs. Barbara Nielson first showed up as a paramour for Galan Zaebos DeSarno. Their relationship apparently began more than ten years ago. It would have been in the mid-seventies based on files. That was right around the first time that Americans became aware of Satanism.

"Galan was another one we could never pin anything on, but at any rate, he was some sort of priest in their order. He died of a heart attack a year ago.

"Your lady moved out to north Atlanta around that time. We checked her out because we thought she might have been involved in his death. A power struggle was touched off in the ranks from what we could tell. She didn't win it."

"So she may have been ousted?"

"Oh that's highly likely. We've pinpointed a new leader, apparently overseeing some of the criminal activities.

"Well, you're giving me an idea of what I'm up against. I guess I need to question Miss Nielson. None of that makes her guilty, though."

"What would bring her out to the middle of Louisiana?" Red asked.

"Beats me. She's just a school teacher out here."

"Well, be careful. She may have killed people. We just couldn't prove it. Have you got a fax?"

He gave her City Hall's fax number.

"I'll ship you what I can on her. Maybe it'll help. I don't know about trained dogs, but I do know The Microcosm has been involved in some strange doings."

"Are you saying there might be real black magic involved?"

"Those are your words, chief. But I'd be careful."

"Thanks. I'll read your stuff before I approach her."

"Good luck," she said. "And God bless."

Sawyer was withdrawn when Barbara approached him in the hallway between classes. He tried a smile, but he didn't wear it well. He was troubled, his face an ashen gray.

"What's wrong?" she asked, feeling knots twist in her own stomach. She liked this man, didn't want him to feel uncomfortable or troubled about their relationship.

"Nothing," he said. "Really."

"Why don't we get together and talk," she suggested.

"I'll fix us something to eat after school."

"I'd like that," he said.

She looked into his eyes for a moment before turning away.

She didn't like the feeling of insecurity. She hadn't expected that from him. She had begun to enjoy his boyish crush, expecting it to blossom when she had time to give full attention to him.

She had not planned—as people so often said—on falling in love. Those emotions were stirring now, though, and the thought of having it evade her was painful.

She had lost too many things in her life. She had lost family. She had lost Galan, she had given up love. There had been too many disappointments.

As she walked back toward her classroom, she felt the anger boiling within her. She had not been angry in a long time, perhaps not since coming to Louisiana, but now she had a feeling things were out of control. She knew she couldn't let that show.

She walked briskly into her classroom, and standing at the board, she scribbled an assignment with chalk as kids filed into the room.

Turning, she scanned the faces. Charlie was not due this hour. With a jerk, she plopped her chalk down in the tray and moved to her seat. She could see the kids were puzzled.

She glared back at them until they stopped staring. Then she looked down at her grade book. After the bell sounded, she called roll without looking up. Then she let them work on their own, staring out the window as the hour ticked past.

It seemed to take an eon.

Sawyer stood in front of his class, finding it hard to concentrate as he explained an equation. He kept getting confused when students asked questions, and finally he assigned some problems in the book and sat down.

He urged the feeling of confusion to leave him, but it would not. It nestled in his abdomen, a dull ache.

Did it matter that she had been a bit aggressive? He had wanted to feel her warmth, to touch and kiss her, but he hadn't expected her to want more.

Sawyer had not dated many women. Petittville was a small town. There were not a large number of girls around. He had always dreamed of finding someone like Barbara, soft and quiet.

The fact that she had set their liaison into motion had rattled him. In one second, it made him aware of a fact he had not wanted to consider.

Barbara had known other men; there could be no doubt. He had not let himself wonder before, but now they hovered in his thoughts, faceless ghosts who taunted him. They had known her, had experienced all of her secrets.

He had never suspected that would matter, had never considered how it would make him feel. Now he could not stop thinking of others between her legs, pumping into her, kissing her naked flesh. Who had been the first? How many had there been? Had she enjoyed it?

He had had trouble sleeping, finally managing to doze off, only to awaken an hour before his alarm sounded. He had never felt pain like this, had never experienced anguish that tried to wrench him apart.

Sawyer had dated a few women, had groped and fondled, but he had never made love, had never had sex. Time had somehow passed him up; he was a quiet man, not aggressive in that department, and so sex had eluded him.

He had not consciously been seeking a virgin, but somewhere inside, his hope had been to meet someone with whom he could discover the secrets of intimacy.

There had been so much he liked about her. She had seemed to be what he needed, an answer to his loneliness, but now he wasn't sure what he should do.

He felt as if there were something inside him, eating away at him. He imagined pieces of his internal organs being bitten away, then more intangible fragments of his being, slivers of his soul, being devoured and digested.

He thought of weeping, but he knew it would have no effect. Even if he left his students and sought seclusion, the release would provide no solace.

He was trapped somewhere within his own feelings—his blossoming love for Barbara and his inability to accept her life before she had known him.

He would have to talk to her. That was the only thing he could envision, the only hope of quelling the pain. He would talk to her, and she would understand, and they would deal with his feelings. He only had to survive until after school. Not long at all. Not long at all.

———

Between classes, Nell called Rice's home. He was tightlipped at first, but she kept asking questions.

"You're going to have to let me handle this from now on," he said.

"I only want to help."

"It's not the job for a civilian. I'm going to question Barbara Nielson after school. I don't want to walk in and yank her out of class and let her know I suspect her. The Atlanta people have been watching her for years and haven't got anything to pin on her."

He briefly explained what he had learned.

"Be careful, chief."

"I'm going to be real careful," Rice said. "Staying alive may be a challenge around here."

When she hung up, Nell telephoned Michael collect. "Have you learned anything else from your friends?" she asked.

"I went back over there," he said. "We talked for a while. They're interesting guys, but they don't really have much to go on yet. They threw out theories, but they want to talk to some more people and look in some more books."

"I have more for you," she said. She gave him the name The Microcosm and The Mopses.

"Maybe they can tell you what kind of spells people of that order would use to conjure hellhounds," she said.

"It's a possibility. I'm finishing some stuff up here, so I'll head over there this afternoon. It's in a shitty neighborhood. The last time I went down there, a gang threatened me."

"Be careful, but tell me something as soon as you can."

"I will. Don't worry. I'm on the job."

"I appreciate your help too. It means a lot."

"Sure. Glad to do it," he said.

"Talk to you later." *Hopefully with answers*, she thought.

Charlie's head hurt. Delia had been threatened. Was it because Miss Nielson had discovered them together? Was she jealous of Delia?

Not just people who tried to harm him were suffering. People who were close to him—his mom, his girlfriend—were being hurt.

Miss Nielson had come into his dreams, and now she had appeared in Delia's. Could that be coincidence?

He'd seen enough horror movies to know it couldn't be a chance occurrence. It was somehow intentional. Miss Nielson had zeroed in on Delia this morning, had known she would find them together. Why did she care?

He was going to have to confront her. If he ever wanted things to be normal, he was going to have to find out what was wrong and settle it.

The only way to do that was ask her. She wouldn't murder him in the middle of the hallway during the school day. She wouldn't unhinge her jaw and swallow his head, so he would ask her. Class was coming up, so he would sit through it, endure her stares, and then stay afterward.

Easy to think, harder to perform, but he would try it. If it didn't produce results, or if his suspicions proved unfounded, he would accept the embarrassment and look for other answers.

His thoughts kept playing with possibilities as he went through his classes, but he was even more convinced when the hour for English approached.

When he moved through the hallway toward Miss Nielson's room, he forced himself to remain calm and steeled himself for discussion.

She was standing in the hallway as he moved toward her door. With her arms folded, she seemed unusually complacent watching him draw near.

He didn't speak as he passed her. She was silent also, but words were unnecessary. She had a knowing look, an assured attitude.

He sat at his desk, not looking at her for the entire hour. Finally, the bell rang, and students began to file from the room.

Charlie stayed in his seat, watching the others leave. He closed his books and stacked them in front of him without making any effort to pick them up. He rested his hands on the text's cover.

Miss Nielson remained at her desk also. The other kids didn't seem to notice, but Charlie could tell she was looking directly at him.

Her eyes had the same gleam he had noticed earlier when she had stared at Delia, and she placed one hand smugly under her chin.

When the last of the students had filed from the classroom, he rose and walked toward her. People flowed past the door, but no one entered. She did not have another class during the next period.

She waited for him to reach her, silent, patient as he approached. A flicker of a smile formed on her lips as he stood in front of her. He placed his hands on the edge of her desk.

"What's going on, Charlie?"

"That's what I was going to ask you," he said.

She arched her eyebrows and pursed her lips. "Well. That seems a bit forward of you. I am your teacher."

"What else are you?"

She laughed. "What are you getting at?"

"Delia had nightmares about you," he said. "I've had nightmares too."

Her eyebrows moved up again. "Nightmares, Charlie?"

He turned away, but only for a second. "What do you want from me? I thought at first you had some weird attraction for me. Now I can't figure out what it is."

"You're a very bright and special student, Charlie. I've been trying to show you that."

"The dog attacks started when you came, and only people who have had some connection with me have been affected."

"Your friends? Your enemies? Your mom?"

"Yes."

"Budd wasn't a good influence on you, was he? He was a crude boy, a troublemaker. He would have gotten you into trouble before long."

Charlie began to tremble. He drew a sharp wisp of breath. What was she saying?

"And those boys who attacked you? Were their deaths any great loss to society?"

He sensed his hands curling into fists at his side. Something in his jaw began to twitch, and he felt more like crying than he had in a long time.

"What are you saying?"

"I'm only making observations, Charlie," she said in a very innocent voice, yet her tone mocked innocence.

"John Tessman was attacked after I told you what happened in the gym."

"He was mean, don't you think? Maybe the dogs can sense that, or maybe they just like you, Charlie."

"What's going on?" he repeated.

"Why would they attack your mom?"

She leaned across the desk now, not smiling, but there was a glow about her face.

"I don't know," Charlie said. "Why?"

"Maybe she's not your mother."

"Of course she's my mother."

"What if she's not? If she's perpetrating a hoax and the dogs are trying to help you, then wouldn't they attack her?"

Charlie turned and took a couple of steps toward the door. He felt his skin igniting. He slammed his hand against the door frame, then spun back toward Miss Nielson.

"What are you saying?" he asked.

She stood and extended her hands toward him. "I was waiting for the right time to tell you, waiting until you were ready, but I guess that won't come."

Charlie almost snarled as he looked over at her. "What?"

"I'm your mother, Charlie."

Lightning bolt, right through the forehead, news he could not understand. Now he raised a hand to the door facing to steady himself.

He was looking at the floor as he heard Miss Nielson's heels clicking toward him. She stopped only a few feet from him, waiting for him to look at her.

When he obliged, he did not find the grin he expected. He could not interpret her expression, but he thought he saw some compassion in her eyes. He didn't find what he wanted, an indication she was lying.

"How can you be my mother?" he asked.

"It was a long time ago, Charlie, and it's a long story. I was put out of my home, and I lived on the street until I fell in love with a man. That was a mistake, but before he died, he fathered you."

"That's not true," Charlie protested. "I've always been with mom and dad."

"Why do you think you're an only child, Charlie? Your mother's uterus is scarred. She can't have children."

"Bullshit!" He spat the word at her.

"She couldn't have babies, but she wanted one very badly. She and your father had only been married a little while, but she was obsessed with having a child.

"Fortunately for her, her father had money, and connections. A man who was taking care of me back then knew I didn't want to give you up, but he knew that you would be in danger if you stayed with me."

"What kind of danger?" he asked. He was still hoping for a loophole, or some flicker that indicated she was lying.

"We were part of an organization, very secretive, very selective. A baby would have served many purposes. Galan DeSarno knew I would refuse to give you up at the command of the elders, so he arranged for you to be sold. He felt your parents would take good care of you.

"I'm sure they have, but now it's time for us to be together, Charlie. I've left The Microcosm, the group I participated in. I want us to have a life together, be a family."

"I don't even know you," Charlie protested. "You aren't my mother."

"You'll get to know me, Charlie. Don't you understand I had no choice?"

Some of the confidence she had displayed seemed to be eroding. She kept her expression unwavering, but she pressed.

"Aren't you unhappy with your parents? They don't treat you right. They don't understand you're special. I've tried to make you see that."

"After you got my attention by pretending there was some kind of attraction. Why am I special?"

"You're brighter than these other kids, Charlie. There are so many things I could show you. The things you can become at my side are unlimited."

"You mean be part of some cult?"

"No. I've left The Microcosm, Charlie. I'm ready to move on, to start a life, a normal life for you."

Charlie felt his emotions twisting around inside him. What if she was his mother? That would explain his father's coldness and his mother's overprotective nature. They had bought him. He was property, and his mother had probably lived in fear of someone showing up to take him away.

Someone like Barbara.

Chapter 26

Barbara's walk was almost a run as she headed home. She felt her emotions imploding, and she didn't want to collapse on the street.

Charlie had not responded as she had hoped. She had been forced to reveal things to him before she was truly ready, and she had only managed to confuse him.

She was going to have to talk to him again soon, convince him that he needed to go with her. She had worked too hard to lose him now, even if she could not keep up with Sawyer.

When she reached her apartment, she rushed into the living room, tossing her books on a table. She sat on the couch, and tears began to flow just as the phone rang. She wiped her eyes and forced composure upon herself before she lifted the receiver.

Sawyer's voice greeted her. "Hi. Hoped you might be home by now."

"Just walked in the door," she said, trying to sound chipper.

"I was hoping I could come over for a while this evening."

She couldn't make out anything from his tone. "I'd like that," she said cautiously. Maybe at least she could get things smoothed over with him. Then they would have a chance to see if the relationship might work out. She had a vision of herself with Sawyer and Charlie.

How perfect that seemed. She could forget about Doss forever, put The Microcosm behind her and the magic. She would not need it any longer. Not once she had Charlie.

She would talk to Sawyer when he arrived. She would explain her past, explain her mistakes and that she had had no choice. He would understand. She would make him understand and tell him that she was falling in love with him.

They'd had only a little time together, but with what she had known in her life, a little time was all she needed. She knew she loved him, knew they could make a fine life together.

She pulled herself off the couch and snatched a tissue, working on her eyes. She would quell the tears and have herself looking calm and normal when he arrived.

She was headed for her bedroom to select something to wear when the knock came at the door.

Too early for Sawyer. Could it be Charlie? She ran her hands through her hair and moved over to twist the knob.

Her heart raced when she looked out to see the uniformed black man facing her. He held a police hat in his hands and nodded politely as he introduced himself as the chief of police.

"I was wondering if I might ask you a few questions, Miss Nielson."

She forced her features to remain pleasant. "What about?" she asked, trying to seem surprised.

"Kind of general stuff," he said. "You're new in town, right?"

"That's right." She tried not to sound defensive. He may just be making routine inquiries. She'd talked to policemen before. You could never tell how much they knew.

Sometimes they pretended to know more than they did, coaxing out information. She had to be careful here. No matter what he knew or suspected, there was no need to volunteer information.

"I'm having a hard time with these dog attacks," Rice said. "I'm the one everybody looks to, but it's not really like investigating a regular murder or anything. With people, I can look for standard connections. Dog attacks seem random, so I've been wandering around practically useless."

"You're not out hunting them down?"

"The sheriff's department has been helping out, but the dogs seem to vanish during the day. They seem to disappear completely unless they're attacking someone."

"How odd."

"Makes you wonder if maybe somebody had trained them or something."

"Could dogs be trained to do that sort of thing?"

"I talked to the vet. He said they can be trained to attack. What we've found with these dogs goes beyond just attack training, though. They'd have to be trained really well, maybe even antagonized somehow. There may be techniques we don't know about."

"Are you getting at something, Chief?"

He shrugged. "Do you know anything about cults that utilize dogs in their rituals?"

She didn't let a reaction show. She shrugged. "I'm sure people do a variety of things in the world today."

"You're from Atlanta, right? They've had reports of a group out there called The Microcosm. Ever hear of them?"

"There are lots of groups. Some make the news. Some don't."

The vagueness was not slipping past him. He'd probably had plenty of experience with evasive people, but what did he know? That she'd been part of a group in Atlanta? That didn't mean anything. She'd never been charged with any crimes, and affiliation there didn't mean guilt here. Even the Atlanta cops had never tried to charge her with anything.

Of course there was the possibility he was only trying to let her know he knew things about her. That could be designed to make her stumble, give something away or panic and make a mistake.

He would probably be watching her closely from now on. That meant caution would be necessary. And swiftness.

"I don't guess you own any dogs," Rice said.

"No. I don't."

"Never thought about a dog for protection?"

"This complex doesn't allow pets."

"I suppose there would be other places to keep a dog if you didn't want him tearing up the furniture here."

"I haven't checked. I really haven't had time to think about getting a pet."

He looked around the room. There was nothing for him to see, but the scrutiny made her uncomfortable.

"Can I get you something to drink?" she asked. "I've got some Cokes. Or you could have a beer. You on duty?"

"I don't care for anything," he said. "Thank you."

He looked back at her, calm, unwavering. He was checking her reaction, studying her.

She sent signals through her body, ordering her muscles to relax. He had nothing. Even if he had checked her work background, that was a matter for the school board, not a matter for the law.

She had no official criminal record. Suspicions didn't count. She repeated that to herself over and over as he lingered.

She felt like the narrator of "The Tell-Tale Heart." She'd been playing English teacher long enough for literary references to flood her thoughts. At least she had no bodies buried here.

Doss was long ago. Everything was long ago, buried far back in the past. No one even cared about his case any longer. It was filed back in some forgotten cabinet somewhere.

She felt a burning anticipation in her stomach. Rice had to leave so that she could get things into motion. She would have to collect Charlie tonight. She would win his heart later.

That ball was rolling anyway. He was confused, but he would soon understand how much she loved him.

His parents couldn't put up much resistance. They had not adopted him through legal channels.

She kept her breaths shallow, less likely to draw attention. Rice still had pieces to put together; he had things to figure out, and that would take time.

She would be gone before he knew what he needed to know. She would have to be, but that could be arranged.

"You like it around here?" he asked.

"It's nice and quiet. Except for the dog attacks," she said.

"Yeah. My sentiments too. I retired here for the peace and quiet."

"I guess this dog business has interrupted that."

"Quite a bit." His tone said that he wanted to get it over with.

Frustration might make him dangerous. He might watch her every move. That might hinder her.

She couldn't warn him to stay out of her way. She would have no choice but to deal with him if he did.

She wondered if he sensed that. Could she project the message, let him know he was better off staying in his home? He was retired. Could he just let her take what she wanted and leave?

She smiled at him. "I'm expecting a visitor," she said. "Do you have any further need of me?"

How much more cordial could she be? Any citizen would get tired of a policeman loitering in her living room after a while. That wasn't a sign of guilt. That was normal.

"I guess I'll be going," he said. "If you will, get in touch with me if you notice anything unusual."

"Oh, I will, Chief."

She ushered him out and closed the door, leaning back against it as she listened to his footsteps descending the stairs.

She had to get to Charlie. If the Blacks weren't willing to let him go even at the threat of having their secrets revealed, she would have to take a different approach.

There were many possibilities to be explored, and she was willing to try all of them.

———

From the apartment complex, Rice drove over to the comics shop. It went against his judgment to consult a kid. It was unorthodox, something he would have never done in New Orleans, but Nell was the best source he'd found in this strange case. He parked in a no-parking zone near the front door and went in.

"When are you going to get those dogs?" a woman asked almost immediately as he stepped inside.

"Working on it," he said.

"You don't need to be watching videos while we're all dying."

"I know."

He walked over to the counter where Nell was sitting. "I've been talking to Barbara Nielson. She didn't twitch a nerve."

296

"And now she knows you suspect her."

"Maybe that will make her act."

"She didn't blow any silent dog whistles while you were there?"

"Nothing."

"I haven't heard back from Michael yet. I hope he's over talking to the men he found about The Microcosm."

"If he knows something, anything that will even let me run her in on reasonable suspicion, it might at least slow things down."

"I'll see what I can do."

"In the meantime, I'm going to watch Miss Nielson. She doesn't know I've been talking to you, but I want you to be careful. Have Matt keep an eye on you."

"I will."

He tipped his hat and headed for the door. He wanted to be back outside Barbara Nielson's house at nightfall.

Nell dialed Michael as soon as Rice was out of sight. She got her friend's answering machine and reiterated the importance of letting her know if he found out anything.

When she placed the receiver back in place, the phone rang. It was Charlie.

"I'm still under house arrest," he said. "With Mom hurt, my folks are going crazy. They're afraid the dogs are waiting for me or something."

"Maybe they are, Charlie."

"They don't hurt me, remember?"

She held her breath. Was there any guarantee they wouldn't hurt him later?

"Miss Nielson talked to me today," he said.

"What about."

"It's kind of confusing."

She realized he was upset and trying to conceal that fact.

"What is it?"

"I need to talk to you. Can you come by? They won't say anything if you drop in."

"Sure. As soon as I can get away from here."

She didn't relish the idea of driving around after dark, but whatever Barbara Nielson had said to him might be important.

She checked out the woman who had ambushed Chief Rice then started watching the second hand tick along. She had no idea how long the night was going to be.

―――――

Michael sat on the train watching a couple of punks bounce about, dangling from the hand straps and bars. They wore black leather jackets with lots of zippers, making them almost interchangeable.

One was wearing a badly faded Anthrax T-shirt, the other one that read POISON. That was about the only way to distinguish them since their dark hair was shaved close to their skulls.

He didn't relish going back to the weird little shop, but Nell needed his help. He'd played games with stories about the bizarre. If something was really happening along those lines, he couldn't run away from it.

He rubbed his hands on his jeans as the train shot along the track, and he jerked himself up by a strap as it pulled into the station.

People began to crowd off in an exodus. He had to make his way to the exit by following a slow line. That made him more nervous.

What made him even more nervous was the fact that Mr. Anthrax and Mr. Poison got off as well.

He didn't like the thought of being on the street with these guys in the neighborhood.

―――――

Charlie came downstairs slowly. He had been playing with a screenplay, scribbling on a yellow legal pad, but he couldn't concentrate.

He felt like he'd inhaled a hurricane, and it was inside him, spinning around, tossing his emotions about. He had stared at the wall for a while, wondering about the things Miss Nielson had said.

It felt strange to have felt attracted to her with this new revelation, even if it was a lie. Maybe she was just deranged, and her obsession with him—whatever the reason for it—was making her come up with strange ideas.

Or maybe she was telling the truth. How much did he look like his parents? There wasn't really a strong resemblance to either of them. He kept telling himself the thoughts were absurd, created by his imagination following Miss Nielson's suggestions. He didn't believe himself.

His mother was resting on the couch, her bandaged leg propped up on a pillow. She had a couple of magazines stacked on the floor at her side, and she was thumbing a copy of *Premier*.

He sat down in the armchair that faced the couch. He stared at her, not sure how to ask what he wanted to ask.

He wasn't pouting, not exactly, but his eyes must have seemed intense, intense enough to make her look at him over the top of the magazine.

"Are you about to make a plea for more leniency?" she asked. "It's not a good idea. My leg's been throbbing all day."

"I wasn't thinking about that," he said.

She placed the magazine across her lap, signaling that she was listening and not reading any longer.

"What's on your mind?" she asked.

"Miss Nielson spoke to me today," he said.

"She certainly is an odd woman. I talked to her just before the dogs got after me."

"She's only been here a few days," Charlie said. "She's seemed to have an interest in me."

"Oh?"

He detected caution in his mother's tone. Could she be worried because Miss Nielson had been interested? Perhaps it was just normal parental concern, or perhaps she was suspicious.

"What did she have to say?" Mrs. Black asked since he made no immediate response.

"She was talking to me, about … the past, I guess."

"What about the past?"

He thought he would just blurt it out, confront her with it, but the words didn't form on his lips. He looked into her eyes. She appeared frightened, yes, it was there, fear.

Would she be this worried if there were not some secret, something she was afraid to have revealed?

"What do you think?" he asked. He was not really angry at her, but he didn't want to volunteer anything. He wanted her to wonder for a minute.

"Did she tell you something that upset you, Charlie?" He glared at her now.

"What do you suspect she might have told me, *Mother*?"

Her eyes widened when he emphasized the word, and it was almost as if he had already asked the question. The inflection did it, suggested that there was some question about the word.

She sat up now, no longer resting casually on her pillows. While the injured leg remained immobile, her hands went to her sides, digging into the couch.

"Charlie, she must be a disturbed person. I'm going to speak to the school board. You know, she was there the other day, and then the dogs appeared."

"You thought she was weird?"

"Yes."

"The dogs started coming around the same day she did, and they seem to only attack people connected with me. Why would that be?"

"Charlie, what are you suggesting?"

"What do you think she told me, Mom? What would she have to tell me, what secret?"

"You're being ridiculous. There's not a secret."

He stood up now and moved to the edge of the coffee table. "She said she was my real mother," he said emphatically.

A snowstorm seemed to sweep across his mother's face, making her features stark white. "Charlie, you can't believe her."

Charlie felt his skin becoming very hot. Sweat streamed through his pores, covering his flesh instantly. "I don't know what to think," he said. "Why would she say that?"

She shook her head. "I don't know."

"She said you bought me while I was just a baby."

"Charlie, that's silly."

No denial. He didn't blink.

"Charlie, you can't believe that woman."

"Is it true?"

"You're my baby. I raised you. I've taken care of you."

"But did you have me or did you buy me?"

"You don't understand that kind of thing."

"Tell me. Tell me the truth! Who am I?"

He was shaking now. It had settled over him without warning, and he couldn't control it. He didn't know who he was, and that was terrifying.

"We were just a young couple. We couldn't adopt, and we couldn't have children."

That confirmed it, shattered any hope that Miss Nielson might have been lying.

"Don't you know what your life would have been if we hadn't taken you? You've had a good home with us, a normal life. You would have been on the streets with her."

"My life has been a lie all these years," Charlie said, tears gushing from his eyes.

"Not a lie," his mother said, pulling herself off the couch and moving toward him. Standing uneasily on her injured leg, she held him.

"We would have told you eventually, let you know. I just haven't felt it was time."

He shook himself free of her arms. "That's why you've always been so protective of me," he said. "You think of me like property."

"That's not true. I love you as much as if I'd had you myself. Your father loves you too."

"He hardly knows I'm alive. He just puts up with me to please you."

She began to weep now also. "No. No."

"She said you were so upset because you couldn't have children you forced him to do something, to find a way for you to have a kid."

"That's insane. That witch is filling your head with lies to turn you against us."

"She's not a witch. She's my mother. My real mother."

Realization swept over her. "You said the dogs only attacked those close to you."

Charlie pushed back from her, his lips pursed tightly. He was trying to stop crying.

"Charlie, she's wanted to take everything away so that you wouldn't have any choice but to turn to her."

"No."

"Charlie, we knew when the lawyer made the arrangements that she'd been involved in some kind of cult. We thought it was some kind of religious group, but the lawyer warned us to be very careful. That's why we left there, why we eventually came here, somewhere small and quiet. But it must be true. She has some kind of evil power. I've always been afraid of that."

"You've been afraid a long time," Charlie accused. "Afraid your lie would be found out."

"We've worried the authorities might know. The other night I was looking for your birth certificate. It's missing, and I was terrified of what might happen if we needed it."

"It's faked."

"Yes, but it's a real document. The lawyer made sure of that."

Charlie lifted a vase from the coffee table and hurled it across the room. It shattered against the wall, spraying glass back onto the carpet.

"Charlie!" She looked at him in horror, startled by his anger and emotion.

"What have you done to me?"

"We gave you a life," Daniel Black said. He had come down the stairs to investigate the screams. "We've given up a great deal for you. We didn't have to."

"I never asked you for anything," Charlie said. Looking at his father was like looking at a stranger.

There had always been a cold edge to the man's emotions. Now the reason was clear. He'd spent fourteen years tolerating a boy not his son.

Now the icy stare had meaning. He was jealous of Charlie, resentful of the demands a son he'd never wanted had made on him.

"I'm sorry," Charlie said. "I never meant to invade your life."

"Well you're here now," Black said. "Were a family." His look softened slightly. "I am your father."

"My real mother wants me to go with her."

"Real mother?"

"It's her," Mrs. Black said. "Barbara Nielson is the woman. She's here in town. She's come for him, like we've always been afraid of."

Black shook his head. "Don't be ridiculous," he said. "How could she have found us?"

"She has," Black said. "Somehow she has."

"Well, she has no claim to Charlie."

"She could ruin everything," Mrs. Black protested. "We're guilty of a crime and she could reveal it."

"Not without revealing her own. We'll remind her of that if she tries to take him."

"Don't I have any say in this?" Charlie asked as he wiped his eyes.

"The woman sold you," Black said. "Now on a whim she's decided to get you back. Is that what you think you want from life?"

"Maybe she loves me," Charlie said, but he had no conviction in his voice. Angrily he added: "That's more than you do."

"I think she's behind these dog attacks," Mrs. Black said. "I think she's trying to make Charlie need her."

"What did she do? Train some attack dogs? That's absurd."

"You remember she was in some cult," Mrs. Black said.

Black laughed. "Don't lose your grip."

"Think about it. All the strange things that have gone on? The dogs got into that school building somehow, and I had just run into her."

"That's no proof that she's controlling killer hounds."

"I think we should get out of here," Mrs. Black said. "Charlie and I can go somewhere. We'll just get a hotel until you can follow. You can get transferred again."

He shook his head. "Don't be crazy. We're fine here. This woman has no claim to Charlie, and she's obviously got a screw loose. She had one loose when she pulled her little sale back then."

"I don't like this," she said.

"You knew there was always going to be some question like this when we made the decision."

"Stop it!" Charlie shouted. "Just stop it!"

He dropped down into his chair, wiping the tears from his eyes. He didn't want to cry anymore. He just wanted to understand. What had happened had taken place a long time ago, but now it was revealed to him. This life he had known for so many years was not real, was not what he had believed it to be.

The storm inside him gained force, threatening to turn him inside out, he felt.

"Let's just settle down," he heard his father saying. "We're all overreacting." He walked over and stood beside Charlie.

"I am your father," he said, his voice softening. "Sometimes I don't show affection well, but it's never been a question of wanting you." He patted Charlie's shoulder. "I love you, son. Understand that."

Charlie remained sullen. He had emotions to understand and deal with, and everything seemed to be channeling into him quicker than he could handle it.

"I'm sure everything is going to work out fine," Black said.

He didn't know any better.

Chapter 27

Rice watched the car pull to a stop at the curb, and Sawyer, the school teacher, climbed out. Maybe Barbara Nielson had been telling the truth. She had a date with a co-worker.

He wanted that to be the end of it, wanted Sawyer to be picking her up for a burger. That way there were only wild dogs in the woods, dogs the deputies would eventually find. He would be able to go home and forget about cults and hellhounds and mystics in Chicago.

Leaning back in the seat, he cranked the window down another turn to let in a little more of the late-afternoon breeze, crisp without being chilled. If they came back out in a few minutes and climbed into Sawyer's car and headed off to the movies, everything would be right with the world.

He reached down and unsnapped the catch on his holster because something told him that he was not going to hear the angels sing.

His gut instinct and his experience confirmed that. Things just didn't go so easily.

She opened the door for Sawyer without checking the peep hole. She knew it would be him even before she saw the gray expression as his face appeared.

"How are you?" she asked.

"Okay."

"Have a seat."

She settled on the couch beside him, not moving too close. She wanted to hear what he would say before she decided how to deal with him.

Whatever happened here, she wanted it to happen quickly. Let him unload his turmoil, then she would determine what she needed to do.

"I've been struggling," he said. "I know it's happened quickly, that we've just known each other for a while, but I think I love you."

She didn't speak. She only looked into his eyes, trying to let him see that she felt the same. Maybe if they loved each other, they could work something out. She could collect Charlie, and they could get out of this little town.

"I don't know how to talk to you about everything," he said. "It's hurting so much inside.

"I've lived a quiet little life here," he confessed finally. Not like what you must have had in the city."

She started to speak, to tell him people made mistakes, but she hesitated, letting him continue.

"I guess I'm kind of old-fashioned," he said. "Or just stalled anyway. There aren't many women around here, you know. The other night, it startled me when you were aggressive. I don't know if I expected you to be a virgin, or pristine or whatever, but it just hit me hard, thinking about you with other men."

She felt something coiling inside her, a fear-tinged pain. She thought about taking his hand but paused. What could she say?

"I just got the idea that that was something you did with all of your boyfriends, and it shook me. I know it's commonplace, but I'm confused. I want to stop hurting. I love you, and I'm trying to accept whatever must be back there, in the past. You're not from here; you're from somewhere more in touch with the real world, I guess."

"The past is gone," she said, though she didn't manage to say it with as much conviction as she would have liked.

"I know," he said. "I just have to deal with it."

He looked over at her. "Have there been a lot of guys?"

"A few," she said, fearing his reaction. Nothing changed about him. He only nodded.

306

"I don't really want to know more," he said. He looked at the floor. "I feel like that guy in *Sweet Charity*," he said.

"I didn't see it."

"Little theater did it once. First he thinks he can handle it. Then he leaves Charity because he can't deal with all of the guys from her past."

She felt her lip trembling. "Is that what you're going to do?"

"I don't know," he said.

She stifled further remarks. No need to give him the satisfaction of seeing her squirm or suffer. Why should he know he could hurt her?

"I don't know what to say," she said, keeping her voice cool.

"Help me deal with this?" he requested.

But how could she help him? How could she tell him what was in the past? If he could not deal with lovers, how could he accept a son, let alone a murder?

Her lack of reaction made him turn, and she saw he was afraid now also. He didn't want to lose her. If he had ever been in love, it had been a long time.

He took her hand. She didn't grip his back. She didn't know what to do, and she wanted to close in her emotions, circle the wagons so to speak.

Now his eyes softened, and he was pleading. He wanted her, loved her, but couldn't reconcile with reality. She picked up the lamp from the end table without a second thought and swung the base of it, bringing it quickly against the side of his head.

It struck with a thud, and his eyes rolled, closing before the surprise had fully registered on his features.

As he slumped sideways, falling off the couch and half across the coffee table, a thin trickle of blood slid down the side of his face.

She rose and reached down with her finger, smearing it with the blood. The crimson reminded her of Doss when he had died. As it colored her fingers while she rubbed them together, she began to think of the hounds.

Michael noticed the skinheads were following him as he moved along the sidewalk. Darkness had settled, and there were few other people on the street. He kept telling himself the guys just happened to be going the same way, but when he looked back over his shoulder, the grim look on their faces didn't comfort him.

He was just wearing jeans and a jacket. He didn't look like he was carrying money, so he couldn't imagine them wanting to mug him. They probably lived in this neighborhood, that was all.

He walked past a knife shop, Shavers and Knives, with a metal curtain protecting its windows. It was the most modern-looking place in the vicinity, and there were no signs of life there.

He wondered if the men following were regular customers. If they truly were from around here, they'd probably visited a few times.

He didn't look back as he passed a demolished building. Piles of rock and debris filled the space where the walls had once towered. He considered picking up something as a weapon, then thought better of it.

Just as he reached the edge of the destruction, however, he reconsidered, and selected a length of wood. It was still firm and solid, approximately four feet long. Devlin would have wielded it a bit more boldly, but he used it like a cane, poking the tip against the sidewalk as a third leg. He hoped his friends had seen him collect it.

He could hear the clack of their steel-toed boots, a constant reminder echoing on the concrete, and they seemed to be moving faster. That was cause for alarm. He still had a couple of blocks to reach the shop, and turning onto the narrow street would isolate him even more, making him a better target.

He tried to pick up his speed, and when he did, the sound of the boots and their clinking, metal decorations, seemed to hasten also.

He gripped the stick, receiving a bit of comfort from the sensation. He didn't want to use it, but it might be necessary. He'd had his characters do battle a thousand times and he'd studied martial arts and sword-fighting texts, but he was not skilled in combat. He had never practiced moves or defense.

Still, swinging a club didn't require much practice, just a matter of sweeping it back and forth, making contact if possible, or if not, at least keeping the subjects at bay.

He began to feel more like Devlin now. The men pursuing him were agents of evil, the same dark figures he had described in his fiction. Now he was being forced to practice what he had imagined.

He reached the mouth of the street and turned, walking along the sidewalk while the echoes of the boots continued.

He was only a short distance down the street when they rounded the corner, breaking into a run when they were sure the alley was deserted. He turned, raising the club as they yanked knives from their jackets.

Nell could hear shouting from the Black house as she got out of her car. She started to get back in, but she was worried about Charlie. She moved up the walk slowly, trying to hear what was being said.

She couldn't pick out words, only emotion—anger. Mr. Black's voice boomed, and then the softer screech of Mrs. Black's tone sounded.

They would not be happy to see her, but maybe she would settle things down. Her presence might make them leave Charlie alone for a while; she felt certain they were screaming at him about something, probably something related to the confusion.

She rang the bell and waited. A moment later the door swung inward with an abrupt jerk, and Mr. Black looked out at her.

"I suppose you're here to see Charlie," he said.

"Yes." She didn't attach a "sir" because she didn't want him to feel any superiority. She didn't have to be pushed around.

"Come on in," he said, pulling the door back.

They were all clustered in the living room, looking angry and flustered. Charlie's face was red and his hair mussed.

He stood when he saw her and walked toward her. "What's going on?" she asked.

"Family discussion," he said sarcastically, looking back at his mother.

"We were busy," Mrs. Black said.

"I'm sorry," Nell said. "I just—"

"It's okay," Charlie broke in.

"You don't have to tell her everything we've been talking about," Mrs. Black said.

"Nell wants to help," Charlie said. "She doesn't know everything, but she knows about Miss Nielson. She knows she's drawn to me for some reason, and she knows more than you do about the dogs."

"What about them?" Mrs. Black asked.

"Tell her about the other night," Charlie suggested. Nell looked at him, then at Mrs. Black.

"Go ahead," Charlie said.

"They don't bother Charlie," Nell said quietly.

"What?" said Daniel Black.

"The dogs don't bother Charlie. They chased us the other night when we sneaked out of here. When they got to Charlie, they cowed down and left us alone."

"Oh, God," Mrs. Black said. She was seated on the couch again and she folded her arms around her abdomen. "It is something to do with that cult she was in."

"What do you think this is? *The Omen*?" Black protested. "Charlie is our son. That's all there is to it. Barbara Nielson, or whoever she is, is just a woman. I don't know why the dogs would have—"

"I had dreams about her when she first got here," Charlie added.

"You're not going to convince me there's some kind of witchcraft involved here," Black said. "Let's all settle down."

"A friend of mine in Chicago is finding evidence that there is some kind of witchcraft," Nell said. "Chief Rice contacted the Atlanta police about Miss Nielson. She's part of a group out there that has historic roots with a cult that involved dogs in their rituals."

"This is insane. This is the real world, sweetheart. Not something out of one of the comic books you push."

"We've got to do something," Mrs. Black cried. "We've got to get out of here, go somewhere she can't find us."

"We're just getting settled here. We can't keep running."

"We have to."

"They bought me as a baby," Charlie volunteered to Nell. "That's what Miss Nielson told me. Apparently it's true."

"Charlie, shut up," Black commanded.

Nell stayed at Charlie's side. It sounded incredible, but no one was denying. They were just angry he had spoken.

The revelation explained a great deal. It explained why Barbara Nielson had come here, why she had had some mysterious attachment to Charlie. It wasn't sexual; she had merely exploited sexuality to draw Charlie closer to her.

"We need to think about what's going on," Nell said, knowing they would probably laugh at her. She was just another kid, a kid who had no business meddling in their lives.

"Maybe you should just go," Black suggested.

"I invited her," Charlie said.

"I don't know. Maybe I really should go," she said. Charlie took her arm, gripping it tightly. She was the only stability he had left, the only friend.

"What are we going to do?" Mrs. Black sobbed. "The whole world is falling apart. We're going to lose Charlie. We're going to lose everything."

"Shut up," Black said. "We're going to work this out. Everything is going to be fine."

Nell shook her head. His denials were not going to make the world normal again. Nothing was. It wasn't a normal place.

They had to realize that.

She hoped they would soon, before there was no time to deal with reality.

―――――

Rice waited a long time for Barbara Nielson to appear, arm entwined with Sawyer's, smiling and laughing. As darkness finished consuming the sky, it became evident they would not reappear.

He wanted to believe they were together, watching television, making love, doing whatever young couples did. The nagging feeling inside him wouldn't accept that, though.

Why? he asked himself.

There was no reason. The fact that he was imagining something wrong should have been enough to convince him it was only imagination, but he couldn't accept that. He popped open his door and slid from the cruiser.

Casually he walked along the street, not wanting to frighten anyone who happened to be looking out a window or anyone who might drive by. He was just walking, not completing an investigation.

He walked up the steps slowly, placing his feet cautiously as he moved along the second-tier planks.

Feeling stupid, like a cop in a television series exercising a plot device, he leaned against the door. He wanted to hear a television, or coupling, heaving breathing, giggling, anything.

Instead, he heard a moan.

That made him knock. When only another moan came in response, he tried the doorknob.

Locked.

He kicked it open and moved inside, gun ready. Sawyer lay in the center of the room. Blood was smeared across his face, and his breathing was ragged.

After a quick spin around the room, Rice found no sign of the woman. Sliding the gun back into the holster, he knelt at the teacher's side.

"You okay?" he asked.

"My head."

"The woman did this?"

"Yeah."

He pulled his handkerchief from his pocket and pressed it against the wound. He was relieved to discover it was not as severe as he had expected. There might be a concussion and need for some stitches, but the skull wasn't caved in.

"I'll get you an ambulance."

"No. I want to talk to Barbara."

"She brained you, son. You sure you want to see her?"

"I hurt her."

"What?"

"I broke her heart."

"So she tried to kill you?"

"Woman scorned. She was mumbling some gibberish I couldn't understand."

"Where'd she go?"

"I don't know. She left me here after she smeared blood off my head."

He picked up the phone and tried the video store. When Matt Bordelon informed him Nell was off work, he tried her home number.

No answer there either.

He'd have to check the Black residence. If Nell had been correct, that was the logical place to look.

She'd committed an assault now. He had a reason to pick her up. That would in turn allow more intense questioning. Maybe he could get to the bottom of this shit.

He started to dial for an ambulance for Sawyer.

"I want to go with you," the schoolteacher repeated.

"I need to talk to her."

"You want to press charges?"

"I just want to talk to her."

"Fine." Maybe that would produce some results. He went into the bathroom for a towel. A strange symbol had been smeared on the mirror in Sawyer's blood.

Nell's theories were seeming more reasonable by the second. He opened the cabinet and selected a hand towel which he dampened.

When he returned to the living room, he helped Sawyer wipe blood from his face and gave him the towel to hold against the nick.

The schoolteacher was able to stand on his own, and he didn't falter as he followed Rice to the car.

The chief decided not to use the lights or the siren. He didn't want the attention, and if Barbara Nielson did possess mystical powers, he didn't want to let her know he was coming.

―――――

"We're not going to leave town," Black said, standing at the center of the living room. "We're going to deal with it."

"What if she does control the dogs?" Mrs. Black protested.

"What do you want me to do? Get a priest?"

"We need to do something."

He shook his head. "Everything is going to be fine."

"Are you telling yourself that so that you don't have to deal with it?" Nell asked.

"Who the hell are you to question me?"

"I'm Charlie's friend."

"The only one I've got left," Charlie noted.

Black ran a hand over his beard. "Let's just settle down. Maybe we can talk to this woman, reason with her. We can make her see Charlie has a far better life with us than she can offer."

"Do I?" Charlie asked.

"Do you ever want for anything?" Black asked.

"We've given you everything."

Charlie bowed his head. He didn't offer any response or reminder about his father's lack of affection. This wasn't a debate.

Maybe if things settled down, they could think everything over rationally. He didn't really want to go with Barbara Nielson, not if she was some kind of witch.

She was dangerous, had harmed people. If she was responsible for the hounds, she'd tried to protect him, but she had hurt people he cared about also.

He rested his face in his hands, rubbing his eyes. He was still rubbing them when the doorbell rang.

Black went to the door and pulled it open. Ice water ran through everyone's veins as Chief Rice stepped across the threshold.

"I was just making sure everything was all right," he said, glancing quickly around the room. He nodded toward Nell, a casual gesture.

"No more dog attacks," Mrs. Black said. She tried to make her voice light and didn't quite succeed.

The policeman turned his hat around in his hands. "I don't suppose you've seen anything of Barbara Nielson."

"Not tonight," Black said. "Why?"

"I'm looking for her. There was a little domestic disturbance between her and her boyfriend. I've got him out in the car."

"Who's her boyfriend?"

"Eugene Sawyer from the school."

"My math teacher," Charlie said.

"She hit him with a lamp."

"Why?"

"Lover's spat, I guess."

Rice's gaze played over toward Nell. Some silent message passed between them, and he gave a slight nod.

"Well, let me run," Rice said. "I've got to get Sawyer some medical treatment, I guess."

He paused a moment more, then moved out of the room.

Black turned to Nell a few moments after the door closed. "What was he up to?"

"He knows the dogs have affected people around Charlie. He knows things about Barbara Nielson. He doesn't know anything about the family skeletons. I didn't know anything until I came here tonight."

Black dropped heavily into an armchair. If she attacked the other teacher, we do have to be careful tonight," he said. "I'll concede that. This occult business is bullshit, but she could be Charlie's mother and she could be wigged out."

He left the party in the living room and made a round of the house, checking doors and windows to make sure they were locked.

"She's out there somewhere," Mrs. Black said. "I know she is."

"It's going to be okay," Nell said. "She won't bother us. We don't know that. What if she comes for Charlie? If she hit that man, she won't have any choice but to act quickly."

Nell couldn't argue with that.

"Why don't I call my friend, see if he's found anything new yet."

"Do it," Mrs. Black said. "Dan won't admit anything's wrong, but we've got to do something."

Nell went to the phone and dialed Michael. His phone rang half a dozen times before his answering machine kicked in with an excuse about finishing up Devlin's No. 33 adventure.

She left the Black's telephone number, hoping he might pick up when he heard her voice. Apparently he wasn't home. She replaced the receiver and returned to a chair. "Maybe he'll call," she said.

Mrs. Black ran her hands through her curls. "Maybe we'll survive."
The night was young.

Chapter 28

Delia was propped against her pillows, a Coke on her nightstand and a new issue of *Glamour* spread in front of her. She was reading about guys since she was home alone.

She was still bummed about Miss Nielson, both in person and in the weird dream. Who was she to mess up things with Charlie?

The princess telephone she'd received for Christmas was at her side on the bed, just in case Charlie called. She kept hoping to hear from him. Normally he would have telephoned by now. She was worried Miss Nielson might have said something about her. What if the bitch had told him Delia was a slut and that he should stay away from her? Would he listen?

Charlie didn't seem like he'd be swayed by that kind of bullshit, but you couldn't tell. Maybe Miss Nielson had scared him. The woman certainly had that talent.

Delia flipped the pages in quick jerks, not really paying attention to the articles or the pictures. She'd read most of the magazine before anyway. She had a subscription and usually went through an issue as soon as it arrived in the mail.

She wanted the phone to ring, wanted to hear Charlie's voice. She liked Charlie, better than she'd liked most of the guys she'd gone out with. He was sweet and kind. She would like to keep seeing him.

She looked down at the telephone, but it did not ring. The sound she heard in the next instant was more like a whisper, or a rush of wind.

She'd been keeping the window closed since the night she'd heard something rattle the screen, so she didn't understand how wind might be audible.

Putting her magazine aside, she slid off the bed and walked to the curtains anyway, curious. She gripped one side and pulled it back, looking out through the glass. With the lamp on, she had trouble seeing outside, so she had to lean against the glass and shade her eyes to prevent reflection.

Miss Nielson was standing on the lawn.

Delia found that odd, so she couldn't imagine why she reached up and undid the latch. Without hesitating, even as she questioned her movements, she lifted the window, watching Miss Nielson move forward and flip the tabs at the base of the screen.

It slid easily from its frame so that they were standing face to face. Delia could feel the teacher's soft, hot breath touching her cheeks as their gazes locked.

"What do you want?" Delia asked.

The smile said that she was silly. It curled up one corner of Miss Nielson's mouth and indicated that Delia should already know what was desired.

"You must come with me," Miss Nielson said.

"Why? I thought you didn't want me around."

"I need you for a little while," she said. "Just to get Charlie's attention."

"What?"

The teacher reached up and touched Delia's cheek, and the girl felt something inside her melt. Her legs almost buckled as they became rubbery, and she leaned against the windowsill for support.

"Come please," Miss Nielson said.

Delia didn't argue. She let the teacher help her through the window, and then she began to walk with her across the lawn. She was wearing socks without shoes; dew began to soak the cloth quickly, but she ignored the chill dampness.

Setting a pace a few steps behind Miss Nielson, she followed through the darkness. Several feet behind them, she could hear rasping breath and faint growls.

They were not traveling alone.

———

Michael jerked to consciousness as the smell of ammonia assaulted his senses. He sat up abruptly and felt needles drive into his temples. The pain forced his head back onto the cushion.

"Welcome back to the land of the waking," Father Alison said. He was smiling down with his familiar grin, a lock of silver curling down across his forehead.

"How'd I get here?"

"Vinoba found you in the street. You had an altercation?"

"A bit of one. I guess I lost." He touched the throbbing knot on the side of his head.

"You've had a rather severe blow. We think you may need medical attention."

Michael checked his pocket and found his wallet missing. "I don't think I have time right now. I'll worry about it later."

Vinoba was standing at Alison's shoulder. He offered Michael a warm cloth. It felt soothing against his forehead.

"Things are getting worse with the dogs," Michael said. "Nell has had more problems since she learned that the woman who may be controlling them is part of The Microcosm. They're an offshoot of something called The Mopses."

"We have been continuing our research," Alison said.

"Have you turned up anything new?" Michael asked.

"We have done some research," Vinoba said. His sing-song accenting of words reverberated through Michael's skull.

Michael massaged his temples. "What have you learned?"

"We have sought in our volumes some method of banishing the hounds you described," Vinoba said.

"Rest for a moment while we cross-reference a few more things to determine if what we've turned up is accurate," Alison suggested.

Michael couldn't argue. He lay his head back, waiting for the pain to go away as he heard the old men shuffling into the next room.

"What would it hurt if Charlie and I went away for just a couple of days?" Mrs. Black asked as she stared across the room at her husband. "We could go to your sister's house, at least until Chief Rice is able to pick up that woman. It might be wise for all of us to be out of town by then. What if she talks?"

"She won't talk to the police about that because she's guilty of a crime too," Black said. "They'll already have her for assault. She won't want to add on to her charges."

"At least we'd be safe until she's not a danger any longer."

"We're safe here," Black said. "We're locked in. If we start running away, how do you think that will look?"

"I don't care. I want Charlie away from here, away from that woman."

Charlie drew his legs up against his chest as the argument continued. Nell knelt at the arm of his chair, touching his shoulder as he tucked his chin down against his chest.

"It's going to be okay," she said. "At least we know what's going on now, Charlie."

"Answers don't help much," he said. "What am I supposed to do?"

"It's going to be okay. Whatever happens. It's best to stick with your parents right now. They may have made some mistakes, but Miss Nielson is a killer, and you know whatever she's conjured with these dogs is evil."

She wanted to give him more reassurance that everything would be fine, but she couldn't say what lay ahead or what price the trauma would exact from Charlie. She could see the discovery of the secret—possible prosecution of his parents and foster homes for him.

That would be difficult, as much a nightmare as the killings. What comfort could she give him, other than reassuring her friendship?

"Things will never be normal again," he said. "You know that?"

"Life changes, Charlie. You roll with the punches. I've learned that. You can still be everything you want to be."

"Maybe. Unless Miss Nielson drags me off to be master of her hounds."

"Don't think that way. Chief Rice will find her. She made a big mistake when she brained Mr. Sawyer."

"Did she? What if Chief Rice goes after her and she sics the dogs on him?"

"I don't know," she said honestly. "I don't think that will happen."

"There are no guarantees."

"We'll figure something out."

"What? What can we figure out? Is there some way you and I can go off together and be friends forever? It can't happen."

She tried to think of some way to hold the world together. There should be an answer, something that would make everything okay again. She couldn't think of it.

"He's always been interested in weird things," Black was shouting. "We should have known there was something about his mother."

"Other boys like monsters. He's as normal as we are," Mrs. Black protested. "He's been raised with us, normal."

"This was a mistake from the moment you ever dreamed it up."

Charlie pulled himself to his feet and jerked his arm away from Nell as she tried to stop him.

"What do you want to do? Just give me to her?" Charlie asked.

His father turned toward him. He was not much taller than Charlie these days, but he was thicker, and he seemed menacing to Charlie's thin form.

But Charlie didn't back down. He faced his father. "You want me out of here?" he asked Black.

"I've devoted half of my life to you," the older man said. "What do you want?"

"I've never really asked you for anything," Charlie said. "You've hardly ever acknowledged I'm alive."

Black moved toward him, and Nell thrust herself between them only moments before blows could be placed. "You're not solving the problems like this," she said.

Charlie looked at her resentfully but nodded and stepped back. "You're right," he said.

Black had to agree. He relaxed his tensed arms and let them hang at his sides, exhaling to show his animosity was subsiding.

"Let's get calm," he said. "Emotion is making everybody nuts here."

"I think the first thing we need to consider is the fact that Miss Nielson presents a real physical danger," Nell said.

"At least for all of you," Charlie said.

"We're locked in here," Black reiterated. "If she does control the dogs, which is a stretch, we ought to be okay."

"They got into the school," Mrs. Black said. "Somebody opened the door for them," Black said. "We're in tight here."

"I'd feel better if I could get ahold of Michael," Nell said. "Can I use the phone again?"

Black nodded, his eyes not exactly forming a scowl. "Just dial direct," he said.

She went to a phone at an end table and left another message on Michael's machine. "If you know anything," she said, "let me know as soon as possible." Then she read the Blacks' number again from the phone base before hanging up.

"So his spook meisters haven't come through for him," Black said.

She shrugged. "Maybe he's with them now."

Black settled into an armchair. "Well, have a seat. Let's all try to rest a little bit. Sleep wouldn't be a bad idea, but I don't suppose anyone is in the mood for that." He checked everyone's face. "I didn't think so."

The emergency room in Penn's Ferry was crowded with virus sufferers, victims of domestic violence, and car wreck survivors. They were all crammed into the narrow waiting area with trays to catch vomit and gauze to stop bleeding while they waited for medical attention.

Rice waded through them and flashed his badge to get attention from the dark-haired woman behind the admitting desk. She was kept from being pretty by the lines etched around her eyes by countless nights of harried business, but her dark hair fell about her shoulders in soft curls, brushing the starched white fabric of her uniform.

"Can I help you?"

"I've got a man with a head wound," Rice said. "I need to get some attention for him if I can. He's needed to identify a suspect, but I want to make sure he's not badly hurt."

She smiled politely, a smile that wasn't reassuring. "We'll do what we can. We're very busy tonight. There's a full moon."

Rice's eyes widened. "I didn't realize that," he said. "I guess I haven't been looking at the sky."

The dew began to sting Delia's feet as well as chilling them while they walked across grassy lawns. Miss Nielson was setting a brisk pace while keeping Delia's arm twisted.

The arm ached, and keeping up was tough. She wanted to rest with the cold air rasping through her chest, but Miss Nielson didn't have any intention of slowing down. "Where are we going?" she asked as they continued to drag along.

"To see Charlie. That's what you want, isn't it? You didn't stay away from him."

"I like him."

"And he likes you. We're going to see if that can't be worked to some benefit."

"You're hurting me," Delia complained.

"We've all been hurt," Miss Nielson said.

"What do you want here? What the hell's going on?"

"I want what's mine. Then I'll leave all of you to get on in your peaceful little world here."

They rounded the corner onto Charlie's street and began to move up the sidewalk. It was quiet, seemingly deserted. Most porch lights weren't even turned on.

Delia thought about screaming for help, but she feared the retribution Barbara Nielson would offer.

She let the woman drag her along the street, trying not to whimper as they approached Charlie's house. She hoped this bitch didn't try to harm Charlie. He hadn't done anything to her. Maybe she was jealous.

When they reached the edge of Charlie's lawn, Miss Nielson hustled her through the grass, twisting tighter and grabbing a handful of Delia's hair.

Unable to stifle her pain any longer, Delia cried. That only made Miss Nielson tighten the knot of hair she was holding.

"Shut up until I'm ready for you to say something," she said.

They moved to a point near the center of the lawn, a point that would make them visible through the large front window. Light was burning through the curtains from inside, but Delia could not catch even a glimpse of movement. The drapes were drawn so that not even a sliver of an opening remained.

She clenched her mouth tightly closed as Miss Nielson positioned herself behind her. Delia's arm was growing numb now, so at least some of the pain was lessening.

Leaning her head back to decrease the strain in her neck, she listened to the sounds of the dogs. They moved up slowly from behind, their breathing coarse and heavy.

She didn't look at them, didn't want to see them, but she could sense their movement. They were lining up, standing shoulder to shoulder on either side of Miss Nielson, and there seemed to be many of them, perhaps a dozen.

A deeper fear began to tremble inside her. Did even trained dogs behave this way? There had been no sound of a command. They were falling into ranks as if they were receiving telepathic messages.

She did roll her eyes sideways now, unable to keep from looking over at them. Smoke burst from their nostrils like steam pipes, and saliva streamed from their jaws.

That was frightening, but her brain seemed to explode when she looked at the glowing red of their eyes. Her breath caught, as if it had become ice in her lungs.

Miss Nielson jerked her head back, forcing a gasp that ended the respiratory arrest. Tears spilled from the outer corners of Delia's eyes since her face was pointed toward the sky now.

She looked into the blackness, the moon's glow touching only the corner of her vision and doing nothing to affect the look of the void. She was looking into midnight, living in midnight.

She felt more tears spilling, and then she felt Miss Nielson's index finger snake into one nostril.

The nail dragged along the septum, tearing the membrane so that blood began to flow. The sting of the cut lasted only an instant, but in a few seconds, Delia felt blood covering half her face from nose to chin.

She wanted to wipe it away, but Miss Nielson had one arm wrapped around her, with her arms to her sides. She had to stand there with the mess on her chin, sticky, dripping. She felt droplets hitting her blouse and knew they would stain.

She was wondering how she would get the stains out when Miss Nielson began to sing out, "Charlie? Are you in there?"

A couple of heartbeats passed before the porch light came on. Then Delia saw a hand reach through the curtains and pull one drapery back a few inches.

Charlie's face appeared in the glass. He had to press his face close to the glass to see out since the lights were on inside.

He would see her. With the porch light and the moon, he would recognize her and make out the blood on her face, and certainly he would try to come to her.

That was what Miss Nielson wanted, to lure him out here. She wanted to take him away. If he came to her, she would snatch him and send the dogs in to get his family.

"Don't come out here, Charlie!" Delia screamed. "Don't do it. I'm not hurt."

With a hand in her hair, Miss Nielson jerked her head back with a rough tug. "You will be. You'll be filling these dogs' bellies in a minute if you do that again."

The front door opened and Charlie looked out. He started to open the glass storm door, but his father's hand fell on his shoulder, stopping him.

Even as he looked toward Delia, and she read the desire he had to come to her, the door closed with a slam.

"You can't go out there," Black said. "Are you crazy?"

Charlie had bolted from window to door almost before he could be stopped. He shook his arm away from his father's grip angrily.

"She's got Delia, and she's bleeding."

"Because she wants you to come out there. Do you want to go away with her and play witch boy? Is that what you learned from all those damned horror movies?" Black had apparently begun to accept what was being presented to him as reality.

"She'll sic the dogs on her if I don't go."

"She'll sic them on her as soon as you cross the threshold. She doesn't have any use for Delia or any of us once she has you."

Finally Charlie nodded. His father was right. As cold and as distant as the man had always been, he was the only one who could really help right now. "What do we do?" Charlie asked.

"Dial 911," Black said. "Get Rice and some deputies back out here."

Mrs. Black picked up the telephone and tapped the numbers, reaching a dispatcher in Aimsley.

Rice's beeper went off while he sat in the hospital coffee shop reading an old copy of *U.S. News and World Report*.

From a pay phone in the hall, he called his wife, who informed him she had beeped because 911 dispatch was looking for him. Hanging up, he tapped out the memorized number on the pay phone's Touch-Tone pad.

"We've just got a call from your jurisdiction," said a young female voice when he identified himself.

"Yes?"

"It was a Mrs. Betsy Black. She said she's seen Barbara Nielson. They'd like you to get over to their house as soon as possible."

He sensed that there was more to the message than they had been willing to leave with a dispatcher. Leaving his coffee and his magazine on the table, he headed down the hall.

326

Back in the emergency room, he found the dark-haired nurse again and told her he had to see the patient he'd brought in. Since he was a cop, she agreed.

He found Sawyer sitting on a gurney behind a cloth partition. A tired-looking doctor who couldn't have been far out of his twenties was finishing up a bandage.

"I was going to recommend that Mr. Sawyer stay overnight—"

"For observation," Rice finished.

The young, red-haired doctor nodded. He had freckles and blue eyes, and his Adam's apple bobbed when he swallowed.

"He can be moved, though?" Rice asked.

"Well, I'm worried about a concussion."

"He has to be somewhere very important."

"I do?" Sawyer asked.

"Charlie Black's mother just called. They've spotted Barbara Nielson."

"I'll go with you," Sawyer said, sliding off the gurney. He seemed fairly steady on his feet.

After several minutes that Rice couldn't spare, they finished signing releases and got the hell out of there.

Once they were in the car, he hit the lights but left the siren off. He could cover the distance to Petittville quickly without noise. No need to announce their approach too early.

Chapter 29

Charlie peered through the crack in the curtains, watching Miss Nielson and Delia. They had not moved much, and Delia seemed to be okay except for the bleeding. He was trying to figure out where it was coming from. Maybe Miss Nielson had hit her in the nose. He couldn't see any cuts on her forehead, but it was dark and they were several yards away.

The dogs were lined up, their heads lowered as they scowled at the house. He felt as if their eyes were boring into him. Dogs couldn't see very far or very well. He knew that from reading about them, but somehow he sensed these monsters with their glowing eyes could see like a superhero.

He wanted to shoot the bastards. He'd never felt that way about anything, but he wanted Delia safe.

He probably couldn't hit them, however. He was no marksman, and the family didn't own guns anyway.

"What's going on out there?" his father asked from behind him.

Charlie turned from the curtain. "Nothing's changed."

"No sign of the police?"

"He had to drive from Penn's Ferry," Mrs. Black said from her seat on the couch. Nell was beside her, trying to comfort her.

"He should have the pedal to the floor," Black grumbled.

"I didn't explain all the details. The dispatcher would have thought I was crazy."

"Didn't they have a deputy to send?"

"The guy working this side of the river is helping a state trooper with a fatality accident."

"Shit."

"They're short-handed because they've had people hunting the dogs all day."

"The dogs are *here*. They got their shifts backwards."

"Charrrrrlieeee!"

Barbara Nielson's voice seemed as sweet as honeysuckle dipped in molasses. It seemed unusually audible considering it was drifting in through a brick wall.

Charlie turned back to the window and looked out. Miss Nielson still had her arms wound tightly around Delia.

"Delia wants to talk to you. Why don't you come out."

"You'll only kill her if I come out."

"No, I won't. I'll let her go, and we can go away together. I really am your mother. You belong with me."

"What kind of life would I have with you?" Charlie asked. "We'd be on the run." He was on the verge of tears, wondering which was the right thing to do.

"We'll find somewhere just like this and settle down. It'll be nice and quiet."

"I don't want to go with you," Charlie shouted back. He was trembling and sweating. He couldn't go with her, yet his anger toward his parents was still simmering.

"You like staying with these people? Do they treat you that well?"

"It's not perfect."

"You're special, Charlie. You're my son. You're superior. You're better than this little middle-class bend in the road. Don't you know that?"

He hesitated a moment, building a response. "It's my home."

"It doesn't have to be. We'll find a place. We'll have fun."

"No. Let Delia go, and just leave us alone."

"You've been brainwashed, Charlie. You think this is what you want, but you need more. You'll never be satisfied.

"I was going to try to show you that you needed me more than anything else, but I've been rushed. I even thought I'd found someone who could be a father to you, but it didn't work out.

"Most things in my life haven't worked out, but I want to start over."

"This won't work," Charlie shouted.

His father pulled him from the window and stood in his place. "Leave us alone," Black said. "Just get the hell out of here."

"Not without my son."

"He's my son," Black said. "My wife and I have raised him. You gave him up."

"I had to. Besides, what kind of father have you been to him? He's not your blood."

Black didn't waver. He stared at her through the darkness. "Maybe I haven't been that close to him, but I've taken care of him. I've given him things. I've been with him on the days that matter. My wife has too. Now you want to just walk in and take him off to play games?"

She pulled at Delia's hair. "You'd better make a decision," she said. "Before someone else gets hurt."

"Just let her go," Black said.

"Give me my son!"

"He's not coming with you."

Nell came over to Charlie's side as the shouting match continued. Taking his hand, she squeezed it. She didn't tell him everything would be okay. That would have been a lie.

"There's not any way out of this but for me to go with her," Charlie whispered.

"Maybe Michael will call in a minute."

"If not, what? The cops come and get eaten too?"

"She's not going to let people live that can chase her," Nell reminded. "We're all Alpo if you *do* go out there."

Rice gripped the steering wheel, shooting through the bends in the roadway. When he could, he glanced over at Sawyer to make sure the guy wasn't going into a coma.

He seemed to be holding up well. A bandage encircled his head, and the blood had been cleaned away. He was pale but sturdy.

He'd be okay and might be helpful when they reached Petittville. Rice had tried for backup and learned there were no units available. Small town cops never needed backup, but he'd never seen a mess quite like this. Bureaucracy and bullshit screwed up most of the police agencies around here, but usually they functioned when there was a real need. He'd encountered plenty of dumb asses with badges and titles, but would have accepted any of them at the moment.

"What do you know about her?" Sawyer asked as they rounded a curve.

"She's a witch. Or something. I think somehow she's controlling the dogs."

"You can't be serious, chief."

"I didn't believe it myself. I've never believed all the bullshit that's handed out about the occult, but there seems to be evidence this is for real."

"I can't believe it. Why would she want to do all of this? Why kill those boys?"

"I don't have answers for that. Maybe we'll find out if we live to question her."

"Dammit. I can't believe all this. She seemed so nice. I thought we were going somewhere. I thought we were in love."

He bowed his head, not crying but on the verge of it. His world had been shattered worse than his head. Rice had to let him suffer in silence as he pressed down the gas. The roadway was at least quiet, allowing him to travel with speed.

He was nearing the Petittville corporation limits.

Once there it would take no time to punch it over to the Blacks' neighborhood. He wasn't sure what he would find, but he prayed it was something he could handle.

"What's she doing?" Black asked.

Charlie was standing at the window, watching her. "Still just hanging around out there," he said. "She's still got Delia."

"Where the hell is Rice?"

"He'll be here soon," Mrs. Black said. "He's due."

Black moved to the window beside Charlie and peered out at her. "Why don't you let the girl go?" he shouted through the glass. His face was reddening now.

"Why don't you send Charlie out?" Barbara Nielson retorted, her tone almost mocking.

"You know that's not possible."

Her head twitched slightly, and suddenly a couple of the dogs detached themselves from the ranks and charged toward the house, their paws kicking up tufts of grass from the lawn as they moved.

Black pulled away from the window, jerking Charlie back as well, and the sound of the dogs thudding against the wall outside echoed into the room.

Cautiously, Black peeled the curtain aside again. He almost screamed when he saw the monster's face pressed against the pane.

Smears from its saliva were streaked across the window, and its breath clouded the pane. Teeth bared, eyes blazing, it peered at him with pure hatred showing in its features.

"We're going to have to figure out something," Nell said. "She's going to start having them charge the house. We need to get ready in here, and we have to think of some way to help Delia."

"She's right," Mrs. Black said. "We can't just let the girl get hurt."

"I know," Black said. "Ideas, anyone?"

"We'd better find some weapons," Nell said.

"Let's check the kitchen," Black suggested. He led Nell through the swinging doorway, leaving Charlie and his mother in the living room.

A butcher knife clung by a magnet to the counter. Pulling the blade free, Black handed it to Nell.

In the pantry, he found a broom on a hook inside the door. He wedged it under a chair at the kitchen table and snapped off the straws. The handle was slim, but it would make a reasonably good club.

"We could tie the knife to that and make a spear," Nell suggested.

Black examined the handle and the blade and agreed. He found some black electrical tape in a drawer of odds and ends and used it to bind the knife into place. Then he jabbed the air with it a few times to test.

"That ought to work for a while," he said.

They moved back into the living room and tried unscrewing a lamp from its base but found from the way it was put together it would not be effective.

A towel rack in the bathroom came apart more readily, providing a cylindrical metal shaft that was not too heavy.

"Better than nothing," he said. He followed Nell down the stairs.

Charlie was back at the window.

"She's got the dogs moving," Charlie said. "Some are headed around back of the house."

"They're surrounding us," Mrs. Black said.

Black and Nell moved to a back room. Looking out, they could see the hounds there, standing shoulder to shoulder, as if waiting for an attack command.

"They can't get in here," Black said.

"But we can't get out either," Nell observed. "We're under siege."

***

Rice's headlight beams washed across the dogs as he rounded the corner onto the street. There were at least a dozen of them, reminding him instantly of the guardians of the gates of Hades. They were large, fierce monsters, larger than he could have imagined.

He floored the gas, breaking only when he reached the edge of the Black's lawn, where he angled the car across the sidewalk and came to a stop on the grass.

He had his gun free as he pulled the door handle, and as he stood, he aimed the weapon across the top of the window.

Some of the dogs turned toward him immediately, snarling as they eyed him. Barbara Nielson took her time in turning toward him, not bothering to relax her grip on Delia's neck.

"Stay where you are," she warned without inflection.

"You need to let the girl go," Rice said. "I'm going to have to place you under arrest."

She smiled. "Are you?"

The dogs facing him began a charge. He fired at one of them, and the slug that dug into its shoulder twisted its course, jerking it around. Its feet slid from under it, but the monster rolled quickly and was coming toward him once again, only a few feet behind the other.

Rice ducked into the car and yanked the door closed before they reached him. In an instant they were on the hood, both of them snarling through the windshield.

"What are they?" Sawyer asked. His fingernails were digging trenches into the dashboard. Rice wished they were deep enough for them to climb into.

"Hellhounds," Rice said before yanking the microphone from its hook. He had to try a couple of times before he connected with the sheriff's office substation, manned by a single dispatcher.

"Get ahold of your base and tell them I need help," he said after giving his name and location.

"Everybody on this side of the river is tied up."

"Then you get me somebody from the other side or you get me somebody from Aimsley or Penn's Ferry. I don't care where they come from, I need backup." The urgency in his voice carried over the airwaves.

"Yes, sir," the dispatcher's voice crackled back.

Rice put the mike back into place, peering through the glass at the monsters. He felt the tightness in his bladder and wished he hadn't had coffee back at the hospital. "What the hell's going on?" Sawyer asked.

"She's a witch, like I told you," Rice said. "That's the only explanation for it. That's the only way this can make sense."

"What do you mean?"

"She's from some kind of cult in Atlanta. I don't know what the hell it is."

"She's a Satanist?"

"I don't know the theology, but apparently it works. Or I'm crazy. Maybe both."

The glow in the red eyes above them seemed to brighten.

Sawyer looked over at him in disbelief, his eyes begging for a smirk or wink to confirm Rice was joking. "How could she be that?"

"She was hiding a lot from you."

"Oh God."

Rice patted the schoolteacher's shoulder. "It's okay, buddy. We've got to think about survival right now, and how we're going to get those people out of that house."

Reaching into the back seat, Rice unhooked a pump action 12-gauge shotgun. The dogs' growls became louder as he checked the weapon over.

Reaching to the plug, he gently began to unscrew it. Sawyer watched, questioning, but Rice did not speak as he slipped the narrow wooden cylinder from the weapon.

"What is that?"

"It's a plug. Takes the place of some shells, but I figure I'll need all the room I can get," Rice said. "You mind handing me the box from the glove compartment?"

Sawyer complied, and Rice slipped seven of the red plastic rounds into the weapon.

"Will those work any better than the pistol?"

"Doubt it," Rice said, "but it gives me something to do."

"Maybe I could talk to her," Sawyer said. "I know she had some feelings for me. Maybe she'll listen to reason. Especially if she knows other cops are coming."

"We'll see if we can get her attention," Rice said.

He reached over and pulled the headlight plunger, flicking the beams on and off until Barbara turned toward the car.

Turning the crank just enough to crack the window a fraction of an inch, Rice lifted his lips toward the opening.

"I've got Sawyer in here," he said. "He'd like to speak to you."

She took a step toward the car, still gripping the girl. "He can get out."

"What about these dogs?" Rice asked.

"They won't harm him without my command."

"Don't know if you can trust her," Rice said. "She bashed you once."

"She was upset."

"Glad to see she's calmed down now."

"Maybe I can do some good."

"Be damned fucking careful," Rice suggested.

Keeping his hands low, he slipped his revolver from the holster once again and slid it across the seat to Sawyer. The teacher looked at it for a moment, then at Rice, who nodded.

Reaching down with a trembling hand, Sawyer took the weapon and slipped it behind his back into the waistband of his slacks. Then he slowly reached over and pushed open his door, closing it back quickly when he was standing so that the dogs would not have access to Rice.

Looking past the dogs, Rice watched the teacher move to the front of the car, standing just beside the front bumper, resting one hand on the fender.

The dogs on the hood turned toward him as he called out to Barbara. They were ready to rip into him if he tried to harm her.

Rice curled his hands around the gun, ready if he had to move, though he didn't expect to do much good.

"Why don't you let Delia go?" Sawyer asked. "We'll talk."

Barbara looked at his bandage, her mouth opening slightly with surprise. Her expression softened, but she shook her head.

"I need her," she said.

"Why? Let's just talk."

"We already talked."

"I was confused."

"It's too late," she said.

He took a step forward. "Please, Barbara. I want to understand. I want to help you."

She looked at him across the lawn, hesitant. Delia bit her hand then, clamping down hard enough to draw blood.

Barbara screamed as Delia slithered out of her grasp and ran, not for the car, but for the front door.

When he saw that, Sawyer yanked the gun out of his belt and fired, not at Barbara or Delia but in the sky. The echo of the weapon confused the dogs for a moment before the one nearest him on the hood lunged for his arm.

He dodged, and Rice was out of the car then. He fired the shotgun, cutting the mutt in half.

"Get back in the car," he shouted.

Sawyer scrambled toward the door, dodging around the mutilated body on the ground. The mutt was still trying to get at him even though it was ripped apart.

Rice fired his second shell into the face of the other dog on the hood, exploding half its brain in a shower of red.

He then aimed again, firing to confuse the hounds on the lawn and Barbara as well. That gave Delia time to make it to the front door. It opened and she was dragged inside before dogs were dispatched.

Lunging back for the car, Rice climbed inside. Sawyer met him in the front seat, and they slammed their doors before the onslaught of dogs came after them.

In a few seconds the car was surrounded, and other dogs were converging on the house. Confusion would no longer be an advantage. The hounds were going to be ready for whatever happened.

Barbara stood at the center of the lawn screaming as neighbors' lights went on. Nobody came outside. They'd been warned. At last somebody was obeying curfew.

Rice picked up his microphone again and asked if they could patch him through to the Blacks' telephone.

Black snatched the receiver from its cradle when the telephone rang, pressing it quickly to his ear.

"Is everything okay in there?" Rice asked. The connection was scratchy, but his voice was audible.

"Yeah, we're scared, but the girl's fine." She was sitting on the couch now between Charlie and Nell, her arms around Charlie's neck as she sobbed.

"Luckily Charlie was watching at the window. We saw her coming."

"Yeah, apparently the dogs and their mistress were confused. That won't happen again."

Black clenched his fist around the shaft of his makeshift spear. "What are we going to do?"

"They're sending some other police units over here, but I'm not sure if firepower is going to be enough. Bullets don't seem to stop these dogs."

"You can't be serious."

"I'm afraid I'm very serious," Rice said. "They don't stop."

"Try talking to the woman."

"She wouldn't listen to her boyfriend. I don't know who else will be able to reason with her."

"We're trapped," Black agreed.

"What the hell does she want?"

"She's obsessed with my son. Thinks he's hers. I can't send the boy out."

"No. By no means."

Black ran a hand over his face. "Look, if you're serious, that there's something supernatural about these dogs, we are waiting on a phone call. Nell has a friend in Chicago."

"She's told me."

"Well, if this isn't all nuts, maybe he'll turn up something that will help. It could be it's all we've got."

"Let's hope," Rice said. "I'll let you keep your line open."

"He's got another car coming," Black said as he hung up. "Won't do much good."

"At least Delia is safe," Mrs. Black said. She had hobbled into the kitchen for a wet towel.

She passed it to Nell, who used it to wipe some of the blood from Delia's face. Some had already smeared onto Charlie's sleeve.

"Charlie," echoed the voice from outside.

He looked over at his father, who nodded. "Go to the window," Black said.

Sliding away from Delia, who was still sobbing, Charlie walked to the window and looked out again. He had been standing there when Delia had bolted, and he had scrambled just as quickly for the door, certain she would be torn apart.

Now he was almost frightened to pull the curtains aside, but he did.

Barbara Nielson was standing closer to the house now, almost at the edge of the porch with a cluster of dogs around her.

"You need to come to me now," she shouted. "People are going to get hurt if you don't cooperate."

"I can't go with you," Charlie said. "You're evil." Her face seemed to melt. The remark cut her. He could see that, and her lips began to tremble.

"I'm only trying to get my son. You don't know what my life has been. I've made mistakes."

"Can't you just leave me alone?" Charlie asked.

"I want you with me. You don't belong here."

"I can't come," Charlie said. He glanced back at his father, who was sitting on the arm of the couch. Charlie let no emotion show to him. This alliance was of necessity, and he didn't want Black interpreting it as anything else.

"You will come. You'll understand later," the woman shouted.

"No!" Charlie protested, taking a step backward.

She lowered her head slightly, her gaze hardening. "You will come," she repeated.

Then the dogs began to converge.

The first sound of breaking glass came from the rear of the house. Black was on his feet in an instant, the spear raised.

"They're coming in," he shouted.

Nell slid from the couch, leaving Delia in Mrs. Black's arms. She followed Black into the back room, where a hound was already standing amid a pile of shattered glass. Shards gleamed on its coat, and blood dripped from a gash on its snout, but its teeth were bared, ready to strike.

Black got the knife blade in front of him before the mutt charged. When its legs pumped, it moved into the blade, the steel piercing its chest.

A gurgling sound issued as the monster tried to bark. Black twisted the blade, yanking upward. It tore out the side of the dog's neck, causing the head to sag to one side. Black expected the body to topple over, but it didn't. The dog kept coming with its jaws dangling at a twisted angle, bright blood spilling through the teeth.

Nell swung the pipe, bringing the iron down across the creature's back. The blow made it stagger, but it didn't divert its course. Black stabbed again, piercing an eye, and only then did the dog slump onto its side.

Together they backed out of the room, Black yanking the door closed as they moved. He dragged a small cabinet from the end of the hall over in front of the door, blocking it as they heard the dog whine. A moment later its weight thudded against the door. It was trying to slam through the wood.

Outside the dogs began to howl, their tones a cacophony of sirens. Then the injured dog began to scratch of the wood. In a moment the others would probably follow it through the shattered window, filling the small room.

"Hope this door holds," Black said. He led Nell back into the living room. Charlie was looking outside again.

"They're all over the place," he said.

"Can you see the chief?"

"He can't get out of his car," Charlie said. "There are dogs all around it."

Just then a dog leapt at the window, flattening its paws against the pane. The nails screeched along the glass, and the monster barked angrily.

Charlie stepped back several feet and felt his father's arm loop over his shoulders. "Let's get something in front of that window," Black suggested.

They moved into the den, where there was a tall bookshelf. Black handed Nell the spear.

Then he and Charlie took separate sides and moved the case from the wall. Some books and trinkets spilled off, but they kept moving, walking it between them.

They had to angle it to wedge it through the doorway, but when they were clear, they hurried to the window and shoved the case into place. It didn't completely cover the space, but it provided some blockage. Grabbing a couple of chairs, they reinforced its position.

Thuds against the side of the house sounded when they began to check other windows and look for ways of covering them.

"It's kind of like *Night of the Living Dead*," Charlie observed.

His father only grunted.

"Maybe we should try to find some planks to nail over the windows," Nell said.

Breaking glass sounded from the kitchen.

"Maybe we should have already done that," Black said, taking back his spear.

Chapter 30

Only one deputy was in the sheriff's patrol car which arrived twenty minutes later. He drove slowly along the street shining a spotlight attached to the driver's door across the lawns.

Rice picked up the microphone and hailed him. The cruiser bumped over the sidewalk and came to a stop across the lawn, facing Rice's car at an angle. The hounds backed up just far enough to give him room without relinquishing their vigil.

"This is Deputy Watkins," he answered. "Where did all these dogs come from?"

"The woods," Rice said.

"Any idea what we ought to do with them?"

"Start blasting. I've got a shotgun in here. That'll scare the bastards."

"Take a look by my tire," Rice said.

The spotlight beam crawled across the lawn, playing on the damp grass until it stopped, some of the light gleaming across the police car's hood.

"There's something down there twitching, but it looks like it's all chewed up."

"I shot it with a shotgun," Rice said. "Guns aren't doing much good."

"Hell, you say."

"These aren't ordinary dogs," Rice said. "I know it sounds loony, but I've been tracking this the last several days, and it's true. I was hoping for more men."

"You're lucky you got me."

"I'll reserve a decision on how lucky I am," Rice said.

Suddenly Barbara moved from the shadows where she had been standing for several minutes. A complacent grin had crossed her features.

Watkins started to get out of his car.

"Stay where you are," Rice commanded.

The deputy picked up his mike again. "She'll be eaten up."

"The dogs are sort of with her," Rice said.

"We need more backup."

"You're quick. That's what I've been trying to convince people of," Rice said.

As he spoke, three dogs detached from the semicircle in front of the house and moved toward the new patrol car. They didn't leap onto the hood, but they stood close to the grill, ready to act if an opportunity presented itself.

"Well, I feel better," Rice said. "Now we've got two cops trapped on the lawn."

Nell helped Charlie place a board, formerly a kitchen cabinet door, over the shattered kitchen window. The dog that had slammed into it hadn't managed to climb through before being forced back with stabs and clubbing.

Quickly Charlie hammered nails into place, then picked up the large barbecue fork he'd found in an almost forgotten cabinet over the stove.

They moved back into the living room, where his father and Delia were helping his mother across the room. She had her arms around their shoulders, and they stumbled forward slowly, headed for the stairs.

"You two drag that loveseat across the base of the stairs and follow us," Black said as he lifted his wife up the first step.

Obliging, Charlie and Nell moved over and grabbed the small two-person sofa from the living area. It wasn't terribly heavy, so they were able to transport it easily to the desired spot. Overturning it against the lowest step, they climbed over and followed the others upward.

Charlie placed a hand against his mother's back, trying to help as they neared the top. Then they headed along the hallway.

"Let's get to the office," Black said. "We can see the front lawn from there."

Charlie moved ahead and opened the door, then turned and helped his mother through, guiding her over to the swivel chair at the desk. Black headed directly to the window, looking out through the blinds which hung there. The multicolored light played across his features as he looked down.

"Another cop's joined them out there, but there are still a dozen of the dogs," he said.

"Where's Miss Nielson?" Nell asked.

"Under the tree. She looks patient."

Charlie walked over to look out as well. The dogs appeared to be rallying. They clustered on the lawn, a black mass of fur. Some of them looked up, as if they knew that someone was at the window, peering down at them.

Charlie pulled back from the glass. They were looking at him. Could they be waiting for a command?

He laced his fingers behind his neck and bowed his head. He felt Nell's touch against his shoulders, an attempt at comfort, but it was not enough.

"My fault," he muttered.

"We're going to figure out something," she said.

"They're going to get in here and tear everybody up, and then I'll have to go with her," Charlie said.

"The hell you will," Black said. "You're not going with that crazy woman."

"How are we going to stop it?" Charlie asked.

"We'll find a way."

Charlie moved back to the window. Barbara Nielson was staring toward the glass. She knew where he was.

Stepping forward so that the tree's branches would no longer conceal her features, she smiled and extended her arms, beckoning to him.

344

He hesitated for a moment, and he knew she could see him, could count every pore in his skin. He could see her just as well, as if he were looking directly into her face.

She was waiting for an answer, an answer that would determine her further actions. Everything to this point had been a matter of example. She had shown that the dogs could be powerful, that they could gain entrance to the house, but she had not commanded them to move forward full force.

Not yet.

But she would.

She was waiting.

Waiting for Charlie.

His hands gripped the edge of the windowsill. Splinters from the soft wood dug into his flesh.

He bit his lip.

She wanted a decision.

He shook his head.

And the dogs charged.

The sound of breaking glass echoed from downstairs, as if simultaneously all of the windows were being broken. The dogs on the lawn were mobile, charging forward as if they had designated targets.

"They're coming," Charlie shouted.

Black lifted the spear. "Let's be ready." He jerked his head toward the door.

Nell flattened herself against the wall beside the entrance, lifting the club over her shoulder so that she could swing it downward if anything broke through the wood.

"It's a hollow core," Black said. "If those things are as heavy as they look, it won't stand up long."

"Let's get the desk against it," Charlie suggested.

"Good idea," Black said. He moved over and pushed the telephone and Texas Instruments calculator off the surface along with some stacks of paper. Neatness wasn't a priority.

With Charlie's help, he shoved the heavy piece across the room, and they positioned it in front of the door. It was in place only a few seconds before a loud thump sounded through the wood, jarring the door in its frame.

Another hit sounded a second later, and then another, and the wood splintered under the battering.

"They can't get in here," Delia shouted. "There's no way." She was nearing hysteria.

"We can't tell," Black said. "Who knows what they can accomplish?"

A loud thud sounded against the wall. One of them was in the next room, butting with all its force. Since the wall was made of Sheetrock, it would not hold long against such an assault. When the next thud came, a calendar held in place with a thumbtack came down.

As Black was examining the spot where the sound rattled through, a thud sounded on the opposite wall, while clawing continued at the door.

"We're not in a fortress," he muttered, then stepped over to the desk, where he began riffling drawers. Tossing out folders and notebooks, he finally selected a small bottle.

"Glue," he said. "Wonder if it'll burn."

He unscrewed the top, pulling out the brush used as an applicator. A clear string of the adhesive dangled down as he let the cap drop to the floor.

Ignoring the stain on the carpet, he sat the bottle on the desk and ripped a strip of cloth from his own sleeve as the battering continued against the walls. Stuffing the cloth through the bottle's opening, he rummaged through drawers for a match and finally located a folder from Robert's Road House in Hickory Hills, Illinois.

"Don't know how these got here, but I'm glad we've got them," he said. He peeled the cardboard open and selected one of the white-tipped matches.

The thundering against the wall continued, deafening coupled with the sound of claws ripping at wood. They were coming through, whatever it required.

Rice watched the dogs charging, some of them diving at the windows, sacrificing themselves to shatter the glass so that others could enter the house. Once the jagged openings were shattered, other monsters scrambled through. There seemed to be an endless supply. "We've got to do something," the deputy said over the microphone.

"Any suggestions?" Rice asked.

"Gonna talk to the woman."

Rice watched him yank his shotgun from his back seat and climb from the car. The police chief shot his hand over to the door handle and climbed out of the cruiser as well, shotgun ready.

"It's time to call them off," Watkins said as he moved toward Barbara.

He had to shout over the howls and the sounds of the dogs ripping at the house. She only looked back at him as complacent as ever as he lifted the shotgun.

"Call them off, lady."

Dogs moved out of the shadows at him, four of them, forming a phalanx in front of him so that he could not move any closer to Barbara.

"Get back in your car," Rice shouted through his window.

"We've got to stop this somehow," the deputy protested, yelling back over his shoulder.

He started to take another step forward when one of the dogs sprang, its teeth bared. He jerked one arm up to protect himself, and the jaws closed around his forearm, biting down like a bear trap.

The shotgun slipped from his hands, and he dropped to his knees as he tried to free himself from the jaws.

Rice balanced his shotgun across the top of his door, but it was not safe to fire. A shotgun blast would rip into the other officer as well.

In a moment, the dog relaxed its teeth, however, and moved back. Blood was smeared across its snout, and it still snarled, but it wasn't trying to kill the deputy. Standing shoulder to shoulder with its brothers, it continued to watch him, ready to strike again, but not relentless in its assault.

With his injured arm clutched in his hand, Watkins scrambled backward, turning when he was sure the dog wasn't following. In a few moments he was back in his patrol car.

Only then did Rice sink into the front seat again. He pulled the door closed with a clunk before picking up the mike.

"How bad is it?"

"Ripped up pretty good," the deputy said. Rice could see him tugging a handkerchief from his pocket to try and stop the flow of crimson.

A patch of the wall crumbled inward in a shower of powder, a piece of the material flopping to one side like cardboard. Nell swung her club toward the opening, but as the dog's head forced through it, he ignored the swing.

With one large paw, he raked at the opening, trying to enlarge it so that his shoulders would follow his head through.

"I can't believe this," Black said, rushing toward the hole. With the spear lifted in front of him, he jabbed at the dog, nicking an ear.

Blood oozed across the black fur, but the hound refused to back off. Its jaws dropped open, shiny rows of teeth gleaming as it growled a deep warning.

Black forced the knife blade into the creature's neck, putting his weight behind it as he attempted to drive the blade deeper.

A new spray of blood shot from the wound, seeping down over the ruined fragments of the wall. The dog's growl turned to an agonized scream, and it did begin to pull back now with the knife tangled into its muscles. As Black held on to the spear shaft, the tape that held the knife into place pulled free.

It was still in the dog's lower shoulder, and the beast carried it with him back through the hole.

Once his head was clear, other claws began to work at the opening, ripping back pieces of the shattered board while snouts gnawed at the upper portion of the opening. Reaching back, Black took the pipe from Nell and began to swing it, hammering at the dogs, trying to drive them back.

Even as he made connections that certainly had to bring them pain, they refused to give up on their quest, and in a moment the thundering blows resumed at other points on the opposite side of the room.

White powdery chips from the ceiling began to sift down, and the vibrations began to rattle through the floor.

"The walls aren't going to hold," Mrs. Black shouted.

Another dog moved through the opening. This time it was large enough for his head to pass, and a portion of his shoulders emerged.

Black began to swing at him with the club, and the dog snapped back, trying to struggle through the opening so that it could manage to bite.

Its right front paw clawed through the hole, and it began to shift and spin its weight. It was coming through, ignoring the blows across its head and upper body. They seemed to have no effect at first, but then the metal crashed down to the side of the skull, breaking the skin. When Black swung again, the club bruised the other side of the head.

Another fragment of wall peeled forward as the dog shoved its weight onward with a thrust of effort. Its features were beginning to lose shape, turning to pulp, but it refused to surrender.

"Dammit," Black shouted, bringing the weapon down harder and harder.

And then, with another push, the dog was in the room, facing him though unsteady on its feet. He swung the club at its head like a baseball bat, the force of it taking the mutt off balance.

Spilling sideways, away from the wall, the dog cried out and rolled, twisting back into a standing position.

Black had the bar in front of him as the hind legs tensed, and when the dog went for his throat, the metal blocked it even as its weight forced Black backward to the floor.

Charlie stabbed the fork into the monster's ribs as it tried to claw his father's face, and its swollen head jerked in his direction.

Mrs. Black screamed as the half-closed eyes locked on Charlie, but Charlie held on to the fork handle, trying to shove it deeper toward the internal organs.

With a grunt, Black forced himself upward, pushing the dog off him. It tried to regain its footing and come at him again, but he scrambled to his feet and kicked it, getting his leg under it so that he had leverage.

The dog was forced back against the desk, slamming into the front of some drawers. Black snatched at the blue container then, fumbling with his matches.

Nell picked up the fallen glass and hurled it at the dog. It bounced off the monster's skull as it let out a loud snarl.

Before it could move forward, Black ignited the match folder and touched it to the strip of cloth before hurling it toward the dog like a grenade.

As the glue burned, it produced a smothering black smoke that trailed through the air. Nell and Charlie began to cough as the canister crossed the dog's back, and the smell of burned fur mingled with the other smells.

The glue spread across the creature's shoulders and spine, and the flames licked over it until the creature was a ball of flame. It rolled onto the carpet, wallowing, trying to extinguish itself, but the effort was to no avail.

It began to screech in agony as the bright orange flames ate through its flesh, consuming.

Taking Charlie's fork, Black moved over to the animal's side, driving the blade downward through its chest, into the heart.

When its writhing stopped, he began to stomp at the flames, trying to keep the carpet from igniting. His coughing was lost in the sound of other dogs hammering at the wall, and before he could turn away from the dead animal, another started through the opening.

Black pushed Charlie aside before the boy could kick at the dog as he had intended. Charlie stumbled backward, watching his father shove the tines into the dog's left eye.

The orb exploded in a pulpy mass, and the hound twisted its head to one side so that it could watch him as it continued through the wall.

He blinded the other eye as well and then shoved the points under the neck, hoping for the jugular.

As the dog's throat was ripped open and blood began to gush from the wounds, the telephone sounded.

Two more dogs slammed against the opening, forcing more of the wall away. Black began to jab at them as well.

It was Delia who pulled away from Mrs. Black where she had been huddled to grab the handset from the floor.

"If that's Rice again, tell him we've got our hands full," Black shouted.

"It's somebody named Michael."

Nell snatched the phone from her hands. "Michael, where the hell are you?"

"I got your message on my machine. I just listened to it. My head's swelling up like a bowling ball. You wouldn't believe—"

"Michael, dammit, we're being attacked. Did you learn anything?" She clutched the receiver to her ear so that she could hear his voice. The connection was static-filled.

"They found something in an old book," he said. "It's called the Cross of St. Roland. There were some monks that were besieged by killer dogs sent by minions of Satan, as the legend goes. They placed it in the window of their monastery to ward them off."

"What is it? Myth?"

"The priest or whatever he was had a book on it."

"If he's got some answers, we need them right now," Black shouted. He and Charlie were using a chair to hold back the dogs.

"Have you got it there?" Nell asked.

"A picture they gave me. It's like a Catholic patron's item or something. I don't really understand special icons."

"What does it do?"

"You have to post it or whatever. They posted the original and prayed for seven days." His voice was growing tense, the sounds of the scuffle evidently traveling to him across the mouthpiece.

"We're not going to last seven days," Nell said.

"Maybe you can draw it," he suggested. "Maybe that'll work."

"I need a pad and paper," Nell screamed. Delia rushed over to the desk and produced a legal pad, then snatched a fallen pen from the floor.

Dropping to a cross-legged position on the carpet, Nell placed the pad on her lap and began to sketch, doing a quick design of a cross.

Another section of wall began to give. Cracks zigzagged through the material from a central point where a blow s had been delivered on the other side.

351

Grabbing a trash can, Charlie scrambled over, pressing the metal against the wall in an effort to provide support.

Black continued his struggle to hold dogs back with the chair.

"Now there's kind of a squiggly line on the cross piece," Michael was saying.

Nell began to etch the suggested marking as he described the flow of the line. When that was drawn, she began to create another design, which Michael described as a flowered cluster.

As she attempted to imitate the symbol he suggested, however, she kept making mistakes, misunderstanding what he was trying to tell her. It was impossible to draw something without seeing it, and she had no idea of how it would work if it was flawed. There was no guarantee anyway.

"It's no use," she screamed.

Delia knelt at her side. "You've got to do it," she said. "If it'll work."

Nell picked up her pen again and turned to a fresh sheet. Quickly she redrew the things she felt were correct then began again on the design Michael was describing.

"Do something fast," Black demanded. A dog was forcing its weight against the chair he was still holding.

Another was ripping through the opening, working its way into the room.

She completed the cluster and began another symbol. "This was the Middle Ages," Michael said. "They did a lot of that kind of ornamental work."

"Dammit, I can't get all this. If it's got to be perfect, we'll never make it."

She stared down at the paper, at the hastily drawn lines. They could hardly resemble the florid, perfect style some fifteenth-century calligrapher would have created.

She was about to try another line when her eyes swept to the corner of the room. The fax machine seemed to glow.

"Is this thing working?" she asked.

Black turned from the dogs, glancing back at her. "It's hooked up," he said. "You'd better hurry. These bastards are going to ruin the whole room in a minute."

"Fax it to me, Michael!" she screeched into the receiver.

She scrambled over to the machine, making sure it was set to receive. Then she read off the number for him.

"I'll hang up," she said. "For God's sake, hurry."

The dogs came through the opening abruptly and took Black down, sinking teeth into his forearm and trying for his throat. He rolled onto his side, tucking his head down to try and protect his jugular. The dogs ripped at his clothing and raked paws across his shoulders.

Spinning, Charlie grabbed the chair his father had dropped and hammered it across the dogs' backs. The blows seemed to do nothing to dissuade their efforts to devour Black's flesh.

Black screamed as they ripped at his skin, and he drove his fist into one's face. Dropping the chair, Charlie wrapped his arms around another dog's throat and yanked backward.

The hound began to struggle to get free of him as he twisted at its head, trying to break its neck. He had to dig his fingers into the fur to keep his grip as the creature bucked and tried to shake him off.

"Stop them," Mrs. Black screamed. "Stop them before they kill him!"

Nell scrambled over to the desk and yanked out the center drawer, swinging it against the side of one of the other dogs. She heard ribs splinter, but he continued to bite at Black's arm.

Blood spurted out the side of its mouth, and Black tried to drag himself away. He couldn't move far because the monster's weight was pinning him.

"Nooo!" Mrs. Black shouted, spilling herself out of her chair and trying to move toward her husband.

A new dog, forcing its way through the jagged opening started for her. Nell blocked his path with the drawer, holding it like a shield and pushing the dog backward.

He began to bark as she struggled against him, and she realized she would not be able to hold out long against his strength.

Delia snatched the fork and jabbed it into one dog's flank, but the beast was not phased.

"Jesus, what are we going to do?" Mrs. Black screamed.

Charlie wrestled the dog in his grasp onto its side and drove a knee down onto its abdomen.

"I don't know," he cried. Tears were streaming down his cheeks. He was doing everything he could do to save Black's life despite his anger at the man.

The sound of the fax's function made all the heads turn, the near silent hum almost drowned out by the dogs. Nell turned toward it, not relaxing her grip on the drawer/shield as she watched the page slowly hiss through the feeder slot.

As it moved in what seemed to be slow motion, she gave a final push to the drawer and then dove, snatching the paper as it fell. The near perfect black and white reproduction of the ancient symbol slid into her fingers, and she clutched it, lifting it.

Whatever the ancient myth Michael had learned of, she prayed there was truth somewhere within it. Then she lifted the Cross of St. Roland over her head.

Something happened, something that made the dogs begin to whimper. Black's attackers almost immediately relaxed their jaws and cowered, tucking their tails as they crept back from Nell.

Some of them leaned against the wall, others tried to slink back through the hole.

Charlie knelt at his father's side, grabbing his head, pressing his hand against Black's throat. The teeth had found their mark, ripping through his skin. His neck was bright red, and more blood coursed through Charlie's fingers as he tried to close the wound.

"Get a rag," he demanded. "Somebody get something."

Black tried to speak, gurgling through the fluid filling his throat. His head tilted back against Charlie's legs, his eyes rolling open.

The stare aimed at the ceiling, and his eyes became like marbles.

The telephone rang again. Nell answered to Michael's voice. "Did it work?"

"They're backing off," she said.

"Be careful," he warned. "The old men said the summoning of the hounds is dangerous sorcery. It takes a lot of skill to manage the necessary spells. It may not be over if they've been driven back toward their source. I'm not sure what might happen."

As the dogs outside stopped their assault, Rice jumped from his car with his shotgun raised. He didn't fire as he watched them swarming away from the house and disappearing into the darkness. He was too amazed.

He heard Sawyer leaping out on the other side as he moved toward Barbara. Her look of complacency was gone now. Her eyes were swollen, bulging with terror. He pointed the gun in her direction, letting her see it.

She didn't seem frightened by the weapon. Her terror came from elsewhere. She pressed back against the tree, her fingers digging into the bark.

"There are going to be a lot of questions to answer, and if the people in that house are hurt, I'm going to do my best to charge you with murder. Now let me read your rights so we can get on with this."

She shook her head. "There's no need," she whispered.

"Come on, lady; I'm placing you under arrest."

"We'll get you an attorney," Sawyer said from the policeman's side. "We'll work it out."

She began to laugh, not coy, not maniacal laughter, but laughter nearing hysteria. Her eyes closed, and as she continued to dig her fingers into the tree so much that she began to break fingernails and draw blood, her head tilted back. With her eyes closed, she laughed more deeply.

"I've failed," she said. "You can't arrest me."

Rice took his handcuffs from his belt and took a step toward her. "I'm going to have to."

He was about to move another pace closer when the front door burst open and Charlie charged through, rushing across the lawn.

"They killed my father," he said through clenched teeth.

Her laughter stopped, and tears stained her face, catching strands of her hair and plastering them across her cheek.

"They did?"

"Yes, dammit. What right did you have to come back here after you tried to sell me?"

"I just wanted us to have a life." She began to weep. "All of us."

Sawyer stepped forward, extending his arms to embrace her. She accepted him, pulling his body close, burying her face against his shoulder.

"It fell apart," she said.

She pushed back from him and looked down at Charlie. She made no move to touch him, but she looked into his eyes.

"If there had been more time, I would have made you understand," she said. "You would have come with me willingly. You would have seen how special you are, how much you could have accomplished at my side.

"I didn't totally control those dogs, Charlie. Your will directed some of their actions. I didn't always know who was hurting you."

He swallowed, still staring at her defiantly. "You go to hell," he said.

"You're angry," she said. "Later you'll see."

"I'll never see anything you tried to show me."

"You weren't loved by that man, and you didn't love him."

"Go straight to hell."

She wet her lips as tears continued to roll down her cheeks. An absent look came to her eyes.

"Not hell," she said.

Nell approached from behind Charlie, placing a hand on his shoulder to support him. She could feel him trembling.

"Just leave him alone," Nell said.

The new voice seemed to jerk Barbara Nielson back to reality. She found a new smile and put in on for Nell.

"I'm leaving," she said. "I have failed the night and there are prices to be paid. Be his friend, Nell, because you are a lot like me. In another life with a different twist I might have been you, but that doesn't matter now."

Rice tried to get to her with the cuffs, but she turned before he could reach her. As the chill night breeze seemed to kick harder, she began to run, following the path of the dogs.

"Hold it," Rice shouted, but she paid no heed. She continued to run, picking up speed, moving farther and farther into the darkness until she could not be seen at all.

In a moment only the howls of distant hounds were audible in the darkness.

Chapter 31

Nell was on her way from school, headed toward Matt's shop, when she spotted Charlie walking. He was moving along the edge of the vacant lot with his hands tucked into his pockets.

She slowed her car, hoping he would look up, but when he did not, she pulled over and climbed from behind the wheel. The coming of winter was not evident today. The sunshine had burned back the late November clouds, and the light breeze was pleasant more than chilling.

The weather seemed to confirm that the bad days were over for Petittville. People were beginning to take walks after dark again, breathing in the autumn air.

Nell had not spoken with Charlie in several days. He had not come by the shop, and she had been unable to get an answer at his house.

The exuberance that had touched the rest of the town did not seem to have lifted his spirits. She could not blame him, she decided as she started toward him. His life had been overturned; the man he knew as his father was gone; his mother was having to make adjustments, find employment.

Rice's official report had skirted reference to Charlie's identity and black magic and to Barbara Nielson's cult involvement, but people talked. Sometimes they whispered behind Charlie's back, she knew. For now they did not taunt him openly. They were afraid. She'd picked up that much from conversations in the shop.

Eventually that would wear off, and he would have to endure teasing. She hoped he could get through it and find some semblance of a normal life eventually.

Counseling would not be a bad idea, but his mother probably wouldn't be able to afford it.

Nell was glad that at least now she would be able to tell him she was available if he needed someone to talk to. She'd never had an opportunity for counseling either, so she knew you got by the best you could.

She called his name as he walked through the tall brown grass, kicking at clumps of weeds. Without taking his hands from his pockets, he turned.

His face was drawn, ashen-looking with dark circles forming under his eyes that gave him the look of a figure from one of the horror movies he liked.

"How's it going?" she asked, moving toward him.

He shrugged. "I'm managing."

"Your mom?"

"Fine. Her leg's getting better. She's going to take a PR job in Aimsley. Money'll be okay, she says."

"I've wanted to talk to you."

He didn't change his expression. "I've been busy. Reading, trying to study some for midterms."

"Me too. That doesn't change when you get to college."

He still didn't smile.

She swallowed, suddenly nervous in his presence. His eyes seemed to have turned hard.

"How's Delia?" she asked.

"Her mother doesn't want her seeing me," he said. "Delia was upset, but she'll get over it.

"I'm sorry."

Now he smiled, a smile that said it was not a loss. "She was kind of a weird girl anyway, bouncing from guy to guy. Who needs that?"

"You'll find somebody. Things will level out."

"Yeah. I'm going to be fine," he said coldly. "Nobody messes with me. I kind of like that. Maybe Miss Nielson was right. I'm kind of special."

Nell realized she felt cold, inside as well as along her spine. "Don't let all this get to you, Charlie."

He chuckled. "Nothing will get to me."

She realized her lips had parted. What was he getting at? She found herself glancing back over her shoulder.

"Charlie, don't let all of her rhetoric change you."

"Maybe it wasn't rhetoric. Maybe I do have a strong will. Maybe everyone will learn it's better not to bother me. The dogs haven't been found and neither has she."

Nell drew a quick breath. "What are you saying?"

The grin used only one corner of his mouth. "Maybe nothing."

"Charlie, you can't call on those dogs if they're still out there. You can't use them to solve your problems for you."

"What? I can't use them to get my enemies?"

"You know you can't. Charlie, what has all this done to you?"

"Made me stronger," he said and turned, setting a slow course across the lot where Budd had died.

Nell watched him only for a moment before turning back toward her car. A cooler breeze seemed to sweep forward out of the forest. She didn't look back, and she tried to tell herself she was only imagining the sounds of footfalls.

About the Author

Sidney Williams is the author of numerous novels including the Si Reardon thrillers, *Fool's Run* and *Long Waltz*. His books from Crossroad Press include the slasher thriller *Dark Hours* and the Lovecraftian action-adventure novel *Disciples of the Serpent*. Sidney's short stories have appeared in numerous publications including *Cat Ladies of the Apocalypse, Love Among the Thorns, Deranged* and the upcoming *Unknown Heroes vs. the Forces of Darkness*. Sidney's first novels were released by Pinnacle Books. Those include *Blood Hunter, When Darkness Falls* and the possession thriller *Azarius*. He wrote several YA books under the name Michael August.

A former newspaper reporter, Sidney is now an adjunct professor of creative writing. He is originally from Louisiana and spent several years in Orlando. He now resides in Virginia with his wife and their cat Zoë Moonshadow.

Visit him at SidIsAlive.com, Facebook.com/SidneyWilliamsBooks for occasional flash fiction or seek him out as Willysid on TikTok for microfiction.

Sign up for his newsletter at sidneyw.substack.com.

Curious about other Crossroad Press books? Stop by our website:
http://crossroadpress.com
We offer quality writing
in digital, audio, and print formats.

Subscribe to our newsletter on the website homepage and receive a free
eBook.

www.ingramcontent.com/pod-product-compliance
Lightning Source LLC
Chambersburg PA
CBHW031133260626
47153CB00021B/164